Always Been Yours

Amada Beach #1

Ashtyn Kiana

This is a work of fiction. Names, characters, places, and incidents are products of the author's imagination or are used fictitiously and are not to be construed as real. Any resemblance to actual events, locale, organizations, or persons, living or dead, is entirely coincidental.

Always Been Yours. Copyright © 2024 by Ashtyn Kiana.

All rights reserved.

No portion of this book may be reproduced in any form without written permission from the publisher or author, except as permitted by U.S. copyright law.

Cover design and illustration by Chelsea Kemp.

ISBN 9798334154490

*to all the kids who started as hopeless romantics
but grew into cynics, I see you.*

Author's Note

My intentions are for this story to be one about healing, love, and finding our home. However, I understand some of the topics throughout the novel may be hard for some readers.

Content disclosures for *Always Been Yours*:

- Multiple explicit open-door scenes between the main characters. These contain on-page sexual content in graphic detail. Turn to page 473 to find out which chapters to be aware of.

- Multiple discussions about divorce and co-parenting between ex-spouses. Some of these conversations involve the children but are mostly had between adults.

- Mentions of cheating and toxic behaviors from a past relationship. None of this is between the main characters and it is not seen on page.

- Mentions of death of a parent. It is brief and it does not happen on the page. Genevieve's father passed away when she was a young child but it is talked about.

- Brief mentions of bullying. It's neither shown on page nor detailed.

Grady & Vivi's Playlist

Are You Bored Yet? (feat. Clairo) by Wallows
You're On Your Own, Kid by Taylor Swift
There's Still A Light In The House by Valley
Fallingwater by Maggie Rogers
Landslide by Fleetwood Mac
All That I'm Craving by Aidan Bissett
Slow Dances by Winnetka Bowling League
Kiss Me by Sixpence None The Richer
Say It by Maggie Rogers
Tongue Tied by GROUPLOVE
Can I Get It by Adele
a boy named pluto by Hailey Knox
Better by Khalid
Butterflies by Kasey Musgraves
Perfume by Del Water Gap
Positions by Ariana Grande
You Make It Easy by Red Hearse
When You Love Someone by James TW
Daylight by Taylor Swift
Guillotine by Jon Bellion, Travis Mendes
Fetish (feat. Gucci Mane) by Selena Gomez
Your Song by Elton John
You All Over Me by Taylor Swift
Dandelions by Ruth B.
Float by HARBOUR

Prologue
Vivi

First night of summer, fifteen years ago…

I settle into my favorite sleeping bag while I listen to Grady fuss over the lantern not being bright enough. The silly thing has turned into a tradition in a way. Every year, Grady buys new batteries for it, even though we only use it for one night, and he's surprised every summer by how dull the light is. He swears he doesn't want me to get lost in the middle of the night when I need the bathroom.

We're camping in my backyard, so I know I won't get lost. I think Grady is scared of the dark, and it may be the only secret he'll never admit to me.

I turn toward him, and the rustling of my cotton candy-colored sleeping bag pulls his attention to me. With my elbow on my pillow and my head propped up by my fist, I give Grady the longest, most exaggerated eye roll I can muster, simply for the fact that he worries when I'm annoyed with him. "You know that's as bright as it's going to get. We bought the damn thing for, like, five dollars at the toy store."

Grady's face warms to my favorite shade of pink, the blush that seems to only happen for me. "I just don't want you to get lost," he says quietly, not making eye contact with me.

Grady always says he can't see the stars as clearly if we leave any lights on.

Sometimes I wonder if it's because he's too scared to hold my hand when it's not dark. When we aren't bundled up in our sleeping bags, staring up into the night sky. When I would be able to see the color that no doubt paints his cheeks when he laces our fingers together. When we can't pretend we're the only two people in the world.

Two years ago, on the last night of school, Grady held my hand for the first time.

Two years ago, I woke up to Grady smiling at me, with our fingers still intertwined, when he told me, for the millionth time, that I'm his best friend.

Two years ago, I realized being Grady Chase Miller's *best* friend wasn't good enough anymore—but it was better than nothing.

Two nights ago, I decided this is the year Grady is going to kiss me. We'll be each other's first kisses. But *I* don't want to kiss Grady. That's too risky. I've loved him since I was five years old, so I've had plenty of time to adjust to the idea of being more than just best friends—but I don't think he has caught up yet. You know how boys are… dumb.

So, I want Grady to kiss me. This summer. On the lips.

He kisses me on the cheek sometimes—usually on my birthday, after I blow out the candle on the cupcake he's brought me every year since I turned eight. The same year we started having our end of the school year sleepovers. One single cupcake to make a wish for the two of us. We split the dessert, and he begs me to tell him what I wished for. I never do, mostly because I've started wishing that he'll love me like his mom and dad love each other.

Before that, I used to wish we would be friends forever. I'm too embarrassed to tell him any of that, though.

He doesn't know how scared I am to lose him, because all I remember, in my almost thirteen years, is Grady.

He's kissed me on the forehead a couple times when we were watching movies in his living room, on the rare couple of occasions we were alone. I think he kissed my knuckles last year in the tent, but I might have dreamed it.

I pull my attention away from the dark curls falling into his eyes as I hear the zipper pull open. I look just in time to catch the pillow one of the twins throws straight at my face. "Hey! Watch it! Ugh, I don't even know why I allow you to come on my camping trip."

"Shut up, Viv," Asher, the older of the twins, says as he makes his bed on the other side of me. "This isn't *your* camping trip. If anything, it's Grady's. He's the one who does all the work every year. Do you even help?"

"Oh, that's rich coming from you," I mutter under my breath.

We'd invited both my brothers to stay in the backyard with us the first year, but they'd said no. Why would they want to sleep on the ground, in their own backyard, when their beds were right upstairs, they had mocked. Well, *Asher* had mocked. Hudson just stood there, silently smirking in agreement. Exactly two minutes after Grady and I had gotten the tent set up and there hadn't been any more work, they came barreling in the exact same way as tonight. Asher always takes the spot to my left and Hudson makes his bed to the right of Grady.

Even though it's another tradition of its own, I can't help the sinking feeling of disappointment that settles in my stomach. I know Grady will still hold my hand, but there's no way I'm letting him kiss me in front of my brothers. I want the moment to be special, not traumatizing.

I look up from my hands twisting in my lap to find Grady's dark eyes pinned on me. He has a small frown on his face, the one that pulls his bottom lip out without him even noticing. He knows I think he looks absolutely pathetic when he pouts like this, but the face secretly makes me want to give him anything in the world, if it means he'll stop looking so sad. I don't know why he's looking at me this way right now, nor what I can do to make it go away though.

He turns his head toward Hudson and tells the group he's going to go make us his famous hot chocolate. Then, without a word, he climbs out of the tent. Hudson follows to help bring the snacks out.

"Why is Grady acting so weird?" Asher asks while fluffing his pillow and getting comfortable for the night.

Grady

Two nights before school starts, fifteen years ago...

My eyes drift to Vivi again. I don't know how many times I've looked at her today, but I quit counting around the time we all stopped for smoothies on the way home from the beach. I spend more minutes than I care to admit looking at Vivi every day, but not usually because it feels like I'm on the chopping block. Eight hours have passed, and I still can't fight the nagging feeling that something is wrong. I'm sure none of her siblings or my sister Blake would notice because from the outside, everything looks fine.

She had me follow her along the shore with a little plastic bucket to collect seashells and shared smoothies with me on the walk back to her house, just like every year.

She's in her honorary place next to me in the bed the six of us made on her living room floor, just like every year.

She's a little more snuggled into my side than what's necessary for us to all fit, just like every year.

Vivi lacing our pinkies together under the sheet is new though. I could feel my face heat up for at least five minutes after. Hudson gave me a weird look, but no one said anything.

The small contact makes me want to pretend that everything is fine between us, but I know it's not. Every time I look at her, I catch her hazel eyes darting away. Every. Single. Time. She doesn't look like she has been crying but the green in her irises are brighter than they usually are, so she's definitely upset. She's been quieter today than she was earlier in the week. Her laughs have been harder to pull out of her, and she didn't even fight Asher for the last bag of kettle corn. I know her siblings won't think much about it, with her tendency to fold into herself sometimes, but she usually leaves a space for just me.

Today, it feels like there is a small corner for everyone except me.

When the ending credits finally start rolling across the screen, I look around to make sure everyone else is crashed out before I gently tug on Vivi's pinky until her eyes flutter open. She starts to say something when I bring my other hand to her mouth. Her brows pull together, but she nods. I stand up and pull her out of the mess of blankets. With our pinkies hooked back together, I guide her to her bedroom and through the window that leads to our favorite spot on her roof.

I sit close enough for our knees to touch and set our linked fingers in my lap.

I don't know if we sit up there for a few minutes or a few hours, but no amount of time ever feels long enough when I'm alone with her.

We don't talk a lot while we sit under the stars, but I can see the tension slowly leaving her body. It turns into overthinking, the evidence written all over her face. Her brows are still knitted together, but instead of exasperation, her eyes are wide like she's trying to visualize every single thought that's fighting, all at once, to make themselves known to her.

"Hey." I bump our shoulders together. "Vivi," I say when she still won't look at me. "Do you want to talk about it?" I know better than to open a conversation with Vivi that doesn't allow her an escape route.

She looks up at me with an expression I've never seen on her face before. The freckles along her cheeks and nose are bunched up together, like when she's confused, but the way she's looking up at me through her lashes is both angry and scared.

"Am I your best friend?"

This feels like a trick. "You know you're my best friend. You do know that, right?" I don't know what I could have done to make her think otherwise, but I would pluck every star out of the sky right now, if that was what she needed to realize that she has always been the most important person in my life.

"Is that all that I am?" She sounds sad now.

"What do you mean?" I don't know what else I can give her, but I can try. All I know is that I want to kiss her. Just like I did when I took her to the beach and surprised her with a picnic for her birthday last May. I know that I've wanted to make Vivi my whole world since last winter when she got caught sneaking into my room. She fell out of my window, cutting her jaw when she landed on her face, and looked up at me with eyes full of tears, before running to the gate leading to her backyard.

I decide to lean in before I know what's going on. She starts to say something to dismiss the conversation and turn her head away from me, but I can't stop myself in time. Our noses bump together, hard, and my lips catch the side of her mouth as she's letting out a soft *fuck*.

I stare at her for a second before turning away. If she could see the color rushing to my entire upper body, I'm sure she would say it's the deepest red to ever grace my cheeks. I'm already thinking of a thousand ways to apologize and beg her to pretend like I didn't just try to drastically change our friendship when I hear her quiet giggle.

When I turn back toward her, she's grinning so wide and lets out one of her high-pitched cackles. My favorite of her laughs and the one that I've only ever heard come out of her because I brought it to life. After a few seconds of staring at her, embarrassed and infatuated, I start to laugh too. My face is still hot when we calm down and she turns toward me.

"Grady, will you try again?"

I slowly turn before leaning toward her. This time I come to a stop a few inches away, just long enough to let her see the smile in my eyes, and softly press our lips together.

Chapter One
Vivi

"My dad says you hate him."

The small voice startles me so much I drop the stapler in my hand. "Holy f—" I start to say as I turn around but stop when I see two girls standing in my classroom. "Holy *funk*. You scared me." I let out a quiet confused laugh, looking around awkwardly. "I can assure you that I don't hate him, but who is your dad?"

As I bend down to grab the stapler the older girl speaks, "Grady Miller." It slips out of my hand again. I don't bother to pick it up before standing and looking at the two girls who wandered into my classroom.

Now that I'm actually looking at them, it makes sense. So much so that I don't know how I didn't immediately realize. His parents mentioned a few months ago that he would be moving back but that was the last I heard. It has been about eight years since I last saw him and if I'm remembering correctly, it wasn't too long after that that his oldest daughter was born.

Even though I've spent the last few years trying to forget his stupid boyish grin, unfortunately, I haven't. And the curious little humans standing in front me are his clones with all Grady's features plastered on their adorable faces. Both girls have his perfect milk chocolate brown hair with loose curls and brown eyes that shine golden when the light hits them just right. The biggest difference I notice is that their complexion is fair, when Grady had always had a natural tan that glowed under the sunset.

Sometimes I wondered if he still did.

Not that it matters.

Not like I've tried Googling him... recently.

Not like there is *anything* about that man on the internet since he was in college and still playing baseball.

"I don't hate your father," I chuckle and finally pick up the stapler. I can't say that I never hated Grady, but I don't feel that way anymore. I tried to stop feeling anything where he's concerned a very long time ago. I quirk an eyebrow at the girls. "But if your dad does think that I hate him, I doubt he knows where you currently are?"

The younger girl looks about five and has big round eyes that probably help her get just about anything she wants. She giggles nervously. It's the first sound she's made since they walked in. "No, he doesn't know where we are because *we* don't know where we are! He gave us money to go to the vending machine, but we couldn't find it, so we turned around and around and around. Stella," she jerks her thumb toward her older sister who rolls her eyes, "said she recognized your name on the door."

Stella turns and leans toward her sister before whisper-yelling, "Ugh, Daisy, please stop talking! You're going to get us into trouble!"

"No, no. Neither one of you are in trouble but I don't want your dad to worry, either." I tilt my head toward the desks at the front of my classroom. "Why don't you take a seat and I'll try to find your dad's extension code?"

I knew I would eventually have to see Grady, but I was not prepared for it today. I look down at my outfit and let out a long sigh.

I opted for a Taylor Swift tee and my comfiest green overalls—which happen to also be really fucking cute. I hadn't bothered with make-up today. It wouldn't have done much anyway. Not after I let my best friend Lexi talk me into staying at the bar two hours later than I had planned. And since I was there, I had two or three more margaritas. It's not my fault that James was bartending last night, and everyone knows he makes the best ones. It was also the first time Lexi and I had time to go out together in a few weeks.

I'm looking a hell of a lot better than I was this morning but it's not my best day by any means.

I don't notice I'm nibbling on my bottom lip until I get the faint taste of blood. I consciously take a deep breath and force myself to stop fidgeting.

I would say that Grady is responsible for like... ninety-three percent of our animosity but I was definitely the one who made an ass out of myself the last time we saw each other.

Which only piques my curiosity more.

I take a seat at my desk and turn the computer on. "Well, since we are at school you should call me Miss Davies." Truthfully, it has less to do with professionalism and more to do with keeping my guard up where Grady—and now his adorable little daughters—are concerned. "Stella?" I flick my eyes from the older girl to the younger one, "and Daisy?"

Stella sighs, "Yes."

"It's nice to meet you both."

"Do I have to tell you how I heard my dad?"

As much as I *really* want to know, I can't in good faith make myself ask.

But if there is one thing I've learned while working with the younger crowd, it's that silence almost always gives you the same information.

I shrug. "No, it's okay. I'm going to find his number."

I usually bring my laptop so I can limit the number of times I have to use the desktop that's supplied by the school, but I hadn't anticipated needing it while decorating my classroom.

It takes about twenty seconds before Stella starts talking.

"I woke up and got scared, so I went to find my dad. I heard him talking to my aunt. It kind of seemed like she knew you too." She eyes me curiously before giving an insolent shrug. In that same moment, I realize she's a fiery little thing.

"Mmhmm..." Yeah, Grady's sister Blake hates me. That's not news to me. We used to be friends, almost as close as me and Grady, but I am pretty sure that friendship's demise is ninety-three percent *my* fault.

"That's all I'm going to say," she huffs in a defiant tone.

I fight back a snort. "Got it."

Chrome is opening at the same moment there is a soft knock on the door. All three of our heads turn toward the disturbance at the same time.

I thank whoever is holy up there that Grady is giving Stella and Daisy a stern look. It allows me time to shake out of the shock from his presence.

I may feel *indifferent* toward him, but I can admit that manhood has treated him well.

I'm too busy taking in his broad shoulders that I don't notice when he looks at me. He says quietly, the same severe expression he gave the girls, but amusement thick in his voice, "And what are you grinning about over there?"

"I'm not grinning about anything." I lean back in my chair.

"Genevieve, you've made that damn face since you were about six years old."

I know what face he's talking about. My poor attempt at a poker face. Considering it's what usually caused our mothers to catch us sneaking out, or something along those lines, I'm not really shocked that he can see through it.

I don't want to be, but I'm weirdly fascinated by seeing this side of Grady. I've known him our entire lives but not like *this*. There was the boy who was my best friend, the teenage idiot and the college baseball player that drunk me, apparently, didn't seem to care for.

But the man standing in front of me now is exactly that.

A man.

This Grady—single father Grady—has a sharp jawline and a light layer of day-old scruff. He always towered over me, but he's even taller than I remember. The mocha curls are a bit longer than they were when I saw him at his parents' vow renewal many moons ago. In one hand, he's holding a very tiny, very lumpy, ceramic mug that has *#1 dad* carved into the side. I'm assuming one of his daughters made it because, even from here, I can see that there's a hole just above the *A*, making it so that he wouldn't be able to fill it more than three-quarters of the way full. The other is casually tucked into the pocket of his forest green chino shorts. The *short* chino shorts. The ones that look almost indecent on a man with legs like that. More specifically, thighs like *that*. Long and muscular. Could probably crack a watermelon if he tried.

My eyes drop to the floor once the heat rapidly spreads through my body.

Get it together, Vivi.

I can't look at Grady like that.

It's a nice pair of legs sprinkled with some dark hair.

Sure, they are thick... and defined... and...

Holy shit, woman.

I get my mind out of the gutter and focus on his shoes. He's still wearing Adidas. Which makes me want to smile, and I hate myself for it. These ones are white with dark gray lines down the side. His High Tides Charter School hoodie also makes me bite back a laugh. He hasn't even had his official first day of working here, and yet it's just so Grady.

He looks good, like *really* good, and I've never hated him more because of it. We all hope that the first boy to break our heart will turn into a smelly, hairy curmudgeon, but I didn't get that lucky.

Once I get a grip on my libido and sanity, I realize something.

"You called me Genevieve," I mutter before I can stop myself. Grady never called me Genevieve. He's the one who started Vivi when we first met at the Fourth of July block party. Before then, it was Gen—which I always hated—or my full name. I was five years old, and Grady was two months away from turning six. His family had just moved to Amada Beach about a year after we did, and he was playing all alone, so I took a plate of hotdogs over to him. I know, it's weird, but it worked for us. We introduced ourselves, he said Genevieve was too long of a name for such a small person. After a few minutes of brainstorming, Grady settled on Vivi, and that was that.

"What?"

"Nothing." I sit up straighter. "Your daughters are a delight. They must get that from their mother." I throw him a smirk before looking at my old computer. The damn thing barely works but it gets shoved to the end of the budget list every year. Grady's mom Selena, who is also the school's librarian, and I talked to a few of the other teachers this year and have requested time at the next committee meeting. Which is in two days.

Grady gives me an assessing look then a soft smile. One that doesn't bring out his dimple but crinkles the skin around his eyes. "It's good to see you, *Vivi*."

I bite back a snarky retort, if only because I told his daughters I didn't hate him.

"Stella and Daisy will be in third grade and kindergarten here, so I'm sure there will be plenty of time for you to tell them all the ways to torment my life." The amused tone is back in his voice. It's the quiet sibling to his playful mood he used to save just for me. Not that anything of his is *just for me* anymore.

And I wouldn't want it if it was.

"Awesome. Can't wait. I'll make sure to go through my childhood diaries for ideas."

I'm feeling more flustered than I care to admit, but I wasn't prepared for this today. I'm tired and close to burnout. It has been weeks since I had time to relax that wasn't for showering or sleep. I don't have it in me for a full-on verbal battle today. Between helping at the bookstore, preparing for the new year, prepping for the meeting, and volunteering at our summer camp program, I'm at the end of my mental rope.

He leans against the door frame, never fully entering the classroom, and takes a small sip from his mug, careful not to spill. "Even I'm interested in reading those."

"No need to waste your time. Imagine all of your worst nightmares, and it will read something like that." I give him a poisonous smile.

He snorts. The bastard actually *snorts*.

"Yup, I'm sure that's exactly what I would find." He stands up straight and looks back at his daughters. "Alright, little ladies let's go. We have to meet Auntie Blake at the house."

Stella stands up and gives me a quick wave before scurrying out. Daisy skips over to my desk and holds her hand out. I take it in mine, and she gives it a frenzied shake. "It was so nice to meet you, Miss Davies!" she singsongs.

"It was nice to meet you, too, Daisy." I give her my biggest smile and shake her arm wildly in return.

It makes her giggle before she skips to her sister in the hall.

Grady softly taps the door. "See you Sunday, *Miss Davies.*" Then he walks down the hall, as if he wasn't waiting there to begin with.

Miss Genevieve Davies,

Thank you for your interest in the University of California, Aurora Hills School Administration graduate program.

We'll be taking applications for next fall in the new year. So, there's still plenty of time to perfect your application. However, I know how important it is to choose the right program for YOU. Especially as a full-time teacher. Attached are all the informational flyers and a list of the required courses. That should be a good place for you to get an idea of what our program entails.

Lacey Hampton is a highly respected educator in our department, and she's spoken highly of you. While I can't make any promises about admission, I would love the opportunity to sit down with you sometime soon. We can discuss the program further in depth, if it seems like something you may be interested in. I can also give you tips on filling out the application

and interviewing for the program. If you're interested, please let me know a few times that work best for you, and I'll schedule you in.

**Best regards,
Kathleen Humble, College of Education Advisor
University of California, Aurora Hills**

Calypso and Lexi are already at my house when I walk through the door, waiting to watch the next episode of our current Netflix show. We like to watch shows together and the desire to finish a series helps to motivate us to regularly see each other outside of the bookstore and obligations. I don't know what I would do without either one of them.

"Hi, Viv." My sister sashays into the small foyer with three plates and forks in her hands. She drops a kiss on the top of my head, which is easy enough for her considering I stopped growing at the whopping height of five foot four when I was thirteen. Calypso continued to grow until she was sixteen and landed at a height of five feet ten inches. She says being so tall isn't always great, but I don't believe her. Calypso still has the body of a ballerina even though she bakes for a living now. She looks exactly like our mom, who is equally as beautiful. Their strawberry blonde locks, and honey brown eyes, are the perfect match to their peachy pale skin. Red is her signature. Today it's a red cropped hoodie and red plaid socks paired with high-waisted black leggings.

"Hey, Lyp." I kick off my sandals next to her Docs.

Lexi is nestled into the couch with her favorite blanket and laptop propped up on the arm. All I can see is her orange flannel and her silky black hair tied up in a messy knot on the top of her head. When she looks up at me with her upturned onyx eyes narrowed, I know I'm not going to like where this is going. So, I choose deflection.

I walk into the kitchen, grab three wine glasses from the cabinet and the big Riesling bottle from the fridge. Between seeing Grady and wherever Lexi's taking this, I know I'll need a couple glasses.

"The store doesn't close for another two hours. What are you guys doing here so early?"

About six years ago, Calypso and Lexi bought the old bookstore near the beach. The building itself is a piece of history around here. Between Lexi's trust fund and Calypso's inheritance from our father's life insurance claim, they were able to buy the building and put in just enough renovations to bring it to this century and add a small kitchen for a bakery.

Now they are the proud owners of Brighter Daze, bakery and bookstore.

"We asked Gavin to close for us. He wants the extra hours before his classes start anyway," Calypso says.

I set the glasses down and start pouring us each a full glass. "Why did you ask him to close?"

"It was slow today. And we wanted to talk to you about the family who came into the store today. You'll never believe who it was." Lexi's giving me her slyest grin.

After an entire childhood of hating each other and then ten years of unconditional friendship, you know someone better than almost anyone else. So, I know she's goading me.

"Grady Miller himself, with two of the sweetest little girls I've ever met."

"They were pretty sweet," Calypso agrees. She isn't necessarily a fan of kids so it's a high compliment.

"He said he was on his way to the school… Have you seen him yet?"

Chapter Two
Grady

The entire drive, I'm distracted, occasionally catching bits of the girls' conversation as they plan the night with their cousins. Mostly though, I'm trying to block out the swarm of relentless memories going through my mind like flies buzzing around a trash can.

The girls and I moved into our house a month ago, the weekend of the Fourth of July, so naturally I couldn't help but think all about meeting Genevieve for the first time on the pier.

We pass the hole-in-the-wall smoothie shack; I'm reminded of all the times that Vivi couldn't make up her mind between a Mango Sunrise and a Blueberry Blast so we'd end up sharing both.

I park on the street outside of Bella Donna's Diner; I'm assaulted by dozens of flashbacks of lunches after long days playing in the ocean with everyone, sometimes just Vivi and I.

Even the pizza joint we are picking up from is associated with countless childhood memories. My sixth birthday when I told Vivi that she was my best friend for the very first time is the featured film tonight. It was also the first time in my life that I recognized the moment as something important, something life changing.

"What kind of pizza are we getting?" Stella's voice pulls me out of my nostalgia.

"I got one for me." Translation: pepperoni with half pineapple and half banana peppers. "One pepperoni, and pepperoni and mushroom."

"Are we getting dessert?" Daisy asks.

"Your aunt is bringing stuff for sundaes, at Millie's request." She smiles up at me as we step up to the take-out counter.

"Grady Miller," a deep voice booms from the open kitchen. "I was hoping you would stop in soon." Carlo, the owner of Tossin' Tomatoes, walks over to me. I stick my hand out for a shake, but he pulls me into a hug. "Come here, son. Your parents let me know you were moving back but I wasn't sure when I would be seeing you." He releases me with a pat on the shoulder.

Carlo has owned the small restaurant long before my family and I moved out here. He has become good friends with my parents and Bonnie, Vivi's mom, over the years. That's kind of how our small community at Amada Beach is, you are, at the very least, friendly with everyone.

"How long has it been now? Are these your girls?" He smiles down at Stella and Daisy.

He looks the same with his full belly and goatee, but his chestnut hair has quite a bit more silver than the last time I saw him.

And if I'm being truthful, that was way too long ago. Something like five years. I was visiting alone, which I did a lot during my marriage. Arielle, my ex-wife, said she didn't feel like she fit in here. I never *really* tried to correct her because it was the truth. It was similar to the way I didn't fit into her family's Upper Eastside lifestyle in Manhattan. It didn't matter how much we liked and enjoyed each other's families either. That was never the problem. It was something between her and I that fit together enough but never felt exactly right. Like when you're down to your last pair of thick, wool socks and all day your shoes feel slightly tighter than usual.

"Too long, Carlo, but we are here to stay now." I place a hand on each of my daughters' heads. "These are my girls. Stella and Daisy."

They both mumble a quiet *hi*, much more subdued than when I found them with Vivi.

He smiles at the three of us with something like pride in his eyes. "I'm excited for the next generation of Miller birthdays celebrated here. Now, if only any of those Davies kids would have their own babies, it'd really feel like old times."

"Well, you know the four of them always have their own plans for things." The fact that none of them are married—sans Calypso's divorce—and are all childless, doesn't surprise me in the slightest, especially not after watching them grow up with a single mother.

"Hmm." He gives me an assessing look. "What about your plans?"

I shrug. "I'm working at the charter school and starting up the baseball team soon."

"Yes, son, I know all that. Your parents told me." I shake my head, not understanding what he wants to know. He glances down at my daughters then back up to me. "Do your plans involve… reconnecting with anyone in particular?"

"My mom might as well start a gossip blog at this point." I roll my eyes, shoving my hands in my pockets.

"Take that up with her," he shrugs back at me. "All I'm saying is you should think about it. Anyway, your pizzas are on the house." He winks at Stella and Daisy, "And I threw in an order of brownies."

Both girls instantly perk up. "We can use them in the sundaes!" Daisy exclaims.

We say our goodbyes, ending with me promising to be around

much more. And I mean it. Not only is my family here but knowing how Amada Beach has welcomed new families cemented my decision to move back to my hometown. I want my daughters to grow up with a community supporting them, not just their dad hundreds of miles away from any family.

"Stell, you're not in trouble," I start carefully. I look at my older daughter in the rearview mirror and can't help my heart from breaking a little when I see our emotional similarities as clearly as I can see our matching eyes. The divorce has been harder on Stella even though she tries to hide it for Daisy's sake. She has been happier since we moved here. Brighter, livelier. But I know that the last two and a half years have also aged her in a way that's not fair to a kid. "I just want to know what you heard the other night when Auntie Blake was over."

She looks out the window for a few moments before quietly explaining, "I just was scared in the new house… I didn't mean to spy on you guys, but I didn't want to interrupt either. I was sitting at the top of the stairs waiting for you to come up." She finally meets my eyes in the mirror. "You were fighting about if Viv—Miss Davies—hated you or not, but the fight didn't really make sense because you both said she did but weren't agreeing on anything either." Giving me her best attempt at looking innocent, she adds, "You know, Daddy, Auntie Blake said a lot of bad words while you were talking… now that you know I heard everything, can you tell her that she owes the swear jar *at least* twenty dollars?" She blinks at me through her lashes and sticks out her bottom lip. It's the same pouty face I make but the difference is, hers is intentional.

I chuckle and consider letting Stella demand twenty dollars from my sister. And what can I do other than insist she complies; those are the rules.

About six months ago, the girls caught me saying *shit* for the first time in their lives. Stella, always the ringleader, decided that was enough reason to implement a swear jar. At the end of every year, she and Daisy get to take the money to the toy store and split however much they *earn*, as Stella described it. I know they were hoping to make out like bandits by January but if the rules applied to only me, they would be lucky to split five dollars.

Blake *was* annoying that night so screw it. "Sure, Stell, I'll let her know."

She smiles triumphantly before turning to look back out the window.

Stella is right, Blake and I were agreeing on the fact that Vivi hates me. She made it perfectly clear the last time I saw her at my parents' vow renewal. She used those exact words, actually.

'*I hate you.*'

It definitely wasn't the smartest idea to try to talk to her when she, Lexi and her three siblings were all plastered before the sun fully set, but I hadn't expected that either.

Blake was still in high school when that happened, and not very close with Vivi anymore.

Blake thinks I'm '*the world's biggest asswipe,*' her exact quote, for taking the job at the charter school knowing that I would be working alongside Genevieve. I insisted I could avoid her for the entirety of the year and my loving sister insisted that I'm '*even more hopeless and clueless and balls-less than even she predicted,*' again her exact quote. When I refused to tell her, for the millionth time, what happened between Vivi and I, she told me that it was *fucking bullshit.*' I then proceeded to ask her what happened between the two of them and she called me '*a fucking busybody who is just as bad as our mother.*'

Most people can't get Blake to have a conversation with them, but I can't seem to make her shut up.

Stella should probably demand thirty dollars, if I'm being honest.

It's not that I'm holding anything back from Blake though. I've never asked her to put distance between herself and the Davies siblings. Our childhood photo albums have just as many pictures of Vivi, Calypso, and the twins, Asher and Hudson, pasted inside as there are of my sister and me. Each one of them was as much her friends as they were mine. I'll never understand why she felt so… hurt? Betrayed? Protective?

It's not only that, but I can't really tell her what happened when I have no idea what happened. It wasn't one fight or one event. After I kissed her on her roof, I felt like I was on top of the world until everything I knew was spiraling out of control.

I wish I could say I don't know who started it but that's not true. I know I did. It was only a month or so after the night on her roof that I went to homecoming with another girl. Vivi was a grade below me so it wasn't like I could take her, which is *obviously* what I would have done. She was still in middle school when I moved into high school. Once we started going to different schools, it got harder to see each other, much less find time alone. It wasn't that we were growing apart per se, rather we weren't growing forward either. Things seemed to just go back to what they were before we ever kissed. I know it hurt her, no matter how much she tried to hide it. I don't know why I asked Rebecca. She was cute and nice, but I didn't like her. At that point in my life, Vivi was the only girl I had ever had feelings for. Sometimes I think too big of feelings for a fourteen-year-old and maybe that was why I continued messing up so bad. Maybe I was just a really, really stupid teenager.

Either way, I'm pretty sure that she would have forgiven me for having a date to a stupid school dance.

The first night of winter break, we were all having one of our movie nights in their living room when Asher made some lame remark about how I kissed Rebecca at homecoming.

I know, I know. I was the one who kissed her when the girl I was pretty much determined to marry one day was at home and sad. I screwed up but Asher never could keep a secret.

I'm still not sure if her siblings or Blake knew we had kissed, but every single one of them knew that Vivi and I were closer... closer than just friends even though we were *just* friends.

That was the beginning of the end.

Things between us never fully recovered after that winter night. On the outside, everything looked the same. We spent countless evenings together and I brought her a cupcake on her birthday the final time that summer. We shared secrets and smoothies. We snuck into each other's bedrooms more than once, wrapped under a blanket while I read to her with the help of a flashlight. But there were also days on the beach when I wanted to kiss her so bad but always chickened out. I wanted to apologize to her, especially when I caught her looking at me lost in her thoughts. Her mood would slightly change, and I always knew she was thinking it. I was embarrassed and cowardly, so I never told her how sorry I was.

The following year, I didn't take a date, but I didn't take her either, even though I could have. *Should* have. But I didn't want her to feel like she was the second option. Now, as an adult, I realize that was a stupid excuse for my fear.

But junior year... that homecoming was a doozy of a night in our friendship. I knew that Vivi would be going to her second homecoming with her new boyfriend–and eventual fiancé—so I did the worst thing I could think of.

I asked her archenemy—who is *now* her best friend Lexi—to be my date.

One thing about Genevieve: she's competitive. As am I—that's the only way to make it as far as I did in any sport—but I used that to push me through my baseball career whereas Vivi focused more on the academic side of things and emotional warfare against said nemesis. Either way, we both love competition. Even if that competition is who can land the lowest blow. I also know that there had never been anything I liked more than riling her up and nothing gets a reaction out of her quicker than losing.

It was an ugly, endless battle with no champion. We were the only two people who understood, *really* understood, how to hurt one another and we used it against each other. I don't know how to explain that twisted game to someone, even Blake.

But I know my sister and she isn't going to let it go. Neither will my mother.

I open the garage door and park the Jeep. Out of habit, I open Stella's door to help her out of her car seat, but she quickly reminds me that she doesn't need help anymore. She's started to ask if she can give up the booster all together, and since the answer is still a firm *no*, she has decided that she's at least old enough to unbuckle herself. She isn't wrong but it still hurts more than I care to admit.

"Stella, what should we watch tonight?" Daisy always looks toward her older sister for direction. Arielle and I were worried for a while that she'd shy away from forging her own path in the world, but we couldn't have been more wrong. She doesn't look to Stella out of fear or conformity. She'll put her foot down and dig her heels in faster than anyone you know. It's clear as day that she genuinely cares about what Stella wants, especially since Arielle officially moved out a little more than a year ago.

They've always secretly reminded me of my other favorite pair of sisters.

"We should watch *Hocus Pocus* again! Millie loves it too!"

"Yesss! I call being Mary!"

"Yeah, okay. Millie likes to be Winifred anyway."

I wait outside for Blake and her kids while the girls go up to their rooms to change and gather their blankets. It has only been a few weeks since we moved into the house, but there have been more than a handful of cousin sleepovers already. It's those nights, more than anything, that have boosted their spirits in the last couple of years.

I start looking through a few more boxes to set aside when my mind starts to drift back to my failed marriage. A lot of the decorations were from the house we shared together. The silverware is from our wedding. The dish towels are the same ones from our honeymoon in Costa Rica. We didn't share my current bed sheets, but they still were used in the townhome we shared in Phoenix.

I make a mental note to take the girls shopping before school starts. There's some money I set aside to let them pick out some decorations and furniture. Home is wherever they are, sleeping soundly at night. I don't care how many floral rugs and *My Little Pony* posters cover the new house if they love it.

Headlights brighten the garage, pulling me from my thoughts. Once Blake is parked, I open the door and begin unbuckling my oldest nephew, Leo. He's already talking my ear off about all the plans he has for us tonight when I scoop him into my arms. Much like Stella, Millie's beginning to crave more independence. I don't offer to help her with her car seat, but I stay close by until she jumps out of the car. She doesn't have it figured out quite as well as Stella but she's a bit younger.

I meet Blake in my living room as she sets her youngest child, Kayson, in his playpen. Stella's looking at me over Blake's shoulder with wide eyes. I huff out a laugh at her attempt at subtly.

"Soo," I start, "we had a little eavesdropper the other night." Blake lifts her head in confusion. "When we were talking about my job at the charter school."

"Oh." Blake blinks. "Okay…"

"Well, you should have listened to Mom all those times she told you to watch your mouth. The girls implemented a swear jar a few months ago, and according to Stella, you owe them *at least* twenty dollars." I don't even try to hide my smugness.

She narrows her gray eyes at me, probably coming up with some pretty creative insults, but she relents anyway. "Of course, Stell. Sorry about that." She gives a sympathetic smile over her shoulder to the kids but turns her dagger eyes back to me.

I start the movie and nod toward the kitchen.

Blake follows me in and jumps on the counter. She watches me put the dishes away and reload the dishwasher. I have a housecleaner who comes over twice a week but if I'm being honest, I try to do most of the upkeep myself. I want the girls to see the benefit of maintaining your own household. But I really hate mopping. So much so, that I hire someone to come do it twice a week, but I feel bad wasting her time. So, I pay for a full morning and tip generously each time.

Dishes are one chore that I didn't realize how much Arielle picked up the slack on, though. Now I make it a point to always do them myself, even when they pile up. It's my own small punishment for my divorce.

"You saw her already." It's not a question.

"Hmm," I grunt in acknowledgement.

"And...?" I can feel her growing irritation with my vagueness already.

And... she's really freaking beautiful. *Radiating,* even. Her hair this time of the year was always my favorite—a little lighter from the summer sun, bringing out the golds more. It reminds me of a wildfire, and that's exactly what she is. Uncontrollable and unpredictable.

But also, bright and burning and captivating.

Even with her sitting down, I could tell that her body is fuller, curvier, than the last time I saw her. She not only looks healthier than that night, but more alive and certainly more voluptuous.

"And it was fine."

"You couldn't even go a week without running into her. Why am I not surprised?"

Maybe because we always seemed to attract each other like a paperclip to a magnet.

"It was probably better we got it out of the way before school started."

Blake hums thoughtfully. "It's okay if it's not fine, you know. I never meant to pressure you to prove something you aren't ready for."

This is another side of my sister that so few people get to see—perceptive and caring.

I nudge her knee with my elbow. "I know that. You didn't. I think I needed to see her. To understand where things are with us."

"And where are they?"

I huff out a dry laugh. "I mean, she still hates me, so I guess six feet below the ground?"

What I'm not telling Blake is that maybe Vivi wasn't happy to see me, but I saw the way she was looking at me before she snapped out of it. She took her sweet time taking me in from head to toe and I let her.

Of course, I let her.

It was probably the shock of seeing me after eight years. I heard Stella talking from down the hall and even after years of silence, I recognized Vivi's voice before I saw her name on the door. There was a rush of nerves for a few seconds, but I realized that I was immediately getting the upper hand when it was me walking into her classroom unannounced.

A large part of me doesn't think it was all from shock though. There was interest in what she saw. Maybe a little amusement, probably because of the Adidas. I've always been slightly predictable, especially to her, and time hasn't changed that. But there was definitely heat. She instantly flushed when she made eye contact with my lower half. Arielle always hated the shorter chinos, but I knew I could pull them off. Vivi's reaction only proved that, as far as I'm concerned.

A small part of me thinks I'm imagining this, but I try not to listen to him as much as possible. I mentally smack some duct tape on the little angel guy's mouth and let his little devil companion take the wheel.

Getting under Vivi's skin, even just a little bit, is still the most invigorating thing I've ever experienced.

Five minutes with her had me feeling more alive than I have in a long time. Years before my divorce even.

And you know what they say about indifference being the true opposite of love, whereas hate is tip-toeing a fine line.

The leather-wearing demon in my head and I agree; Genevieve feeling *something* about me is better than her feeling nothing

Chapter Three
Vivi

Taking a few more deep breaths, I slip my sweater on over my head and sit on the edge of my bed. Lexi won't entertain more than five minutes of me locking myself in my room, but I plan to use every last second. I've been preparing myself for weeks. For all the questions that will be asked. For all the memories flooding my mind.

Where do we even stand now? Last time I saw him, I was about eight tequila shots deep before nightfall and none of us—Calypso, my brothers, Lexi, and I—stopped there. We each made some… choices that night. Some were better than others. I was drinking to help me loosen up in anticipation of seeing Grady for the first time since he left for college. To say I overcompensated would be an understatement.

There is a long stretch of time during the party that I don't remember, and that's probably for the best because what I do remember is horrible enough.

One second, I'm sitting on the steps of his front porch, trying to sober up at my mother's request, and the next he was standing in front of me.

I'll never forget what I told him no matter how much I wish I could.

"*I* hate *you*."

He took a step back, as if I landed a physical blow to his chest.

"I really don't know you anymore." *He chuckled but it was dripping with poison.* "I'm embarrassed to have ever known you."

I barked out a dry laugh. I was never the one who lied to him. I was never the one who cut the other out of their life. I was never the one who secretly spoke such ugly words about the other.

No, that was him.

And he was embarrassed to know me?

After all those years, I still knew where to hit. "The best thing you ever did was leave for college. I don't want you here. We're all better off without you."

Grady stared at me for a long moment. "Don't worry. I won't be visiting very often anymore."

"Good." *It hurts every time you do.* "My wish for us every birthday is that you stay far, far away. It's been that for years."

Lie. Lie. Lie.

Grady stared at me like I killed his hypothetical puppy, before he softly nodded his head, and walked past me to the party inside.

I had never seen Grady close to tears and maybe I was still drunk, but I think I made him cry that night.

I went to my childhood bedroom soon after and cried myself to sleep. At some point, Lexi found me and curled up around me. Even when I got the last word, I somehow still lost when it came to Grady.

"You know, I've always liked Grady. Personally."

Calypso snorts, then mutters, "Here we go again," and fills her wine glass almost to the brim.

"No, we aren't going there again," I state as I snatch the wine bottle out of her hand. Lexi has only brought this up a few times in our ten-year friendship. The first time, when we were drunk in the studio apartment we shared and decided to lay our past out, once and for all. We needed to make sure we weren't going to murder each other before moving in together. The other time was about two years after the vow renewal, Asher told us how he ran into Grady on the beach that morning and Lexi was trying to get something, *anything*, out of me about what happened on the Millers' front porch. The provoking didn't work, neither did bribing, threatening, or ignoring me. "We all know that you have always liked Grady. It was made painfully obvious when you guys had your tongues down each other's throats at homecoming." I can't stop my eyes from rolling when I notice the looks Lexi and Calypso are giving each other over their wine glasses.

Lexi's says, *I thought she didn't care.*

Calypso's response is, *just as expected.*

Lexi's eyes cut back to me, and she gives me a shit-eating grin before declaring, "Trust me, Viv, there was nothing painful about making out with Grady."

I know she's trying to rile me up with intentions to get me to chug my wine, but I do it anyway. Drunk Genevieve doesn't usually talk about Grady—I have anything related to him under lock and key—but who knows what will come out after seeing him. He still had some of his boyish features and softness the last time I saw him. I often wondered how that would transform into manhood. It was better than I could have ever imagined. "You're disgusting."

Lexi takes on a serious tone, but her features are still bright with mischief. "All I'm saying, maybe for the last time but probably not, is that Grady was the best guy I've ever made out with." She puts her hand up in a '*scout's honor*' gesture. "He was like, sixteen when it happened. Either the male population is really as hopeless as we have considered," Calypso raises her glass to that, "or he's just that great and has definitely only gotten better."

"I don't really understand how you decided those are the only two possible situations," I say slowly, "but I'm going to put my money on the former."

"It doesn't matter what you think. It matters what me and Calypso think. And I think you should find out if he's still a good kisser. What do you think, Lyp?"

Calypso is plating a serving of one of my favorites of her desserts—dream squares, also known as graham cracker-almond-mandarin-orange-coconut pudding-*heaven*. She offers me a plate and I know she brought it to soften me up. Unfortunately, I'll allow it.

"I think I want to stay out of this." She stuffs a spoonful of pudding in her mouth, rendering it otherwise useless.

I know my sister, and she won't be quiet for long. Her silence is more daunting than Lexi's pestering.

They may be friends because of me but they have that annoying oldest sibling connection, so I'm still the one who gets ganged up on.

"I've kissed Grady before. It was… fine." After we almost broke each other's noses, the kiss was quick and soft but was anything other than *fine*. It was like what I imagine Aurora felt when she woke up from her sleeping curse.

"Mmm, no. Bumping noses doesn't count as kissing anyone." I roll my eyes at Lexi. "You guys need a re-do."

"Over my dead body."

"It's been like, fifteen years, Viv." As if that should change my mind.

I stare at her for a few seconds before saying slowly, "Exactly. It's been fifteen years, let it go."

Lexi is about to speak, probably to tell me to *let it go* when Calypso says, "Maybe if you just tell us how it went today, this one will shut up for a second."

Lexi grumbles in response but crosses her arms and waits expectantly.

I take a large gulp of my wine and tell them how Stella and Daisy snuck into my classroom, accused me of hating their father and then Grady came to pick them up.

"That was… anticlimactic," Lexi says before sipping from her glass.

"I don't know what you were expecting. It was… fine."

"I doubt that it was fine, Viv." Calypso, ever the attentive older sister.

"I don't know what you guys want me to say."

"You could tell us more about what happened. People in high school get boyfriends and girlfriends. It was kind of ridiculous to think that you would be each other's *only* relationships, or nothing at all." Lexi cringes away from the dirtiest look I've ever given her, including our mutual years of hatred toward each other. "I'm so sorry. I shouldn't have said that. I just mean… I don't know."

It isn't that I expected Grady and I to be each other's *only* anything. Except maybe I did. I was young. And when it wasn't Grady, I believed it could've been Brody. It definitely wasn't him.

"You don't have to tell us anything that you don't want but I think what Lexi is failing to say is just that…" Calypso picks at the cat hair on the throw blanket. She and my two cats have a mutual dislike for each other. Cinnamon and Vanilla are currently locked in my bedroom. "Was whatever happened between you and Grady really so bad? He was your best friend for years. It was obvious that you both liked each other." Calypso takes another bite of the dessert before saying, "It's just hard to imagine what could have ended that."

I sit back in my velvet armchair and look out the window.

I don't know how to explain to them that, *yes*, Grady asking another girl to homecoming his freshman year really had been so bad. Or that I cried in my bedroom the entire night while all my siblings and Grady were dancing to T-Pain in some gymnasium because I felt like I was losing something important.

And I've always hated to lose.

Sure, maybe I would have gotten over the date. Asher and Hudson always took girls to homecoming. I asked Asher about it once; he said '*it's just what you do.*'

I know that he wouldn't have been allowed to take me anyway, I was only in eighth grade at the time, but why did he have to take anyone at all? Why did he kiss me on my roof just to never even try again? Why did he kiss her? Why didn't he take me the following year?

And that was only the start of it.

I spent my entire childhood chasing Grady and being chased by him. Sharing secrets with him. Planning ten lifetimes worth of adventures together.

I spent my entire childhood believing that he was *mine*.

That had been the night I realized that Grady Miller wasn't mine at all.

Chapter Four
Vivi

Selena and I are standing in the lobby of the auditorium where the committee meetings are held. A few of the other teachers, who helped us prepare for the presentation, are also here.

Different organizations formed over the twelve years since High Tides opened, each one supervised by a different member of the faculty and many of the non-athletic ones were in favor of updating the computer systems this year.

I finally decided at the end of last year that we needed to push this at one of the committee meetings. Selena, an angel, has been helping me put this together all summer. It was a long shot I would even be approved to take the floor. As much as I love High Tides, the principal, Mrs. Gable, and I aren't exactly on the best terms. Teachers, parents, and students from all grade levels love me though, so it really isn't in her best interest to get rid of me either.

Applying to graduate programs in Educational Administration is on the list of things I need to do this fall. I'm only twenty-eight, but I'll be the principal of this school one day.

To be fair, Mrs. Gable has done a lot of good for the school and has been the principal since the school opened twelve years ago. She was head of the movement to expand to all grade levels and has pushed our athletic department into a fast growing and highly respected program.

Looking in from the outside, you would see that our school is continuously in the top fifty for test scores and graduation rates. Not just in charter schools but in all California schools. The yearbook I supervise has been nationally recognized three times since I started. The STEM club makes it to the finals in their competition every year but has yet to win. One of the more recent newspaper editors is now working as the editor for *Princeton Beat*.

Our students are overflowing with talent, and the least we could do as their teachers is help them hone those skills.

Unfortunately, the budget has already been finalized—and I'm sure it includes brand new jerseys for each sports team just like every single year. I've wasted more than enough breaths trying to convince Mrs. Gable, and the rest of the council, to move updating the computer systems and software higher on the priority list, but it falls on deaf ears each year.

This year I'm taking a different approach: grants and fundraising.

It isn't that I haven't thought about it before but to replace every single computer will be a feat. The numbers we have ran multiple times, going as far as having my brother Hudson take a look at them as well, will barely cover the price of everything and that's if we're accepted by every single grant and can hit our goal through fundraising.

It's all we have right now though, so we have to try.

I'm still silently hyping myself up when I hear Selena. "Vivi? Genevieve!" When I finally look over at her, my nervous hazel eyes connecting with her calm gray ones, she gives me a small smile.

"*Mija,* are you okay?"

"Yeah, I'm just going over everything in my head one more time."

Deep breaths.

Inhale. Hold. Exhale. Repeat.

She gives my arm a comforting squeeze, knowing me just as well as if I was her own daughter. "We'll need to go in soon, but let's stay out here and get some air a little longer, okay?"

I nod. I hate public speaking but when it's six against one, you buck up and do what you have to do for the greater good. In this case, the students and school.

That's enough of a reason for me to put on my big girl panties and face the committee.

"We've gone over this a million times now," Selena says quietly, just loud enough for me to hear. "You're the best choice for this, *roja*. It was your idea and you've put the most work into the entire presentation. I'm really proud of you." I stand a little bit straighter and give her a nod, forcing more conviction into my movements this time. I don't notice Selena's attention snag over my shoulder until she says, "What are you doing here?"

I turn my head to look but I know who it is just from the goosebumps that break across my arms and neck.

Stupid, foolish, traitorous body of mine.

We don't react to any man's presence, I tell myself, but absolutely not Grady's. Especially when all he did was walk into a room.

"Hey, sorry I tried to get here as soon as possible." He sounds slightly out of breath like he ran to get in here. "I know there's only about ten minutes until the meeting starts but I needed to show you this."

My eyes are ping-ponging from Grady to Selena, but his eyes are glued on me.

"What are you doing here?" I repeat Selena's question, ignoring the small knowing smile spreading across her face.

He takes a deep breath and looks like he's contemplating running back out of here. "I didn't learn about this board meeting until about a week ago." That kind of surprises me, considering Selena has been helping, but everyone has always been understanding about us keeping our distance from each other. "The principal from the school I was working at in Phoenix was recently promoted to the district leader and felt that she owed me a small favor. I finally cashed it in." He gives a nonchalant shrug that makes me think there's more to that statement.

"Grady, is that supposed to mean something dirty?" I blurt out but Selena's surprised laugh makes me bite my lip to hide a smile.

"What?" He shakes his head and starts to blush. "*No.*"

"We only have a few minutes until the meeting starts. Can this wait?"

"No, it can't, Vivi." Back to business, he shoves a stack of papers toward me, and says, "Just—hold on. I looked at your presentation, and it's good. No, it's *great.* I wouldn't have expected anything else. But you only found large charities. It will be harder to get approved, especially as a charter school in a middle-class neighborhood. Laurie, the district leader, got someone from her office to pull up records of different organizations the schools have worked with out there. She even reached out to some people she knows at the charter schools. I went through them already and only included the ones that are national. The highlighted ones work with charter schools specifically."

Selena takes the stack from me, but I'm just staring up at him in shock. I shake my head, not knowing what to say or how to adjust my presentation to fit all of this.

"That's not all. There is a small tech company located in Portland that buys old computers from schools. With the older hardware, the school could still get a hundred dollars, at least, for each one." I don't think he's taken a full breath since he started. "And there's another tech start-up, this one is in Seattle, that helps schools pay for the software. That could potentially allow us to splurge a little."

"Grady…" Even if I wanted to argue with him, I can't think of a reason to, as much as I hate the fact that I didn't find this information. This was so incredibly kind and thoughtful. But… "It's too late. I can't remember all of this and readjust my presentation." I take a deep breath and look toward the doors that people have slowly started to file through. "They are going to call us in."

His face falls and I can see the rebuttal forming on his tongue.

"Why don't you do the presentation together?" Selena asks, a little too innocently. "They approved time for two speakers, but it was all you anyway, Viv."

"Selena…" I can feel myself starting to hyperventilate.

This was *not* the plan.

"Vivi," Grady says quietly. "You can keep to the original plan if that's what you want." After so many years he still knows me. It isn't fair. "What do you want to do?"

I close my eyes, take a deep breath and count to ten.

This is not about me. It's about the kids and the school. Not my nerves.

I open my eyes and give Selena a small nod. I meet Grady's gaze. "No, it's better with the information you gathered. Thank you for that. I'll start. You said you looked at the presentation? Follow my lead and I'll give the microphone over to you toward the end, when I'm talking about the charities I found. It will make the most sense. Deal?"

I can see the triumph blazing in his eyes, so I remind myself again that this is not about me. I school my expression into cool detachment.

From him, from my anxieties, from the dress that suddenly feels too tight, from everything that's not about getting up in front of the committee to present.

"Deal." He smirks and sticks his hand toward me.

I swat it away and turn toward the doors. "Don't make me regret this, Grady Miller."

Selena's airy laugh follows me to my seat, but it's Grady's searing gaze that has the hair on the back of my neck standing up.

Grady

Well…

The committee meeting went great, but I can't say that Vivi doesn't regret her last-minute choice to make me the other speaker.

She did amazing up there from the very beginning. I don't know what she was so nervous about. All eight of them looked interested in her solution and she was able to answer the few questions they had at the end. They loved her idea to host a winter fair at the end of the semester. I don't know if my contribution helped sway them necessarily, but they were interested in having more opportunities for grants to come through. Somehow, the little mastermind finessed the committee to agree to the terms that every school organization and sport has to participate since the computers will be utilized by all of the students. From what my mom has said about some of the coaches they won't be happy about that.

I like the idea of my team fundraising and volunteering in the community. It's important for them to learn about mutual support and the need to give back. I'm hoping my assistant coach Knox, will have the same feelings toward it. We've yet to meet.

I glance down at her without turning my head. We're waiting for my mom outside while she talks to some of the other teachers, and it feels eerily like we're kids waiting to be picked up again. I followed Vivi out here to try to talk to her but when I felt the anger radiating off of her, I decided to keep my mouth shut.

When her eyes flash up to me, I immediately look away but not fast enough to miss the fire blazing behind her pupils. Not the kind of heat when I saw her in her classroom unfortunately.

No, this is a fire from hell. One I'm sure she's imagining I'm currently burning in.

Even the devil on my shoulder is cowering.

"Look, Vivi," I turn toward her. She narrows her eyes and I flinch back. I didn't think it was possible for her to hate me more, but she can, and she does. The optimistic part of my brain tries to remind me that it's better than her being cold and indifferent. I throw my arms to the side, and she crosses hers in response. "I didn't know that they were going to come to that conclusion."

I'm not lying. How was I supposed to know that the committee would assign Vivi and I to manage this project *together*? Not even in my wildest dreams—or maybe nightmares—did I predict this.

There was a short-lived moment of hope when they first announced their decision, but it died as soon as I smiled down at the fuming troll doll next to me. Vivi has never delegated well, and it appears that's another thing that hasn't changed.

She doesn't say anything. Her eyes just continue to burn holes through my head.

"I'm really, really sorry. I don't want to ruin this for you. We…

we can find someone else to fill my role or… or I can sign a legal binding agreement that says you're fully in charge, and I'm your mere peasant to do as you say."

She tilts her head and thinks it over.

"*Anything* I say?" she asks a little too silky but it's the mischievous glint in her eyes that really scares me.

"Within reason, yes," I say it slowly, to not poke the bear, but sternly. "This is your winter fair. I'm at your will."

"Fine." She sticks out her hand to shake on it and captures me in a death grip. "But I have the right to end this agreement at any point so don't get in my way."

"Got it." I rub my knuckles. "You're weirdly strong," I mutter.

She looks up at me. "I kayak a lot," she says matter-of-factly, like that explains her superhuman grip.

I'm quiet for a moment, knowing it's better to not cross the troll's bridge… but I'm curious.

"When did you start kayaking?"

Her eyes drop to the ground, and I figure she's done talking to me.

"When I was a junior." Her response surprises me. "I went on a random date to the coves up in La Jolla, but I fell in love with it."

We both know who she's talking about.

"Cool," I lamely reply, not knowing what else to say. The last time I tried to ask her about what happened with Brody I was ruthlessly cut down. I learned that lesson.

Instead, I stand quietly next to her. My mom finally makes her way toward us about five minutes later. She lets us know, as expected, only a few of the coaches attended the meeting but the teachers who were present agreed and are on board with Vivi's plan.

Part of me feels like I should try to talk to her about the project, but I know today isn't the time. Four months really isn't that long to plan a fair and apply for multiple grants. Not to mention my daughters and coaching. I need to be as present as possible for Stella and Daisy, especially right now. It was unsettling enough when Arielle moved back to Manhattan, but we were in the only home they had ever known. This is a completely new world for them. I've been planning on starting conditioning and try-outs early, as well. Getting a brand-new team adjusted to each other and starting the program from the ground up is a huge feat, and they deserve their best chances.

I climb into the driver's seat and take a second to process what just happened. I know I said I wanted to bug her a little bit here and there, but I didn't mean planning a fair like this.

Look, I'm as competitive as they come, but I like to believe I'm a smart man. And a smart man would not even *think* about standing in Genevieve's way on something like this. Even if I knew what I was doing, I can guarantee that she would still do it better. Not that I'll be admitting that to her.

There's a possibility that she will murder me—and I'm positive she could get away with it—but I don't want her to find anyone else either. It should be seen as a public service, really. I'm saving some other poor chump from getting in over their head.

And I won't lie and say it wasn't a humorous surprise dropped right into my lap because it is. I don't have a death wish so I won't screw with the fair, but I was handed ample one-on-one time. I plan to take advantage of it. There are a million ways I can get under her skin that doesn't include work.

She's going to hate every second of it.

Or really love it.

Chapter Five
Grady

"Let's gooo!" Daisy is yelling from the backseat.

From the rear-view mirror I can see that Stella looks about as excited as I feel at the prospect of walking into that house. She turns her head toward me and asks for the fourth time, "Who all is going to be here?"

I turn in my seat to give her another round of reassurance. "Gramma and Grampa, of course. Gramma's best friend, Bonnie, will be here with her four kids. I don't know if Hudson will be here actually, but Vivi will be. So will her other siblings, Asher and Calypso." She grimaces as Daisy makes an excited squeal. After five minutes of interacting, she's declared Genevieve as her new favorite person.

Miss Davies is pretty and funny.

Plus, she liked her classroom—it was rainbows, rain clouds, suns, and moons—more than the jungle theme that her teacher picked.

"Millie won't be here?" Stella asks, twisting her seatbelt in her hands.

"No, your aunt isn't coming to dinner tonight." Blake avoids uncomfortable situations, and truthfully, I don't blame her after everything she's been through. While I wouldn't say that Vivi and her siblings are mean, they are intimidating and stick together through anything. It's not hard to become the odd man out with them, and that's not a situation Blake likes to put herself in.

"Why do we have to come to dinner with all of these people then?" It might surprise you that Stella's extremely shy because she radiates confidence most of the time, but she hates new situations.

I take a deep breath, picking my words carefully. I want them to know that the Davies family were important to my childhood because I promised myself to always be honest with them the first night we spent without their mom in the home. I'll keep that promise right now. I just don't want them getting too attached to any of them. My entire family seems to be susceptible to each one of their charms. The girls don't need to feel like they lost anyone else right now, and I can't guarantee how much they'll be around.

I take another deep breath, starting to panic. Was this a huge mistake? Am I complicating the girls' lives too much too soon? Are they going to grow attached to this magnetic family only to be let down when they aren't around more than a couple times a year?

"Can we go inside? Please?" Daisy starts to whine, getting antsy in her car seat.

I nod but look back at Stella. "We are coming to dinner tonight because your grandparents asked us to. Because they want to spend time with you. And because Bonnie is your gramma's closest friend to the point that she was basically my second mother. Bonnie's amazing and I know she really wants to meet you."

She glances between the front door then me. Nodding, she starts to unbuckle herself.

"It's going to be so fun!" Daisy singsongs, skipping up the stairs.

I'm not at all ashamed to admit that I used my youngest daughter as a buffer when I stepped into my parents' house. There weren't any other cars in the driveway but they most likely will park at Bonnie's. Our houses are neighbors, with the Davies' house directly behind us on the next street up. When I was eight, my dad installed a gate between our backyards, and I know our moms still use it.

It's been over a decade since I had to attend a meal with the Davies family. The anniversary party doesn't really count. It wasn't a small event. It didn't feel *intimate* like this. It didn't remind me of Christmas mornings and countless birthdays spent with just our two families.

I can hear Daisy squealing in delight from somewhere in the house when Stella pulls my sleeve, stopping me at the front door.

When I look down at her, she pouts up at me. Her face is saying, *do we* really *have to do this?*

I know that she liked Vivi, even if she isn't as vocal about it as Daisy is. I know she's scared, though, so I grab her hand in mine and walk toward the kitchen with her.

To both of our delights, only three people—not including my daughter—are in the kitchen. My dad is holding Daisy and spinning around the kitchen to the music. He used to do the same thing with Blake and I, and I don't doubt that he's danced with all of her kids many times now. My mom is cutting vegetables on the island. Her brown hair and tan complexion are the same shades as mine, but her eyes are a sharp gray. Blake got that from her, but she has our dad's fair skin and black hair.

Sitting across from my mom is a familiar face—strawberry blonde hair, light brown eyes, oval face with high cheekbones, and the warmest smile I've ever seen. Bonnie looks exactly the same as the last time I saw her, which was around four years ago now. There are a few more lines around her mouth and eyes, but she has always been beautiful.

"*Hola, nena.*" My mom makes her way to pull Stella into a hug. Her little arms wrap around my mom's neck as she places a soft kiss on her cheek. When we first moved back, Stella asked if my mom and sister would teach her Spanish and she's picking it up much better than I could've ever dreamed of.

"*Hola, Abuela,*" she says in a near whisper. Quietly, her and my mom talk to each other and after a few seconds, Stella starts to giggle at something she says.

Bonnie steps off the chair and kneels down beside them. "Hi, are you Stella?" She gives my daughter her biggest smile, but I can see the emotions in her eyes.

Stella nods once, clinging closer to my mom.

"I'm Bonnie. It's very nice to meet you."

Stella tentatively sticks her hand out in front of her, and Bonnie gives her a small handshake.

"And I already met Daisy," Bonnie smiles over her shoulder at my dad and Daisy. She moves toward me with open arms. "Come here right now."

I wrap Bonnie into a hug, ignoring the tight feeling in my chest. She was collateral damage when I started avoiding Amada Beach and visiting my family less. It's on the list of things I feel guilty about toward the end of my marriage—right alongside hardly seeing my parents, putting off Blake's visits, and not telling anyone about the divorce until it was practically finalized.

My distance never stopped Bonnie from reaching out, calling every birthday, and sending a card each Christmas. She still makes all four of her kids dress up in matching sweaters and take a photo on her front porch.

"Stell, wanna learn how to grill?" My dad grabs the tray of steaks, corn, and jalapeno peppers. "Daisy is going to help too."

Stella gives me a small smile and I lightly ruffle her hair. "Go on, it'll be fun."

I, personally, hate grilling, but she'll enjoy the time with him.

She skips out back, falling into a silly conversation with Daisy. Something about the animal hospital they were running in Stella's bedroom before we left for dinner. Daisy is listening closely and nodding to whatever Stella is saying about Princess Pumpkin Pie.

Once they turn the corner, Bonnie pulls my attention back to the room. "They're beautiful, Grady." A tear slips out, but she quickly bats it away.

"Aw, come here, Bon." I put my arm around her shoulder. I make it a point to not look at the tears building in my mom's eyes now or I'll be done for. "I'm sorry this is the first time you're meeting them. It was long overdue."

Bonnie leans into the hug for too short of a moment. "No need to apologize. Just promise that you will bring them around more. There are no excuses now." I nod. Her hand lifts to softly pat my cheek. "I'm happy you're home, Grady."

The girls, the last I checked, are inside sitting on the island eating fruit salad out of the bowl. I can hear my mom and Bonnie singing along to ABBA while they cut vegetables and make sangrias.

It's a sight I grew up seeing almost every Sunday, but it feels like the first time all over again. I can add this to the list of things I missed without even realizing how much.

"How're you feeling about seeing everyone tonight?" My dad is wholly focused on the grill, flipping the steaks and corn over. Stella and Daisy didn't even last long enough to let the grill heat up. I don't blame them but unfortunately, I'm stuck out here. It isn't completely horrible. I'm enjoying a cold beer from the local woman-owned brewery and he's enjoying one of his favorite hobbies.

"What do you mean?"

I know what he means. Of course, I do.

He obviously knows I've seen Vivi already. There's no way my mom could keep that secret even if it hadn't been work-related. He probably doesn't know I've seen Calypso and Lexi at Brighter Daze but that was a quick interaction.

The girls wanted to get some new books and I may have used that as an opportunity to see the inside of the store for the first time. The big chain bookstore is only fifteen minutes from us, so it wasn't like I didn't have another option.

The only people I haven't seen yet are Asher and Hudson. They're easily the two I have the least apprehension about reconnecting with. We haven't stayed as close as I would've liked over the years, but we've stayed in touch regardless. We went to get lunch about three years ago, only months after Arielle asked for a divorce. Of course, I didn't mention anything about it then, not even when they asked about my life, or Arielle, or my daughters. It would've gotten back to my parents, and I didn't want anyone worrying about me. Especially not with something that no one could help or change.

Asher should be showing up anytime now. And from what my dad was telling me a few minutes ago, Hudson's on some solo adventure in Sedona. He's always been sort of a loner and extremely picky about who he lets into his life, so it doesn't surprise me. Regardless of his stoic demeanor, Hudson and I were always a little bit closer because of baseball. So I make a mental note to reach out to him sooner than later.

"To see Vivi. Here, in this house. I'm sure it'll bring up some memories for you."

Um. Okay. Not exactly what I was expecting. He isn't usually so straightforward, and I don't appreciate the knowing look in his eye.

Doing my best to keep my tone even, I say, "I saw her at the vow renewal." *And we all know how well that went.*

My dad gives me a small nod. "And I don't think that went all that well, from what I was able to pick up."

I stiffen at the blatant call out. "What did you *pick up*?"

He opens his mouth, but the voice I hear doesn't come from him.

"G! Man, I was happy to hear you'd be joining us."

Asher daps me up before turning to my dad, giving him a firm handshake. It doesn't matter that my dad practically raised them—both of the twins have gone as far as saying that Tim Miller taught them how to be men worth being proud of—he still expects a strong handshake before he pulls you into the loving hug. I'm his legitimate son and I get the same greeting when he isn't holding his grandchild.

"Even if my mom had allowed me to miss the dinner, I would have still been here." I shrug, trying to let the guilty undertones of that statement fly off in the light breeze.

"Yeah, our mom didn't give us much of a choice either. Except Hudson since he's on his little *finding myself* journey. Again." Asher rolls his eyes in a playful manner but neither my dad nor I can stop the soft chuckles that vibrate our chests. Asher has always been the clingiest of the siblings. It never bothered me much... except when I wanted time alone with Vivi growing up. "I'll be honest with you," he says before taking a sip of his root beer—he stopped drinking alcohol a few years ago. "*She* tried to plan a last-minute trip, but my mom wasn't in a compromising mood by that point."

I lift my eyebrows, shocked that Asher not only told me this but also that she wants to avoid me that bad and we have to work together. I shouldn't be surprised but I am. I wasn't expecting us to be friends or for her to have forgiven me necessarily. But it's been *eight* years since we had last seen each other. Granted, that last time wasn't worth remembering but I didn't think she would actively avoid me. That makes me feel like it's something more. Vivi can bounce back from an argument faster than anyone, especially when she gets some good blows in and the last word. She got both that night. Not that anything I said was particularly pleasant, even if my intentions were good.

"Is she here?"

Asher looks over my dad's shoulder. "No, Lyp picked me up. She should be out any time now. Lex had to close down the store and Vivi is picking her up." He takes another sip before his expression morphs into confused amusement. "Dude... Are you sweating?"

"No." I am. Just a little. I'm suddenly really nervous again. "It's the humidity. I'm still getting used to the weather out here again." That's a lie if I've ever told one. Every day I lived in Phoenix, I missed the weather out here. The sea salt air, overcast days when the tide is high, and summer afternoons looking for shells during low tide. The best part is the sixty-to-seventy-degree weather year-round.

Asher and I haven't talked about my life out there any of the times we've seen each other so he wouldn't know that I'm lying. That doesn't stop the skeptical side-eye he gives me.

Unfortunately for me, my dad does know me and is standing right next to us. "Son, it's sixty-four tonight. Not to mention, I know for a *fact* that you hated the dry weather in Arizona. It was all you talked about when you came home for a visit."

My dad and mom have never referred to Phoenix as my home. Even when I was married and owned a townhouse out there. Home has only ever meant Amada Beach. Arielle hated it. It was one of the many reasons that she stopped visiting with me—not that I wanted to mix this part of my life with her. Even if it was always the largest part of my life, outside of my Stella and Daisy.

Calypso sashays out to the patio in that exact moment, saving me from having to poorly avoid more questions.

I've never been attracted to Calypso but even a blind man couldn't deny that she's as gorgeous as the rest of her family. Her strawberry blonde hair is cut to her shoulders. She's dressed as if she was ready for a night out in a cropped leather jacket and her red lipstick she started wearing when she was a senior in high school. It warms something in me that she still does, like maybe more things than I anticipated have stayed the same here. I have a lot to catch up on but maybe it won't be hard to find my place here again.

"Hey, Grady." She slides up to us, a glass of red sangria in her hand.

"Hey, Calypso." I give her a side hug before I think too much of it. It's awkward for half a second, before she gives me a tight squeeze back.

My dad gives Calypso a quick hug and excuses himself to go check on the food inside. He hands me the tongs on his way inside. From the look of apprehension on my face, Calypso must realize that I don't want this job. She snickers and snatches them out of my hand.

"Isn't it a rule when you become a dad you automatically love grilling?"

I shake my head. "The grill master gene must have skipped a generation."

"Dude, your poor daughters. Are you just going to deprive them?" Asher says in faux disappointment.

His sister pokes him with the opposite end of the tongs. "You have *never* cooked a day in your life." She turns to me. "He has literally gotten coupons for being one of DoorDash's *most loyal* customers."

I chuckle at his furrowed brows. "I've never heard a single one of you complaining about it when we have movie nights."

There is a weird tug in my heart to hear that they still have movie nights. I would bet almost anything that the hangouts turn into sleepovers at least a few times a year. The majority of my childhood is the simple memories of blanket forts and fighting over the last bags of kettle corn.

Calypso folds her hands under her chin and says in a saccharine voice, "That's because you and Hudson are the only two who ever want to pay."

"Yeah, we *want* to pay." He looks at me but points in a *can you believe her* way.

She shrugs, turning back to the grill. "I'll pay next time then."

Asher rolls his head in exasperation. "No, none of you are paying. Hudson and I'll pay."

Calypso smirks at me over her shoulder. It's never mattered that she's the oldest or that she helped Bonnie with her siblings, especially Vivi, until she graduated. The twins have always been just as protective and accommodating to both of them.

And from what they told me when I saw them a few years ago, the surf shop known as The Shack, that they bought almost nine years ago, continues to grow every year. They expanded their merchandise to include other water sports, such as kayaking—probably for Vivi now that I know it's one of her favorite hobbies—but they didn't stop there. They sell and rent roller skates, bikes and longboards for the tourists who don't want to spend time in the water.

The fact that they're well off and choose to spend that money on their sisters doesn't surprise me, especially since neither of them has been in a relationship recently.

There is a small crash coming from inside, followed by muffled arguing.

Both of the blondes standing in front of me turn with amusement across their features.

"Are you ready to see her?" Calypso asks. Her voice is sympathetic, but her face says she's delighted at the prospect of a show at dinner.

"Yeah, why wouldn't I be?" I stuff my hands in my pockets, trying to appear casual. I don't believe for a second that Calypso doesn't know I've already seen Vivi.

"Nah, don't let him fool you," Asher pipes in. "He was sweating earlier when I mentioned Viv."

Calypso's grin grows more feral in anticipation. "Oh, I don't mean her."

"Wha—"

I'm immediately cut off by the low, sarcastic voice of Lexi Hart. "Well, if it isn't my *favorite* homecoming date."

I slowly turn around, taking in the mischievous glint in Lexi's eye. Other than the time we went to the dance together—which was obviously a mutually beneficial ploy to piss off Vivi—we really don't know each other.

What I do remember is that she's always got off on instigating situations. I doubt that has changed.

Just as I see Vivi's red hair peek around the corner I retort, "It is *my* parents' house."

Calypso turns back to the grill while Asher looks down, shaking his head. I can hear all three of the Davies siblings laugh under their breath.

"Hm, I don't know, Grady Miller. I'm pretty sure I've been here quite a few more times than you in the last few years."

Genevieve finally speaks up, "She's honestly probably Selena's favorite." She's talking to me but never manages to make eye contact.

"Why do you keep calling me by my first and last name?"

"I don't think we are on a first name only basis yet."

"Okay well, I'm back now, *Alexandra Hart,* so I'll be taking back the title as my mom's favorite."

She laughs, as if the thought is so incredulous. "Sure, sure. Whatever you think."

Vivi turns and walks back inside before I had a chance to properly greet her.

Asher notices, elbowing me and shaking his head. "That could not have gone worse," he says loud enough for only me to hear.

Chapter Six
Grady

Sun, Aug 7 at 5:55 PM

Arielle

Hi how are the girls?

Hey. They are good. Both are very excited for school to start.

When is that again?

In two days.

Right. I wanted to order them a surprise to come home to

They would love that.

:)

> And how are you?

> I'm good. Thanks. You?

> I'm good...

> I don't have a show tonight. Can I FT you and the girls?

> We're having dinner with my parents. Won't be home until after 1am your time.

> I'm in Dallas. Call whenever I'll be up

> Ok.

In the twenty minutes it took for all of the food to be ready and the patio table to be set, Lexi asked me about every aspect of my life in the last decade except my marriage. I mean *everything*. She asked if I started on a teaching track—started as an Econ major. How I tore my ACL—running the bases—even though I am almost positive she's seen the video. If that was why I didn't go into the MLB—mostly, no elaboration. How we came up with the names Stella and Daisy—we both had great-grandmothers named Stella and we found a field of daisies on our first date.

There were at least ten more.

Vivi was inside helping our moms the entire time, but I could hear my daughters talking animatedly to her through the open door. Daisy was telling her about their animal hospital, and that tomorrow it will probably be a circus. Stella gave her a very detailed explanation of all the stuffies' diagnoses. She played along the entire time, asking questions and acting shocked at the medical miracles happening.

Even now, sitting across from Vivi at the table, my heart feels like it has grown three sizes. I would never want someone to replace Arielle, because she's a great mom and I don't begrudge her for wanting to follow her lifelong dreams. But I know that's what my girls miss the most. The love and understanding that a mother brings.

I don't expect Genevieve to give that to them, but it reminds me how important it'll be for my future partner to have a good relationship with Stella and Daisy, to be someone that they trust.

"How was yesterday, *mijo*?"

My mom's question pulls me out of my thoughts. I start cutting Daisy's steak for her and nod at my dad in gratitude for helping Stella. "Hm?"

"Didn't you take the girls furniture shopping? I swear, Grady, if you didn't go then I'll be picking everything out for you tomorrow. That house is completely bare, and he's been in it for a month now," she tells the table.

I'm a grown man but that doesn't stop the color from staining my cheeks at being chastised by my mother.

"No, mom, we went. I promise. You can come see all of the boxes getting delivered tomorrow if you don't believe me."

"Well? How was it?" She takes a sip of her sangria before giving me a stern look over the rim. "Did you go to the stores I told you about? There were a lot of great sales this weekend. I hope you didn't spend too much money. Oh, and *please* tell me that you didn't go with purple again." Arielle's favorite color.

That earns my mom a stern look from me. *Not in front of the girls*, I silently reprimand. Her eyes glance between Stella and Daisy before she gives a guilty nod.

The entire table is looking at me now and I fidget with my silverware under the attention. It's very unnerving to have the full attention of all the Davies siblings. Lexi is a solid replacement for Hudson at this moment, definitely more menacing.

There is nothing to be embarrassed about. I know that. We bought some couches and new bedroom stuff. Nothing that needs to remain a secret but there is something emasculating about having your mother still treat you like a kid. And that's coming from the man who has bi-weekly tea parties in costume jewelry and tiaras.

My youngest daughter doesn't have any of the same worries, bless her innocent heart.

"It was so fun!" She gets on her knees to sit even higher on her chair. "We got so much!"

"Did you pick it out yourself?" Vivi asks in a sweet voice.

"For my room, yeah I did. Stella picked her room and Daddy picked his."

"What did you choose?"

Daisy perks up more, slightly puffing her chest out in pride. "Pink sheets and a forest print blanket." I smile, sliding her plate toward her. The light pink sheets are a pretty contrast to the white duvet cover that has a dainty forest design on it, a mix of plants and animals. I guided her choices with everything else—a bamboo bed frame, mustard yellow curtains and a soft green throw blanket that matches her painted walls perfectly. "You should come see it sometime," she shrugs casually, not realizing that she just dropped a bomb of awkwardness at the table.

When I look up, Vivi is smirking at me but quickly looks down at Daisy. "It sounds like the perfect room." She leans forward, pushing her ample cleavage up enough to make it almost indecent, even in a shirt as modest as hers. I do my best not to look… but her breasts are hard to miss especially when she's wearing a dark shade of green that makes her loose copper hair glow. "What about you, Stell? How did you decorate your room?"

If Stella is surprised by the use of her nickname, she doesn't show it. It throws me off for a few seconds—though, I don't know if I appreciate the gesture or should be worried about a mutiny forming against me.

Instead of shining in the attention like her sister, Stella sinks down in her chair a little, but her voice is steady when she says, "I just picked a pink blanket and white sheets. It matches the white flowers on my walls. Daisy and I have the same curtains though." She shrugs, as if her pink haven isn't just as precious. Daisy likes to change things more often than Stella, so she wasn't allowed to pick wallpaper yet. Stella picked a pink background with large white cartoon-style daisies. It's simple and adorable, just like her.

"That sounds cute and cozy," Vivi says with a wink.

I turn to my mom, feeling less nervous with Vivi's attention somewhere else. I tell her about the dark blue couches we bought because the girls wanted something colorful, and I wanted something that wouldn't stain. She asks me to describe everything else we bought down to the curtain rods we chose. "I just want to make sure the girls have a *home*, Grady," she reminds me.

"Thanks, Mom." But there's no bite behind my words.

She truthfully isn't a controlling person, but I know that she's just looking to be a part of as many aspects of our life since we're close enough for her to be. And I don't want to block her out anymore.

I have all the patience in the world for the sweet woman until she asks, "And your bedroom? How did you decorate that?"

It's an innocent question but the fiery woman sitting across from me makes me feel like I'm answering something intimate.

Not that it matters, but *what if* she doesn't like it?

She will never see the inside of my room, that's not what I'm insinuating at all. I'm not delusional. But I don't want her to have more negative opinions about me.

I clear my throat. "Mom, I'm sure that no one wants to hear how I decorated my house."

Lexi chimes in with, "Oh, I'm absolutely invested in this conversation." She places her head on her fist, and Calypso follows with a cheeky smirk. Silently Lexi adds, "Daddy," with a wink, causing Asher to choke on his bite. Vivi slaps him on the back, continuing to pretend like she isn't paying attention to this conversation, but she's biting her lip, hard, to fight a laugh.

I keep my attention on my mom. "You can come see it next weekend. Maybe even come with us to look at kitchen stuff."

"Yeah, Gramma! Come shopping with us!" Daisy begs.

"Of course, *mi amor*," she smiles toward my daughter before her stern eyes turn back to me. "But I want to know. So go on."

I know my mother means well but she isn't dumb. I just don't know what she's trying to prove. There is no point in fighting with her though. She always gets her way. Ask my dad if you don't believe me.

I huff out an annoyed breath. "As you know," I start, trying to appease the maternal monster, "I decided I may as well get a new bed." She nods, thankfully not bringing up the conversation we had a few weeks ago. She agreed that I shouldn't keep anything that Arielle and I shared, you know, for the comfort of my future partner. *'Whoever that may be'* she said in a casual tone, but she was smiling through every word.

I tell the table, keeping my eyes on my mom, about the walnut mid-century modern bedframe with a matching leather cushion back. The olive-green duvet that matches the light gray sheets. The Turkish rug brings in some color and contrasts the black walls nicely.

Lexi and Calypso are grinning like fiends behind their glasses of sangria. Asher is giving me his idea of a subtle thumbs up. When I make eye contact with Vivi, there is a faint blush on her cheeks, but she turns back to my daughters. She's giving them tips on how to run a successful classroom of stuffed animals—as if their father isn't also a teacher.

Thankfully, after the verbal home tour, the attention moves away from me.

Chapter Seven

Vivi

<u>family meeting</u>
Sun, Aug 7 at 6:45 PM

Lexi

> A man who knows how to decorate?

> Say less, daddy

Calypso

> LMAO stop with the daddy.

> I am begging you. I practically raised him.

Lexi

> Get on your hands and knees and I'll consider it

Hudson

> What the fuck did I miss?

Asher

If you weren't on some BS self-journey you'd know

Selena loves to embarrass her children

She made Grady tell the table how he decorated his house in detail so she could decide if she needed to redecorate

Hudson

Why can I perfectly imagine that?

> Probably because mom was the exact same way when you two moved out

Lexi

Awwwhhhhh

Look at Viv defending her bestie <3

Asher

We were like 18 not 28

> Lexi. I will crash the car on the way home I swear to all that is holy

Calypso

Vivi's heaven probably looks like a mid-century modern room with black walls

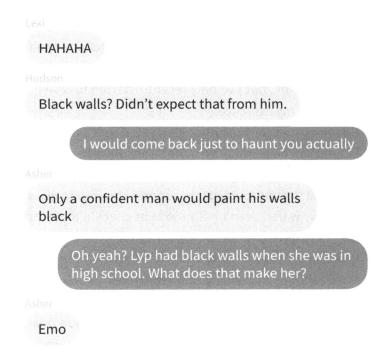

I walk into the kitchen, bringing more plates inside, when I catch Grady slightly opening the window to the backyard. It allows the happy sounds of our mothers to pour through the crack, filling the kitchen with the soft echoes of their laughs.

Selena's laugh is light and airy, as if she doesn't have a care in the world, whereas my mom has a playful and mischievous snicker. It's a little high-pitched and quiet, almost identical to Calypso's.

I don't know if I *remember* my dad's laugh, but it feels like I do, mostly because my mom and siblings say that I have his deep belly-laugh. One of those laughs that starts in your toes, and you feel it throughout your entire body to the point that you can't keep it in. Hudson always told me that it was a sign of how much our dad and I loved life, but I've only recently started to love it again after years with my ex-fiancé.

Sneaking up beside Grady I quietly say, "That's one of my favorite sounds in the world." The perfect mixture of the two women sitting on the bench swing with their glasses of sangria.

He jumps at the unexpected interruption, dropping a glass back into the sudsy water. I can't help the faint chuckle that works its way out of my throat at the same time he clears his. "You scared me." He shakes his head, continuing with his task. "But it's one of my favorite sounds as well. I didn't realize how much I missed it until tonight."

I nod in understanding. I wasn't away from Amada Beach for nearly as long as Grady but those four years at UCLA were hard, even with Lexi. I missed my siblings. I missed my mom and Selena singing in the kitchen. I missed Tim's warm hugs and his deep soothing voice. I don't know how he stayed away so long.

Without thinking much about it, I open the drawer to the right of the sink and pull out a dish towel. We work together in a companionable, slightly awkward silence for a few minutes.

After the sixth time that we lift our heads at the same time in response to our moms giggling like two schoolgirls together, I decide, *fuck it.*

"Why didn't you visit more?" I can hear the disappointment in my voice no matter how hard I try to remain neutral. "It was hard for her. For your dad and my mom too but especially for Selena."

He doesn't say anything, just focuses on the dishes. He scrubs one cup for longer than necessary and I can tell he's lost in his own thoughts.

If he doesn't want to talk to me, then that's *fine*. I don't particularly care to open myself up to him again either. I'm about to finish drying the last dish when he finally turns toward me.

He leans one hip on the counter and faces me head on. I swallow down my sudden awareness of him, of his earthy masculine scent, of his assessing eyes taking me in with one full sweep.

When I finally turn to meet his eyes, he begins talking. "It was... hard coming back while I was married. Arielle is a really great mom—" It's hard to believe when she isn't here with her daughters, and he must see that in my expression. "I know how it must look to people, with me here as the sole parent and her across the country in Upper East Side Manhattan—that's where she's from. Her parents and sister all live there in glamorous, way too high penthouses and very little privacy. I didn't want that. I can understand why people like that lifestyle—the hustle and bustle, never feeling alone because you aren't *ever* alone in a city like that. But I didn't want that, and I didn't want that for my daughters.

"On the same note, Arielle didn't like the laid-back lifestyle of California. She especially didn't like the feeling of being known, even if there are less people. There isn't emotional privacy in a place like Amada Beach." I hum in agreement. There has probably never been a family with less privacy than mine out here. It all comes from the heart and good intentions. The community saw a single mother of four moving in and decided that we were Amada Beach's family now. We've never known a moment of feeling unwanted since we moved here, and I'll always be thankful. But that also comes with a few hundred people constantly checking on you, finding out your business and having opinions on things that don't involve them.

"I can understand how our little town can be... jarring for people."

"It's always been my favorite place in the world," he says with sincerity. "When Arielle and I got divorced, I knew that I was going to bring the girls here. They have cousins here… a community. Arielle wants to be on Broadway." He shrugs lightly. "She has a real shot, but she's getting a later start than most. *That* was her dream." He's quiet for a moment, looking at his hand that's clutching the counter. "She's a great mother but she was just a little girl with big dreams. I want her to explore that, and I want to be *here* with my daughters."

I feel choked up at his honesty, at the vulnerability he granted me, when he doesn't owe me anything. I'm not sure that I would've laid myself so bare to him if he asked.

Fuck, I *know* I wouldn't have. I can't even bring myself to be open with Lexi or my siblings most times.

"And what about you? What happened to the little boy with big dreams?" Grady wanted to join the MLB. He talked about playing for the San Diego Sharks our entire childhoods.

He says instantly, as if he has given it a lot of thought already, "Dreams change, Genevieve."

I know he means his daughters. Or when he tore his ACL and was probably forced to find a new dream. Or maybe both.

Yet that husky voice wraps me like a vice for the second time now. It doesn't even bother me that he used my full name this time. How could it when he says it in that voice that belongs in a bedroom, whispered directly in your ear?

I'm about to ask what his dreams are now, or even *who* that dream involves regardless of the alarms flashing in the corners of my mind. I know it isn't fair to demand answers from him when I can guarantee that I'll refuse to answer anything he asks me, partly from self-preservation and partly from spite.

Lexi walks inside a moment before I was about to embarrass

myself, and I've never been so thankful to see her perfect—albeit smug—face before.

Slowly, she asks, "What's going on here?"

"Nothing. Are you ready to leave soon?"

With her signature shit-eating grin that's growing by the second, she nods and turns back outside. Presumably to start the goodbyes.

I take a step toward the door, offering Grady a weird closed-mouth grin. It probably looks more like a constipated grimace, but it's all I have in me right now.

"Vivi?"

"Hm?" There are a few feet of space between us now, but I still feel too close to him. It's suffocating, like he takes up the entire room and his cologne is the only air available.

"When is a good time to meet this week?"

I don't say anything, but I take a step toward my purse. He doesn't follow me, instead watching from the island. I pull my tablet out and open the planner app. I could use the calendar app but this one is as customizable as a physical one. It holds almost every minute of my life.

I quickly scroll through the next week, looking for any sort of availability I can swing that's not the first thing tomorrow.

With classes beginning on Wednesday, I know that the later into the week, the less time I'll have. I just... I'm not going to be ready tomorrow. Not after tonight. Not after everything he told me. Not after the expectant glint in his eyes as he waits for an answer.

But this isn't about me. This is about the students, and the school, and the promise I made.

So, I'll spend the night mentally preparing and show up tomorrow.

"It's last minute but tomorrow at eleven works the best for me."

Just because I wake up early doesn't mean I like having to rush my morning routines on the days that it's not necessary. "I have two free hours. Not that I think it will take that long, but we won't have to worry about running out of time either."

"Eleven works for me. Let's meet at the school. I have some things to finish up."

I wonder what *things* he means, but I give him a thumbs up and another closed-mouth smile before turning quickly on my heel and walking outside.

"That was interesting," Lexi says from the driver seat of my CrossTrek, never letting her eyes leave the road. She's the safest driver I know.

"I guess so." I give her a noncommittal shrug, connecting my Bluetooth. I usually wouldn't bother for the short drive, but I already want to drown out her curious voice.

"What were you guys talking about?"

"When?"

"In the kitchen?"

"We were doing the dishes."

She pauses, contemplating her next line of attack. "What were you talking about when you finished the dishes?"

"When we're meeting for the fair." Not a total lie but not the part of the conversation I know she's asking about.

She knows it too. The large breath she huffs out is a dead giveaway of her frustration and I can't help but smirk in response.

"God, you're fucking annoying sometimes, do you know that?"

"Your fault for taking in a pathetic little stray ten years ago," I tease.

Lexi's laugh reminds me of those rare thunderstorms over the ocean—booming, wicked and slightly rumbly. "Wish I could say I regret it."

"Ah, but you don't. Not even for a second," I say in a sweet voice, folding my hands under my chin.

"I hate when you and Lyp make that G.D. face."

I tilt my head back, laughing at her exasperation. "It works just as well on you as our brothers."

"Fuck you guys and your perfect faces." She gives me an annoyed look, but I know she doesn't mean it. She would be bored without us tied to her hip constantly.

Lexi only has one brother whose twelve years younger than her. Regardless of how close they are, I know the age gap creates a different type of relationship than my siblings and me.

We sit in a comfortable silence for a few minutes, letting the soft voice of Maggie Rogers flow around us. The irony of the lyrics after the last couple weeks are not lost on me. And from Lexi's next words, I know it isn't lost on her either.

"When you're ready to talk about it, I'm here." I give her a side-eye look and a quick nod. "I won't bring it up again. Just… seriously, Viv, just come to me. Don't hold it in."

I nod again, looking back out the windshield. "I will. If there is ever something to tell." Or if I ever figure out my own feelings. "Tell me about your date last night."

Lexi laughs, shaking her head in amused exasperation.

"It was not good. I don't want to say terrible because she was nice, but it was… bad."

"Did she try to order for you? Oh god, did she make you listen to her ex's voicemails for half of dinner like that one guy?"

She barks out a laugh, and I can't help but follow suit. "No, it wasn't that bad. So maybe not *terrible*." I wait patiently for her to go on. Lexi has never had a serious relationship, not unless you count a few months of exclusively hanging out with one person until it inevitably ends. Either due to her getting bored or annoyed, or them being put off by her independence and aloofness. She's my favorite person in the world, and almost anyone who knows her would agree. I know she will find someone when the time is right—and by that, I mean when Lexi decides she wants something serious.

"Listen to this shit… She said she got busy at work and asked to move the date back half an hour. That was fine. Until she was still twenty minutes late! I swear, my server was about to kick me out. But she finally showed up. And let me just say, she's *gorgeous*. She's a few inches shorter than me—you know I love that with women—and curvy. She wore this tight little black skirt with a slit on the side." She rolls to a stop and grabs my arm for emphasis. "Like drop dead sexy enough that you would let just about anything go, right?"

"Oh-kay… So what went wrong?"

She laughs and I can't help but follow along without knowing what happened. "She walked in at the same time as this guy, but I didn't think much about it. There were a few parties who looked like they were still waiting. But—"

"Oh no. Oh god, please tell me she didn't bring a friend," I plead to the universe on behalf of my best friend.

"No, she didn't bring a friend." I'm about to let out the breath I'm holding in anticipation when she says, "She brought her *brother*."

"Nooo!" I shriek and throw my head back in a cackle. "Who the fuck takes their brother on a date?"

"Apparently Marlene. That's who."

"Did you leave? You left… right?"

"Remember when I said she was beautiful? Like, ignore-red-flags-beautiful? She smelled so sweet, like sugar cookies, I could only imagine what her cookie tasted like."

"Alexandra, tell me right now that you didn't go home with her and her brother," I say in my teacher voice.

"Chill out, Miss Davies. Have some faith in me, goddamn."

"Oh, thank whoever is holy up there." I put my hands together in a prayer pose. "How long did you stay?"

"Well," she drags out slowly. "I stayed until the end of dinner. Her brother paid for all of it, which was really nice. Honestly, I stayed because he was way cooler. A much better conversationalist than her with a wicked sense of humor. I wish I had dated him instead." I roll my hand in the air, in a *get on with it* movement. "After he paid, he went to the restroom, and she asked if I wanted to go home with her. I was considering it, you know, wanting another round of dessert."

"I'm not Asher. Please just get to the fucking point."

She snickers as she pulls into our shared garage. "She said that her brother could drive us back to *their* apartment." She puts her car in park and turns toward me. "She, a twenty-nine-year-old woman, lives on her brother's couch."

I blink in response, shocked. I last less than five seconds before my head is tipped back and there are tears forming in my eyes.

Lexi is reaching for her bag in the backseat, chuckling at the ridiculousness of her dating life. "*I know*. I told you it was bad."

"No, I would put that up there with terrible, Lex."

"Whatever, I'm cursed," she dramatically whines but there's humor in her voice. "Make me tea and love me. Don't I deserve it?"

"Fine, you can sleep in my bed tonight. But I'm watching *Parks & Rec* and working on my planner."

"Your pillow talk is unparalleled," Lexi says with a cheeky grin over her shoulder as she goes to change into pajamas before hogging my bed for the night.

Chapter Eight
Grady

"Sorry I'm late," Vivi says as she turns the corner into my classroom.

Her arms are full of two bags of classroom decorations, a tote bag completely full of who knows what and a bunch of artificial flowers. Her cheeks are red, I assume, from walking as fast as she could from the parking lot.

She's wearing a loose pink sweater, the sleeves rolled up her forearms and tucked into a white floral print skirt that hangs just above her knees. Her tan wedges add a few extra inches to her short height but still not enough to bring her to my eye level. And just like everything else she wears, it's demure but with the right amount of femininity to even it out. I would even say it's a little bit sexy with the way everything clings to her curves. Her face is bare of any make-up except for a light shimmer on her cheekbones and the inner corner of her eyes.

She's radiant. There simply isn't another word to describe her warmth and beauty.

"No reason to apologize. I was just writing down some of my ideas."

She sets all of her bags down on a nearby desk and turns a raised eyebrow at me. "Your ideas?"

There is a teasing lilt to her voice, but I know she's not totally joking.

"Calm down, killer." That gets me an eye roll. "Just come sit down and let me show you what I was thinking. You can veto anything and everything."

I hook my foot around the leg of the chair I placed next to my desk and pull it a little closer.

She narrows her eyes at me and crosses her arms, not taking a single step forward.

I huff out an exasperated breath and kick the chair back a couple inches.

She smirks at me and finally takes a seat. She pulls the chair closer to my desk, right where I had positioned it, getting a better look at my laptop.

Now it's my turn to roll my eyes.

"Well? Are you ready?" she asks in an impatient tone.

"I wasn't the one who was late," I say matter-of-factly. She tilts her head in a way that reminds me of a predator—albeit a small one—sizing up their prey. As fun as I'm sure going down that road would be, I move the conversation along to save us both time.

"Did you have an idea of where you wanted to host the fair?" I ask as I take a small, careful sip from the mug Daisy made me about six months ago. It's disfigured and barely holds half a cup of liquid in it, but she seems to love pottery and I don't want to ever discourage her from that. The way Vivi's eyes twinkle as she watches, I know she thinks the tiny dish is just as humorous as I do.

She leans back in her chair, crossing her arms and thinking it over. "Yes, but I don't know if it's possible." She hesitates, seemingly not sure if she wants to tell me more. "I don't know much about city permits and things like that, but I thought it would be perfect to have it on the pier. They used to host block parties and events on it all the time when we were kids, remember?" I nod. The end of the pier was where Vivi found me for the first time at that Fourth of July party. "I don't know why they stopped but I'm assuming it was just easier to do it closer to the businesses. I think it would be really fun and nostalgic if we could host it there…" She scrunches her nose and gives me an unsure look.

"I think that's brilliant. I was thinking about the sitting area across from where the food trucks set up daily. What is that called again?"

"The Loop," she answers quickly. I've been there a couple of times since moving back and I recognize most of the trucks from when I was a teenager but the small property some of the owners bought and turned into an outdoor seating area a few years ago opened about two years after I left for college. It's a local and visitor favorite though, according to Blake.

"Right. But the pier is more family friendly and would probably attract a larger crowd."

She sits up straighter. "That's what I was thinking. If we make it a High Tides-only event, we are turning away a lot of potential guests and donations before we even start."

She's right. Summer is the busiest time of the year in Amada Beach, much like it is along the entire coast of California. The weather doesn't change drastically throughout the year, but the cold water is still only appealing to the most committed surfers during the winter months. Between Thanksgiving and New Year's, the community typically gets a small spike in tourists who are looking for a West Coast winter rather than a White Christmas.

The conversation flows for a while and Vivi is much more open to suggestions than I had anticipated. I promise her that I'll take care of the permit and getting access to the pier, and she will focus on reaching out to the faculty members. Some of the teachers, and most likely some of the students, won't be thrilled about having to participate. It's impossible to make everyone happy. I say that they have to get over it. Vivi says that we should try to meet them halfway where we can, starting with letting each club choose what they want to do for their booth at the fair. She's right... like always. And it's another thing that hasn't changed in all these years.

By the time we are wrapping up our first meeting, I'm feeling confident and even a little excited about this project. Partly because it allows me time to spend with Vivi without really having to ask. It's more than that though. When I started teaching at the school in Phoenix, Arielle and I were already having problems in our marriage. I was too focused on that to put much effort into making a name for myself there. Once we divorced, I knew that I was in limbo while I figured out what was next for Stella, Daisy, and me. There was never a reason or time to become attached to my position there.

That's not the case now. Amada Beach has *always* been my home even when I was trying to run away. I want to make this my daughters' home. I want to become a part of this school; in the same way my mom has been since it opened and Vivi has in the few years she has been teaching here.

"Should we meet again next Monday?" I ask.

"Hmmm," she contemplates to herself, pulling her iPad out of her purse. I try to look at the screen—wondering exactly what she puts on that thing—but she shifts it slightly. Just enough that I can't read it. "How about the Monday after next? It will probably take me some time to talk to all of the coaches and teachers anyway."

I don't like the idea of not having a reason to spend time with her for two weeks. It feels just long enough to undo the little bit of progress we have made.

"Yeah, that works for me," I shrug.

She starts packing her bag and I panic. I don't want her to leave yet. This meeting was way quicker than I had expected. Plus, she said she had two hours blocked off.

I want at least *one* full hour.

The nervous sweat that's beginning to form at the base of my neck is distracting and I ask the first thing that comes to my mind, "Do you plan what time you go to the bathroom on that thing too?"

Slowly, ever so slowly, she turns around. Her mouth is gaped open in offense but the gleam in her eyes shows amusement. "Excuse me?"

I point toward the tablet she's slipping back into her purse.

"Only on days I'm really busy," she retorts, pushing her hair over her shoulder.

My eyebrows quirk up.

There is no way she actually schedules that, right?

"Wow, you're an idiot. No, I don't plan when I go to the bathroom. Though, if I didn't know any better, I would wonder if Lexi or Asher put you up to asking."

"They don't like your planner?"

She takes a seat next to me again, pulling out the tablet. "Hm, I don't know why you have such an issue with how I live my life—"

"No problems here." I hold up my hands in surrender.

She unlocks it and hands it over to me. "You can take a look. It isn't a secret." There's a light blush on her cheeks, making me think that maybe it *is* a secret. That only piques my interest more. I tentatively go to grab it.

Her hand releases it easily and I immediately am blown away

by the articulate organization of it. Its color coordinated—green for work, blue for personal, yellow for appointments, orange for volunteering, purple for her family, gray for exercising, which is mostly kayaking, and pink for dates. As I scroll through her calendar, it brings me an immense amount of selfish satisfaction to see that she hasn't used pink in at least three months. There are little blurbs for a new restaurant she tried with Lexi, the books she's currently reading and how she likes her coffee from different shops. I can guarantee that she's spent money on this planner app. There are hundreds of stickers, fonts and note options. It's dorky and a little neurotic. But I can't stop myself from finding it completely adorable and endearing at the same time.

"And just so you know, Lexi and Asher *hate* my planner…" I'm only half listening, too distracted by an appointment she has in a few days. I pull the tablet further from her reach and read the title: *UCAH Advisor Meeting, 10:45 AM, Teaching & Admin Building.*

"Are you going to school again? My mom didn't mention that." She gives me a questioning look and I can't stop the heat rising to my cheeks.

She raises her eyebrows, giving me a slow once over before meeting my gaze with a cheeky grin. "Ask about me a lot?"

I roll my eyes but don't deny that *maybe* I've casually asked about her a couple of times recently. "Are you looking at graduate programs for teaching?"

"No," she shakes her head and slips her hands under the thighs. She's *nervous.* "In school administration."

The lightbulb in my head immediately flicks on. "You want to be a principal?"

She bites back a smile and nods.

"Are you going to leave High Tides?" There would be a couple years at least before that would happen but it doesn't calm me down either.

She shakes her head, giving me a shy smile.

I tilt my head, about to ask what she means when it finally clicks. "You want to be the principal at High Tides?" I whisper it. I don't know why I do but it reminds me of when we would whisper to each other while her siblings and Blake slept around us on those summer nights.

"Yeah, I do. I really do. I love this school so much." Her eyes drop. She's waiting for my reaction.

"I think that's amazing. I know I have no right to say this but I'm proud of you, Viv." A light flush quickly works its way up her neck and face, but she tentatively preens at the praise.

After a few seconds of her assessing me, looking for any hint of mocking, she breaks out into a grin.

Not just a grin.

A smile.

A beaming smile.

A smile brighter than the sun and more beautiful than the sunset over the ocean.

"Thanks, Grady." Her voice is soft, a little breathy. "Applications are due in January but the principal from the private school where I used to be a teacher's aide, knows one of the advisors at UCAH. She's going to meet with me. Give me tips and stuff like that."

I nod, leaning back in the chair and setting her iPad on my desk. "For what it's worth, my mom has mentioned more than a few times that she thinks you should move higher up on the faculty ladder."

She chuckles and shakes her head. "She tells me that often, same with Knox." I catch the very second realization dawns on her. She lightly places her hand on my forearm. Our eyes both drop to the contact. To my delight, she doesn't remove her hand right away.

"He's your assistant coach. Have you met him yet?"

"No, I haven't. I'm going to try to meet up with him later this week."

"He's kind of the best." She slips her purse over her shoulder. "I think you two will be a force to be reckoned with. And maybe start to sway some of the other coaches' attitudes." She shrugs, acting like the pushback I know they constantly give her isn't frustrating. "I need to get going, though."

"Your planner didn't have anything else planned for another hour." I test my luck. She doesn't sit back but she doesn't stand either. "I was actually hoping that you had some ideas about what I could do with my classroom."

She gives me a curious look. "You want my help with decorating?"

"Yeah." I lean back and cross my arms. "I don't think rainbows and stars will translate great to a high school history course but other than a couple maps on the walls I'm clueless."

She gets comfortable in her chair, not planning to leave so soon after all. With her signature smirk—part mischief, part sass—and a silky voice, she says, "Didn't seem like you needed any help decorating your room the other night."

I know my cheeks are warm again, mostly because Vivi is the only girl who has ever made me blush. I don't let her win this round though.

"Have you been thinking about it?"

"No," she huffs too quickly. "But black is a bold choice for your walls."

"I like a dark room to sleep in. And it feels cozy and intimate, somehow. You should try it out." It takes me a few seconds to recognize the insinuation I made.

I look at her, expecting her to get annoyed or maybe even laugh in my face. "Not my style. Much more Calypso's." I know she's just deflecting, but for once, I'm appreciative. "As far as your classroom… I agree that rainbows aren't your thing. You should go to Golden Age and look for some globes and vintage maps." I recognize the store name as the small antique shop that opened while I was living in Phoenix too.

"That's a good idea."

"I know. Write it down."

Chuckling, I grab a pen from my desk and a notepad from the drawer. I make a note of her suggestion and motion with my pen for her to go on.

Mon, Aug 8 at 4:26 PM

Hey, the girls were hoping to FT you again tonight.

Arielle

Yes, of course! I was going to see what your plans were after rehearsals.

Does 7pm my time work?

Yup. Can't wait to see you :)

Once both girls are bathed and ready for bed, we all crawl onto the couch and FaceTime their mom.

Arielle was studying English and theater when we met at Arizona State University. She's an amazing actress, but she has always wanted to write plays too. She's more than talented enough.

When we were juniors in college and only a couple weeks after I tore my ACL, we found out she was pregnant with Stella. I'd be lying if I said it wasn't terrifying but there has never been a role in life that was more right for me than being a parent. I knew before Stella was born that she was going to be my entire world. The first time I held her, it only solidified that unconditional love. I wasn't sure how much bigger my heart could get until Daisy was born. It doubled in size and feels like it's split in two places outside of my body.

Arielle was happy being a parent, too. I know she loves the girls. I have never and would *never* question that. I think that hurting my knee and knowing I was going to make big changes to my life plan had helped me prepare for parenthood. Arielle wanted to join a touring theater group and work her way toward Broadway. And she could have. She's doing just that now.

Never achieving that goal was starting to eat at her, and it was obvious. She was happy with our daughters but that was just about the only thing in her life that made her happy. I wasn't making her happy anymore. We were comfortable and good friends, but we weren't *happy*. I certainly wasn't in love with her anymore. The thought of all of us moving to New York City came up when we attended couples counseling but neither one of us was sold on the idea. Arielle would have loved for the girls to go with her but we both knew that our relationship was coming to an end. Arielle deserves a real chance at accomplishing her dreams, and the girls deserve a parent whose schedule better fits what they need right now.

I want my daughters to know that their mother both loves them and achieved her goals.

That doesn't make this transition any easier for them, though.

Arielle's face pops up on my phone and both girls squeal at the sight of her beautiful face.

And she is beautiful. She's only a couple inches shorter than me and has a very elegant, quiet beauty to her. She has sharp features and a thin frame. Her hair is a dark brown, similar to mine and our daughters, but with cooler undertones. Her skin is milky with few blemishes. I always thought she was interesting to look at.

Seeing her after spending time with Vivi makes me realize everything is different now. Or maybe it has always been this way and I spent years trying to forget.

She isn't only gorgeous. Genevieve is fucking sexy. There has always been this underlying wildness about her. An untamable energy that has driven me crazy my entire life. Now, with her womanly body—soft hips, full chest, and round bottom—she's irresistible.

"Grady?" Arielle tries to get my attention. Both girls are staring up at me, looking like they are waiting for an answer. "Would that be okay?"

I don't know how long I zoned out of the conversation, but I don't want to agree to anything I might regret later. "Sorry, what was that?"

Arielle gives me a long, weird look before repeating herself. "I was thinking that I would visit for a few days around Stella's birthday in December. Our tour is ending in Northern California, and train tickets are pretty cheap. I can fly out of San Diego in time for our string of local shows in the city."

It feels weird to mix Arielle in with my life here. Even while we were married, I hardly ever brought her back home and when I did, I made sure that there would be no Davies family members around. But I have to remind myself that it's *our* life—mine and my daughters'. They deserve to see their mom whenever they can.

"Of course, that would be okay. It would be nice to spend Stell's birthday together.'

"Mom, you can stay here!" Daisy shouts, bless her young heart.

Arielle and I look at each other, still able to communicate silently when it comes to parenting. Stella is the first to speak up.

"No, Dais, Mom's probably not going to stay here…"

I give my ex-wife a small nod and turn to our daughters, "You're right. Mom won't be staying *here* but she will be visiting every day, or we can visit her wherever she decides to stay."

"Can we have sleepovers with Mommy?" Daisy asks quietly, giving me her sad eyes.

"Of course, darling. You guys still need to go to school but you can spend every night over there if you want. I'm sure you're ready for a break from me," I tease and tickle her side.

Arielle gives me a small smile before talking, "We can have a girls' night every night you come to stay with me. Remember when we used to do the DIY spa? We'll do that again. Even a paint night!"

The three of them continue making plans for the visit and my mind starts to drift again.

Another thing therapy helped me realize is that I'm sadder about losing my marriage than I am about losing Arielle.

I would have stayed in that marriage forever just because I didn't want to fail.

But that wouldn't be fair to her or I. Or to our daughters.

Moving back to Amada Beach is quickly making me realize that I don't want to feel *content* in a relationship. I want to feel like my heart is split into a third piece.

Chapter Nine

Vivi

The first day of school has always given me a specific sort of thrill, even as a teacher. I don't know how to explain it.

It's a certain type of anxious excitement that only happens when you know you're stepping into a new experience. And every year is exactly that.

The kids are one year older, gaining new knowledge, meeting a friend for the first time. The teachers are meeting a new class and getting another year to help these kids find another part of themselves.

I'd be lying if I said every class is an easy fit. Some years, it takes more adjustment. And that's okay. Those are usually the years that there are a higher majority of kids who need more. More attention, more praise, and more encouragement.

This year I get the feeling that the students are going to get along pretty well and are excited to be here.

I've been teaching for five years now, and there are some things I've learned about how to base what the school year will be like. For example, this year's class loved my silly ice breakers and we spent longer than I had planned playing two truths and lie, once they figured out the rules a bit. Heads Up Seven Up is another classic way to get the kids interacting with each other and learning names quickly.

The more excited and open they are on the first day usually means that they will feel that way throughout the year.

I sent out the email to all of the supervisors and coaches during my lunch, and a few of the supervisors have gotten back to me already, letting me know that they will have their ideas by the beginning of next week. We usually try to hold off on starting after school activities until the second full week of classes, allowing the students some time to get settled.

Not at all surprising, none of the coaches have replied to the email. Even though I *know* a lot of the coaches believe in accessibility to all students and the prioritization of education, I also know that Harper can be a bully and is the leader of the sports pack.

He constantly wonders why I won't give him a chance.

He's the type of man who not only peaked in high school but feels entitled to any woman he meets. Mrs. Gable loves him because he's taken the football team to multiple state championships. And Knox, Grady's assistant coach, and I are certain that she has a crush on him.

"Knock, knock."

I turn toward the soft tap on my classroom door and smile at the friendly voice I recognize easily.

The very man himself.

"Knox!" I jump from my chair. He's easily my closest work friend even if I've refused to let that expand outside of the school. "How are you? How are Lucas and the boys? How was Hawaii?"

He chuckles and opens his arms to give me a tight hug. "It was amazing! Remind me to have Lucas email you the photos of Matty and Jake kayaking for the first time. Matty got a little sick but pushed through. Jake hated it but refused to give up."

"Oh, no," I laugh. Matty is in kindergarten at the school, and Jake was in my class two years ago. "Let Matty know that I was sick for *weeks* when I first started to kayak but you get used to it eventually. If it's something he likes, I would love to take you guys around the coves up in La Jolla sometime."

"You angel, Matty would love that. But you know, Viv, that means *actually* spending time with me outside of work," he jokes.

Rolling my eyes, I take another step back. "Just let me know when. What are you doing on the munchkin side of the campus?"

High Tides accepts students from kindergarten all the way to twelfth grade, but the classrooms are designed in a way to separate the younger kids from the older students.

"Oh, right." He laughs awkwardly, glancing around my room. I raise my eyebrows, waiting for him to tell me what's going on. "I was actually looking for Grady... Grady Miller. I haven't had a chance to meet him since I got back to town. Selena said if he isn't in his classroom to maybe check yours..." He lets the sentence drift off but gives me a curious look.

Selena, ever the meddling mother.

After everything that happened with former best friend Molly and ex-fiancé Brody, I haven't allowed anyone into my life after Lexi. And as thankful as I am for her, at the time it simply was due to necessity. Knox and his husband Lucas have invited me to dinner multiple times and have encouraged me to meet someone at every single work function. I always refuse. He says that I'm an angel, but really, it's him. Knox is one of the most patient men I've ever met. The fact that he doesn't hate me after I've blown off his offers every time should say enough.

I knew from the moment I heard that he would be coaching with

Grady that they'd be fast friends.

I try to break the tension with a teasing eye roll, and I turn back to the whiteboard, trying to keep myself busy in hopes that I can hide my reaction from him.

"Is that what the rumor is?"

"I mean, I wouldn't call it a rumor. If anything, Selena seemed hopeful. Any idea what that's about?"

I shoot him a sharp look over my shoulder that he answers with a grin. "No idea at all. As you can see, there's no one in my classroom."

I turn to face him now, and we give each other a long stare, waiting to see who'll break first.

Knox is not nearly as stubborn as me. "Fine, I can see he isn't here. I guess I can go check his room now." He gives me a faux guilty look and backs toward the door. "I figured I would check in here first."

"You and Selena spend too much time together. Busybodies, I swear."

Knox stops before turning the corner into the hall and gives me a wide smile, "You could be a busybody with us if you ever attended dinner at my house. We love to gossip." I give him an exasperated look, but we both know I don't mean it. "This will be the year, Vivi. You will be my friend. Not my work friend, my *real* friend."

I shake my head but can't hide the smile that blooms on my lips.

Sometimes I hate Brody and Molly, not even for what they did with each other, but for what they did to *me.* They ruined the trusting girl that I had been and helped create the secretly cynical woman I am.

A mixture of terrifying nerves and unconditional hope fall into the pit of my stomach as I think about what it would be like to be *real friends* with someone like Knox Barker.

Maybe this will be the year I push through my distrust of… well, everyone.

I don't know how many times she walks by my door before I notice her from behind my computer.

"Daisy? Do you want to come in?"

She looks up with wide eyes, as if she's surprised that I saw her. She gives me a small nod and walks into my classroom.

"Bring one of those chairs over here."

She quickly does so and takes a seat. "Hi," she says quietly, a solemn look on her face.

I don't know what she needs in this moment, but I don't love it when people force me to talk about things before I'm ready, so I go for subtlety.

"My day was craaazy," I drag out the last word for emphasis. It was actually pretty calm, but I can see that it piques her interest. "How was your day?"

"Hm." She's quiet for a second and swings her short legs in the chair. "It's been okay."

"Oh. Okay, like boring? Or okay, like not very good?"

"Not very good," she whispers.

"Do you want to talk about it? Or do you want to hear about how I bought popsicles for my class and now I have sticky messes everywhere and even a few stains on the carpet over there? My year is off to a great start, too." I give her a little wink.

She gives me a genuine laugh, but it ends too quickly. She looks out the window and I almost can't hear her. "All of the girls in my class already know each other. No one asked to play with me all day."

I'm quiet for a second because I'm worried I might actually start crying for her, and working with kids has taught me enough to know that crying in front of them only makes them cry harder.

She continues, "I saw Stella at recess, but I didn't want to bug her… She looked like she'd made a lot of friends."

I take a steadying breath before talking, "Yeah, that must have been really hard, Daisy. I'm sorry your first day wasn't what you had imagined." I give her a sympathetic smile. "I bet a lot of the kids in your class were feeling the same way."

She gives me a disbelieving side-eye, "Really?"

"Really. Starting kindergarten is scary, even when you know people. It can be weird trying to meet new friends and a big school can be really confusing. I'm sure that at least a few of them were just as nervous as you. Give it a few days and you'll know all the kids in your class. And they will want to know you, too."

She looks at me for a few seconds. "Are girls mean? In Phoenix there were some girls who made Stella cry."

I love kids. I work with kids. I've never wanted to push a few kids down a hill more than right now.

"Sometimes, yes, girls—and people in general—can be mean," I answer honestly. "*But* more often than not, when someone is being mean it's because there's something going on with them. It probably doesn't have anything to do with how they feel about *you* and more to do with how they feel about *themselves.* Does that make sense?"

She stares out the window for a long moment. "Yeah, I think it does."

"You met my best friend, Lexi, the other night at dinner. We used to not get along at all. Not until after we graduated from high school. We never played together, and we would compete against each other all the time. It was really exhausting."

"But she's your friend now?"

I think back to how Lexi and I became friends. Everything I told Daisy was true. We fucking *hated* each other from the moment we met in kindergarten. Most young girls would bond over having the same *Lisa Frank* backpack but not us. The winter recital was announced a few weeks later and we were the only two kids in the class who wanted the solo. We ended up splitting it, and that was the beginning of twelve long years of emotional warfare.

We probably could have done some evil genius shit if we had put our energy into something productive rather than beating one another. Spelling bees, prom queen, class president. We fought through it all, clawing each other down until one of us was on top.

That was until we entered our first year at UCLA and we were in an Ethics lecture together. The only people we knew in a room of five hundred strangers. I somehow caught her eye from my seat while she was walking up the stairs. We took one look at each other, I moved my bag from the chair next to me, and she sat down.

It wasn't that we took an immediate liking to each other, not by any means. We didn't speak a word to each other for the first month until Lexi missed a class and asked for my notes, but we sat together three days a week without question.

"Oh, yeah, Lexi's my best friend now. We even live next door to each other."

"She's so cool," Daisy perks up a little.

"I know, she totally is. But Lexi and I had to grow up and change before we could be friends. And, Daisy, your *best* friend right now might not be a girl. And guess what? That's okay."

"I don't want a *boy* as my best friend. Who is going to play with dolls with me?"

I chuckle softly, thinking about the little brunette boy that tried his hardest to hide his excitement about getting to play as my Barbie's husband. "You would be surprised what a boy will do when he likes you, and what he may even like doing. Your dad was my best friend when we were kids, and he played house with me."

Her little legs kick back and forth, she twists her hands in her lap and finally, after almost a minute of silence, she looks up at me and says, "I wish you and my dad were still best friends. It's weird at the house without my mom."

I'm not at a loss for words very often but at this moment, everything I can think of falls short. I blurt out the first thing that comes to my mind, "Can I give you a hug?"

Tears fill her perfect brown eyes, bringing the gold out, but she gives me a genuine smile before flinging herself off of her chair. I kneel down in front of her and wrap my arms around her. Her little fingers twirl my hair. "Thank you," she whispers.

We stand there hugging for a long moment before there is a light knock on the door and Grady clears his throat.

We pull a part and look up at him. I don't know how much he heard but I hope I didn't overstep.

Getting to my feet, I turn toward my white board hoping he doesn't see the tears threatening to spill over. "I was going to call you or Selena in a minute."

"It's okay, Vivi. I saw Stella on the playground, and I had an idea where my other little lady must have run off to." He smiles down at Daisy who is now clinging to his leg. I can't stop myself from smiling down at her, too.

"I'm sorry, Daddy. I know you told me to stay with Stella, but she was playing with her friends and I… came here…"

He looks up at me and we share a moment of mutual understanding. "How about we add this to the lists of places you're allowed to go? If that's okay with you, Vivi."

"Of course, it is. You guys are welcome in my class whenever you want." I don't specify that I don't only mean his daughters.

From the look that Grady is giving me, he caught the subtle gesture too.

"Dais, why don't you go find your sister and meet me by the front bench?"

She nods and skips off, seeming a little brighter than when she first entered.

"I didn't mean to overstep. I can't li—"

"Thank you."

We both stop abruptly and stare at each other.

"What?" I whisper.

"Thank you, Vivi. I heard… some of the conversation. I didn't mean to eavesdrop or burden you with my problems, but I want the girls to talk to someone, even if it isn't me." I nod, suddenly dumbstruck.

"You can't lie about what?"

"What?" I ask again, louder.

"You were about to say you can't lie about something."

"Oh, that." I clear my throat. "It's nothing." By the way he leans his weight against the doorframe, I know he isn't planning on leaving until I tell him. "Fine, okay? God, you're pushy."

He looks down at his feet and chuckles softly. When his eyes move back up, he takes his sweet time sweeping them up my body.

I don't know what Grady's type is, and it doesn't matter either way, but I've noticed the way he looks at me. Sometimes it makes me feel like I might as well be in that lacey green set I bought a few months ago.

Desirable. Hot. Wanted.

The way he's looking at me right now? In my yellow midi overall dress and white sneakers? It makes me feel naked. It makes me feel sexy and seen and *exposed*. Just from the way he drags his eyes along my curves, pausing for only a second on my large breasts. It would be easy to miss if I wasn't hyperaware to all of his movements right now.

When his eyes finally find mine, he's slightly smirking but his face is a couple shades warmer than normal. He moves his hand in a *let's hear it* motion.

"I was going to say that I can't lie about how quickly your daughters are growing on me." He straightens up slightly. His expression shifts into something of surprise, maybe a little gratitude too. "Grady, you have some of the coolest kids I've ever met. And I clearly know a lot of them." I laugh softly and his eyes drop down to my mouth.

He stares reverently at my lips before giving me an intense look. One that I can't deny has more of an effect on me than I care to admit. His eyes are full of hunger and appreciation. "Thank you," he says in that low, husky voice. It never fails to send a shot of heat straight to my core.

I don't say anything, I just nod slowly again, never breaking eye contact.

"I should go," he says in that same tone. "See you tomorrow, Miss Davies."

Chapter Ten
Grady

As soon as I step into the vet clinic, I know my dad is swamped. He keeps the clinic open late three days a week, in hopes of making up for closing on Sundays now. I told him that I would stop by with his favorite; carne asada tacos from Gringos Tacos food truck down at The Loop.

It's a small place that my dad opened when we first moved to the neighborhood. Amada Beach had never had their own animal hospital, and the town used to travel at least forty-five minutes into the city for an appointment. I can't imagine what happened when any of the pets had an emergency.

The success of my dad's clinic wasn't only for the convenience that he brought. The people simply enjoyed supporting local businesses in the community. Between the local support and the high volume of yearly tourists, of the small businesses in town do extremely well.

I brought some extra food, not knowing how many people were going to be working tonight, and I immediately know I made the right call when I see three of the exam room doors closed and Krissy, the vet tech, taking the vitals in the front lobby of some of the pet patients while the owners are waiting.

My brother-in-law Adrian is in the break room, filling up his water bottle. "Hey, man. I wasn't planning on staying but I think I might jump behind the front desk for a bit."

He looks over at me and I can see the instant gratitude in his dark brown eyes. My dad's the one who introduced Blake and Adrian, a little over seven years ago. Adrian was looking for his first job while working on his D.V.M. My dad apparently knew right away that Adrian was the man for his daughter, much like he has said throughout my life, that he knew Vivi was the girl for me.

It wasn't that my parents didn't like Arielle, but she just never fit in with my family. Much like I never fit in with hers. They weren't unwelcoming or disapproving at all, neither were my parents. It was just another thing between Arielle and I that never worked itself out in the long run.

Blake's husband never had those problems. He fits in with the Millers as if he was always meant to be a part of our family, and his parents love my sister just as much.

Adrian really is one of the best men out there—he's patient, outgoing, trusting, and easy-going. Al the opposite of Blake's hard exterior but he's softened her up over the years, in only the best ways, without trying to silence the storm.

Not to mention, Adrian is objectively one of the most good looking people I've ever met. He's around six-foot-three-inches tall, lean but with broad shoulders, and his deep mahogany skin is only a few shades lighter than his eyes. He usually cuts his hair close at the start of summer, letting it grow throughout the year. Right now, it's just at the edge of a buzz, the early hint of curls making their way back.

"Has anyone ever told you that you're my favorite Miller sibling?"

I huff out a laugh. "Please let me be in the room when you tell Blake that."

"Yeah, sure. Might as well hand her the divorce papers while we're at it." I laugh while I set the bags down. Blake is *picky* with just about everything. To most people, it would've seemed crazy for a nineteen-year-old girl to get married less than a year after meeting her boyfriend because it does sound crazy. But Blake isn't an impulsive person—never has been, and my parents came to the realization fairly quickly—but she is an *impatient* person. Not only that, but Blake also didn't really give anyone an opportunity to say otherwise.

Blake made up her mind about six months after they started to date. She wanted to marry Adrian and she was sure enough that he wanted to marry her that she wasn't going to wait around for the *appropriate* amount of time to pass. She went to his parents and asked permission to propose to their son. Apparently, his mom immediately started laughing and both were overjoyed. At the small wedding, Will and Cami said they weren't at all surprised that Blake decided to take matters into her own hands. Blake's conviction is quiet but heartfelt and strong.

She's not always an easy one to get to know but over time Adrian cracked the hard exterior that is Blake. He learned about the years of bullying to the point of transferring to online classes. He knows about the years of loneliness and exclusion before the torment began in high school. He saw Blake for all that she is, including the saddest, darkest parts, and has loved her fiercely every day since.

"Your dad mentioned you were stopping by..." Adrian says as he peaks over my shoulder.

"I bought extra. I wasn't sure who all was going to be here."

He grabs a plate and loads a few tacos on top with salsa and lime. "Thanks, man. As you can see, we're swamped tonight."

"Yeah, I didn't see who else was here other than my dad and Krissy." We call it a clinic, since that's how it started over two decades ago, but it's grown almost three times in size then. It's a fully staffed pet hospital now.

He nods, taking another bite of his food. He scarfs down as much as he can as quickly as he can, and I leave him to it. On nights like this, he only has a few minutes to get a bite in and I don't want to distract him. Instead, I make my way to the front desk so Krissy can focus on prepping the animals while I check them in.

I have always known that I didn't plan on taking over the clinic, or becoming any sort of medical care workers, but I helped out after school and during summers from the time I was old enough.

I've been here for about three hours by the time I finally get a moment with my dad. We're sitting in the breakroom, talking about the fair and the first day of classes. I know from the look in his eye he wants to ask more about the meeting with Vivi, but he takes pity on me, letting me deflect from that topic as long as I want.

Impatience is a trait that Blake gets from my mom.

"Dr. Miller, sorry to interrupt but Lexi's here with Sage."

"Oh, crap. I lost track of time. Will you grab Sage's vitals for me and get them settled in exam room two?"

"Absolutely." Krissy turns her back to us and I direct my attention to my dad.

"Don't start. Lexi's a good girl." *Said no one ever,* I think to myself. "A bit wild but aren't all the best people?" he chuckles. "She's a better friend than that Molly girl ever was to our Viv."

Our Viv. My parents have claimed each of the Davies, just like Bonnie has done with me and Blake, but it was always a little different with Vivi. Not that they loved her more but maybe they had different expectations for her. For us.

"Lexi's cool. And I never liked Molly, so I'll take your word for it. I'm going to head out, anyway. Mom's been with Stella and Daisy all night and I know how exhausting they can be."

He throws his trash away and we make our way back toward the front together. "Oh, you know your mother will be more upset that you're taking them home than she ever will be about getting to watch them for a few hours."

I know he's right. It's another reason that I know moving back home was the right decision for the three of us.

"Hey, Tim. Grady." Lexi greets us. A large white and brown pit bull is sitting off her leash next to Lexi's feet.

"Hey, Lexi." My dad takes a step away and pats his leg to call Sage to him. "I'll get the exam going and see how those antibiotics are treating our friend. Meet me there whenever you're ready."

After the door closes and it's just the two of us in the lobby, Lexi finally looks back towards me but doesn't say anything.

I break the silence first. "You *would* have a giant pit bull."

Her dark eyes narrow and she sharply retorts, "And you *would* get another woman pregnant, but you don't hear me making any comments about it."

Rolling my eyes, I slip my hands in my pockets. "We went to homecoming together *one* time, Alexandra, and that was like ten years ago. You need to move on."

Her hand flies out and hits my chest but even she can't hide her chuckle. "You know that's not who I meant, Grady *Idiot* Miller." I rub my chest and shrug nonchalantly. "So, it was nice seeing you at dinner the other night. I'm sure your mother agrees."

"Did she tell you that?" I snap. I like Lexi, I do. We've never had any problems with each other, and we even had a good time at homecoming—arguably the best time I had at a high school dance. But I'm tired of everyone making subtle comments about Vivi and how much time I spent away from here.

No one knows, nor cares, that I was trying to do what was best for my daughters. Only that I clearly failed somehow.

"She didn't have to," Lexi says in a rare compassionate voice. "I won't sit here and pretend I know your parents better than you because of course I don't. But it doesn't take a rocket scientist to know that your mom has been happier the last few weeks than she's been in years."

I don't really know what to say to that, so we just stare at each other in silence for a few seconds. She nods, a mix of deep-rooted exasperation and unfair disappointment crossing her features.

She stops a few steps from the door. Turning toward me with a popped-out hip, she states, "Vivi and I force her siblings to go to karaoke with us every few weeks. Hudson and Lyp don't sing, as I'm sure you would guess, but they like to drink. Asher doesn't drink but he has the best stage presence you'll ever see. You should come."

"Oh… I don't know." I don't want to impose on something that's hers.

"She won't mind. She may act like it, but you can see past that. I know you can. Friday night, eight o'clock, Spotlight Lounge." She turns toward the exam room before I can say anything. With her hand on the doorknob, she looks at me over her shoulder. "Don't let us down, Grady."

She walks into the room and closes the door behind her, leaving me stunned and gawking at the spot where she was standing, unsure of what to do with the offer.

Chapter Eleven
Grady

"Can I expect you to bring me lunch every day? Because that would be amazing," I tell my mom as I shovel another bite of menudo into my mouth.

Her laugh is light and airy. "Oh, *mi amor*, I don't spoil you that much anymore."

"Why did you even make menudo? It isn't Christmas." Menudo, mole, and tamales are just one reason I'm excited to spend the holidays back home again.

"I know that. It's for Knox. His birthday is on Sunday so I told him I would bring him enough to take home this weekend."

I huff out a laugh. "Wow, I didn't know I could make demands for my birthday."

"You can't." She gives me a sharp look. "He would never make any sort of demand. That's why I offered, *tonto*."

I'm about to make a retort that would probably get me hit over the head regardless of the fact that we're at work, when Vivi walks in with a teacher I've never met before. She's looking up at him, with a large smile across her face. I don't pay attention to what he's saying but I feel the sharp sting of jealousy when she barks out a beautiful laugh in response.

Not the breathy cackle I love.

But her deeper belly laugh, that means whatever she's hearing brings her pure joy.

When I take a good look at the two of them together, the envious feeling only grows.

She really is gorgeous. Her copper hair is in two buns on top of her head, with a few strands framing her face, allowing a clear view of her round face and soft features. She's in a light pink shirtdress. It doesn't cling to her body, but it doesn't need to. She fills it out perfectly.

The tall man next to her is dressed nicely but without a lot of flair. He's in slim-fit dark blue pants and a white button-up shirt. His dark brown shoes perfectly match his belt. It's a simple outfit but much crisper than what you'd typically see a teacher in. His dark blonde hair is a little long but perfectly tousled to look like he didn't put any effort into it. His olive-green eyes cut to my mom and me.

Vivi is breathtaking and the man next to her is handsome, there is no denying that fact. They look good together.

And I hate it.

Her head falls forward once her laugh comes to an end, and she sees my mom and I sitting at the only table in the breakroom. "Oh, hello." She's still smiling as she walks further into the room.

"Hi, *roja*. How is your week?" Before Vivi can answer, my mom is already turning her attention to the man that walked in as well. "Knox, I made you menudo. Plenty for you and Lucas. It's in the fridge with your name on it."

The jealous feeling in my stomach crawls back to its cave, only leaving the wanting and confusion behind.

I feel slightly embarrassed, even though I haven't said a word since I felt my heart fall out of my chest.

I pull my eyes away from Vivi just in time to see my mom giving me a knowing look. One I don't necessarily appreciate.

My head snaps back toward Knox when he says, "Thank you so much, Selena. Looks like the boys are getting chicken nuggets tonight."

My mom and Vivi both laughs.

"Were you two able to meet the other day?" Vivi asks Knox, pointedly ignoring me.

"No, we didn't." I stand up and put my hand out.

Knox gives it a firm shake. "Good to meet you. Selena has told me a lot about you. Vivi, too."

He nudges her with his elbow, and she gives him a look that says otherwise.

I choke down a laugh. "I've heard a lot about you too. Do you guys want to join us?" I ask as I take my seat again.

Knox takes a seat, but Vivi goes toward the fridge instead. "I'm on recess duty on Fridays. So, I should get out there." She grabs a small lunch bag before turning back toward us. She stops to give my mom a small hug from her chair. "Knox, stop by my classroom later. I have some stuff from one of those teacher subscription boxes. I think the boys will like it." She pats my mom's shoulder and looks me in the eye for the first time since she walked in. "Bye."

"Bye, Vivi," I give her a pathetic wave.

She stops at the door to look back at us. Some of the hair framing her face gets stuck on her smiling lips.

I imagine what it would feel like to push them behind her ear, letting my hand settle on the nape of her neck.

My mom puts her hand on my shoulder, getting my attention. "Honey, are you breathing?" There is a mischievous glint in her eye.

I decide to not entertain her and turn my focus back to Knox, who is also smirking. "How many children do you have?" I ask.

"My husband Lucas and I adopted two boys about four years ago now."

"That's amazing. How old are they?"

Knox and I'll be spending a lot of time together, and I hope to build a friendship with him. The fact that he has a family gives us some common ground.

"Jake is in fourth grade. He turned nine while we were in Hawaii. Our youngest Matty's in kindergarten."

"My youngest is in kindergarten. Who is his teacher?" There are only two teachers for each of the elementary grade levels.

"Mrs. Verma."

"Oh, okay. Daisy's in Mrs. Waymier's class. Stella's in third grade."

"You should bring them over for dinner sometime. Matty's been nervous about making friends."

"That'd be great. I think Daisy's been feeling the same way."

We talk for a while after that, eating menudo and getting to know basic things about each other. Knox and his husband moved to Amada Beach about a year and a half ago. Lucas is a lawyer at the local family practice and originally from here, but he was a few grades ahead of me, so I don't think we've ever met. I know his dad Stanley, the owner of the hardware store and construction company. Both are small but handle almost everything in our small community. His mom is the owner of the law office Lucas works at and will be taking over one day according to Knox.

We don't talk too much about baseball, but we make plans to have lunch next week to start discussing our plans and coaching styles. Any lingering anxieties are melting away though.

After some time, my mom heads back to the library but Knox

and I apparently have the same afternoon prep hour. A small group of coaches walk in as I'm packing my things up, including Derek Harper. None of them pay us much attention but I can't fight my curiosity anymore.

I ask Knox if he wants to prep in my classroom today, wanting to ask him some questions about the politics at this school. Normally I don't like to get involved with such things but implementing a new sports team and helping Vivi with the fair puts different pressures on me.

When we get to my classroom, I take a seat at one of the students' desks and Knox follows.

He doesn't waste any time getting to the point. "So, I assume you want to understand that clique better." He lets out a dry laugh and I immediately know for certain that I hate Derek Harper.

"Yeah, pretty much. Mostly Harper, I guess. He seems to be the ringleader of sorts."

"Yeah, he is. He's also Gable's favorite faculty member." He takes a second, thinking through his words. "She only cares about sports. Which is good for us, in some ways. She's willing to put quite a bit of the budget into sports and has the rest of the committee wrapped around her finger on that. She isn't all bad, but her priorities are not aligned to most of the teachers here anymore."

I nod, remembering my mom mentioning something similar more than a few times.

Knox continues, "Harper took over the football department three or so years before I started working here, so I don't know much about his time before then. What I do know now is that he's an arrogant prick. He doesn't care about education—he barely cares about his P.E. courses if I'm being honest. He thinks he's some sort of God because the football team has won multiple state championships since he started working here. Most of the other coaches fear him because of Gable's favoritism but some of them—like Kramer and Hayes, the cheerleading and boys' basketball coaches—do agree with him.

"Truthfully, it's the way that he bullies everyone that's a problem. If you're a man, you either kiss his ass and he sees you as inferior or you keep your distance, and he sees you as a threat."

"And women?" My blood runs a little cold at the tense grimace that takes over Knox's features.

"And women... well... there isn't any good way to put this so I'm just going to say it. There are three options with women. He either finds them attractive, meaning they become a conquest that he feels entitled to. Or they also fall into the *ass kissing* group, and he uses her as sway, like the men. Or he doesn't find them attractive or useful, so he pretends that they don't exist." My eyebrows pinch together in disgust, Knox catching it. He nods in acknowledgment. "I've seen him flat-out ignore more than a few of the teachers here while harassing others at every turn."

I can't help but wonder which of those categories Vivi falls into. I know she doesn't kiss his ass, mostly because that's not her style. I don't know which of the two options I hate more, though. Vivi either being treated like a piece of meat to be eaten at his own leisure or not being treated like a human at all.

I decide it's better not to have this conversation with Knox and add it to the long list of things I hope I get the chance to talk about with her one day.

Toward the end of our prep hour, I throw caution to the wind.

"Hey, do you and Lucas have plans tonight?"

Knox thinks it over a second, putting his weekly course plans into a divided folder. "No, we don't. Why?"

"My... friend," I stumble, using it for lack of a better word, "invited me to Spotlight tonight. I'm not really one for karaoke but I was thinking I could go for a drink. You and Lucas should come."

"Yeah, sure," he starts walking toward the door. "Thanks for the invitation. By chance, do I know this friend?" He stops at the door with a smirk on his face.

"Honestly, I don't know."

He looks slightly confused by my answer, probably assuming it was Vivi who invited me, but I really don't know if he knows Lexi or any of the other Davies.

I wasn't even sure if I was planning on going to Spotlight tonight until I asked Knox. Somehow it feels like I have back-up. And that doesn't even make sense considering he's friends with Genevieve and I hardly know him.

Regardless, I decided to call Blake and ask her to watch the girls tonight. I knew that she'd say yes. Millie's been sad that she goes to the public school rather than the charter school. She said she was willing to give up all her friends to go to school with her cousins. We have compromised with weekly sleepovers. Sometimes more than one.

I'm on my way back home after dropping them off. My plan is to take a quick shower and change before heading out. I've only been to a karaoke bar once. And that was years ago.

My college teammates and I went to New Orleans together for a fall break trip during our junior year of college. One of the last stops of the night was the Cat's Meow where five intoxicated D1 athletes performed "BedRock" together. The crowd was nice enough to cover Nicki Minaj's part for us.

I swore that once was enough for my lifetime, but I guess tonight proves just how much I'm willing to do to get back into the good graces of Amada Beach.

I could say it's for Asher and Calypso but there doesn't seem to be much animosity there. Hudson's always preferred to stay out of other people's business. I don't anticipate him having much to say either.

I know that tonight is about working my way off Vivi's blacklist.

My phone pulls me out of my thoughts, ringing through Bluetooth.

Arielle calling... flashes across the dashboard.

I can't stop the soul-aching groan that spills out of me.

There truly isn't any bad blood between us. Once we both accepted that we wanted a divorce and agreed on where the girls should go, the divorce was easy enough. We both were given a trust fund when we graduated from college and bought a house with a small portion of those. The financial separations took the longest to work out. Cutting emotional ties was the easiest. Which is really depressing considering we had a life together.

The girls and I are adjusting though. Even before we moved out here, the three of us had routines. We had a life together even if it was only us three. Even if I felt like I was carrying the entire world on my back and didn't have anyone to turn to.

That's what I miss the most from my marriage—having someone to talk about these parental struggles and someone who understands.

I'm beginning to wonder if what Arielle misses the most is the company that comes with marriage. The knowledge that someone's there, waiting for you, present for you.

Since we moved home, Arielle has been calling more. And texting more. She's always tried to stay as present in the girls' lives as possible but that's shifted back to me. The calls and texts will start with the girls but quickly move to questions about me, my life. And I don't really care to have those conversations with her anymore.

I need the separation.

But my guilt always gets the best of me.

So, I answer.

"Hello?" I don't know why I always answer my calls like that when I know who it is. That's what caller ID is for. It's always bothered her no matter how much I tried to break the habit.

"Hi," she replies in a tense voice. *Yup, annoyed by my greeting.* She clears her throat then uses a lighter voice, "How was your day?"

Maybe it shouldn't but it feels really freaking awkward.

"It was good. I just dropped Stella and Daisy off with Blake for the night." I always try to bring the conversation back to our daughters.

"That's nice. I'm sure they'll have fun…" she trails off, probably wondering how to keep the conversation going.

I take pity on her. "How was your day?"

"It was pretty good," she perks up. "We're in Phoenix for the next two weeks. I called some of the girls to plan dinner." *The girls* would be the three mom-friends Arielle made through the PTA.

I let her tell me about her shows and the plans she made and a lot of other things I only partially hear while I drive home.

When I pull into the garage, I finally cut her off. "Hey, Arielle? I'm sorry to end the call so abruptly," I start cautiously, even though I'm not, "but I just got home and I'm kind of running low on time right now."

I can feel the shock before I hear it in her voice. "Oh… What are you doing tonight?" She doesn't really have a right to ask that, and she knows it. She immediately backtracks, "No, no. I'm sorry—inappropriate. It's just a habit."

We both know what she's really asking: *are you dating anyone?* And it isn't fair. She's the one who voiced the idea of divorce. She's the one who set us up with a lawyer and who moved out of the house, running back to New York City. I've never, and would never, cross those boundaries with her.

And even though tonight isn't a date, it still feels like the start of something. Maybe my new life. Maybe a step into my old life. I don't know but her place in it has changed. And I find myself hoping someone will soon be taking that spot.

So, I don't answer. Instead, I gently end the call and I go upstairs to get ready to spend a night out in my hometown. And for the first time in a long time, I feel excited.

Chapter Twelve
Grady

I get to the Spotlight Lounge and immediately make my way to the bar. I'm feeling nervous to the point that I'm nauseous, and I don't know why I showed up at all.

It probably had something to do with the way Lexi said, '*don't let* us *down.*'

I obviously know who she was talking about. And honestly, I don't want to let Vivi down.

But I also have a weird feeling that Lexi didn't let Vivi know about the invitation.

"Hey, what can I get you?" the young bartender asks, pulling me out of my head.

Looking over at the taps, I clear my throat. "Whatever IPA you have is fine," I tell her, knowing that I should probably stay away from hard liquor if I'll be seeing Genevieve tonight.

"You got it." She returns a few moments later with a glass, letting me know that it's from Clear Horizons, the woman-owned brewery next door. I give her my card to open a tab then take a seat at the end of the bar.

Waiting for Knox might be the best idea. I *know* that Vivi likes him. She'll be excited to see him even if she doesn't feel the same way about me.

It isn't Knox who finds me first, though.

It's Hudson.

He slips into the stool next to me and gestures to the bartender for another beer.

"Hey," he says in his low voice.

I give him a nod in acknowledgment, and we sit quietly while he waits for the bartender to bring his drink. She returns with something dark and creamy.

"For some reason, it doesn't surprise me that you're a stout guy."

Hudson gives me a sidelong look and glances down to my glass. "Yeah, well it doesn't surprise me that you drink beer that tastes like piss."

A surprised laugh falls out of me. He's one of the funniest and most sarcastic people you will ever meet when he opens up to you.

"I wouldn't expect to see you here," I admit to him.

He lets out a loud huff. "Lexi and Vivi threaten me every single time."

"Threaten you with what?" No one's ever had Hudson and Asher wrapped about their finger like Vivi, but she apparently told them once in high school that she was just training them for their future wives and children.

"To egg my house. Like fucking children." He pauses and looks at me. "You know she would do it, too. She loved doing that shit with Asher."

That makes me smile. It was quite the talk of the town when her tenth-grade biology teacher's house got TPed after she didn't place in the science fair. No one could prove it was her—Vivi's way too smart for that—but we all knew.

"Lexi practically threatened me into coming tonight as well. Is that what I should expect?"

He chuckles and shakes his head. "No… I'm sure whatever they would have planned for you would be way worse. Let's go, before you have to find out."

I don't consider what he means by that, but I follow him either way.

He falls into his seat at the table with his three siblings and Lexi. "Look who I found."

I sit in between Lexi and Calypso. "Hey," I say, giving Lexi an annoyed look when I notice the surprise on Vivi's face.

When I turn my head back to Vivi, sitting in between her two brothers, I'm relieved that there doesn't appear to be any anger or discomfort. Just shock.

Lexi nudges me with her elbow. "It's good to see you."

Vivi gives us a weird look I can't decipher. "Hi, Grady."

I clear my throat. "Knox and Lucas should be meeting us here as well."

"Oh, thank God you invited that poor man. He's been trying to be Vivi's friend for years now," Calypso teases.

"You guys aren't friends?" I ask.

"We are friends." Vivi rolls her eyes. "He's asked me over for dinner a couple times and I wasn't able to make it."

Lexi snorts, "Yeah, a few times."

"They invited me over for dinner sometime too," I say.

"Oh, I think I see them actually." Asher stands.

We all turn toward the entrance and find Knox walking toward us. He's holding the hand of a slightly taller, just as handsome man and pulling him forward. Lucas looks like what I could vaguely recall—short brown hair and clean-cut scruff over a sharp jaw.

Asher is already up and dragging another table and two more

chairs over to make room. I get up to help him as Knox and Lucas join us.

It isn't until we're all settled with a drink that Lucas, unknowingly, picks up exactly where our conversation left off.

"You know, it's really good to see you, Viv, but I'm a little hurt that it only took Grady one lunch to invite us out." Calypso snickers and Knox shushes his husband.

I look down to my left, having ended up next to her when we sat back down. She's putting on her best effort to be annoyed but she clearly isn't. Genevieve always wanted to be everyone's friend, so I'm confused why it seems like she isn't closer to Knox. I haven't heard a single negative thing about him.

"I'm sorry, okay? I don't like to impose on anyone." Lucas huffs out a breath and before Knox can comment, Vivi continues, "Either way, everyone at this table will tell you that Grady has always been the more gracious one between us."

She smirks up at me and I quirk an eyebrow in response. It almost feels playful. The thought alone makes my cock twitch.

"Hell, isn't that the truth?" Asher pipes in from across the table, causing Calypso to laugh out loud this time, followed by asking Lucas about their trip to Hawaii.

"It was amazing, and I hate to be so bougee, but we took the nanny, and I don't feel remotely bad about it," Knox confesses.

"We were out there for a week and let her have half the time off and bring her boyfriend for free. There's nothing to feel bad about," Lucas shrugs.

Lexi claps her hands together under her chin. "Please, adopt me. I promise I'll be a good girl."

"Please, shut the fuck up," Vivi attempts to say seriously, but can't hold a straight face for a second.

Lexi shrugs and leans back. "One day they'll finally take pity on me. I've always wanted two daddies."

"Please... Shut the *fuck* up," Calypso snaps but there is no bite in her tone.

Lucas just rolls his eyes and turns back to Calypso. "Have you ever been to Hawaii?"

"No, I haven't but Asher has." Calypso nods her head in Asher's direction.

"Surf competition a few years back," Asher confirms. "That was the only time, but it was amazing."

"Speaking of surfing," Lucas begins, "Matty loved being in the water so much that we already asked Vivi if she would take him kayaking but he has been asking about surfing non-stop, too. Do you think we could get him signed up for some classes?"

"Oh, swimming too," Knox follows up. "Grady mentioned that you're teaching his daughters." Vivi's head turns toward me, a questioning look in her eyes. I brought up the idea with Asher when we had dinner at my parents' house, but we hadn't finalized anything yet.

Smiling, Asher replies, "Sure. I'm teaching Daisy to surf myself—while Blake does the indoor swim lessons—but if it's possible to have you all meet at the same time, I think that would be great. Otherwise, I can get you hooked up with one of the instructors."

"Should be easy enough to work around practices, if you're okay with that, Grady."

"Yeah, sure. I think it would be good for Daisy to have a friend to learn with. She's already excited to surf but Stella isn't interested at all."

From there, the conversation flows freely, naturally moving between group conversations and breaking off into pairs.

It doesn't happen for a while but eventually, Vivi and I are left sitting together quietly, while everyone else is distracted by their own conversations.

After a minute or two, I clear my throat to get her attention. I'm looking down at my glass on the table, but I can feel her eyes on me.

"Lexi didn't tell you I was coming, did she?" I inquire, lowering my voice so only she can hear me over the music.

Her head snaps toward her best friend before turning back to me. She takes a drink of her margarita. It looks like a dark, almost crimson color, and I find myself wondering what all her favorite flavors are.

She peers at me like she's trying to see into my very soul. I make eye contact with her and let her read what's lying there... Hoping it's whatever she's looking for.

"No, she didn't," she admits. "I figured it was Asher. *Maybe* Hudson, but that seemed unlikely."

I couldn't fight the curiosity that takes over. Both of her brothers seemed happy enough to see me. "Why was that unlikely?"

"He doesn't even want to come here himself, and he isn't cruel enough to subject someone else to this torture."

We both laugh quietly, and I look at her, really look at her, for the first time tonight. I'm on my second beer by now and maybe that's why I let my eyes glide slowly down her body knowing she's watching.

Her lips are painted a crimson red and she's biting the lower one. She has thin but dramatic lines across her eyelids. Her cheeks have a pink blush to them that would look natural if I didn't know what her actual blush looks like. Her hair flows around her in soft waves, appearing like she left it to dry on its own accord.

I'm thankful for the dark room as soon as my eyes run down her chest and ribs, which are showing more than I had originally realized. She's perfectly filling out a black floral print dress that stops just above her ankles, from what I can see sitting down. The top, however, feels almost indecent in the best way.

I've never seen Genevieve's naked chest but lately I've found myself thinking a lot about her perfect breasts.

And there is no doubt in my mind that they are *perfect*.

Considering the times we've seen each other at work or at my parents' house, it makes sense that her tops have had higher necklines. But that's not the case tonight.

The front of her dress brings two triangles over her chest, coming to a bow in the middle. I don't know if it's sewn together but it looks like I could pull one side and get a perfect view. There's another triangle that's cut out across her sternum and lower ribs. Her soft freckled skin in plain sight and her waist highlighted beautifully.

When I look back at her face, it's faint but there's a real blush creeping up now.

I can't hide the satisfied grin that spreads across my face when I ask, "Does it bother you that I'm here?"

I can see her throat dip with a swallow. "No."

"Good."

"I really don't care," she retorts, grabbing her drink, taking a large gulp, and not looking back at me.

I lean closer to her ear. "Why are you blushing then?"

Her glare snaps to me. Her cheeks burn brighter.

"Maybe it just makes me uncomfortable when someone ogles me," she hisses and finishes off her drink.

I smirk down at her, calling her bluff. "Fine, I won't look anymore."

My head flicks back to the karaoke stage—some college kid is singing what I assume is the newest pop hit—but I can feel the frustration in her small body growing.

Genevieve doesn't like to be denied things, especially attention.

"I'm going to go get another drink. Would anyone like anything?" Vivi asks the table.

Everyone shakes their heads, Lexi looking between the two of us. Vivi heads to the bar, and everyone returns to their previous conversations.

I try not to watch her, but it feels impossible. Like I'm a moth and she's the bug-zapping lantern hanging out front. I can see everything going on around me, the signs to *stay away* but I can't stop myself from wanting to fly right toward her.

A man puts his hand on the small of her back and it immediately pulls me out of my wandering thoughts. My eyes are focused on that hand, gripping just a little bit tighter when she flinches away. As I pull my eyes up to his face, my blood boils.

I look around the table, but everyone seems preoccupied by their conversations. Too distracted to notice that Harper's slipped up to Vivi.

And while I'm *sure* that Genevieve is someone that can handle herself, Knox didn't give me the impression that Harper was the type of man to take *no* as a suitable answer.

I look back at the bar, debating if I should go over when I feel a light kick to my shin. Across from me, Lexi catches my gaze and tips her chin toward the bar, toward Vivi who's still trying to pull back from Harper.

Without giving it another thought, I stand up as casually as possible and walk toward the bar. I can't hear what he's saying but he leans toward her, one hand on the stool behind her keeping her trapped. The annoyance portrayed on her face quickly turns to anger.

If there's one thing that Vivi *loathes,* it's being backed into a corner—mentally, emotionally, or physically. It doesn't matter.

Once I reach the bar, I place my hand on the counter in between their bodies, my own turned toward her. "I changed my mind about wanting a drink."

I could have slipped my arm around her shoulder, but she isn't mine to claim.

Not yet, that pesky voice insists.

Vivi's head tilts back, making eye contact with me.

Harper's arm slips off the stool to avoid bumping into me. He clears his throat, breaking our connection.

"I was just offering to buy her a drink," he states in a matter-of-fact tone.

My eyes drop back down to Vivi and hers flash up to mine.

At this moment, it almost feels like no time has passed. I can read all the thoughts floating through her pretty little head.

We both hold neutral expressions, but I can see in her eyes that she's screaming, *I don't want* anything *from him.* I try to make her understand what I'm trying to say back, without moving my face a centimeter: *I'll handle this.*

When she looks around me to a very disgruntled Harper, I take that as her reading my mind.

This time, I place my hand on the counter behind Vivi. I make sure not to touch her, but the intent is there. "That was nice of you, but I'm here now." I pull out my wallet and flag the bartender over. "I'll take another IPA. And Genevieve?"

I look down at Vivi to finish her order. "A blood orange margarita on the rocks. Oh, with salt! Thanks." *That was the reddish color I couldn't place.* Turning to me, she says shyly, "Thanks for the drink."

I smile down at her and bring my arm a little closer in. Glancing over my shoulder, I nod at Harper. "I got you, man. What are you drinking?" It's a lazy move to turn the power scale back in my favor but it hits his ego all the same.

"Nah, I think I might head to Yellow Cab actually." That's the New York City themed bar around the block.

"Have a good night then." I step around Vivi, successfully blocking her off from Harper while we wait for our drinks.

Chapter Thirteen

Vivi

If Harper walks away, I don't notice. The entire world could be burning down, and I wouldn't notice anything except Grady's gaze searing me. I hate to admit how hot his little masculine display was but *holy fuck,* it was sexy. I've never been attracted to the possessive caveman thing until right now.

Anytime Brody tried it, it was grating. Not anything like *this.*

I can faintly hear someone talking behind me, but I don't process the *excuse me* until she's sliding onto the stool directly behind me. I tip forward into Grady, but he catches me with a light hand on my elbow.

"That was my first real conversation with him, and I think I hate him." Grady's confession surprises me, making me laugh in response.

"Yeah, he's the worst." I don't mention anything specific but I'm sure that Selena has filled him in on some of Harper's horrible traits.

"Does that happen often?" His voice is so low that I shouldn't be able to hear it over the music and conversations. Yet, I can hear him as clearly as if he were whispering in my ear.

"What?"

He wags his finger between me and the space next to us. "What just happened with Harper, Genevieve."

The use of my full name and his husky timber send a chill down my spine. I'd rather go on a date with Derek Harper than let Grady Miller know how much he affects me though.

I stand a little taller and lean an elbow on the bar. "He thinks he can bully me, and he can't."

"That's not what I asked."

I roll my eyes at him. "It happens pretty much anytime he can corner me alone. He doesn't take *no* for an answer. I'm not the only teacher he bothers—some of them are even married. Do you think Harper cares? Nope, it doesn't deter him for even a second."

"And from what I understand about Mrs. Gable..." Grady starts.

"She turns a blind eye in favor of the football department and her inappropriate crush on him," I frown, finishing his thought. "Thanks for stepping in. I can usually handle these situations," I quickly add, not wanting Grady to see any weakness in me, "but he can be pretty relentless. He doesn't respect women or our right to say *no.* Usually my brothers or Knox step in."

I peer around him, seeing everyone at the table deep in conversations. I don't believe for even a second that they're all ignorant of the fact that Grady and I are missing at the same time. I shake my head at the thought.

"I changed my mind about the drink." Grady shrugs and slips his hands in his pockets.

"Mm, okay." I play along. It isn't that I expected Grady to outright admit that he came over here on a proverbial white horse, but the deflection is disappointing anyway.

Don't be ridiculous and don't expect anything from him.

Grady

I slide into the stool next to her, and let my arm fall on the counter behind her.

"You don't have to act like this." She takes a small step back and waves her hand between us. "Least of all with me. There are plenty of girls here to flirt with. Maybe even one to take home."

I flinch back at her assumptions. I mean, sure, while single I've always been a naturally flirty person but by no means would I describe myself as a man who goes out prowling for women. Even the few one night stands I've had were random and coincidental, never a plan for the evening.

"Considering my two daughters are expecting me to pick them up bright and early, I'm not interested in that tonight." She opens her mouth to speak up, looking slightly guilty, but I cut her off. "And not that it's anyone's business but there hasn't been anyone since my ex-wife. There's been no time or privacy. Even if there was, I'm not looking to confuse my daughters by introducing them to someone that I have no intention of knowing a week from now."

A look of wary realization washes over her, and it isn't lost on me that I willingly introduced my daughters to her family. Yes, they stumbled into Vivi's classroom, but I was always planning on going to dinner at my parents' house knowing full well who all would be there. But my worries weren't that I wouldn't want them in Stella and Daisy's lives, but that Vivi and her siblings wouldn't want to be a part of the girls' lives.

"Thanks for the clarification," Vivi says before turning to flag down the bartender.

"Another shot?" I ask.

"No, just a margarita." She orders from the bartender, James, apparently. The way she's leaning forward on the bar pushes her backside out toward me. When she catches me staring, a scowl pulls across her face but is undermined by the tiny smirk she can't hide. "What do you want to drink?"

I lean around her and say to James, "Two waters, please."

"Water?" she asks in disgust. "It's your one night out in forever, or so it would seem."

"I drove. And even if they don't know the difference, I don't like to be drunk or hungover around the little ladies when I can avoid it."

"Ooh, so responsible." The admiration in her eyes is a contrast to her teasing tone.

As most single fathers would probably tell you, there's a majority of straight women that swoon at the sight of you with a child. I think even for the women who don't want children of their own, it shows a promise of maturity.

I typically wouldn't use my daughters to win me brownie points with a woman, for many of the reasons already stated tonight, but I know that Genevieve cares about them already. In this case, is it so bad if I use my parenting skills to sway her a bit? Maybe... but with this one woman, I don't really feel guilty about it.

"I don't think it surprises anyone what a great father you are." The comment and the sincerity catch me off guard. It's the first real compliment that Vivi's given me in years and it's the one that means the most to me.

"Thanks." I clear the gravel from my throat. "I don't know what I'd do without them. My entire being is pretty much wrapped up in them now." Throughout my marriage and since the divorce, I haven't wanted to be anyone, or anything else, besides their father. Before that, I thought I wanted to be a catcher for the San Diego Sharks. Tearing my ACL and accidentally getting Arielle pregnant ended up showing me how unhappy I would have been with my original plan. The problem was, I never had any ideas for who I wanted to be further down the line.

Until I moved back to Amada Beach. Now I want to be someone who matters, who is a part of the community and has roots keeping them here.

And truthfully, I don't know what I could give someone right now when I'm barely holding it all together for the three of us. The more I think about Lexi's request the more I want to listen to her. I want to *try* to be whatever Vivi needs. Even the simple idea of being her friend again sparks hope in my chest.

"I assume that's how it goes when you become a parent," she muses.

Growing up, Vivi always wanted kids. We spent many afternoons playing house in either one of our bedrooms. And if it wasn't that, then we were playing with her dolls. Regardless, it always ended with me as her husband and at least four children.

The bartender returns with Vivi's margarita, two glasses of water and two shots. James points to them and says, "Those are from Lexi." He walks away and Vivi grabs one of them, taking it back with a sharp exhale. She offers the other to me, but I shake my head. She sets it next to her but makes no move to drink it yet.

"Who is that for?" She points at the extra glass.

"You."

"I hydrate *before* I go out."

"That's the stupidest thing I've ever heard. It's important to hydrate during. You're going to have a hangover tomorrow."

She shrugs irreverently. "That's not your problem."

The truth of that statement grates at my nerves, but I make it mine anyway.

Slipping off the chair, I step into her space. I place my arms on either side of her, forcing her back into the counter. I don't touch a single inch of her, despite how desperately I want to, but she can't walk away either.

"What… what are you doing?" Her voice is breathy in a way I've never heard before. It belongs in a dark bedroom and that thought sends all my blood to my cock.

"You need water."

"And what? You're going to *make* me drink it?"

I grab the glass and hold it to her. "I can't make you do anything. I know better than that. *But* I'm not really in a rush to get back to the table."

"Why not?"

"The only company I came for is right here." My voice is pure gravel, my body only inches from hers.

"You could have stayed home to hang out with yourself," she retorts.

"You think you're so funny," I pinch her side.

She playfully nudges my hip. Instead of letting go, she pulls me closer by hooking her finger through my belt loop. We still don't touch but are less than an inch apart now. "I don't mind the company either."

Every nerve in my body is telling me to touch her but her fingers are still innocently fidgeting with my pants. Spooking her isn't worth the loss of contact. Plus, there is a more important matter at hand right now.

"Drink, Genevieve." I thrust the glass toward her again. She rolls her eyes with a cheeky smirk but gulps down half the glass anyway. Immediately after, she takes the other shot with a smile the entire time. I playfully roll my eyes, pushing the water closer to her.

We stay at the bar while she drains another glass and I help her finish the margarita. We don't make it back to the table until I accompany her to the restroom—where I wait outside.

    Nobody says anything about our absence, but I wouldn't care if they did.

Chapter Fourteen
Vivi

"Who was that girl you went home with on Friday?" Lyp asks Lexi as she scrolls through her phone.

This is a normal part of our routine. Every Sunday, the three of us come to Bella Donna's for brunch. Lexi tells us about her latest hook up—if any—Calypso swears to be the single wine aunt for the rest of her life, and I silently question which one is saner. My sister's plan definitely sounds easier, and I don't need a man to have kids. There are plenty of options nowadays. But even if Lexi swears she's only dating because she enjoys the noncommittal sex and fleeting connections, there's something brave about her willingly putting herself out there, time and time again.

The only thing that's not a part of our normal routine is the excited glint in Lexi's eye as she looks over my shoulder.

Calypso and I turn in the direction of the entrance at the same time Grady walks in with his daughters.

And the sight is devastatingly perfect. My eyes make their way from the top of his head down to his shoes. His hair looks bed ruffled and not in a styled sort of way. In the natural, *I-was-pulled-out-of-bed-by-a-five-year-old* way. He's wearing a gray short sleeved button up and a pair of those short chino shorts that show off his muscular thighs. And you can't ever forget the pair of Adidas.

I turn back toward the table and note more than a few women who are staring at him while he waits for the hostess. It doesn't take a rocket scientist to figure out that the sight of Daisy cuddling into his shoulder and his hand attached to Stella's head only adds to his overall panty dropping presence.

I sit up a little straighter, turning back to our table, as the feeling of bitter jealousy runs through my veins. I hate that all these women notice him. And I *hate* that it bothers me.

Suddenly, a small brunette pops up at my side.

"Hi!" Daisy waves and twirls next to our table.

"Hiii," the three of us singsong back.

She looks at us expectantly but doesn't say anything. She just smiles and waits.

"Did you guys get a table?" Lyp cautiously asks. Looking confused about what to do with a child.

"No, not yet."

"Do you want to sit with us?" Lexi asks. "If it's okay with *Daddy*, of course."

Calypso snorts into her coffee. "Jesus effing Christ."

Daisy beams at us before turning around. "Dad!" She waves them over. "They asked us to sit with them!" Turning back to us she adds, "I wasn't allowed to ask but you offered so…" She shrugs her shoulders.

Marcie, our favorite server, comes over and moves a small table over to ours as I shake my head at Lexi. But my usual annoyance is only half-hearted. From her satisfied smirk, she knows it too.

"Thanks for inviting us." Grady takes the seat next to me. "Daisy and Stella were excited when we saw you three."

Daisy bounces in her seat from excitement but Stella looks embarrassed at the mention of her name. I give her a small smile. "How have you been, Stella? How do you like your class?"

She nods like that's an answer. I don't push her to answer but Grady helps on her behalf.

"Stella's joining the spelling bee." His eyes move from me to Lexi before setting on Calypso with a smirk. She doesn't even try to hide her snicker.

Lexi and I make eye contact and I don't try to hide the smug grin on my face. Who cares if it's been twenty years? I won that shit fair and square.

"Don't even start," she points a finger at my face. "*Tropical* was a hard word for an eight-year-old."

"T-R-O-P-I-C-A-L," Stella chimes in at the same moment Marcie drops off two kids' menus and crayons. She picks one up and hands the other to Daisy without even looking in our direction.

After a moment of amused shock, Calypso and I tip our heads backwards in a fit of laughter. Grady simply rubs his daughter's hair, looking at her with pride.

Lexi rolls her eyes all in good fun and turns toward Stella, "You're gonna kill it if you can spell words like that already."

Stella preens in her chair but continues coloring with her sister.

Once we're sure that they're fully invested in the sheets, Calypso turns toward Lexi again, "As you were about to tell us, the girl from Friday?"

She's vaguer in her wording but Grady picks up on the topic at hand. "After I left?"

"Yuuup," I answer for her.

"A bee farmer, apparently," Calypso adds.

"You guys are so annoying," Lexi picks up her menu. "It was good. We had fun. But she lives in Georgia and is visiting her cousin who lives in La Jolla. We agreed to a one-night thing." Lexi shrugs. They aren't all failures, but they never lead to more than a couple weeks lately. "It was the guy last night you should really be asking about."

"Oh, good god. What was his name again?" Lyp leans forward.

"Adolf?" I contemplate. It was something that started with an A and was *horrible.*

"Like I would ever swipe right on a dude named Adolf, no matter how hot he was." Lexi cringes. "His name is Abaddon."

A laugh bursts out of Grady and he shakes his head at the absurdity. "That name alone probably caused him so much trauma."

"What the fuck is wrong with parents?" Calypso mutters.

"That's a dollar for the swear jar," Stella says.

Our three heads turn toward her, but Grady doesn't even look up from his menu.

"Children are *always* listening," is his only response.

"I don't have any singles," Calypso looks in her wallet and I'm honestly surprised she's playing into Stella's demand. "But give us until the end of the meal… I'm sure all three of us will owe you at least ten." She throws a wink at her. Stella blushes at the attention but giggles anyway.

"If it wasn't the name that scared you off, what was wrong with the man?" Grady asks Lexi.

The fact that he's genuinely invested in her story and a willing participant of this conversation does something funny to the pit of my stomach.

It feels like he could fit into this routine. Not every Sunday—I'll never be ready to give up all my alone time with Calypso and Lexi—but a normal part of my life regardless.

"Grady, do you prefer boneless or traditional wings?" Lexi asks him in a very serious tone.

Calypso and I know exactly where this is going. And so far, it has been one of her best theories into dating.

"Uhm… this feels like a trick question?" We each keep our faces blank, waiting for his answer. "But I like bone-in wings. Half habanero mango, half garlic parmesan if you want me to be specific."

Lexi nods her head in approval. "The flavor isn't important but maybe I should research that next," she muses.

"Did I pass?" Grady looks at each of us.

"Yes," I confirm.

He nods his head like he has any idea what's going on right now.

"There's something to be said about a person who's scared to get their hands dirty," Lexi wags her eyebrows.

"And if they just like boneless more?"

"Then next time we can save time and money and go to McDonald's for their chicken nuggies."

"I'm guessing your date did not order traditional wings?"

"No, Grady," she solemnly shakes her head. "He did not. And that was only the start."

This is the part of the meal I've been dreading the entire time—the end. Grady handed Marcie his card before she had the chance to put the split checks on the table, asking her to put it all on his card. I was the only one who argued but he shot down all my attempts. Lexi and Calypso simply shared an impressed look but kept their mouths shut.

"Well," he pats Daisy's head, who crawled into his lap a few minutes ago. "Thanks for letting us sit with you."

"Thanks for paying," I add with a begrudging smile.

We don't break eye contact for a few seconds, and I can't help but notice all the small changes from the years—the lines around his eyes and the sharp jawline and day-old scruff.

Suddenly I'm pulled back to my childhood when I could've happily stared at his perfect face forever.

"We should be getting to the store soon…" Calypso says, and I know she feels guilty to be ruining whatever moment she thinks we might have been having. But there wasn't a *moment.* And no reason for her to feel bad.

I nod and lean to grab my purse.

"Your bookstore?" Stella perks up.

"Yeah, we have to work," Lexi tells her with a fake sad face. Lyp and Lexi love being at Brighter Daze, it's never a chore for them.

Stella's eyes swing to her dad, and she gives him a perfectly practiced pout—one I'm more than familiar with. *The sad puppy face.* "Dad, can we please, please, *please* go with them?"

Daisy sits up, setting one hand on each of his shoulders. "With cherries on top!"

Grady chuckles and looks at his older daughter. "Did you finish the book already?" Stella nods. Grady looks at me and clarifies in a shy voice, "I introduced her to May-Bird and the Ever-After."

The shock is written across my face, I'm sure of it.

Not only was that my favorite book series when we were younger, but it's what we were reading the night I snuck into Grady's room and fell asleep next to him in fifth grade. We were in so much trouble when Selena found us the next morning, but it had been worth it.

The memories of young Grady reading to me under the blanket while I held the flashlight are some of my favorites to this day.

"I only have the first book. Do you think you have the second?"

Stella looks toward my sister and best friend.

"Yeah, we actually do. That was Vivi's favorite book growing up, so I make sure to keep it in stock," Calypso smiles at me.

"Let's go!" Daisy hops to the ground, and we obediently follow behind her.

As soon as Grady walks through the door, both of his girls run to the children section at the back of the store. It's one of the few areas Lexi and Lyp decided to put money into fully renovating. Not that they don't dream about updating the entire space but most of their money went into just buying the store and setting up the bakery. And while they are successful, it's nowhere near Asher and Hudson yet.

I'm equally proud of all four of them, and it isn't a competition. The store that Lexi and Lyp have created is amazing, but I know that they both wish they could afford to throw more money into Brighter Daze.

They've met with Stanley, the owner of the construction company and hardware store in Amada Beach, more than a few times. He keeps most of the plans for the building that he, Lexi and Lyp have designed together. No one except the three of them has seen the blueprints but I'm positive that they are *gorgeous* and modern and a perfect mix between the two of them. Calypso's feisty consistency and Lexi's lively mutability.

Daisy skips up to the counter and watches as Calypso sets up her materials. "What are you doing?"

"I'm going to frost this cake. Want to help?"

"Yes! Can Stella help too?"

"Of course, she can. The more the merrier."

It's interesting to see Calypso interact with children. She's never rude to them and has more respect for kids than some teachers. But I've never seen her willingly offer her time to a child either.

Once they're set up and busy at work, I wander toward the cash register. Lexi is talking to Gavin, my favorite of their employees, about the courses he's taking at UCAH.

"Sorry to interrupt but have you gotten anything new?"

Lexi nods toward the romance section. "There are some new romances highlighted on the table you might like. Also, a new fantasy author I think you should check out."

I'm about to thank her and turn away when Gavin leans forward. "But you won't be needing those novels pretty soon, huh?" He fails at subtlety when he tilts his head in Grady's direction.

Lexi playfully shoves him with her hip. "We can only hope."

"He's hot," Gavin whispers, clearly checking him out by the bakery counter.

I roll my eyes in fake exasperation and turn away from Tweedle Dee and Tweedle Dum behind the register counter. Over my shoulder I say, "Whatever she told you is a lie. You should know better by now, Gavin."

It takes no more than sixty seconds until Grady steps up next to me in front of the shelf I'm skimming. Internally, I smile *and* groan.

"It should surprise me that you're a romance reader, but it doesn't."

Oh, Grady, if you only knew what I read.

"There is nothing wrong with enjoying love stories," I retort.

He turns his head toward me, assessing me. "Never said there was but you seem to have sworn off love in any form."

His observation makes the hair on the back of my neck stand up. It's the truth but I hate the call out all the same.

"A person can believe in love and not be sure if they want it for themselves." And that's also the truth. I can acknowledge that romantic and platonic love stomped on my heart, leaving it bleeding in my chest but there are good people and couples with happy endings. Grady's parents are a perfect example.

"I guess so," he turns his whole body toward me now. It reminds me of when he surrounded me at the bar, forcing me to drink water by flirting with me. "It's disappointing when I've *never* met a person more deserving of being loved though. Or a little girl who wanted it as badly as you had."

My mouth forms a small O at his sober confession. It was easy to blame Friday night on the alcohol, even if he had only a couple drinks. But in the light of day, after sharing a meal together, I can't deny the way my body heats up in response. I so badly want to believe that Grady has *ever* felt that way about me, but it goes against a lot of what I know about our history.

Before I can think better of it, a disbelieving laugh bubbles out of me.

Grady's brows scrunch at my response. I quickly shut my mouth, but I don't look away.

He doesn't look angry. Just confused.

"You can believe whatever you want. For now."

Now I'm the one left confused. I don't do anything while I watch him walk back toward the bakery counter. He stays over there until the cake is finished and gives us a simple goodbye before whisking off with his daughters.

Chapter Fifteen

Vivi

The email from Harper is open on my computer screen while I wait for Grady to meet me. It's been ten days since we went to Spotlight and eight days since we ran into each other at Bella Donna's. During that time, we've barely talked—excluding the few lunches we awkwardly got roped into with Selena—so I have yet to find any clarity into whatever the fuck is going on with Grady and me.

Thankfully, I don't think she has any ideas about what's going on—because I'm still telling myself it's nothing—she's just a hopeful mother and doesn't change her mind often.

That week and a half clearly didn't give Harper time to cool off after what happened at the bar. I'm not scared of Harper, and I don't need anyone to defend me, but I really don't know what to do about Harper's threat. Especially when it involves the other coaches.

So as much as I hate it, I have no other options than to ask for help.

The longer Grady takes to arrive, the more anxious I get. It's the largest project I've overseen, and four months really is not a long time to put something of this magnitude together. With Harper's backlash, it's only going to make things more difficult. It doesn't matter if the board says they *must* participate. They can drag their feet the entire time and make it impossible to reach our goal.

I'm about to start tearing apart my craft closet to find a brown bag to breathe into at the same moment that Grady walks through the door.

He senses my panic and pulls a chair to my desk. His hand goes to the back of my chair and even though I can't feel it, the gesture helps relax my chest a little.

"What's wrong?" He scans my entire body as if he's expecting to find blood oozing onto the floor.

"I…" Not able to put together a sentence, I shake my head and point to the computer screen.

Grady slides his chair close enough that I can feel his warmth and smell his earthy amber cologne. He leans toward the screen and reads the email from Harper out loud, "*Genevieve,*" he says in a disgruntled voice, and it almost makes me smile despite my anxiety. He turns toward me. "Has he ever called you that?" I shake my head. Grady officially owns all my names in some way, and he knows it. "Yeah, I didn't think so." He turns back to the computer and continues, "*I've talked to the other coaches on your behalf*—what a butthead," he says it with the straightest face, and I can't help but laugh. He graces me with a small smile. "*And we have decided that the athletic seasons are our top priority. We won't risk potential losses by forcing our athletes to split their focus when a majority of their time is already focused on their education.* He says that like we don't work at a school, but okay. *I'm sure you can understand our need to be excluded from this little gathering. We can reconvene after you talk to the committee members. Thanks in advance.*"

Grady stares at the screen for at least ten seconds before he turns toward me. He stares for another five seconds.

"What a fucking asshole. I hate that douchebag."

His outburst takes me a moment to fully comprehend but once my brain catches up, I almost tip out of my chair in laughter. Grady *rarely* curses. I don't know why but he never has. It has always made me giddy when that proper exterior cracks for a second.

At the same second my outburst happens, a shocked little gasp comes from the door. Grady whips around to find his daughters standing just inside my classroom. Daisy has her hand over her mouth and wide eyes from shock. Stella's mouth and brows are set in hard lines.

"Dad," she says in a very stern voice, making me want to lose it all over. "*That's* a bad word." She holds up two fingers. "Two bad words actually!"

Grady looks at me over his shoulder with an expression that says, *do* not *correct that statement.*

I bite down on my lips, but a few snorts sneak out. Grady's doing a much better job at keeping a straight face even if his shoulders are shaking.

"You owe the swear jar money now."

Grady nods his head in defeat and amusement.

Her eyes and accusing finger swing in my direction. She has Selena's disapproving glare which is a little scary but mostly funny on such a small human. "Are you going to be a bad influence on my dad?"

I look at Grady and back at Stella, shaking my head.

We were always bad influences on each other. It was mutual.

"Stella," Grady says in a reprimanding fatherly tone I've never heard before. "Be nice."

Stella rolls her eyes and I suddenly realize that there's something going on here. It's not my place to ask… and if I'm in any way at the heart of it, I don't think I want to know.

"Can we go home?" Stella asks. Daisy looks between them with a pout.

"I'm not done with my meeting. You can sit down if you don't want to go to the playground."

I stand up and go to the cabinet where I leave coloring supplies. Some of the kids from past years come to visit occasionally so I make sure to always have paper activities that are age appropriate. I place the stack on the table in front of the girls and give them a small smile.

"It's good to see you both," I say quietly.

Daisy gives me her signature smile and Stella just flips through the sheets.

When I take my seat next to Grady again, he nudges my leg to grab my attention. He gives me a look that says *I'm sorry about that.*

I shake my head and give him a sympathetic smile.

Shaking it off, Grady surprises me with his next statement. "I have an idea about how to handle the coaches." I lift my eyes in question. I'll graciously take help this time. "The board made the right decision, and we know that. If they aren't going to choose how they'll participate then we'll make the decisions for them. The final list is due next week." He shrugs in a humble way.

Nodding, I tell him, "I like that idea."

"And I think that the football team should host the dunk tank. And isn't it so nice that Harper volunteered the three football coaches?"

I gasp in delight. "I *love* that idea, Grady."

"As the notorious vandal around here, I thought you might," he remarks with the sexiest, most evil smirk I've ever seen on him.

Rolling my eyes, I scoff, "First of all, eggs and toilet paper hardly count as vandalizing."

"The judge would probably disagree with you. And now I'm questioning if we should trust you with America's future."

I point a finger at him. "I teach outstanding little citizens, okay? And second, everyone knows Asher went with me. Why doesn't he get any of the blame here?"

"Sure, he went with you but it's funny how it was never any of his teachers."

Giving him a quick shrug, I simply retort, "It would have been a full-time job if we egged a house every time he failed a test. Plus, most of my teachers had failed him at some point." I chuckle.

He shakes his head at me with an amused grin. "Let me see the list of the other clubs, you little troll."

Grady and I spend the next hour going over the details of the booths and planning when we can take a trip to city hall for the permit. I don't know when we decided that we'd be doing that together, but it was a silent agreement that we would.

I guess we're taking a field trip next week.

As he's about to stand, he stops and turns toward me again. "How did that meeting with the advisor go? I'm sorry, I should've asked."

I'm slightly taken back that he remembers but to be fair, Grady's always given me his full attention when we talk. It doesn't matter if we were whispering secrets or throwing barbs back and forth. He always made sure to hear each word.

"It went really well," I smile. "I'm working on my essay and getting some letters of recommendation together now. I have a few months, so if I plan it right, there shouldn't be any problems." I nod, more to calm my own nerves.

"I'm sure you already have the next three months' worth of

work perfectly planned out in your cute little planner. You don't have anything to worry about, Viv." Grady's knee knocks into mine before standing and my entire body bursts into flames. At least it feels like it.

Am I really that desperate for touch? I mean, it's been a while since I've been with anyone. More than a year for sure. But a *knee*? A fucking knee? That makes me think it has a lot more to do with the man who that joint is attached to. And that's so much worse than being horny.

Chapter Sixteen
Grady

Daisy's squeal from inside pulls me away from my dad and the grill—no complaints on that one. I walk inside to find Vivi, Lexi and Calypso walking into my parents' house. Lexi walks in first without a care in the world. Certainly not one for the giant boxes the other two are cradling between them.

"Alexandra!" Calypso scolds in that tone that takes me back to all the times she babysat us growing up. "I told you to hold the door, not slam it open so it ricochets back!"

Lexi waves her hand over her shoulder at them but gives me a sweet smile. "Haaappy birthdaaay."

"Don't look at me like that," I tell her. "It's scary. And it's not even my birthday yet." That's tomorrow. I take a step toward Calypso and Vivi. "Do you need help?"

"I should say no, considering it's *your* birthday cakes in here but that would be great," Calypso huffs.

I grab the boxes—a smaller one taped onto a larger one making it easier to carry—and walk toward the kitchen island. "Did you say cakes? As in plural?"

"Your mom asked me to bake two for you." She leans against the counter and tilts her head.

"Why? How many people are coming tonight?" She hadn't mentioned if she invited anyone besides my sister and the usual group. The only group that we have ever had, plus Lexi. I wouldn't be upset if it was Knox and his family, but I think he would've said something to me.

I selfishly don't want anyone else here. I've missed out on years with these people. Yes, Vivi, *of course.* But not only her. My family. Her family. My people.

"Just us, I'm guessing. She only invites guests over for the bigger parties. Not family time." My chest tightens at the phrase.

"The second cake is probably to take to the school tomorrow," Vivi says from the other side of the island. My birthday falls on the day after Labor Day this year so we're celebrating on the holiday instead. "The school year typically ends before my birthday, so she brings a strawberry cake on the last day to celebrate." She rolls her eyes but it's full of affection.

"That makes sense," Calypso says more to herself. "The second cake is a plain chocolate cake." German chocolate is my favorite, but the school has a safety policy against tree nuts and peanuts.

"Is it mean that I'm kind of embarrassed?"

"*Si, tonto.*" My mom slaps the dish towel against the back of my head. "I might just share it with the entire staff, while you don't get any."

Before I can apologize Lexi pipes in from her spot on the counter. "You should give *two* pieces to Harper, Selena."

That evil instigator.

Vivi grimaces at her friend. "Grady could commit murder and Harper still wouldn't deserve a piece of birthday cake in comparison."

My mom points to Calypso and Lexi. "Will you girls come help outside?"

Vivi takes a step toward the back patio, but my mom stops her. "Oh no, can you get the fruit from the fridge and start cutting it?"

Vivi gives her a skeptical look but nods anyway.

As she's grabbing everything with her back turned to us, my mom comes to give me a small kiss on the cheek. "*Feliz cumpleaños, mijo.*" Her eyes shift toward Vivi before she walks out. Over her shoulder she says, "Just relax in here while we get everything ready for you. The girls are helping Bonnie set the table out back. Don't worry."

Right as the door closes Vivi turns back toward me and rolls her eyes with a small smirk. "She couldn't be more obvious if she tried."

"Is it so bad being stuck in here with me?" I place my hands on the island and lean toward her.

She tilts her head and scrunches her nose. "I guess there could be worse."

"That's not what you said a few weekends ago," I tease without missing a beat.

"I was drunk. You can't use that against me." Her head is down, keeping her focus on the task at hand, but it doesn't hide her cheeky grin. I bet if she looked up, her eyes would be sparkling in that familiar glint she always had when she teased me.

"I remember you saying at least three times that you were, and I quote, '*a little buzzed but otherwise completely sober.*'" Her chest shakes so hard with silent laughter that she has to put the knife down. The more she tries to hide it, the more I start to laugh. "What does that even mean?"

"I have no idea." She *finally* leans forward on the island and laughs out loud. It isn't quite her all-consuming belly laugh but more of a giggle. It's really freaking adorable. "That should have been your first and only sign that I was in fact drunk. So, you can't use anything I said that night against me."

I press my forearms down on the counter and lean a little closer but we're still on opposite ends of the long island. "What about when you came twirling out of the bathroom, pulled me in by my belt loops and told me how happy you were that I was there?" I smirk at the flush quickly creeping up her face.

"That didn't happen," she says with so much conviction I almost believe her.

"It did." The memory of her drunk and happy that night has lived in my head rent-free over the last couple of weeks. She really did twirl down the hallway, smiling more freely than I've seen in a long time. Smiling to herself, *for* herself. It was a beautiful sight. She looped her fingers through my pants, pulling me close enough to be overwhelmed by her berry vanilla scent. It was sweet and fruity and so goddamn intoxicating. From the way she was looking at me, I knew she wanted to kiss me. I wanted to kiss her. Not like our first and only kiss. Not in a way that would have been appropriate at a bar with her siblings down the hall. And not at all when she was drunk. So, I took a step back.

"You wish," she says in a sigh, attempting to seem bored.

"I don't have to wish, because it happened."

"You're annoying," she mutters, but I see her small smile as she goes back to cutting the watermelon. Eyeing me for a long moment, she changes the subject to a safer topic—work.

Not long after Vivi and I were left alone in the kitchen, Blake and her family showed up. I don't know how long it's been since she spent time with the Davies family, though I'm sure it has been more recently than me.

She and Vivi were polite enough when they saw each other but it was Adrian who introduced their kids to Vivi and her siblings. I guess Blake had done a good job at keeping her life completely separate. Except from Bonnie, if the hug they shared and the excitement her kids expressed when they saw her, are any indication.

Adrian doesn't appear to have any ill feelings toward Vivi or her siblings. He gave each of them a hug and has been catching up with Asher and Hudson since they arrived.

Now as we all sit around the table, Millie's placed herself beside Stella who's next to Vivi, with Daisy on her other side. Despite the fact that she's sitting right across from me, she has barely talked to me since she walked out of the kitchen with the bowl of fruit. She's given both of my daughters and my niece all her attention since then.

Stella is different with Vivi when she thinks people aren't paying attention. There's none of her snark from earlier in the week. She doesn't roll her eyes or cross her arms.

She doesn't smile as freely as Daisy or ask as many questions as Millie, but she pays attention to Vivi like she's the most important person at this table. Stella hangs onto every word and offers small smiles instead of giggles. I try not to stare. Stella caught me once and immediately crossed her arms and turned away for a few minutes.

The endearing and affectionate feelings only fight off the irrational jealousy so much.

Am I seriously jealous of my daughters right now? Unfortunately,

I think I am. I'm also annoyed with my sister for her horrible timing. Usually, I'm happy to see her. But not tonight. And not with the questioning look she immediately gave me when she took in the scene.

"When are you starting tryouts?" Hudson asks from the other side of Daisy.

"This week. For three days starting on Tuesday." Vivi and I are going to talk to someone about the permit for the pier on Monday. I don't mention that, but I don't miss the side-eye she gives me.

I know her well enough to know that she wouldn't want our parents and family to ask questions. It'll spook her. Maybe enough to ruin the potential of even a friendship. And I agree, if only for my daughters' sake. I really couldn't care what anyone else has to say about it. I'm quickly realizing that even if I don't know what I can balance as a single father, but I know that I don't want to let this chance slip with Vivi. I can make excuses for the teenage boy who hurt his best friend but that's no longer the case. I'm old enough to acknowledge a good thing when it's in front of me. And whatever is happening with her is life changing, I can feel it in my bones. Whether it's for better or for worse will be entirely up to me and my actions.

"What positions did Knox play?"

I have a feeling I know where this is going. I was going to ask him anyway, but I wasn't sure if he still enjoyed baseball enough to want to be a part of it.

"Outfield mostly," I say easily. Hudson played shortstop.

"I don't know if it's allowed at the school, but the store doesn't need much from us anymore." He tips his chin toward his brother. "So, if you want an infield coach, I can help out."

"I looked into that already and there are no rules against it for assistant coaches. You'll just need to get a background check and fingerprint card before you can start."

Hudson nods as I text Knox with the news. I assume that it would be okay, but I know that I should check with him anyway. Discreetly, I pull out my phone and send a quick text.

Mon, Sept 5 at 7:26 PM

> Hudson offered to coach the infield. He played shortstop when we were kids until we graduated.

Knox

> Please tell me you told him yes.

> I did. I just wanted to make sure it was cool with you first.

> That's why you're going to make a better head coach than me.

> Seriously, I trust your calls going forward but I appreciate the consideration.

After the meal, we're all sitting around the table while Calypso brings out the cake.

Everyone takes their seat at the table again, and the beginning of the universal birthday song starts in a melody of off-key voices—before Stella insists that everyone who can, sing the Spanish version too—but it's one of the best sounds I've ever heard. Maybe even *the* best sound with the sweet voices from my daughters mixed in.

When the song ends, I glance around the table and shamelessly let my gaze fall on Vivi for a few too short seconds before I take a deep breath and blow out the two candles that spell out 2-9.

For the rest of the night my wish plays through my head on repeat.

For my best friend back—for her to take a chance on me again.

Tue, Sept 6 at 5:02 AM

Arielle

Happy birthday, Grady! I hope you have a great day.

Thanks, Arielle.

What are your plans for today?

Just having dinner with the girls. I was with the family last night.

They're probably so happy you're home.

Wish I was celebrating another year with you.

Chapter Seventeen
Vivi

I'm currently huddled between Asher and Lexi while we watch the Seals play against one of the other charter schools in the San Diego area. High Tides plays some of the smaller public schools in the area throughout the sport seasons, but they try to partner with as many of the alternative schools as possible.

It's colder than usual for late September and to say that none of us came prepared is an understatement.

"Look who I found," Calypso's voice rings out over the cheering crowd, carrying another round of apple ciders. "They had the same idea as us, only smarter."

"No surprise there," Asher jokes.

Knox throws a blanket toward Lexi at the same moment Calypso hands me my drink.

"You, my dear, are an angel. Have I told you that before?" Lexi wraps herself so tightly that there isn't room for anyone else. I scoot down and snuggle between Knox and Lucas, who places another blanket around my shoulders.

"Yes, yes. You want two daddies to tuck you in at night," Knox waves a hand in her general direction but wraps an arm around me. I stick my tongue out at her, like a child. As much as we love each other, competing and pestering is seared into our DNA by this point.

I've been making a conscious effort to spend more time with Knox and Lucas. I even went to dinner at their house this past week and scolded myself the entire time for not going sooner.

I could see the questions swimming in Knox's eyes all throughout dinner, but he took pity on me and didn't mention Grady once, except to tell me about how the first week of practice went.

'Oh, good enough,' Knox had said, *'but it's going to take a while to get their little pecking order in line. Grady and I are leaning toward Jeremy for team captain.'*

I thought it was a great idea. Jeremy's been working at Brighter Daze for almost two years now, and he's best friends with Lexi's little brother Johnny. When I told them, Calypso and Lexi couldn't agree more that he was the right choice.

The only downside of the night was when Lucas asked me about Brody.

I know Lucas grew up here, but I didn't think they knew each other. Lucas was a football player and in Calypso's grade. But I forgot that Brody's dad worked for Maddon Construction for over fifteen years.

I do my best to avoid seeing or hearing about my ex-fiancé at all costs, but I was thankful that they let me know they had seen him in town recently, hopefully just visiting his parents. After we graduated from UCLA, I have successfully avoided him and Molly, despite the fact their families still live here.

I didn't ask how or what they knew about Brody and me, but between the sympathetic looks Knox couldn't hide and the flames burning in Lucas's eyes, they knew *enough*.

Just like the rest of this town.

"Where's Grady?" Knox's asks his husband.

I'm not *avoiding* Grady per se, not again. We saw each other a few times at lunch, with Selena, in the break room and we had gone to city hall to get a permit for the pier together earlier in the week, but there's something different between us.

There's always been a sort of taut pull toward Grady, a tug that I've never been able to ignore, but now it feels like that string between us is on fire. And we could either succumb to whatever it is or let it burn right through that invisible thread holding us together.

I don't know what to do with that. Not after his birthday a few weeks ago.

"I haven't seen him since yesterday. I didn't realize you were coming to the game together." I try to sound indifferent, but I know from the way Knox's arm momentarily tightens around me that he knows I'm anything but.

"We can go sit somewhere else… if you want."

"Don't be silly." I wave his suggestion away. "I see him walking up now."

I watch Grady make his way up the bleachers toward us. Toward me, if the way he won't look anywhere else is any indication.

He looks warm in his perfectly fitted jeans and High Tides hoodie with a light parka over it. And of course, his Adidas with the green stripes down the side. It still makes me smile to think he hasn't grown out of his favorite shoes.

He doesn't only look warm though.

No, Grady looks handsome with his boyish charm most days but when he lets his eyes sweep across my body like a lover's caress and bites his bottom lip to hide his growing smirk, Grady looks fucking *delicious*.

I want to run my tongue across those smug ass lips until his face is heated in the way only I have ever accomplished, and his hair ruffled from my hands rather than the wind.

From the way his eyes darken as he gets closer, I'm sure he can read every filthy thought running through my mind.

I don't get up when he joins us, mostly for the fact that it's cold, but also a little bit because I'm too busy clenching my thighs together in hopes that my pulsing center will calm down.

None of my siblings or Lexi get up either, probably not wanting to get booted from the large blanket they're currently having a silent war over.

Lucas quickly gives a haphazard reason to go sit beside his husband, leaving the seat directly next to me empty. Skeptically, I shoot him and Knox a look, but they pretend to be interested in the game.

Grady sits, and I silently unwrap the blanket from my shoulders and lay it across my lap, offering him half.

"Thanks," he mumbles. He takes the corner I offer and slides a few inches closer to me. "I forgot that it actually gets kind of cold here."

That makes me chuckle for some reason. "Yeah, I've never been to Phoenix, but I can imagine it's a shock to your system some days."

"It is. But it's nice, too. The only thing Arielle," he starts as he shoots me a questioning look, unsure if this is an okay topic to breach, "and I agreed on toward the end of our marriage was that the dry heat was far worse than the humidity we were both accustomed to."

I've never allowed myself to ask questions about Grady's ex-wife after that first dinner at his parents' house. The mere thought of her has always been a bucket of ice water to my nervous system. Even hearing her name roll off his lips so naturally is grating my nerves, but I can't fight the curiosity any longer.

Plus, *he* brought it up first.

"Last time, you said she's not from here?"

"No," he shakes his head. He doesn't look sad necessarily but maybe… guilty? Discouraged? "She's from Manhattan. That's where she moved back to."

"Why?" The question flies out of me before I can tamper down the anger I hear in my voice.

Grady's small smile tells me that he understands what I'm asking. "She was studying theater and English when we first met, and she was able to still graduate on time after finding out that she was pregnant with Stella, but she was never able to use those skills. To chase *that* dream."

'… *but she was just a little girl with a big dream.*'

Grady's words from that dinner ring through my mind.

"And you're okay with that?" I can't hide the disbelief dripping from my tone.

"I'm not *okay* with the fact my daughters are growing up thousands of miles away from their mom. But I'm more open to the idea of my daughters seeing their parents happy as two separate people than unhappy in a marriage." He pauses, seeming to think his next words over. "I would rather my daughters know what it's like to have a mother who's proud of herself and who chased her dreams rather than resentment grow between all four of us for choices we made and those that were made for us."

All I can do is nod. It does make sense. I don't know Arielle and I've never asked about her, but I know that if there was anything so horrible about her, I would've heard.

And maybe this is my first step to trusting Grady again, because I do trust that he'd never make a decision that would harm those little girls, even if he had to rip his own heart out.

"It just didn't work out, Viv. I've spent enough time being angry at her, and myself, that I don't want you wasting a minute of your energy on that." Under the blanket, he gives my leg a little squeeze.

I scoot a few inches closer toward him and catch his hand between my thighs, rendering it motionless.

I hear the almost inaudible sigh he lets out right before his hand spreads to its full width and his grip tightens. Not hard enough to hurt but hard enough that I can't fight the images of what his hands would feel like on other parts of my body.

Neither one of us talked much throughout the first half of the game but we sat there in a comfortable silence while my siblings, and our friends, conversed around us and the crowd continued to cheer. His hand stayed on my thigh the entire time and at some point, I let my pinky wrap around his.

Just like we used to when we were hiding under covers during movie nights.

"Jeremy looks so handsome!" Calypso declares before we all jump out of seats to cheer for this year's homecoming king.

"I can't wait to embarrass the shit out of him with this for the rest of his life," Lexi teases but I know she's happy for him—especially as a former homecoming queen herself. I, on the other hand, won prom queen our senior year.

Knox offers me some skittles and asks, "Are you chaperoning the dance tomorrow? I thought I saw your name in the email that was sent out."

I nod while watching the homecoming court walk across the field in their crowns and sashes. It's only a requirement for teachers to volunteer for school events if it involves their grade levels, but sometimes the teachers will trade chaperone duties for other things. "Mr. Sparks offered to cover my bus duty for a month if I chaperoned the homecoming dance for him."

It was an easy decision.

"That man really has the worst social anxiety. Nothing is worse than afterschool bus duty," Knox laughs.

I chuckle thinking about Mr. Sparks handing out paper cups of punch and making small talk with the other teachers for an entire night. He's a sweet man. Short, slightly heavy-set, and unfortunately resembles a toad. We tried for a few years to convince him to play Santa for the elementary students, but he declined every time. Now Pete, the owner of the tourist shop, Just Visiting, comes to the school every year in a red suit and beard. He doesn't quite have the right build for it, but we make it work.

"Are you chaperoning?"

"Yup," Knox replies with a sly smirk, popping the *P* for emphasis. "We both are." He waves his hand toward Grady.

"I didn't know that," I say, as my head turns back toward Grady.

His cheeks are pink, probably not noticeable to anyone except me. "Yeah, I'll be there." Knox turns back to his husband and Lexi, knowing his instigating work is done for the night. Grady clears his throat and quietly asks, "Can I give you a ride tomorrow?"

Chapter Eighteen
Vivi

family meeting
Sat, Sept 24 at 5:23 PM

Asher
> Vivi and Grady sitting in a tree…

Lexi
> 1st comes love, 2nd comes marriage <3

Calypso
> Next comes a baby in a baby carriage! (ew)

Hudson
> You forgot the part about kissing.

Lexi
> Who cares about kissing when there's fucking?

> You're worse than my 7 y.o. students

Calypso

> What are you wearing tonight?

Asher

> You can't ignore us I'll drive to your house with a camera

Lexi

> Omg the homecoming photos they never got to take!!

If you show up to my house, I will take eggs to each of your cars. Don't tempt me.

Hudson

> Leave her alone. Viv, have fun and try not to eat the poor man's heart out.

Asher

> Yeah be nice to the guy

I think he's excited about getting to "take" you to homecoming

Lexi

> The little green dress you bought makes your boobs look *chefs kiss*

Like two fluffy clouds I wouldn't mind getting lost in

Calypso

> Wear protection.

I've been staring at myself in the mirror for fifteen minutes now, but I can't look away.

I love this dress, but I picked it out before I knew Grady was also chaperoning the homecoming dance. And before he asked if he could give me a ride tonight.

I said yes, even though my mind instantly had gone to a different type of *ride*.

But now, I'm standing in this green floral dress, feeling both beautiful and nostalgic. I doubt that Grady will remember the color dress I wore to my junior—his senior—prom but I do.

This dress is shorter, with a small slit up the thigh and bunches around my breasts before coming together in dainty bows on my shoulder. It's a lighter shade of green than the emerald gown I wore to prom but the dark leaves in the pattern feel like they are mocking me and my memories.

The sound of the doorbell pulls me from my anxious thoughts but does nothing for my nervous system.

I make my way down the hall while putting my earrings in, opening the door without really looking and leaving it for him to follow me inside. "Let me just put my shoes on and we should be good to go."

I don't realize that he stopped just a few feet inside until I turn back toward the door. "Is… is everything okay?" I look down at my dress and gently pat my hair. Everything seems like it's in place, but Grady's still looking at me.

"Yes, everything is fine." His voice is gravelly, and he tries to clear it. Twice. "You look beautiful in green. You always have."

That comment sends a mix of emotions through me. Satisfaction, confusion, lust.

And it's at that moment that I realize that Grady isn't looking at me like something's wrong.

He's looking at me like I'm the most beautiful woman in his world.

"Thank you, you look very handsome yourself," I say shyly. He looks more than handsome. He's striking. In his all-black outfit consisting of a form fitting button up shirt, suit pants, a belt and dress shoes. It's simple but let me tell you, it's *working*.

"Thanks," his voice is still incredibly low. "I wasn't sure what color you were wearing, and I didn't want to clash." One side of his lips tip up and his eyes snag on my neckline. The dress is slightly less demure than what I would wear on a school day, but it isn't immodest by any means either.

Yet somehow, when Grady looks at me with his bedroom eyes, so clearly full of desire, I feel like I might as well be laid out bare for him.

And there is no possible way to deny that this is more than a simple carpool any longer.

I bubbly laugh spills out of me as we walk into the gymnasium. Prom is held at the local theater every year, but homecoming doesn't have as high of a budget. And only about two weeks to prepare compared to the month allotted for prom.

But this year? The dance committee did amazing.

The theme is *Enchanted Forest*. There are papier-mâché trees with lights wrapped around them, a full moon backdrop for photos, moss and butterfly jar centerpieces, a flower arch near the entrance and seating areas made out of logs.

"This is incredible," I breathe.

"It really is. I knew that a lot of the clubs came together for the dance, and some of the businesses even donated decorations and food, but I never would've imagined this."

I'm beaming up at him as we walk further into the dance. "Isn't this the best school you have ever worked at?"

It's only the second school I've ever worked at but there isn't a single ounce of me that would consider looking somewhere else.

"Yeah," he gives me a soft smile in return. "Let's see where they need us."

Two hours later, I wish that Grady and I hadn't asked about our stations. I'm helping the art teacher, Kara Lee, and the other eleventh grade history teacher, Lily Dawson, at the photo station. As distracted as I've been, it hasn't been a bad night. Both of them are the supervisors of their own organizations, art club and book club, respectively. I've been so busy recently there hasn't been much time to talk to any of the teachers about the fair coming up, and the complaints are always so much louder than the praises. So, it's been encouraging to hear their positive thoughts, and that the students are just as excited to raise money for new computers.

Grady was assigned to the beverage station with Knox. I've snuck glances at him throughout the night and every single time, he's staring back at me. The last time I caught him, I was looking over my shoulder toward him, but his eyes were glued to my ass. It took him a solid five seconds to notice my attention was on him, but for once Grady didn't blush. He gave me a sultry smirk and a quick wink before responding to whatever Knox was telling him.

I should be ashamed of the wetness between my thighs, even

after fifteen minutes, just from a look. Granted, a look I almost swear I felt coasting along my curves and wrapping around my neck.

Instead, I promised myself that I would *not* look in his direction again and I'd focus on helping the students fix their hair or ties and taking photos. Nothing else.

Until I feel a looming heat crawl up my back and a familiar presence crowd me from behind.

I let out a shuddering breath before Grady even has a chance to speak.

"Will you dance with me?"

I only turn my head toward him, but it's enough to get a whiff of his musky amber scent that's so intoxicating I might as well have downed two shots.

"I'm helping with photos," I say quietly.

From the tightness that creeps into his shoulders and the way his lips thin, I know he wants to argue with me but before he gets the chance, Lily encourages me to go.

"Don't worry. It's slowing down enough that Kara and I can handle it until clean-up," she says with a sly smile.

"Are you sure?" I ask uselessly. Lily's already pulling the camera from my hands while Kara nods in a dismissive way.

I turn fully and look up at Grady. His eyes are the color of my morning coffee, and his short curls are starting to fall on his forehead.

"Dance with me, Genevieve."

Damn him for using my full name in that low voice that instantly makes me think about him between twisted bedsheets.

I don't trust myself to talk right now so I nod and offer him my hand.

He wraps my small, soft hand in his large, rough one. I follow him toward the dancefloor and count my blessings it's a slow song; something modern that I recognize from the radio though couldn't tell you who the artist is.

And none of that matters anyway.

Because, fifteen years later, I'm dancing with Grady at a homecoming dance. And it's everything I had imagined it would've been.

We talk quietly about mundane topics and keep a couple inches of space between us, but it still feels perfect in a way that my imagination was never able to grasp.

The song comes to an end, and I mentally prepare myself to walk out of this moment we created together.

Until the next song starts playing and all I can do is stare at Grady.

Does he remember? Did he plan this?

He chuckles softly, muttering, "A very serendipitous moment." Then he pulls me back in for another dance.

Except this time, he tucks me into his chest and guides my hands to the nape of his neck before settling his on my lower back. My head is resting on his chest and all I can think about is that one fateful night many moons ago.

I was sitting in my backyard, hiding from my mom, and thanking whoever's holy up there that my siblings were away at school.

Not a single person in my family liked Brody. Not even my best friend Molly liked him, and she liked every boy we had ever met.

Actually, Hudson was his friend but didn't like him for me. *Which was stupid and didn't make sense.*

I used to think my mom's problem with Brody was the simple fact he wasn't Grady. In her mind, no one would ever compare to the boy-next-door for her youngest child.

I didn't allow myself to think about Grady very often or else I'd also start second guessing my relationship.

And I didn't need the reminder of what could've been on prom night.

No, that night Brody made sure I had been doubting our relationship without any help. He insisted we skip the after party at Harry's beach house to go straight to the hotel instead. You know because 'that's what people did on prom night.'

As if it wasn't something Brody and I had been doing, safely, for over a year now. Sometimes it felt like it was all Brody ever wanted to do.

But this was my first year going to prom, and Molly and all our friends were going to the after party. Harry had the best house for parties and parents who were conveniently out of town this weekend. It didn't make sense why we couldn't go there first, but he said that if we went to the party, he wouldn't be able to drive us back to the hotel afterward.

Which, okay that made sense. I hated when Brody would drive home after a party, even if it was 'just one beer' or 'a few hits from the bong.'

I told him I didn't care about a stupid hotel room. I cared about making memories.

He didn't like that.

Brody never yelled but his silence was almost worse. Sometimes it would last for days depending on how much I disappointed him. He always came back apologizing and making big gestures, but I think he secretly knew what that word did to me. How much I hated disappointing people to the point that I started having panic attacks a few months after we started to date.

The car ride back to my house had been quiet, and I was surprised he hadn't burned out when he was driving away. I hadn't even gotten to the porch steps by the time he was down the road.

Not that I had planned on using the front door. I didn't want my mom to worry about me or ask why I was home when she had given me permission to spend one night with Brody. Something I had been begging her for months to let me do.

I spent a lot of time wondering if her answer would've been different if I was dating the brunette-boy-next-door.

Instead of spending what should've been one of the most magical nights of my high school career dancing on a pool table with my friends and drowning in the affections of my boyfriend, I was sitting behind the tree in our backyard.

It was a risk, but I didn't have a lot of options. My mom couldn't see me from here, not unless she walked out toward the gate leading to the Millers' yard, but Selena and Tim would be able to see me from their kitchen. Even worse, Grady could see me from his bedroom window.

Neither of those outcomes would be worse than my mom finding out, and inevitably my siblings, that Brody left me crying in my gorgeous emerald-green gown that my mom almost didn't buy me because it was so expensive.

I've never hated Brody more than I did in that moment and that only made me cry harder.

Sometimes I didn't know if I loved Brody at all. Or if I was just attached to the idea of him.

But we had been together for two years by that point. And I really believed that he loved me. Otherwise, why would he come back even after I disappointed him, or after he didn't talk to me for days? He'd always tell me he just needed some space sometimes and nothing would keep him away from me for long.

It felt so romantic and addicting at that age.

I don't remember if it was the thought of Brody leaving me or the thought of being alone that caused the horrible sob that crawled *out of the deepest part of my chest, but it couldn't have been worse timing.*

I heard the gate between our backyards unlock but I'd been too emotional to really process what was happening.

Until I felt the hand on my cheek and heard the soft, familiar voice that I hardly recognized. "Vivi?"

His gentle tone and even gentler touch only made me cry more.

"Are you hurt?" *I didn't have to look at him to feel the fire in his eyes.* "What did he do to you?"

Shuddering breaths and gasping sobs were his only answer. Aggressively shaking my head was the only answer I could give at that moment.

I wasn't physically hurt—Brody never laid a hand on me—but emotionally, I was broken. Partly due to the boy standing in front of me.

He was still holding my cheek, brushing the tears away that were falling too quickly. "Stand up, Viv."

Viv. It had been so long since I heard him call me that. Since I heard him call me anything. It was shocking enough to break me out of my emotional stupor.

The gasping and sobbing slowly receded but the tears were still flowing.

I couldn't form the word, but I mouthed silently, "What?"

"There's something I promised you a very long time ago, and this is my last chance to make it happen." *I stared up at him for a long moment.*

I shook my head again.

Not in argument but in disbelief.

There was only one thing that Grady promised me he'd do that night.

"Please." *The desperation was apparent in his eyes.*

Even when I hated him, I didn't have the strength to deny Grady anything.

And I didn't want to deny him this. I didn't want to deny myself this.

I moved to stand up and grabbed his hand that was waiting for me. We stood a few feet apart while he searched for the song.

He dropped his phone in the front pocket of his suit jacket, leaving the volume just loud enough that we could hear it but not get attention from either of our parents.

He pulled me toward him, wrapping his other hand around the middle of my back.

"You remembered," I whispered into his chest.

"Kiss Me" by Sixpence None the Richer was playing, and I was taken back to the summer before I started middle school. It was the girls turn to choose the movie, and Lyp, Blake and I were on a Freddie Prinze Jr. kick. Ten years too late.

After everyone else had gone to bed, Grady and I were awake and left whispering secrets for only us to know. Movie nights usually ended like that.

I told him that the final prom scene of She's All That was the most romantic thing I had ever seen.

Sue me, I was like ten at this point. It was the most romantic thing I'd seen at that age.

I don't know if Grady thought it was silly. He probably did, but he never told me so. Instead, he leaned in and hooked our pinkies. "I promise to dance with you under the stars when we go to prom."

I always thought we'd go to together but at that moment, I didn't care about who he had gone to dances with, nor was I thinking about my high school boyfriend. I only cared about Grady Chase Miller and how warm his arms felt; how gently he rubbed my back through the entire four-minute song.

We swayed together, and he even twirled me around a few times. But as soon as the music stopped, so did we. It was about a minute later that Grady pulled away from me.

His arm was still around my back, but his other hand moved up to my cheek, wiping away more tears I didn't know were falling.

"I'm sorry, Vivi," he whispered, like a guilty admission and a heartbreaking finale.

Neither one of us had anything else to say so he turned around and closed the gate. I sat under the tree, staring at his bedroom window and feeling cold in a way that had nothing to do with the temperature. Thirty minutes later, my mom finally turned the lights off and I snuck into my room, where I laid in bed and continued staring at his bedroom window. And I could have sworn I felt his eyes on me the entire time.

I know the song is coming to an end and I know I need to take a step away once it does.

I feel like I'm drowning in everything that Grady is, has been and could be.

"Thank you, Grady," I whisper into his chest.

He's rubbing my back gently, just like he did after prom. "For what?"

I do my best to swallow the lump in my throat, but my hands tighten around his neck. "The dance."

The jury is out on whether he knows which dance I'm talking about, but it's not the one we just shared.

Chapter Nineteen

Grady

I wanted to hold on to Vivi a little bit longer after our dance, but she walked away too quickly. And as much as every nerve in my body is buzzing to go to her, I know that I need to give her some space right now.

All I wanted from tonight was to finally take Genevieve to a homecoming dance, even if it's fifteen years too late. But Vivi wearing her pretty green dress and the DJ playing that song at that moment? An amazing coincidence, even if it wasn't prom.

I could tell from the way her hands tightened in my hair and her soft '*thank you*' that that dance meant as much to her as it did me. And I don't need anyone to tell me when to not push Vivi.

So, I'm cleaning up the trash left on the floor and bleachers while Vivi is helping Mrs. Lee with the tablecloths and centerpieces. As it always goes when I'm in the same room as Vivi, my attention is on her even when I'm doing something else.

My entire life I've been consumed by Genevieve Briar Davies, and even after years of silence and a failed marriage, she's still the only woman who has this hold on me.

"You making up for missed opportunities?" Knox smirks at me

from behind the trash bag he's holding out.

I don't know what, or who, Vivi has talked to about us, but it seems more likely my mom would have gossiped about it.

"I don't know what you're talking about," I shrug.

All of the amusement fades from Knox's expression. "Look, Grady, I know this isn't my business," he pauses, seemingly knowing that it isn't, but continues anyway, "but clearly you two have a long history I don't know about. I'm not asking you to give me the details. From what I just saw," he waves his hand toward the dance floor, "there is something there. Something that a decade couldn't break."

"I don't know what you're talking about," I repeat. He gives me a frustrated look at my childish response. It's the closest to anger I've ever seen from Knox. "It was technically fifteen years, by the way," I add, deciding to throw him a bone.

Instead of anger though, he rubs his hands across his eyes. "Good god, man. Are you serious?" Taking a deep breath, he looks at me. "She doesn't deserve to sit around waiting for a man to make up his mind. And I don't think she's the type of woman to do that. You'd only be disappointing yourself, and her."

"I know," I say in a gruff voice. He gives me a disbelieving look, opening another trash bag. "I do, okay? There's just a lot that happened between us. And now with my daughters…" He nods in understanding at that. "I'm figuring it out."

He looks over my shoulder. "Well, don't take too long with that."

I turn to see what he's looking at and the blood in my veins immediately boils when I see Harper leaning toward Vivi. From where I'm standing, he's about to brush the hair out of her face when she pulls her head away.

My head whips back toward Knox and he gives me a look that says, *what are you going to do about it?*

I may not have earned back the right to lay claim on Vivi, but my feet are already moving and there's no stopping the possessive monster from coming out of his cave now.

"Are you ready to go, love?" I ask in a sharper tone that I intended.

I've never called Vivi love. I've never called anyone love.

But *love*... I like how that sounds for her.

A lot of things happen all at once, and if I didn't know her better, I might have missed something.

Her eyes slightly widen, and she swallows. *Relief.*

She quirks her eyebrow and slightly tilts her head. *Curiosity.*

Her cheeks flush and she bites her bottom lip. *Desire.*

She gives me a small nod and takes a step closer.

Harper puts his hand in front of her and my eyes drop to where it is before meeting his hard gaze. "We were talking, Miller."

"I didn't hear anything but from the looks of it, Vivi's ready to leave, and you need to let her."

"She's a big girl. If she wanted to leave, she could tell me."

Vivi clears her throat and looks him in the eye. "I've told you multiple times, while I was flattered, I have no interest in going on a date with you and that hasn't changed since you asked me a few weeks ago. Now if you'll excuse me, I'm going to leave with *Miller* now."

That's my girl.

And there's no more denying that Vivi is mine. She's belonged to me since that first block party when she found me sitting alone.

And more importantly, I want to belong to her.

I don't try very hard to hide my smugness as I place my hand on the small of her back and lead her toward the exit.

"We aren't done cleaning," Vivi leans toward me and whispers.

I look around until I make eye contact with Knox, and he grins before giving me a quick nod.

"No, they can handle it. I want to get you home."

A full body shiver rolls through her, the typical response when my voice drops a few octaves I've noticed.

I'm not expecting anything from her, and the girls are expecting me home tonight. I also have no plans of rushing things with Vivi. I don't want one night together. I want her, all of her. Every morning and night. All of her thoughts and pleasures. Mine.

Neither of us brought a coat and while California has pretty nice weather year-round, it has been raining more this year causing the chill to creep in early.

At least that's the excuse I tell myself when I pull her a little bit closer to me, tucking her under my arm.

The possessive beast in my chest hums in satisfaction when she willingly snuggles in closer and reaches around my back to hook her finger through my belt loop. It's a small gesture I maybe wouldn't have noticed from anyone but it's such a natural, intimate gesture from her.

"Thanks for saving me back there."

"Mmm, you're welcome," I mumble into the top of her head, laying a small kiss on the crown. I used to place kisses on her head a lot growing up, but this is the first in years. "I hate that I have to save you from him, but I always will."

"Did you have fun at your first High Tides mandated event?" Her voice is lighter than it was earlier.

"I had a really good time. Thanks to you, Viv." I give her waist a little squeeze before releasing her. I open the door and help her inside, leaning across her to buckle the seat belt. As I'm leaning back, I stop just an inch from her lips. "It was long overdue, and that was my fault, but I'm here to make up for a lot of lost time."

"What else?" she asks, a little breathless.

I pull back just enough for her to see the playfulness. "I have some ideas, but you'll have to come along for the ride if you want to find out."

She rolls her perfect hazel eyes and I choose to take that as a *yes*.

Without even thinking about it, I drop a kiss on her temple and shut the car door.

It's a quiet ride after that, but it's a comfortable silence. Like we both are just soaking in the presence of each other.

After a few minutes I test my luck at putting my hand on her thigh like I did at the game last night, reveling in the way she interlaces her fingers with mine.

The few times I've glanced over at Vivi, there's a soft smile on her face as she looks out the window.

The drive to her place is coming to an end too quickly and I don't have any reason to prolong it.

Our perfect bubble pops as I pull into her driveway.

She unbuckles herself but my hand squeezes her thigh before she can get out of the car.

"Wait."

I open my own door and walk around to her side. She not only accepts the hand I offer as help, but she pulls me toward her front door.

I want to tell her how badly I want to go inside. How I want to fall asleep with her and wake up next to her, and everything else that may, or may not, happen would be an added bonus. I just want her in my arms for more than a few uninterrupted hours.

But instead, I follow her up the few stairs and decide not to make any assumptions.

She unlocks her door and starts to say '*good night,*' but I don't let her finish.

With one hand still laced in hers, because I refuse to lose the physical contact until the very last minute, I bring my other hand to her waist and gently push her up against her door frame.

She releases a sharp breath, looking up at me through her lashes.

We're half in, half out of her foyer. I was so captivated by her earlier I didn't notice much about her place. From where I'm standing, I can see her living room perfectly—her mismatched velvet armchairs and magenta couch, the shaggy boho rug and small coffee table with what appears to be stains from wine glasses, and the dozen of plants and books laying messily around any surface available.

I can't help but think how perfectly our two styles would blend together under one roof.

My eyes cut back to her. She's watching me take in her space, her teeth nibbling on her bottom lip and one eyebrow quirked.

I jerk my chin toward the room. "It feels like you."

"Mmm," she hums softly and glances inside. "I'm going to miss this house."

"Are you moving?"

My mom hasn't mentioned anything about it, and I know that Vivi loves her teaching position, so it doesn't make sense why she'd leave. Maybe she decided to apply for a different graduate program. Either way, the idea of her leaving after we just reconnected has my anxiety ready to spiral.

The idea of her not telling me causes a streak of hurt to cut through the growing panic.

"In February. Lexi's parents want to sell the lot—they get offers all of the time and have graciously let us stay here for way less money than it's worth." Her knee knocks into mine and she teasingly says, "Don't worry, Grady Miller, it'll be harder to get rid of me this time around." When I look at her, I don't see any signs of joking on her face. I see insecurities and vulnerabilities battling in her eyes, begging me to calm them before they overtake her.

"Good." I bring my face down to hers, until our noses are brushing against each other. "I don't want to get rid of you."

"You say that now," she replies with a cheeky grin, but the usual glint in her eyes is absent.

She tries to take a step away from me, but I don't let her. I'm not anywhere near ready to lose the feel of her body in my grasp.

My grip tightens around her waist, and I push her back into the doorframe. My eyes drop to her full lips at the same second her skin flushes, starting at her chest and moving up toward her cheeks.

"Not so fast. I'm not done with you."

I'll never be done.

I brush some hair off her face and let my hand settle along the column of her neck. I count to five, giving her enough time to pull away if she wants.

She doesn't.

Her eyes move from mine to my mouth. The hand she was using to skim my chest has tightened around my shirt. But it isn't until she whispers, "Try again, Grady," so quietly, that my control snaps.

It's almost exactly what she told me, after we bumped noses the first time I tried to kiss her.

And I don't waste a second.

My hand tightens along her neck, and I drop my lips to hers. The kiss is sweet and soft. Neither of us are in a rush. Her other hand runs up my arm before tangling in my hair. The hand I have on her waist slips to the small of her back, pulling her closer to me.

We're tangled together in this moment, and I'd freeze time right now if I could. I'd live in this second and be the happiest man on this earth.

And from her soft, desperate moan that escapes when I pull away slightly, I know she'd agree.

I tilt her head to the side a little, allowing a better angle. And she takes advantage of it immediately.

Her tongue is running along the seam of my mouth, trying to get access to more, but I quickly realize that teasing Vivi like this is my new favorite thing.

She's always liked for things to be her way, and she's still as impatient as ever. A smile breaks across my face when her teeth start to tug on my lower lip. More a demand than a request.

I open to her and give her exactly five seconds to take what she wants before the control becomes mine.

My grip on her neck and waist tightens. I step into her space, forcing her further against the doorframe, her front flush against mine.

I deepen the kiss, plunging my tongue into her mouth and find myself already addicted to the sweet taste of her.

All I know at this moment is Genevieve Briar Davies.

Her rich berry and vanilla scent. The way her hands grab onto any part of me that they can. Her soft, needy moans matching each of my deeper, and equally desperate, groans.

And even though it feels like I'm a dying man in the desert turning away from a needed oasis, I know that I have to pull away before I lose track of reality.

The whimper she makes when I take my lips from her is almost enough to make me fully step into her house. To bury myself so deep within her body and heart that we're never able to separate who is who again.

But I can't. Not tonight.

"Fuck, Vivi." I place a small kiss on her mouth.

She blinks up at me and giggles. "You… you cursed. Again."

I chuckle and rub my nose along her cheek. "Because you drive me so crazy. I don't know how else to express it."

She lightly pushes at my chest, adding unwelcomed distance. I catch her hand and hold it against my chest.

"You owe the swear jar a dollar when you get home."

"Says the girl with a mouth like a sailor. You'd owe them your annual salary if we had to pay when they aren't around to hear it."

"Sorry," she shrugs irreverently, "that's not happening." Her cheeks start to turn a light shade of pink and she shyly gazes up at me through her lashes, but her voice stays steady as she contemplates, "I guess you'll just have to think of another way to punish me if you want me to stop swearing."

Yeah… this is a game I would love to play with her.

"I can think of more than a few mutually enjoyable ways to punish you but unfortunately, I love your mouth the way it is."

She smirks but I don't miss the shiver that runs up her back, nor the sharp inhale that I cut off with one last kiss.

I pull her away from the door frame and guide her through the door with a taunting smack on her ass. Her eyes are wide when she turns toward me, one hand on the doorknob. "Who are you?" she whispers but I can hear the mix of amusement and desire dripping from her voice.

She peeks at me through the crack in the door, and gives me a shy smile, but the next words out of her mouth don't fit the coy demeanor. "It's a good thing I know all the best and quickest ways to get under your skin."

"You're already there."

She slowly pulls away from the door and singsongs, "Good night, Grady."

I don't take my eyes off the sliver of her I can still see when I tell her, "Good night, love." My feet feel cemented to the ground but the knowledge that two of my three favorite girls are waiting for me at home as me turning toward my Jeep.

Though the satisfied grin and my lingering arousal stay with me most of the way home.

Sat, Sept 24 at 10:37 AM

Arielle

Good morning :)

What are your plans this evening? Can I FT you and the girls

> What time were you thinking?

7 your time again?

> I won't be home but I can ask the babysitter if she will bring her tablet.

No, don't inconvenience her. Maybe tomorrow.

> Sounds good.

↓ **New** ↓
9:02 PM

Can you jump on FT now?

10:56 PM

I know you had plans tonight I just idk. I thought maybe you would be home by now

11:49 PM

Is everything okay?

Yes, didn't mean to worry you. Just wanted to talk. Are you just getting home?

The girls are in bed.

I figured lol. I wanted to talk to you

About what?

Just to see how you're doing, catch up, talk about things

We do all of that when you FT the girls. We can catch up tomorrow. I'm getting ready for bed now.

Good night, Grady

11:52 PM

> *photo attachment of the swear jar with a twenty on top.

> I decided to be nice and throw in a little extra for the girls on your behalf.

Vivi

Thanks but if you're just going to pay for me I don't really see the point of letting you introduce me to some allegedly enjoyable alternatives

> Next time, I won't have to leave you after only a kiss. Patience, Genevieve.

That's never really been my strong suit

> Trust me, I know.

> Maybe I'll have to find a mutually enjoyable way to teach you that lesson.

I must ask again...who are you?

> Not the little boy next door anymore.

I've noticed

Good night again ☾

> Good night again, love.

Chapter Twenty
Grady

"What are you doing here?"

Vivi's clearly surprised to see me standing on her porch, almost soaked to the bone. I didn't bother to grab an umbrella or rain jacket when I impulsively decided to come see her.

We've barely talked since I dropped her off last weekend, but she's been on my mind every minute of every day since. Dating with two young daughters is hard, especially when I get the impression that Vivi doesn't want people to know we're dating. If that's even what you can call this now. I hope so. Who knows what she thinks?

I'm fine with giving us time to get on the same page, but I won't allow it to break the growing trust between us. You don't get a chance to push a woman like Genevieve against the wall and kiss her like your very life depends on it only to ignore her afterwards. Absolutely no reason is good enough.

Sure, I kissed her and kind of ignored her once before. But there was definitely no pushing up against any walls. Plus, we were *teenagers.* This is different.

I sent her a few text messages throughout the week, and I

surprised her with her favorite coffee and pastry from Brighter Daze—large iced dirty Chai tea latte with oat milk and an extra shot of espresso and a bear claw, *thank you Lexi*. She smiled so bright when I walked into her classroom, that it took every ounce of self-control I had to not kiss her.

I didn't want a possessive, consuming kiss.

No, that morning when Vivi was standing at her dry erase board, in her purple wrap dress and her natural waves flowing down her back, all I wanted was a soft and affectionate brush of her lips.

I'm not saying that I'd ever be opposed to the chance of bending her over her desk—my dick knows I think about it enough—but I don't only want her hot, pleasure-filled moments. I want her quiet mornings, sleepless nights, and everything in between.

"The girls are gone for five days. The house was too quiet."

I dropped my parents, Stella, and Daisy off at the airport this morning before my classes began. It's fall break as of this afternoon, and my parents were gracious enough to fly to Seattle for a long weekend with the girls, so I didn't have to.

As much as I hate being away from them, the truth was… I didn't *want* to go. I didn't want to spend a weekend co-parenting with Arielle. I'm thankful we get along and things are amicable between us, but I'm ready to move on with my life and the girls' lives.

And I'm looking at who I hope holds that future in the palms of her pretty little hands.

When I got home from work, and the house was silent, I lasted thirty minutes before I felt like I was going crazy. Before the feeling of my heart being a thousand miles away from me took over. Before I realized for the first time since my daughters were born, my heart was split into three and one of those pieces was five miles from me.

Without thinking, I got in my car and drove here. The promise of

Vivi's laugh like a siren song pulling me toward her.

She pushes the door open and gestures for me to come in. I walk inside and take in the room again. I can see her small bright orange kitchen to my right and a hallway to my left with three doors.

"But what are you doing *here*, Grady?" She slowly closes the distance between us, one hand slides to my chest and the other plays with my belt loop, not seeming to care that I'm dripping water all over her tile flooring.

The simple touch has my tongue dry and my chest tight. "Thunderstorm," I mumble, not taking my eyes off her lips.

Fuck, I want to kiss her.

She chuckles, "Didn't realize you were still a big weenie." Her voice is teasing but her hands are possessive.

Saying the first excuse that comes to mind, "I wanted to make sure you had a generator… in case the power goes out…" If she doesn't have one and the power goes out, there isn't a damn thing I could do.

She gives me a knowing smile, "I do have one. Hudson installed it for us when we first moved in. We've never needed it before." We don't get a lot of thunder or lightning storms out here.

"Oh… okay…" I don't know why I thought showing up to her house was a good idea. I just wanted to see her and now that I have, maybe there's no reason to stay. "I can go then. I don't wan–"

She fists my soaked shirt. "Don't you dare, Grady Miller. What if *your* electricity goes out? I know you're scared of the dark."

That makes my head tip back as I laugh. "I am not." I step into her space. "Nor have I ever been," I remark, one of my arms wrapping around her waist, "afraid of the dark, you little troll." My other hand slides to her chin and I angle her face up to mine. Her smile is so bright it's almost blinding, but I couldn't look away if my life depended on it.

"Are you going to kiss me?"

I huff out a laugh. "Impatient girl."

A small smile plays on my lips as I lean toward her. I gently brush my lips against hers for half a second. Her eyes are closed, mouth barely open, waiting for me. I lay a soft kiss on the tip of her nose before taking more. My fingers tighten around her jaw and her hum of approval only urges me on further. She opens for me, and I don't waste a second before slipping my tongue in, getting tangled with hers.

For such a simple kiss, my cock is already rising to attention.

From the moans slipping out of her, I wonder if she's as ready for more as I am.

I don't know how long it takes me to realize that the house is darker, and the soft melody of Taylor Swift stopped.

I pull away and rub my thumb along her swollen lips.

"Huh, I guess you need that generator now," I tease.

Vivi's eyes fly open as she takes in the dark, quiet room.

"Ummm," she says in a quiet, almost embarrassed voice, "I actually don't know how to use it."

I stare at her in disbelief, "You were so cool and confident when I got here."

Her arms drop to my waist and pull me closer to her. She buries her face in my wet chest, and she's so goddamn perfect I can't help myself. I plant another kiss on her temple. "I just didn't want you to know how happy I was that you were standing at my door. It reminded me of summer days… remember when you would pack picnics and surprise me?"

The memory makes me smile. "Those were my favorite days."

I honestly didn't have any coherent thoughts when I decided to drive to Vivi's. Actually, it was all very caveman of me.

Vivi.

Must see Vivi.

Go to Vivi.

Next thing I knew, I was parking my Jeep in the driveway and running through the rain to get to her.

But the fact that it means this much to her? That just needing to see her made her remember those perfect, warm summer days?

That makes me feel good. Better than good. I'm on top of the world right now.

"Are you saying that you want more surprise visits and beach picnics?"

She nods against my chest. "I haven't had a picnic on the beach since that last time we went, around my fifteenth birthday."

I squeeze her tight. "I haven't either, Viv. I promise to take you on as many beach picnics as it takes to make up for the years we didn't go."

"Okay, Grady." She kisses my chest, right where my hearts beating for her. "I can show you where the generator is but that's all the help I can offer."

"No, love, that's okay. Just point me in the direction of the garage."

She points down the hallway to the door on the left.

As I'm about to turn the knob she pokes her ahead around the corner—it's too dark to see anything, but her hair is like a burning ember—and warns, "Just so you know, it's a shared garage with Lex. I don't know if she's home."

"Guess we'll find out," I mutter.

I like Lexi, more now that I've gotten small glimpses into her friendship with Vivi.

I don't like the idea of Lexi deciding to spend time with us tonight.

I want Genevieve to myself for once.

Using my phone flashlight to find the generator in the corner, a sigh of relief falls out of me when I realize that it's similar enough to the one I had in Phoenix.

As I'm switching the fuel valve on, I hear someone walk into the garage.

Without looking up I say over my shoulder, "Hey, it'll just ta—"

"AHHGH!"

I jump up, looking for the wounded animal that must have gotten trapped in here because that's the only thing that would make a sound like *that*.

I shine my light around until I see a figure standing in the door—not the one that I came out of.

"*Fuck*, Lexi," I mumble, rubbing my chest. "Are you trying to give me a heart attack?"

"Excuse me?" she screeches at the same moment Vivi sticks her head in, phone flashlight in hand. "This is *my* garage, Grady Miller. I was going to turn on the generator. I wasn't expecting to find an ax murderer hanging out in here."

Vivi puts two and two together, cackling at the scene. "Oh my god, I was really worried for a second."

Lexi doesn't dignify that with a response, instead she stares at me, clearly waiting for me to explain what I'm doing here.

"First of all, you didn't find an ax murderer," I scoff, rolling my eyes even though she can't see it. "You found *me*. Second of all, I'm not *hanging out here*. I'm trying to get this started for you since apparently neither of you were paying attention to Hudson." The frustration is dropping from my tone.

"What's up his ass?" Lexi turns toward Vivi.

"He's mad that we don't know how to do this ourselves and are two helpless women living alone susceptible to ax murderers. *Obviously*."

"It's California. We never get storms like this," Lexi states in a matter-a-fact tone.

"Yup," Vivi pops the P. "That's exactly what I said."

"You both can go back inside now, thanks," I mutter.

Of course, they ignore me, so I turn back to the generator.

I feel Lexi's assessing look before I hear her accusing tone. "What are you really doing here anyway? Did you show up just to check on our generator?"

I turn and give her an annoyed look at the same time the lights flicker back on.

Once she clocks my expression, a shit-eating grin slowly pulls on her lips, but it isn't until she looks at Vivi's horrible poker face that she loses it. "Oh, that's too predictable, even for you, G. But it's appreciated."

"Whatever." I don't walk toward Vivi. I don't know why but I don't like the pressure of Lexi's knowing eyes right now.

"Don't get embarrassed. We've never had a man to take care of us that wasn't one of her brothers." She steps back into her side of the duplex and starts to close the door. "I'll just… leave you guys to your… night or whatever."

I don't need to look at her to know that she's not only amused, but smug.

"I was going to order pizza and watch some TV tonight, maybe get my schedule prepared for next week." I nod, prepared for the dismissal I can feel coming but to my surprise she asks in a quiet voice, "Want to stay and hang out?"

"Yes," I close the distance between us in only a few strides.

Later, I might be embarrassed at how eager I came off just now, but that's a worry for another day. Tonight, I'm focusing on Vivi and that addictive berry scent.

Chapter Twenty-One
Vivi

Grady abruptly stops with his foot halfway through the door. He slowly looks back at me with a surprised expression on his face.

"What?" I follow his gaze back to the shelf next to the door.

He picks up a Ziplock bag that I'd forgotten about.

"This yours?" The amusement is thick in his voice as he takes in the joint that Asher left for me months ago.

"Technically, it is, yes." The truth is, I haven't smoked since college. And even then, it was *rare*. I know that Lexi and Calypso like to hang out with Asher when I'm not there. They think I don't know what they're doing but I do. I'm not dumb. I just don't care.

"Technically?" He raises his eyebrows but doesn't put the bag back on the shelf.

"Yes," I say slowly. "I had a pretty bad anxiety attack awhile back. Lexi called Asher; it was that bad… He was able to help me calm down without it. He said he was going to leave that for me since he likes to smoke when he's anxious. He finds it helps." And it does help *Asher*. I've found it's better to avoid that when I feel anything other happy.

He bypasses the questions I can practically see on tip of his tongue, instead asking, "You haven't lit it yet?"

"Obviously not."

"Why?"

"What do you mean? Because I'm a teacher."

"It's legal in the state of California, Viv."

"No shit, Sherlock. That doesn't mean it's *federally* legal. Plus, it always made my anxiety worse."

"Always?"

"I mean, not *always*. Sometimes in college, when Lexi and I would get in comfy clothes, order a lot of pizza, it would be okay. I wouldn't have to leave my blanket cocoon so there wasn't anything to be paranoid about. It worked about half the time."

He nods slowly, trying to fight the smile creeping across his face, but he still doesn't put down the bag.

"Do you… do you want to get *high*?" I whisper, for no reason at all.

He gives me a smirk and a small shrug. "No one would know. Except maybe Lexi."

"I mean… we are ordering pizza anyway…"

"Wow, that didn't take much convincing at all." He's smiling wide now.

"Shut up," I mutter and take the bag out of his hand. "You cannot tell *anyone*; do you understand me?" I point at him. "Not only could we be fired but our parents could find out."

He stares at me with disbelief clear across his face. "You know you're a twenty-eight-year-old woman, right? What's Bonnie going to do? Ground you?"

"You would be surprised," I huff.

"Come on, Vivi." He gives me his sad puppy face. He hasn't used this on me in over a decade, but desperate times call for desperate measures apparently. He sticks out his lower lip just slightly more than what's natural, tilts his head to the side, and I can feel myself cracking before his eyes. "We can add it to the list of things we would have done together in high school."

"*Fine*. But I'm ordering pizza first."

He plants a quick kiss on my nose. "Deal."

After the pizza has been delivered and I change into my comfiest silk pajama set and Grady borrows some of Asher's sweats and a t-shirt he left here after a movie night, we get comfy in the small sunroom attached to my kitchen. I can keep all of the windows open without having to worry about a lingering smell.

"Viv, we don't have to do this." He leans his head back and tilts it toward me. "I don't want to pressure you into anything."

I look back at him while I think it over.

Sure, he was the one who suggested it and gave me that goddamn sad puppy face. So, on one hand, I didn't stand a chance at saying no. On the other hand, this *is* something we would have done in high school. And it's not like I never thought about the joint that Asher left for me. If I'm being honest, I just didn't want to smoke with them because they do it fairly often and I always got a little… giggly when I got high.

But with the rain continuing to pour down and Grady here at my house as if we never wasted all those years, it feels right. I feel calm and in a good headspace.

I want to have fun with Grady. I want to be a little irresponsible with him too.

"I know, Grady." I give him a small nod. "Light it up."

Grady

"Are you sure you're okay? I can get some water." I do my best not to laugh but Vivi's been coughing for probably five minutes. Every time I think she's getting better, it gets worse.

She's going to be stoned, alright.

"No, I'm fine." She takes a deep breath and holds it. Only to start coughing three seconds later.

"I'm getting you water. If you die, I'll definitely get fired *and* grounded."

She flips me off when her death glare is undermined by the tears rolling down her cheeks.

God, even like this she's beautiful. I could stare at her all night, waterworks and all. I haven't been able to take my eyes off of her once, even while trying to hold it together as she hacks up a lung.

"Earth to Grady," she sputters out.

Oh.

Oh crap.

I was actually staring at her for who knows how long.

"Huh?" It's the only coherent thought I can get out.

"I think I actually need that water." She gives me an embarrassed look in between her coughing.

I push myself off the chair and tug on the hair piled on top of her head. "I'm on it."

Vivi

"Mmm," I contemplate over another bite of pizza. "I don't *really* believe that's your favorite romcom."

"Why would I lie about that?" In his defense, he truly seems slighted.

"It seems like a staged, fake ass answer, honestly."

I don't know why it bothers me so much, but *it does*.

"*Drive Me Crazy* is my favorite romcom," he says it with such conviction and heart that I don't question him again. He clocks my resignation, continuing with an infuriating boyish grin, "Why wouldn't it be my favorite?"

"Hm, let me think about it." I tap my chin, pretending to put some thought into it. "Two childhood best friends who fight over whatever adolescent reason only to make up later, realizing that they not only truly are best friends, but they're actually meant to be. It's a cliché and one I think you're using to tug on my heartstrings."

He shakes his head, his messy waves falling over his forehead. "No, I promise. It's my favorite. Yes, everything you said is true and fair. But I don't know… it's more than that. It's a story about how opposites attract. Nicole and Chase are weighed down by the social expectations of their friend groups. Don't you remember being in high school and feeling like you had one box that you had to fit yourself into? Even when it was suffocating and only held enough room for one small part of you? But they saw each other for who they are… the good, the bad, the surprising."

He shrugs lightly. "The scene when he takes her to that local all-girls rock show is probably my favorite. It's something neither of them really expected her to enjoy but she does. Plus, his name is Chase." He lifts his shoulders again, as if a character having the same name as his middle one is reason enough.

"Hmm. I guess that's a good analysis. I'll accept it." I take another bite of pizza but I'm assessing him from the corner of my eye.

"What about you? What's your favorite?" Before I can answer he adds, "Oh, wait. *She's All That*. Is that still your favorite?"

It's a sweet gesture that he remembers and makes me even more sure that the dance we shared last weekend wasn't a fluke.

I open my mouth to answer but it suddenly hits me why his favorite romcom bothers me so much. It's all of the similar tropes to one of mine.

"Let's hear it, Viv. Spill your secrets to me." Again, with the handsome grin, that I can't decide if I want to trace with my tongue or smack off his face.

"*She's All That* is one of my favorite movies." His eyes bore into me, waiting for me to tell him the other. "It isn't really a *secret* but if you must know…" I pause, taking a deep breath for dramatic effect, "*13 Going on 30*."

My face is warming at the admission. It suddenly feels like my deepest secret. I turn for another piece of pizza, hoping to hide the pink that's tinting my cheeks.

When I turn back around, the complacent tug to Grady's mouth is the most infuriating—and sexiest—thing I've ever seen.

"That's interesting… two best friends who fight for *whatever* reason only to go back in time after figuring out they, not only are best friends, but are meant to be." He leans across the island and plants a soft kiss on my nose. "Sounds pretty familiar to me, Viv."

I take a large bite of pizza and give him a half-hearted '*fuck you*' around a mouthful of food.

That makes him break out into something very similar to a giggle. Before I know it, the hazy feeling takes over my mind and body again. I sink deeper into the stool and start snickering with him.

Not because anything is funny but because I'm *happy*.

At this moment, staring at the handsome brunette man across from me, leaning in to place another kiss on my nose, before he stuffs almost the entire slice of pizza into his mouth; I'm happy.

Grady

Vivi is star-fishing on her living room floor next to me. I don't know how long we've been here. It could be a minute. It could be hours.

My brain feels like it's floating to Saturn, and I have to mentally tie a string to the end like a balloon to keep it down on earth. I try to tug it down… down… down so I don't lose it.

My body feels heavy and grounded to the hardwood floor and I imagine being rooted right here, in the middle of Genevieve's living room. Where I could see her every day and hear her thoughts that she refuses to voice anywhere outside these walls—because I *know* she talks to herself.

I feel soft velvet skim across my fingers. My head turns faster than my eyes but once they catch up, my gaze is locked on the light green fingernail drawing shapes across the back of my hand.

I look at her face and she rolls onto her side to meet my gaze. One of her arms is tucked under her head, while her hand makes its way up my arm in a torturously slow pattern.

I open my mouth to say something—I don't even know what. I want to hear her voice more than ever.

Something down the hall catches my eye though.

I shoot up to a sitting position and try to get a look toward the end of the dark hallway.

"Um, are you okay?" Vivi sounds more concerned than she has since we smoked half of that joint.

I don't want to cause her to panic so I take a deep breath and lay back down. "Yes, love. Everything is fine." Immediately after the words leave my mouth, I see another movement down the hall.

Now *I'm* starting to panic.

I sit back up and she follows this time. "Grady?"

I turn my head to her, and I know my fear is apparent. "Did you see that?"

"What?" Her voice is a whisper, and she peeks toward the hallway.

"I saw something move." I wait for her to react. She doesn't. She just looks mildly confused. "Twice," I add.

She *giggles* in the face of my fear. "Oh."

Vivi stands from the floor and walks up the hallway.

"Wait, don't go back there. I should be the one who confronts the ax murderer."

That makes her breathy cackle come alive. When she walks back, she's still slightly wheezing and holding... two cats?

She has cats?

"You have cats?" I ask.

"Yeah." She's beaming at the two balls of fur who are hanging from her arms. "This one is Cinnamon." She lifts the smaller, less fluffy cat. She's orange with green eyes. "And this is Vanilla." The white cat is almost double the size as the other one with yellow eyes and a lot more fur.

"How long have you had them?"

"I got Vanilla when I moved back about six years ago. Your dad knew I wanted to get her a friend, so when the strays were brought in four years ago, he let me choose who I wanted first."

Vivi sets them both down on the floor and they assess me before walking over.

"And just so you know, they aren't killers. So far, they have never been violent toward anything except Calypso."

I pet their heads and Vanilla rolls into a ball on my lap. "We've all been there," I start to chuckle before I can even get the comment out. Vivi shoves my shoulder but laughs.

Vivi

Cinnamon and Vanilla took to Grady faster than even Asher—their favorite man until now.

He had to *gently* lug the hefty white fluff off his lap. I could tell he considered staying there all night to not disturb her. My entire body was bursting with warmth at the sight of Grady making himself a part of my little home.

That was until he started to get restless and wandered to the bookshelf that spans the length of one of the walls. Hudson installed it when I ran out of room. It's almost to the brim with books but my little home is at its capacity. Almost all of them are romance novels—because let's be honest, the best literature is always romantic.

And I've never, and will *never,* be ashamed of reading what I do. But that doesn't stop my entire body from lighting up like a fire alarm when he goes straight to some of the smuttier books.

I stand ramrod straight with my back to the bookcase while he flips through a particularly spicy book about an NHL player and his teammate's little sister. He doesn't seem to be skimming any of the pages so that's a plus.

"Have you ever even dated a hockey player?" He grunts like a caveman. His jealousy sends fireworks through me.

"Nooo, I haven't," I say slowly. "But I've never dated a billionaire or a single father either. Doesn't stop me from reading about them." I give him a cheeky grin.

He rolls his eyes and turns back to the book.

Slowly his head tips up to meet my eyes, and the fire I see burning sends a heatwave straight to my core.

"You read this?"

"Yes," I answer slowly.

He takes a step toward me. "This book talks about…" His eyes skim the page again before looking back up at me and reciting, "…*my hard cock pumps into her over… and over…*"

I really have to give it to him; he got through that entire sentence without stuttering.

"Are you going to make fun of me?"

He gives me a goofy, endearing grin and shakes his head slowly. That thick lock of hair falling over his forehead again. "If anything, your porn makes me like you more." He leans forward. "Plus, it makes you blush, and I *love* that." He plants a soft kiss to the apple of my cheek.

He turns back toward the kitchen and calls over his shoulder, "I want kettle corn. Do you have any?"

Grady

I have two sleeping cats in my lap and a large bowl of extra butter popcorn sitting between Viv and me. I'm higher than the moon after smoking the rest of the joint before we got snacks. Or *munchies,* as Genevieve insists on calling them.

I should be happy.

But I'm not.

I'm betrayed.

"I can't believe you've lied to me our entire lives."

"Well," she argues, tilting her head back and forth, "you've been lying to me all of these years too, Grady Miller."

I can't hide the guilty twist to my lips. *She isn't wrong.* I don't think either of us remembers how it all started, but I was under the assumption that kettle corn was her favorite kind of popcorn. And even as a kid, I wanted any reason to sit next to her. Share her bowl of snacks. Have something in common with her.

So yes, for over two decades I let her believe that kettle corn was my favorite kind of popcorn too, because it was supposed to be *her* favorite.

She's giggling now.

Probably thinking about how she was under the same assumption and chose kettle corn for *me.*

I can't help but laugh with her. We were just two infatuated kids who would rather spend years not eating salty, extra butter popcorn than chance someone else sitting by them during movies.

Vivi

"No fair, you're cheating!" I point an accusing finger at him.

A few minutes ago, I slid—yes, *slid,* my head doesn't feel as foggy but my body refuses to get off the floor—to the other side of the kitchen to see who could catch more pieces of popcorn in their mouths. Except Grady is much better at this than I am.

I always beat Lexi when we play. Granted, she catches about one for every ten.

But still, I thought my sixty percent rate wasn't bad.

It isn't even comparable to Grady's nine out of ten catches.

"How would I even cheat?" He laughs at the accusation.

"I don't know," I huff out, crossing my arms like a child. "You played *baseball*, Grady. Throw better."

His smile is so bright and goofy I want to crawl to him and kiss it off.

"Yeah, I did play baseball, *Genevieve.*" He lets his voice drop an octave when he says my full name. "But if you remember correctly, I was a *catcher*." To prove his point, he tosses another piece in the air and leans to the side to catch it.

And I hate him for making such a valid argument.

"Whatever. Rematch."

Grady

Vivi didn't win.

I lean back on her couch, my feet propped up on her coffee table, while I watch her get another snack ready. Her feet shuffle from cabinet to cabinet as she looks at the contents. Her lilac pajamas hug her body like a glove but my favorite thing about her at this moment is the small smile that she can't wipe off her face.

She comes back with a container of ice cream—non-dairy phish food—and two spoons.

She hands me one and takes the lid off.

I watch with an ache in my chest as she dips her spoon in and takes a bite.

"Mmm," she moans quietly and nods her head in approval. As if she didn't buy this flavor. As if it, most likely, isn't one of her top three flavors if she has it stocked at her house.

She tilts the carton toward me, and I grab it from her hands.

I watch her as I take a bite.

It all feels very intimate. Like I'm looking into someone else's life, getting a glimpse of what could've been.

Maybe what could still be.

"This is good," I say in a husky tone.

"I know. It's my second favorite flavor."

Knew it.

Smiling, I ask, "What's your first?"

"Mint Chocolate Cookie."

"Nice. I like Cherry Garcia."

She crinkles her nose. "Really?"

"Yup." I watch her think about it, licking her spoon far more seductively than she's probably aware of.

She nods, tucking that piece of information away for later. When she isn't stoned and can dissect it in whatever way I know her mind inevitably will.

We fall into a comfortable silence, with just the sounds of Vivi's indie playlist quietly coming through the speaker.

From the corner of my eye, I can see her begin to pick at the throw blanket on her lap. I turn my head as her face starts to turn more serious, her thoughts growing louder.

I want to give her the space to open up to me when she's ready, so I sit patiently. I don't stop myself from scooting a little closer or from rubbing my thumb along her neck.

She suddenly spits it out. "What are you scared of?"

"Are we talking like I'm scared of clowns and snakes–"

"Don't forget the dark," she retorts with a teasing smirk.

"Right, *of course* I can't forget the dark." I play along.

"But no." Her serious tone comes back. "I'm talking about real-life fears."

I think about that for a second. "I guess, right now, my biggest two? Always my daughters. They're with their mother and my parents right now, but I just feel this… worry that I can't explain. It's almost painful to be away from them. But not just for their physical well-being but their emotional well-being too. And it scares me that I may be putting that at jeopardy." We haven't talked about Arielle tonight and I don't plan on starting now. Not tonight. This is for just us.

"And your second one?" She's whispering again, even though it's only the two of us.

I turn my entire body toward her, demanding her undivided attention as well. "I'm scared that I won't be able to make up for all of the lost time."

"With your family?"

I nod once. "Yes, them. But with *you* too, Genevieve." My eyes drop to where my thumb is still rubbing her neck. "The time that I owe you goes back a lot further than when I left for college."

"You're already making up for it, Grady." She places her hand on my chest. "But I'll happily take whatever time you're willing to give me."

My hand moves to the nape of her neck, gripping tighter. "You can have all of it. Every second of the rest of my life belongs to you if you want it."

A small smile plays on her lips, but her eyes are glued to mine.

I slowly pull her into a kiss, needing to be closer to her. There's so much I should say but I couldn't even articulate properly with a clearer mind. For a sweet minute, she leans into me as my tongue explores her mouth deeper.

Slowly, as if she's coming out of a fog, she pulls away. "Not like…" She shakes her head, holding her hands to her swollen lips.

"*Not* like this," I agree. I'd never want any of our firsts to happen when we're under the influence of anything. Those are moments I want to remember every second of.

Suddenly, she blurts out, "I was supposed to put my laundry away tonight." She jumps off the couch, turning toward her bedroom.

I fall back against the cushions, dramatically groaning in exasperation.

"And you're helping!" she singsongs as she turns the corner.

Vivi

One thing I'm quickly learning tonight: you make dumb decisions when you're high.

Like ten minutes ago. When I decided that I could force Grady to help me fold my laundry. I didn't think much of it at the moment. I figured we could put on a show—*Parks and Rec*, of course—and he would help me cut the time in half.

What I didn't think about was all my *delicates*. My lacy bras and cotton thongs.

What I also didn't take into consideration was how particular I am about *everything*.

So, when Grady went to throw my favorite black set into a pile to the side without making a big deal about it, I almost had a heart attack. I couldn't just let him chuck them as if they're a pair of socks. I spend a lot of money on my lingerie, even the everyday pieces.

I wasn't surprised when Grady laughed at my declaration that I fold everything, including those.

I *was* surprised when he declared that he would focus solely on those pieces.

And even more than that, I hate that he's folding each one impeccably.

Every time he catches me giving him a scathing side-eye, he gives me a saucy look in return.

"I'm learning a lot about you tonight," he says as he picks up a satin bra with a dainty floral design embroidered across. I raise my eyebrows in question. "One, we have the same favorite sitcom." He nods toward the TV. I didn't tell him that Leslie Knope is a kindred spirit but considering I know almost all the lines, I would say it's obvious. "And two, you have an aversion to padded bras."

We both look at the bra he's currently holding then our eyes drop to my breasts at the same time.

"I don't think I need any padding."

Grady graces me with my favorite sight—his blush.

"Trust me, I know that." He clears his throat, but his eyes are glued to my chest. "But you know... nipples."

What the fuck?

The laugh starts as a quiet chuckle, more confused than anything. But the longer what he said sinks in, I can't help the throaty cackle. From the mortified look on his face, I know he doesn't know what the fuck to think either but his eyes shine at my amusement.

"You know," I try to keep my tone steady, but I can barely fill my lungs in between fits of laughter. "I have no fucking idea what you mean."

His goofy smile breaks open, finally showing humor at his own expense. "That didn't make sense." He clears his throat, trying to act serious now.

I furrow my brow, trying to keep my grin at bay. "No, it didn't." Another giggle bubbles out and I slap a hand over my mouth. In a muffled voice I say, "Go on."

"*I meant,*" he huffs, sounding exasperated, as if I'm the one who blurted out *nipples* like I was on a dirty game show. "There isn't much to hide your..." he trails off, suddenly shy.

"Nipples."

"Yes," he clears his throat again. "Especially when they're..." He waves his hand in my direction and my eyes drop to my chest again.

"Hard," I finish for him.

"They sure are," his voice is thicker now.

I pull my shoulders back and answer his initial point. "They're just nipples, Grady." I grab the see-through red one from the pile. "These bras are much more comfortable. And I'm not going to be ashamed of my body."

He swallows and drags his eyes back to my face. "You definitely shouldn't be."

I'm struck speechless at his lustful honesty.

His eyes track the heat rushing across my cheeks and I'm glad he can't see the other parts of my body that are affected by him.

I could take a couple of steps and close the distance. Let whatever is burning between him and I engulf us both in the flames.

But tonight isn't that night.

I don't feel like my head is disconnected from my body anymore. I know I wouldn't regret anything we did by morning. But I would regret not being completely absorbed in every second. Because I know, without a doubt, that it'd be the most intimate first time I've ever experienced with someone. I think about all of the ways Grady is gentle with me. The soft kisses to my nose. When he guides me through a room with his hand on the small of my back. How his breath feels when he whispers in my ear. Those sultry looks he gives me in rooms full of people. But it's more than just that.

It's the desire in his eyes that would burn my whole world down if I let it.

No, Grady wouldn't be gentle with me in this aspect. And I love that.

And I want to remember it.

"Thanks," my voice breathier than I intended. My chest is rising and falling as I attempt to gather my laundry. "I'm going to put this stuff away really quick." I point over my shoulder toward my room.

Grady

It takes Vivi about twenty minutes to put her laundry away. But if I'm being honest, I feel like she's avoiding me. We were having a good night—the best night I've had in years—and I hope I didn't ruin that by pushing her too far.

She's been driving me crazy all night even if she doesn't mean to. She probably has no idea how she's making me feel. Emotionally and physically.

I got so worried that she was uncomfortable that I figured she was going to want me to go home. Sitting on her couch, I start scrolling through Uber, not wanting to risk driving, even hours later. I'm prepared to ask her for my clothes from the dryer and call a car. I'll go home with my tail between my legs and work out a plan to fix the inevitable tension.

When she makes her way back to the living room, she sits down on the couch, not as close as she was sitting before, and looking more nervous.

I'm positive that the dismissal is coming but once again, it doesn't.

She just tucks her feet under my thighs and throws a blanket across both of us. I tentatively place my hand on her knee, and she snuggles deeper into the couch.

"Do you want to watch a movie?"

I nod and hand her the remote from the coffee table.

At some point during *Tinkerbell and the Great Fairy Rescue*—her choice—we abandoned the couch and made a haphazard attempt at a bed with the blankets and pillows she had in the living room. There are more than any sane person would need, but they're all smaller throws.

    We're making it work. And with Vivi laying on the floor next to me, her head on my shoulder, I really don't have any place I'd rather be. Our bodies don't connect anywhere else, but I feel content with what we have going on.

    I lean down to plant a soft kiss on the crown of her head, not able to stop myself from showering her in affection. She hums in appreciation and snuggles a little closer into my side.

    It's sporadic small gestures for now. But when she gives me the go ahead that I so desperately want, I'll show her how I'd worship the ground she walks on for the rest of our lives.

    Everyone thinks I was infatuated with her when we were kids? That's nothing compared to what it would be like now. What I could give her now.

    "I think Tink should give Terence a chance. He's the sweetest cinnamon roll. Just look at how he looks at her!" She points toward the TV.

    This may not come as a shock, but I know quite a bit about Tinkerbell and Pixie Hollow, thanks to my little ladies.

    "I don't think it's obvious to Tinkerbell how he feels about her, though," I say in a soothing voice but I'm trying not to laugh.

    "But it's *so* obvious," she retorts.

    "I know, love." I put my arm around her, finally pulling her body flush to mine. My heart swells when she immediately relaxes against me.

    I know Terence's pain. Wanting a woman who doesn't see your feelings even if you think they're flashing like a neon sign. But a part of me knows that Genevieve sees my intentions clear as day, but she isn't ready. And that's okay. I can be patient with her. I owe her that much.

    But I want to guide her a little closer to being ready.

"Maybe Tink knows but isn't ready to admit her feelings for Terence." She huffs, as if it's a ridiculous suggestion. "And that's okay," I whisper into her ear. "I think that Terence will wait for Tink. No matter how long she needs." I place a kiss on her temple. "I know I would."

Her head turns a fraction of an inch toward me but it's all I need. I grab her chin and turn her mouth the rest of the way.

Our lips meet in a chaste kiss. It isn't frenzied or all-consuming. This one is a quiet promise. One of patience and possibilities.

Chapter Twenty-Two
Vivi

The light through the crack in the curtains is blinding even while my eyes are closed.

I feel a weird mixture of the best sleep I've had in months and grogginess that's threatening to pull me back under.

Who knows when I'll get sleep like this again though?

Slowly, I turn to my other side to hide my eyes from the morning sun.

I bump into the wall, causing me to fall onto my back.

Except my bed isn't against the wall. And it's softer than what I'm currently on. My terracotta satin sheets are a lot lighter than this itchy knit blanket too.

Hesitantly I open one eye and peer around the room, last night slowly coming back to me.

Grady showing up on my door. Grady kissing me and the power going out. Grady and I smoking that joint. Grady and I having fun after we smoked that joint. Grady kissing me again. Grady whispering in my ear and pulling me against him.

The only thing I don't remember is falling asleep out here. I'm almost positive that my plan had been to go to my room at some point.

As I glance at Grady sleeping peacefully next to me, I can't find it in me to care at all. Not only do I feel like I slept on a cloud, the sight of my childhood best friend asleep is one I haven't seen in forever. It's still one of my favorite things ever.

I guess Grady isn't *just* my childhood best friend anymore. If I'm being honest, he hasn't been for a while now. Maybe since the moment Stella and Daisy marched into my classroom.

It's been a long time since I've stepped into this world of dating and even longer since I allowed myself to stay the whole night with a man, so I don't really know what comes next. But I don't want it to end.

I close my eyes and move closer to Grady's chest. He's wearing the shirt I let him borrow but I really wish he had taken it off at some point. From what I've been able to see through his clothes—muscular arms, thick thighs and even his ass looks like he's still playing catcher on a daily basis—I bet he's toned and gorgeous underneath.

He starts to shift around me, and I realize that I'm using one of his arms as a pillow. My heart breaks a little as his arm moves under my neck but I lift my head so he can pull it out.

My body and nerves melt as soon as he scoots his arm further under my neck and wraps his other arm around my waist, pulling me close. He falls forward a little, now half laying on me and tangling our legs into a knot I never want to unravel.

I want to remember the feel of his body wrapped around me and the pressure of his weight over me. It's like the warmest anxiety blanket not even money could buy.

I let one of my arms wrap around him and the other settles between us, twisted into his shirt to keep him close.

It doesn't take long until the comfort of his protective body lulls me back into a deep slumber.

Instead of the harsh light from outside, this time I wake up to a hand lightly brushing through my hair.

My eyes crack open slowly as I'm brought back into consciousness. The first thing I note is that Grady and I are in the same intertwined mess, but I'm lying on him now. Practically straddling him.

I try to slip off of his chest but his hand falls from my hair to my back, stopping me.

He presses a soft kiss to my forehead and murmurs against my skin, "Good morning, love."

"Good morning."

He nods, like he's confirming something to himself he already knew. "I like how you sound in the morning."

"Only in the morning?" I jokingly chastise him.

"No, all the time. But especially right now. It isn't my favorite but it's in the top three, easily."

I tilt my head to get a better look at his face. "What are your top two?"

He doesn't think about it, just says, "My second favorite is the little squeal you make when someone tells you good news or you see something you like. Like the new book in that series when we were at Brighter Daze a few weeks ago."

I didn't think he was paying that much attention when I found the new inventory Lexi was bringing out. But of course he did. I'm starting to accept that Grady's just as trapped in this magnetic force between us as I am.

"And my favorite," he continues on, "is that breathy cackling laugh. It's your least used but most genuine one." I pull myself closer to him. "I can't tell you how happy I was the first time I heard it again."

I don't need him to tell me, I already had an idea. Even when we were kids, my witchy and obnoxious laugh was one of the few things Grady allowed himself to shower in adoration openly.

"Thanks for last night," I breathe.

"I had fun."

We just sit there staring at each other for a moment, neither of us ready to pop the bubble we've created on my living room floor.

"Can I come back tonight?" He looks a little shocked by his own request and tries to save face, which is equally funny and infuriating. "I mean, there might be another thunderstorm, you know. That's what the weather report said this week."

"Yes, Grady, you can come back tonight." I take a steady breath, trying to emit more confidence than he currently is. "In fact, I would love that."

"Me too." He breaks out into one of the most beautiful grins I've ever seen. "Okay, cool. Cool cool. I have to run home super quick but… what time should I come back?"

I chuckle at his eagerness. "Whenever. I have to go to the grocery store, but I can go now if you want to give me a few hours."

"I can go with you. Give me two hours and I'll be back with breakfast."

"Yeah?" He nods and kisses my nose. "That sounds perfect. We can cook tonight then."

The thought of doing something domestic with Grady is a lot more appealing than it's ever been with anyone—more than I ever thought it could be.

I start to push off his chest, but Grady quickly pulls me back down. I fall against his chest at the same moment his other hand gathers my tangled hair at the nape of my neck.

I try to squirm away, but his arms are like a vice. "I have morning breath. It's too soon for that. It will *always* be too soon for that."

"Mmm, no. Sorry, don't care." I begrudgingly relax against him as he murmurs against my lips, "Anytime I wake up next to you, I expect a kiss first thing. Understand?"

The demand in his voice is the sexiest thing I've ever heard. I couldn't say no if I wanted to. I nod and place a soft kiss on his lips.

"I need more than that, love." His hand tightens in my hair.

I lean into him, giving him the control and time to deepen the kiss.

He takes and takes until he's satisfied, making sure to give back just as much.

When his grip loosens in my hair, I place one final kiss on his scruffy jaw before pushing off of him to start *our* day.

Chapter Twenty-Three
Grady

As I pull into Vivi's driveway, I can't help but smile down at my passenger seat.

I promised her that I would bring breakfast, so I stopped at The Loop to grab breakfast sandwiches and parfaits from Morning Munch. But that wasn't it.

Before I left the house, I FaceTimed the girls and Arielle took them to get doughnuts and chocolate milk for breakfast which reminded me of last night when Vivi said that doughnuts were her *favorite dessert ever.* She was half feral when she was describing all the different flavors Calypso makes on Saturdays.

I was pretty sure she said doughnuts on Saturdays and strudels on Sundays. I decided to take the chance.

Lexi wasn't surprised at all when she saw me order half a dozen. I ordered three of the flavors I remembered Vivi mentioned—key lime, strawberry shortcake, and rocky road—and took a chance on three that practically had my mouth watering. Fruity pebbles, mixed berry, and German chocolate. As Calypso was wrapping up the pastries, thinking nothing out of the ordinary, Lexi came up. She ordered Vivi's favorite drink for me—on the house and to-go.

She hopped up on the counter, looking smug as hell.

It took Calypso a solid ten seconds to stop glancing between us. Once she picked her jaw off the floor and lowered her eyebrows from the ceiling, she made me the dirty chai with oat milk. I figured there was nothing stopping me now, so I ordered a cappuccino and gathered the items. Before I could turn away, Lexi cleared her throat.

When I turned back to her, I raised my brows in question.

"You know who loves fresh flowers on weekend mornings?"

Calypso gave me an encouraging grin and quick nod, but thankfully didn't push further.

Even if I didn't know for a fact that Calypso and Lexi would be expecting to see the flowers, I would've stopped by Sunday Blooms anyway. I want to give Genevieve all the best mornings. Every day. Forever. Whatever she's willing to give me.

That's how I ended up with an array of options for her this morning, all wrapped into a plastic bag next to the coffees and marigold bouquet.

I'm taking a chance on the duffel bag full of clothes in the backseat. I don't want to assume anything, and she had only asked me to come back. But I *really* hope that she wants me to stay the night again.

I'd happily sleep on her living room floor by myself with her tucked into her own bed. Anything to just be near her.

I consider leaving it in my Jeep but figure we were working our way toward putting it all on the table. No more games, no more secrets. And sure, we're still working on breaching some subjects, but I can let her know that I want to be with her tonight.

She opens the door and looks more gorgeous than anyone should have any right to. My hands are full but that doesn't stop me from taking a long minute to soak in the sight of her.

Her hair is wet, slowly drying into her natural waves. She has minimal make-up on, most of it used to bring the green out in her eyes. Except for the dusty pink lipstick. It's just natural enough to resemble a bratty pout. I'd love nothing more than to kiss it off her.

Her outfit is what's really about to bring me to my knees right here, right now.

She's wearing a light green button-down sweater and short set. The material looks light and soft. It hugs her curves in all of the right places but is just loose enough that I could easily slip my hands around all of my favorite spots. She has it unbuttoned enough to see a white lacy bra underneath—one I now recognize.

She looks cozy and adorable but somehow sexy and tempting as hell. Just looking at her has me half hard on her front porch.

"I love you in green," I tell her in a husky voice.

She gives me a beaming smile. "Thanks, it's my favorite. What can I help with?" She motions toward all the things I'm balancing.

"Oh, uh." I try to hand her the bag of food, but the coffees are blocking it, so she goes for the duffel bag instead.

"Wow, I can't wait to see what Grady Miller wears to bed," she teases.

I guess that answers my question about staying the night.

She sets my bag down by her couch.

And that answers the question about where I'll be sleeping.

I'm okay with that. Even if my cock would like to fall asleep buried deep in her.

"Nothing special compared to what you wear to bed." I've been thinking about her little silky set all day. The lilac color against her milky skin. The way the soft fabric wrapped around her hips and left just enough cleavage to tease me all night.

She shrugs and meets me at the island. "I'll be the judge of that. What do we have here? Quite the breakfast spread."

"You said you love doughnuts. And Lexi wouldn't let me leave without getting your *daily fuel*." I glance up to see how she reacts to the fact that Lexi brought up that we're together in front of her sister.

She doesn't seem put off by it. Instead, she has a small smile while she reaches for her drink. "Ah, one of the reasons I decided to keep her around."

I want to ask about that. *Them*. It's been killing me. But it's early in the day and I want to enjoy it.

So, I pick up the breakfast sandwiches while she inspects the doughnut flavors. "Bacon and avocado or sausage and hashbrowns?"

"Bacon and avocado, please." She sticks out her hand without looking up. I grin at her demanding nature.

I hand her the sandwich and tell her about the girls' trip to Seattle. She tells me about the yearbook's progress. And it doesn't only feel easy, but it feels *right*.

At some point, the cats make their way in for breakfast. Vivi's still eating and points me in the direction of their food rather than getting up. All I can do is exactly as she says and wish that all of my mornings will be spent getting bossed around by her.

That evening, Vivi and I are in her sunroom again. This time we're eating homemade pizza and sharing a variety pack of Clear Horizons ciders.

We spent the afternoon at the grocery store and then we took a nap on a slightly more comfortable floor bed. While we were cooking dinner, she mentioned an air mattress in her garage that I could use later. No mention of where she would be sleeping, and I didn't ask.

We've been working our way through the different cider flavors—starting with watermelon—and discussing the many differences between teaching second grade versus eleventh grade history.

"High school kids don't randomly throw up," Vivi muses.

"Kids do that?"

She looks at me accusingly. "You have children, how don't you know that? And don't you remember in like, first to third grade there was that one kid throwing up once a month?"

"The girls only throw up when they're sick. It's rare though. And kind of. Not *that* often though."

"Just last week, two kids threw up." She gives me a pointed look. "Neither had a fever or a cold. It wasn't food poisoning. One puked on their desk during reading hour and the other made it to the trash can ten minutes after getting dropped off after a doctor's appointment."

I click my tongue. "His mom needs a new doctor."

"That's what I said. But tell me what beats *that.*"

I grimace and sit up a little straighter. Looking her straight in the eye I say, "I'm sure you've *never* overhead your students talking about their very... colorful sex lives."

"Oh no. No, no, nooo." She covers her face and groans in discomfort. "I would've *never* considered that!"

"Yeah, well—"

The door to the sunroom opens and Lexi walks in. She's holding a plate with two slices of pizza and a blueberry cider. She plops down in a chair like this is her daily routine. It might very well be.

"What are we talking about?"

"The sex lives of Grady's students," Vivi says in fake outrage.

"Ew, don't be a pervert, Grady. It isn't a good look on you," Lexi chastises.

"I didn't realize being a pervert was a good look on anyone," I shrug. She rolls her eyes, but I can see a smile playing on her lips.

"We were talking about who has it harder because our work problems are so different, you know?" Vivi cuts in.

Lexi doesn't even think about it. "Oh, high school for sure. Don't you remember what we were like? At least in elementary we were cute and goofy and not having sex."

"But *puke.* Projectile vomiting." Now Vivi's actually outraged that no one sees her side.

"Nope. Doesn't beat horny teens. Sorry, babe." Lexi suddenly sits up a little straighter, sniffing the air like a bloodhound on a scent. "Why does it smell like pot in here?"

Chapter Twenty-Four
Vivi

Grady and I are sitting like two kids in the principal's office—another adolescent experience we missed out on together.

"You promised." Lexi points an accusing finger at me.

I cringe in response. "I know. It wasn't planned. I completely forgot Asher left it in there."

"I didn't forget," Lexi snaps, pointing at her chest. She finally turns her attention and finger toward Grady. "And *you*. I hope you had fun. Vivi's one of the funniest people to get high with. You better know how lucky you are."

The handful of times that Lexi and I smoked together were always fun, but I've almost always felt somewhat paranoid at some point, no matter who I was with. It has happened with Lexi, Asher, and Calypso. Even when I was with all three of them. After the giggles and random thoughts, the worry and dread always came next. It's a major reason why I don't smoke pot—and you know, *my job.*

Except for last night.

I felt comfortable and content with Grady. I felt *safe* with him. In a way I don't think I ever have with anyone else.

"Do you remember the first time we smoked together?"

"Yes," I say in a flat voice. "I had only been living there for like a week, you fucking twat." Lexi's booming laugh is her only response. I turn toward Grady and give him an exasperated shake of the head. "It was a week after I moved into Lexi's studio apartment. We got way too high, and I just wanted to eat my Jell-O cup in peace, but this bitch wouldn't give me a spoon."

"She forgot where they were and was on the verge of a meltdown." She chuckles at the memory. "I was laughing too hard to offer any sort of help."

"Do you know how hard it is to eat a Jell-O cup without a spoon?" A few giggles pop out at the memory, but I bite my lips to hold together my annoyed demeanor.

His face is lit up with amusement and I hate how much I love that goofy grin.

"That was the night I decided *for sure* that I would keep my little stray," Lexi says in a genuinely affectionate voice.

"Not the first night? When we got drunk? We really let each other have it."

"Nope. Too much crying." She looks at Grady and points at herself. "Not me. I don't cry."

Rolling my eyes, I ask, "How about when you brought your boy toy Troy to force me out of my dorm?"

Grady's eyebrows raise in question, but he doesn't stop our banter.

"No, I wasn't one hundred percent yet. I just knew you couldn't stay *there.*"

"Huh." I sit back and consider that. "That's fair. I was sure I wanted to stay after we got drunk." Lexi shrugs me off and I smile in response. Not saying it never happens, but it's rare that Lexi and I hurt each other's feelings anymore.

Grady doesn't look as convinced of our good standings.

He clears his throat and waits for both sets of eyes to fall on him. "I have some questions."

I suck in my cheeks, looking at Lexi with a raised brow. *Knew this was coming.*

Lexi glances at me then back to Grady with a shrug. "We figured you might at some point."

"Go ahead and ask, Grady." I look at his face, but I can't get myself to meet his eye. Instead, I stare at his flawlessly proportioned nose, letting my eyes skim over the light sprinkling of hair along his jaw. It was trimmed when he came back with breakfast, but I can tell by morning it'll be back to my favorite scruffy length.

Looking back at Lexi, I can't help but think about the last ten years we've spent together. Even though it's strictly platonic between us, I've never been more committed to anyone like I've been to Lexi—not even my ex-fiancé.

I love her so fucking much but I hate that the beginning of our friendship is tangled up in so much bullshit. And I don't even mean *our* bullshit.

A decade later, I still hate talking about this. I hate the insecurities it brings up and the numb feeling in my bones. I hate the memories I have with Brody and Molly and the memories from the weeks after without either of them.

It doesn't matter that I wasn't sure if I wanted to marry Brody. Or that I was starting to feel the shift in my friendship with Molly. Or that I don't miss them at all.

It was the worst betrayal I've ever experienced.

"I mean," he chuckles awkwardly, "how did you two become friends?"

I bite my cheek and look down at my hands twisting in my lap. I can feel both of their eyes on me, but it doesn't stop the bone-deep chill that creeps in. I concentrate on calming my nerves before the anxiety causes me to start shaking or hyperventilate.

Somehow this is the worst part—that ten years later, what they did still has this power over my nervous system. I can go months without thinking about that night but as soon as I do, my body can't decipher what's in the past and what's in the present.

Grady tentatively wraps his strong hand around the base of my neck, lightly running his thumb along where the nape of my neck meets my hair. I glance up at Lexi and she's giving me a small smile. Their encouragement and support give me strength to open this wound.

After a few seconds I start, "I'm sure you know that Brody proposed to me a few weeks after graduation." He nods. I shrug. "Molly and I were already locked into a dorm, and I don't know. It felt better than moving in with him. I told Brody I wanted a long engagement, the three of us went to college and that was that, so it seemed."

"Ah," Lexi gives him a Cheshire smile. "And then I came along."

I can't stop myself from chuckling as I flip through the mental catalog of my friendship with her.

"I was sitting in my first Ethics and Humanity lecture. It was a large class, with a few hundred people, and there were a few seats left but I knew as soon as we made eye contact that Lexi was going to come sit next to me. Misery loves company, and all that, you know?"

"And just like that? You were friends?" He doesn't give either of us a chance to clarify before adding, "I remember you two tackling each other during the spirit week powderpuff game. And you were on the *same* team. Not to mention the spelling bee—"

"Tropical was a hard word, dammit," Lexi mutters to herself, causing me to laugh.

"It's hard to believe that you could sweep it under the rug so easily," Grady continues.

"God, no," Lexi chimes in. "We were stubborn little shits. We sat next to each other for about two months without saying a word."

"She missed a week of lectures and had to make the hardest choice: ask me for my impeccable notes or a stranger for their mediocre ones."

"Ethics are stupid, and I had a C in the class. I couldn't take the chance." Lexi rolls her eyes.

I laugh and turn back to Grady. "Asking for notes slowly turned into talking about assignments and studying together at the coffeehouse. The study sessions turned into talking about a lot more than our classes. It was a slow progression. We were both reluctant for a while, to say the least. Lexi was struggling in the class, and I was having a hard time with my English class. It was Rhetoric of Film Making."

"She barely even knew who Tim Burton was."

I roll my eyes. "I don't pay attention to those things. You couldn't even ask me who my top Spotify artist is."

"Taylor Swift," Grady and Lexi say at the same time.

"Whatever," I mutter. "We agreed to have an all-night cram session together and help each other. I hadn't planned on going back to my dorm." My stomach drops at the memory. "I forgot something, who knows what. But I went back on my way off campus. It was *my* dorm room," my voice carries a hint of anger. Well-deserved anger. "So, I walked in. On Molly straddling some guy. She was wearing a pair of underwear we had gotten at the semi-annual sale together the weekend before." I always remember that detail for some reason. Like the fact that she wore our matching pair of panties makes the offense that much worse. I let out a bitter laugh. "And that guy just so happened to be Brody." I shake my head as my stomach roils at the mental image.

Grady is quiet for a moment, but I can feel his eyes on me. "What happened?"

"Nothing that night. I was in shock, honestly. They weren't really going at it yet, but I left them to it. I didn't even grab whatever I needed. I just... I turned around and walked out. Neither one of them came after me. Neither one called me to explain what the fuck was happening. They just let me leave. So, I went to Lexi's—can't even remember how I got there but I didn't have anywhere else to go." He gives my neck a little squeeze.

And that's the most embarrassing part of it all. The two people who had been in my life the longest at that point didn't give a single fuck about breaking my heart. I don't doubt that they finished what they were doing.

"She knew immediately that something was up," I give my best friend a wry grin. "I guess after years of being the cause of each other's misery, it only made sense that we'd be able to recognize it."

"They never said anything to you?" Grady's voice is dripping in anger.

"Not that night. Molly was waiting for me in the dorm the next morning, but I had to get to my Ethics final. Brody was waiting for me in the courtyard afterward and..." I can't help the laugh that bubbles out of me.

"I threw my much-needed coffee at him," Lexi says in a way that makes me believe that it might be one of her favorite moments. It's definitely one of mine.

"You... threw your coffee at him?" Grady looks torn between terror and admiration.

"Fuck yeah I did." She raises her can in a salute.

"She didn't just *throw her coffee on him*. She ripped off the lid and chucked it at him from five feet away." Laughing, I relax a little.

"That's... amazing." He chuckles at the thought and Lexi just smiles smugly from her chair across from us.

"It was," I agree. "The only reason she didn't get arrested, or something, was because of the two football players who were walking out behind us and heard me tell him I didn't want to talk at least five times before she threw it. But they did eventually try to talk to me." I take a deep breath and Grady hooks his foot around the leg of my chair, pulling me closer to him. "They said that they bonded over the fact that they felt *'left behind'* with my growing friendship with Lexi." She bows in her seat. "And they couldn't forgive her for all of the *'horrible things she did to me.'* So, they did something way worse than she ever did. And blamed me."

"And me, by association." Lexi looks way too happy about it.

I don't bother to go into further details with Grady. Not tonight.

I don't want to tell him how I cried so hard that I threw up for hours. Or that Lexi had to retake the course because I couldn't pull it together to tutor her. The only reason I passed my English course was because we had to write an essay instead of taking an exam, and Lexi finished it for me that night after I eventually fell asleep. Or how we overheard Molly at a party talking about how *'sometimes you make a sacrifice to get what you want in the long run.'* Ten fucking years of friendship only to be sacrificed for a boy who couldn't stop partying enough to make it to the MLB. Or the weight I lost and the food I stopped eating because Brody said it was my fault that he was more attracted to other women, and any boy would feel the same. I quickly learned that he was wrong, and those *men* could get me off better than he ever did. Or how I probably would've taken Brody back simply for the fact that I was terrified of being alone and unloved, even if that's exactly what I was in my relationship anyway. I was pathetic, and I don't need to confirm something Grady already knows.

Lexi suddenly sits up, pulling me out of my spiraling thoughts. "What time is it?"

"Um." I pull out my phone. "Almost seven."

"Ugh," Lexi draws out and slouches in her chair. "I have to get ready. I've another date tonight."

"Another?" Grady asks.

"She went out last night," I reply.

"Don't even remind me of the train wreck that was last night."

"Ooh, do tell!" I shouldn't get so much entertainment out of the garbage fire that is Lexi's dating life but when she's constantly meeting the worst or weirdest people, it's hard not to. And Lexi isn't desperate. She's gorgeous and intelligent and successful. She fucking knows all of that. She thinks it's just as comical as the rest of us.

Grady looks skeptical but he has no idea the type of people Lexi has met on her journey to fuck anyone willing in the San Diego area.

"We called his mom," she says with a straight face.

"What?" The word comes out through my chuckles of anticipation.

"What?" Grady asks at the same time, clearly suddenly invested.

Slowly she says, "We called his mom." She cringes. "Almost immediately after we fucked—which was unfortunately so good. And he had a bedframe, four pillows *and* a shower curtain."

"What kind of people are you dating?" Grady asks but we don't bother responding. He obviously has no idea how bleak the dating world is if we're to believe I'm the first woman since his divorce.

"He pulled out, said how amazing it was, threw the condom away and then pulled his phone out. I didn't even have pants on, but I know a dismissal when I see one."

"He wasn't dismissing you, was he?" I try to hide my laughter behind my hand, but it spills through my fingers all the same.

"No, he didn't dismiss me. He FaceTimed his mom to introduce her to the girl he's dating now." I can't fight it anymore. Lexi's misery washed the last bit of discomfort I was feeling from the earlier conversation, and she knows me well enough to know I needed the deflection. "I left while she was in the middle of telling him their plans for the holidays. I think she saw my bare ass, but I had to get out of there and block him."

"And this is exactly why we made the rule that you would *not* be bringing dates back here."

"Yeah, good rule. Anyway, I'm going on a date with the owner of that little fruit stand you love at the farmer's market."

"Wait, the girl with the agua fresca?" I go practically feral for it every time we make it to the market in La Jolla. Even just thinking about it has my mouth watering. "Please, *please* let it be love, Lexi. I'm begging you."

Lexi winks, "You know I love that. Get on your knees." I kick her, laughing. To Grady she adds, "Just kidding, G. But *you* should make her beg. I promise she will."

I scoff but to my horror Grady sits back in his chair looking smug as hell. "Noted." He holds his can up to cheers her.

Ugh, I would though. I so fucking would.

With that, she stands from her chair and makes her way to the door. Before she leaves us in my small sunroom, she looks over her shoulder with a sickly-sweet smile. "Don't do anything I wouldn't do."

Once the door closes Grady looks at me with uncertainty. "I'm getting the idea that there isn't much Lexi wouldn't do."

I love her crazy ass but he's right. She isn't leaving us with a lot of rules tonight.

Chapter Twenty-Five
Vivi

I've been laying in the dark for who knows how long. After Grady dozed off, I figured it was time for me to go to sleep too. Except I couldn't sleep, and I didn't think going to my own room would help the problem. It probably would've only made it worse.

Instead, I've been laying on the air mattress, staring at the ceiling. My mind has been ping-ponging between different thoughts without any sort of coherent direction. But it keeps coming back to that one year when it was storming on the last day of school, so Tim set us up in their living room. We were still in elementary school, far too young to even begin to understand romantic feelings, but it was the one, and only, sleepover Grady and I got to have alone. Not including the times we snuck into each other's rooms. We never meant to stay the night together those times.

Since we laid down tonight, we've stayed close with our sides touching while we watched TV, but neither one of us crossed that line, despite everything.

Another thing my mind keeps going to: did that last conversation change something between us? Rationally, I know that seems crazy. He's been so open about everything that it seems unlikely that he'd be swayed by my own complex history.

That doesn't calm my insecurities though. The ones that tell me I'm too much. My history is too convoluted. That no matter what, I'll never be loved in the way I've spent my life dreaming. In the way I grew up watching Tim love Selena. That not even Grady could want me, despite all the broken pieces.

And I don't think I could stand to lose Grady again. Not now.

Maybe I haven't fully confessed my feelings toward him, but we crossed a line tonight. I put my trust in him and if he pulls away now? I'll never recover this time.

"What are you thinking about?"

I turn my head toward his voice. "Aren't you sleeping?"

"I was. Your thoughts were too loud, they woke me up." I can hear more than see the playful smirk gracing his face.

"You tell me what they're saying then."

"It sounded like gibberish."

I chuckle quietly. "Yeah, that's pretty much what it's like all the time."

He pauses for a few seconds. "Can I hold you?"

"Yes," I whisper, pulling in close to him. "You don't have to ask."

He wraps his strong arms around me, instantly making me feel safe. "I do. I don't want to push you too far after everything this weekend. Those weren't my intentions when I showed up this morning."

I smile even though he can't see it. "I know that. Quite the difference from last night, huh?"

"Yeah," he mutters but I can feel him smiling against my forehead. "Is that a bad thing though?"

I consider this, letting my hand trail up to his jaw and run my fingers through the short hair there. "No, not bad. Probably good, right?"

"Probably, yes. Do you think you can sleep now?" He kisses my nose.

I turn around, spooning him. "If you hold me like this, then yes. I think I can fall asleep."

It isn't lost on me that we could go to my bedroom and sleep on an actual mattress. But I'm not ready for... that. That sort of vulnerability.

Grady hasn't asked yet. He hasn't really pushed me at all. He's been patient in a way that only Grady ever has been with me. He's taken all of the *next steps* but waits until I make it pretty clear that's what I want.

But right now, in his arms, I want more. I want *him*.

He says that he'll be here as long as I want but he's wrong.

I'm at his mercy whether he knows it or not.

I want all of him even if I'm too scared to ask for it.

But tonight?

Tonight, I'll take a little more.

I slide backwards, straight into his chest and pull his arm tighter around me.

"Comfy?" he asks in a husky voice.

"Hmm, getting there." His chuckle turns into a tortured groan as I settle my ass along the top of his thighs. *Slowly* I scoot up just enough to settle my bottom along his half-mast cock, feeling him harden against me.

His hand clamps down on my waist. "Genevieve," he warns.

"I'm getting comfortable," I retort in a breathy whisper.

"Okay," he resigns skeptically.

I take in his amber scent, noticing a hint of driftwood, and nuzzle into his warmth, building the nerve to kick my leg over his waist. The motion pulls me back into his hardness again. A moan escapes out of me at the same time I hear him groan against my neck.

"There's no way you're comfortable," Grady places a kiss on my neck, squeezing my soft thigh.

Fuck, I want him to move his hand up.

No, need. I *need* him to touch me.

I nod. "This is what I want, Grady." I punctuate my point with a roll of my hips.

A sharp sting on my shoulder makes me yelp. Grady's teeth press down further before letting go and I whimper at the absence of the pain.

"I thought you were just teasing me when you changed into your *pajamas*." He runs his hand up my thigh, along my silk shorts that flutter around the tops of my thighs and a tank top that falls just a little too low on my cleavage. They're similar to what I wore last night… if you cut more than half the fabric off. "I need you to tell me what you want. We're only going as far as you want."

Over my shoulder I whisper, "What do you want?"

"Everything. All of you. *Finally*," he says, like a man coming off a life-long fast. "But I'm not in a rush, Genevieve."

Holy fuck. The sound of my name, in that voice, while he's actually wrapped around me is better than I could have ever dreamed.

"I want you to touch me." I tentatively grab his other hand that's wrapped around my shoulder and slip it under my shirt.

His hand slips down to my nipple, and he rolls the tight bud between his fingers with a gentle reverence.

The very next second I'm gasping and rolling my hips again as he pinches *hard*.

The confidence in his movements leave no room for my doubts. I feed off of his surety and use my leg to better position him while I grind my ass against him.

Maybe I should be embarrassed by my desperate panting and how close I already am to a climax, but I'm lost in the euphoria that is Grady's hands on me.

"What else?"

I shake my head, words beyond my mental functions right now.

"Show me what you want, Genevieve."

I grab the hand still gripping my thigh and move it to my center, rubbing his fingers over the fabric.

Grady slips out of my hold and moves my hand to the back of his neck. "Don't move from here," he says, a note of authority in his voice, but I don't like when other people make the rules.

"I want to touch you," I whine as I begin to slide my hand back down, but he grabs it, roughly setting it back on his neck.

"I don't care about what you want anymore. I'm going to give you what you need." I want to roll my eyes at his arrogance but if anyone can figure out what it is that I need, it would be Grady.

With an exasperated huff I tighten my hold on his neck.

"Good girl." His teeth nip my ear lobe. "I'm in control of your body right now, do you understand me?" I shakily nod. "Exactly like that, Genevieve. I want to fucking devour you but only if you allow me."

That sounds like the most delightful form of torture.

I nod and pull his mouth to mine. Against his lips I plead, "Touch me. Please, Grady. I *need* to know what your fingers feel like inside me."

He huskily grunts in affirmation and slips his hand into my shorts. I never sleep in panties, so there's nothing else between his skin and mine. His fingers stop at my clit on their descent.

When he makes a few swipes along the bundle of nerves, I cry out in bliss and agony.

"Just let me take care of you, baby." I pull his mouth to the spot at the base of my neck, relishing in his kisses. "That's all I need."

Grady bites down *harder* as he pinches my clit. It hurts but only in the most delicious of ways. I'm still pulsing from it when he slips a finger into me.

His deep groan is the perfect counterpart to my needy moan.

"You're soaked, baby. I can't believe this is all for me." His finger moves in and out, falling into rhythm with my hips still rolling against him. "Have you touched yourself to the thought of me before?"

"Yes," I admit in a breathy whisper. "*Oh god, yes.*"

I don't bother to clarify that the first time I climaxed to the thought of him was years ago—junior year of high school when I saw teenage Grady without his shirt, saltwater dripping down his chest as he shook the excess out of his hair. It was the star of all of young Vivi's wet dreams. And more than a few times his scruff and mouth between my legs have been on my mind in the last two and a half months.

"And how were those fantasies?" His voice is gravelly, but the smug tone is impossible to miss.

Whimpering, I try to pull myself together long enough to give him what he wants. Maybe what *he* needs. "Good but nothing compared to this," I confess.

Grady must like my answer.

His control snaps further. With his finger driving inside me and thumb against my clit, his other hand palms my breasts. Hard and slow. Spending time on soothing the swollen bud after playing roughly with it.

Grady slips a second finger into me, and I lose control of my body.

All I know is that I feel full just from his hands and I still want *more.*

I pull his mouth to mine and demand entrance. He grants me what I want and matches me stroke for stroke, nip for nip. My hips begin to move more frantically, my ass bouncing on his thick length, that I desperately wish I could get my hands on. Or my mouth.

The movement makes my breasts and belly jiggle. Grady pulls away from our kiss as his hand tightens on one of my breasts. His dark eyes slide along my torso, revealed at some point during all of this. I want to cover up or pull him back to my mouth, anything to get his eyes off the soft rolls. But he refuses.

When I try to pull him back to my mouth, his grip on me tightens to the point of near pain, never leaving that gray area of pleasurable. "I want to look at you."

The lust in his eyes and his ragged breaths tell me everything I need to know. At that moment, I let all of my inhibitions truly go.

"Grady," I whine.

"You're so goddamn gorgeous, Genevieve. There are no words for it." He begins to roll his hips, pressing his cock against me at the same pace his fingers fuck me. "Ethereal. *Radiating.* Still doesn't do you justice."

No one has ever used those words to describe me. Nothing even close to that sort of reverence has been spoken about me before.

And it's just enough to bring me to the edge of my climax.

My moans and whimpers turn into silent screams as Grady does exactly what he said he would: he takes control of my body and gives me exactly what I need.

"That's it, baby. This perfect pussy is squeezing my fingers so goddamn hard." I'm *right there,* ready to come from his words alone. "Just imagine what it's going to feel like when it's my cock filling you."

"Grady," I plead, begging him to push me off the cliff.

He pumps his fingers in and out of me, faster, harder. His teeth and lips and tongue leave marks anywhere he can reach. His other hand tugs on my nipple.

But it's Grady's husky demand, "Be a good girl and come on my fingers, Genevieve," that causes my release to wash over me like a tsunami.

I grab his wrist, not letting him pull away until I ride out this wave of pleasure to the very end. It pulls me down until it's almost too much but at the same moment, I hope it goes on forever.

"I'm not going anywhere," Grady groans into my neck, still rubbing his cock against my ass.

It's all too much—a level of ecstasy I've never met before—but more than anything it feels *right*.

As I come down from the euphoric high, Grady's movements become more frantic, his breathing even more ragged. My body is shaking from the best orgasm I've *ever* experienced but that doesn't stop Grady as he continues to grind into me. His fingers slip out of my throbbing center, and he puts all of his attention on my sensitive clit—rubbing and pinching at the perfect speed to bring me to another climax without pushing me too far.

Except this time when I come from Grady's fingers, his body goes rigid against mine and he lets out the sexiest sound I've ever heard. Deep, guttural, *primal*.

I relax into his body and watch his hand slide out of my shorts and up to his mouth. "*Fucking perfect,*" he groans as he sucks my arousal off of his dexterous fingers. When he notices me watching him, his hooded eyes drop to my mouth. "Want a taste?"

I nod my head, my lips parted for him.

He slips his still wet thumb into my mouth, and on instinct I suck.

"Taste what I do to you." He slips his thumb a little bit deeper, and I catch it between my teeth.

When he pulls his hand back, we stare at each other for a long moment. There's no need for words at this moment. What Grady and I just shared feels long overdue yet like a dream I'm scared to wake up from.

I sheepishly ask, "Did you... uhm..." I don't want to embarrass him, but I also want to make sure that he found his pleasure tonight.

He gives me a small, sleepy smile. "Yes, Genevieve. Finger-fucking you made me come in my pants like a teenage boy. Which is fitting, considering you were the star of teenage Grady's spank bank."

A disbelieving laugh slips out. "Yeah, okay," I say as I pull him tighter around me.

"I'm serious," he chuckles. "The things I've dreamed about doing with you, *to you*, are filthy."

"Just like your mouth, apparently," I tease but the memories of a few minutes ago sends another jolt of wet heat straight to my core.

"You bring out a different side in me," he whispers while gently brushing a lock of hair behind my ear. I like the idea that only I've ever brought this disciplined man to his breaking point. That his dirty words and possessive arousal are *mine*.

I attempt to turnaround, ready to strip and straddle him right here, but he gently settles me on the floor next to him and hovers above me. I watch his silhouette through the dark, confused for only a second before he places a soft kiss on my cheek.

"We are going to bed now. Like I said, I'm in no rush with you, Viv. I'm going to drag this out until you're as addicted to me as I am to you." *Too late.* Grady already feels like my own personal form of heroin. "But I promise you can have my cock however you want next time."

Content with his promise, I snuggle in for the night, the high of my climax replaced with satisfied exhaustion. "In my mouth is preferable," I murmur.

His tortured groan makes me laugh. He pushes to stand and tells me he'll be right back. With the light of his phone, he makes his way to the bathroom. There's some rummaging around and the faint sound of the water running. A small smile plays at my lips because I can guess what he's doing. It's only confirmed when he comes back out, places what I assume is his underwear in his bag, and crawls back into our makeshift bed.

Without a word, he pulls the blanket back and quietly asks, "May I?" I nod, still doing my best to watch through the dark. He slides the warm, damp towel up my loose shorts, but this time, he's cleaning the wetness that lingers. It's the perfect amount of affection to contrast his earlier possessiveness.

And I want more of it.

Finally, after he's done getting both of us ready for bed, he crawls back into the space next to me. Without a moment of hesitation, he slips one arm under my head and the other around my waist, holding me close. Holding me like he never wants to go even a day without this again.

I kiss the bicep I'm using as a pillow and close my eyes. I drift off to sleep surrounded by Grady's warmth, with the pleasant soreness between my legs and his fingers lightly running against my neck like a silent lullaby.

Chapter Twenty-Six

Grady

I'm helping Knox and Lucas clean up after dinner as the kids play on their new trampoline. It's the least I can do after they invited the three of us over and cooked a homemade lasagna. Knox swears that he doesn't cook, he only drinks. The cooking is all Lucas.

It surprised me at first, but I really don't know Lucas. He grew up in Amada Beach and was in Calypso's grade, but they were never friends growing up. So, everything I do know about him has come from Knox, who is a lovesick husband and gushes about him constantly. It's adorable and nauseating. Mostly because I don't think Arielle and I were *ever* like that. Not even when we were newly dating, before my ACL tear, before Stella was born, after the girls were born. Never.

The only other times I've seen people this in love are with my parents and Blake and Adrian.

It's a feeling I've always wanted for myself, and maybe that was another reason why I kept Arielle away from my family. Visiting always made it glaringly obvious that my marriage was not like that at all.

Not for the first time, or even the hundredth time, I think about how my dad said he *knew* that Adrian was the man for his daughter. And how my dad has said the same thing about someone for me. Someone that I didn't marry.

"When is your dad going to step down?" I hear Knox ask Lucas by the sink. I'm wiping off the table but turn around at the news that Stanley's planning on leaving his companies. Lucas's dad is the owner of the construction company and hardware store in Amada Beach. It's been a staple to the community before my family even moved here.

"Early next fall, most likely," Lucas replies easily.

"Why is Stanley retiring?" He hasn't been on job sites in years, from what my parents have said. He mostly does the administration work and runs the store now.

"It's just time," Lucas shrugs. "My mom is getting ready to leave the practice in a few years too. My sister and I are both working there now. It's always been the plan for us to take over when she retires—if we wanted to. We do," he chuckles. Lucas's sister, Brooke, is four years older than him and Calypso if I remember correctly.

"What about your dad's businesses then?"

"There was never really a plan or any pressure when it came to that. My dad was never angry that we both took an interest in law over business. But my cousin Liam's an architect up in Portland. He double majored in construction management on top of that."

"He's taking over then?"

"Yeah." Lucas goes to the fridge and offers me another beer. I shake my head, knowing that I'm leaving with the girls soon. I never allow myself to have more than two drinks at a dinner when I'm with them. Even that's pushing it.

"Liam came out here every summer starting his freshman year of high school," Lucas continues as he wipes off the counters.

"He started to help my dad for some extra cash, and he actually really liked it. I think the work helped him in more ways than just financial. He even continued working in construction throughout undergrad and the summers between his graduate courses." He turns toward us and leans back onto the counter. "I don't think my dad ever put much thought into whether the businesses would go to the family or not but it's definitely a solution we're all happy with."

"That's great then. Is your cousin moving out here soon?"

"That's the plan as of now." Lucas looks at me a little sheepishly. "No one around Amada Beach really knows yet…"

He doesn't have to finish his thought for me to know where this is going. "No problem, I won't say a thing to anyone."

"Thanks."

"You should tell us something," Knox muses, "for the information you eavesdropped on."

I know Knox well enough to know when he set a trap for someone. For better or for worse, he reminds me of Lexi more often than not.

Narrowing my eyes, I say, "You were talking about it in the same room as me."

"Whatever." He waves his hand like that point is irrelevant. "I want to know… something about…" He pretends to think it over but we both know where this is going. His face lights up and I shake my head in exasperation at him. "Vivi."

Lucas hits him in the torso with the dish towel and gives him a wide eye look. The universal look in a marriage that means *shut the fuck up right now*. Turning back to me he says, "Excuse my busybody husband."

"I plan to," I tell Lucas. Turning to Knox I add, "I'm not going to gossip about Genevieve with you."

Her full name slips out, a habit now. *Vivi* will always hold a place in my heart. That's always who she'll be to me at the heart of things—my best and oldest friend. But *Genevieve* holds the promise of a future I would very much like to see play out, like maybe I was always just waiting to use that name.

"Ooh, Genevieve, is it? I thought she hated to be called that?" he teases.

"She does. Except by me," I shrug. "There's your piece of information."

His eyes glitter like he just received the answers to world peace. "I'll take it."

I roll my eyes at the same time all four of the kids come into the kitchen.

"Dad, guess what!" Daisy is bouncing on her feet. A shy red-faced Matty is standing still next to her but grinning like a little fool.

"What, darling?"

She squeals in excitement, shaking her fists in front of her. "Matty has a lizard! A pet *lizard*!"

Daisy is a fan of all things creepy and crawly. Their oldest son Jake is standing behind them next to Stella, and from the looks on their faces, neither seems too excited at the thought. The two of them have been arguing all evening but refuse to leave each other alone. Instead *choosing* to pester the other into insanity.

Maybe one day I'll feel that fatherly protectiveness you hear about when it comes to daughters, but I don't think so. At least not for a while. For now, I want them to relish in the giddy innocence of your first childhood crush. Because that's what's clearly happening right now, and I'm not at all surprised by the different reactions to their new feelings.

"A lizard?" I glance at Knox and Lucas. "Really?"

"It's a gecko," Matty pipes up.

"What's its name?" I ask with a small shrug and a smile.

"Duckie."

"That's cool," I say. After a second, I add, "Why?"

"*Pretty in Pink*," Knox answers with a chuckle.

I turn toward him again. "The movie?"

"Yeah. He loves it. Especially Duckie."

I look at them with confused amusement and turn back to the kids. "Good taste, bud." He beams at me in response.

"Can I get a gecko?" Daisy asks.

"No," I shake my head.

She pouts for three seconds before asking sweetly, "Can I go see the gecko?"

"Duckie," Matty says.

Chuckling, I nod. "Sure, go meet Duckie for ten minutes. Wash your hands before and after."

They walk down the hallway, Stella and Jake tentatively following behind them. Jake says something I can't hear but I do hear Stella whisper-shout, "You're so *dumb*!" Jake laughs at her response and Stella flicks his forehead before walking into Matty's room.

I turn back to Knox and Lucas, embarrassed about their encounter. "I'm so sorry she called your son dumb." They don't look mad at all, if anything slightly amused, so I add, "And flicked him," with a chuckle and shake of my head.

"Don't worry about it. He can be a little shit sometimes—as most little boys are. He recently got brave enough to say *shit* and we made the mistake of laughing in surprise."

Knox shakes his head, "Now he knows he isn't really in trouble no matter how hard we try."

I place my hands on the chair behind me. "How did he use it the first time?"

Lucas actually snorts. "We were at Subway for lunch after *he* chose to go there. I don't know what was wrong with his sandwich, but he decided he didn't like it, so he muttered, '*I didn't realize I ordered a shit sandwich.*'"

I don't try to hide my laughter as they both tip their heads back, practically howling at the memory. It reminds me of the time Vivi was ten and shouted '*motherfucking shitballs*' after losing a game of who knows what to Asher. It was really only the beginning for her.

But watching Lucas and Knox deal with the uncertainties of parenthood makes me realize that I miss *that*. I don't miss Arielle and I don't miss our marriage. But I do miss having someone to laugh with and vent to. Someone who gets it because they're feeling all the overwhelming emotions you are toward your child.

My chuckle dies off and I look down at my feet. "Stella's been acting out lately. I'm not surprised considering… everything." I wave my hand in the air for emphasis. It feels weird and wrong to open up about the struggles I'm having but since moving back, I'm trying to do better by what the girls need. Not what I'm comfortable with. "Not with cursing. She likes making a buck off of that, so Jake better be careful." They laugh lightly but don't interrupt me. "She's bordering on the line of disrespectful, sometimes slipping her toe over just enough to make a point without warranting a more severe punishment."

Lucas nods his head in sympathy, but his parents are together like mine. I understand the divorce from a relationship point of view, not from a child.

Knox looks unsure for a second before he decides to say what's on his mind. "Grady, it's going to be hard. I was angry for *years* when my parents got a divorce." I'm taken back by the knowledge.

Knox often talks about both of his parents, but I guess now that I think about it… never them *together.* "I was suspended from middle school multiple times for fighting. And those were only for the times I was caught. Even after I started playing baseball more seriously in high school, I was still making a lot of stupid choices because I was so fucking angry."

I don't know when this is supposed to get better or what the big lesson is supposed to be, but I don't say that. He must see it written on my face though because he continues, "When I started dating Lucas," he begins, tipping his head toward his husband, "he kind of gave me an ultimatum. It sounds bad but it wasn't. Therapy or we break up. It was good. It was *needed.* And it was long overdue."

I nod, too dumbfounded to say anything more.

How have I not thought about putting both *of my daughters in therapy?*

It may not have saved my marriage to Arielle, but it definitely helped us get to the somewhat amicable situation we're in now. I need to tread lightly here, knowing that Stella can often feel spooked and will close herself off. But I can barely process my own emotions sometimes. I can't imagine how overwhelming this all must be, especially since moving to a new state and introducing a boatload of new people into their lives.

Arielle and I made this choice so the girls wouldn't be alone and would have support. So, I'm going to keep my promise and look into child and family therapists tomorrow.

Fri, Oct 7 at 8:02 P.M.

Vivi
Did u have a good dinner :)

9:13 P.M.

I did. I can't believe it took you YEARS to go over there.

Shut up

What did they cook for u

Homemade lasagna. What about you?

Tomato basil soup, vinaigrette salad AND bruschetta

Sucker

You're lying.

Nope

photo attachment of Vivi's hand holding a glass of wine in front of a spread of food on Knox's dining room table

The whole world really does revolve around you.

Please Grady don't be ridiculous

> Not the WHOLE world

You're right. Just mine.

> I thought I told you not to be ridiculous

Good night, love.

> Good night, bane of my being ☾

7:49 P.M.

Arielle
> Can we FaceTime tonight?

The girls would be happy to.

> I meant you but of course I want to see them as well.

↓ New ↓
9:48 P.M.

Sorry, just got the girls down and I'm going to bed. I'll have the girls FaceTime with you first thing tomorrow. Let me know when you're awake.

> When can I FaceTime you though?

Chapter Twenty-Seven
Vivi

Bending down next to one of the child-sized desks, with Kacey Musgraves quietly playing in the background, I wonder why I thought it was a good idea to give seven-year-olds googly eyes, liquid glue, and confetti all at once.

I feel Grady's presence in the room before I hear his quiet knock. When I turn toward him, I catch his eyes glued to my ass. Which is directly pointed to him as I'm crouching to see under the desk. When his eyes sweep up toward my face, he doesn't look the least bit embarrassed. *The smug bastard,* my mind shouts even if the rest of me is heating at the sultry gaze.

"What are you doing, love?" he asks me, leaning against the door and his gaze moving back down.

I may or may not make a show of standing up, remembering the only useful advice Molly has ever given me–*when bending down, always remember the three-step rule, down-booty-up,* she told me once in high school. We proceeded to practice in the dressing room mirror in her parents' closet while giggling uncontrollably. It's one of the only memories of Molly I've allowed myself to keep close to my heart.

But I don't want any memories of Molly or Brody to stain this moment. This very inconsequential moment where Grady is looking at me like I'm the most beautiful woman he has ever seen. *Radiating* was the word he used at my house. And this isn't the first time he's looked at me like that.

This look is mine, and only mine. I refuse to share it with anything, not even a memory.

"We were doing arts and crafts earlier." He gives me a sympathetic shake of the head. One only a parent or primary school teacher would be able to truly muster.

He takes a step closer to me and gives me a one shoulder shrug. "Point me to a desk. Preferably one behind you." That sexy smirk graces his face again.

I laugh, trying to ignore the growing wet heat between my legs. It only makes Grady smile wider.

I point to the desk a few down from me. "Did you hear back from any of the volunteers?" Along with our families, a lot of the employees from Maddon Construction, and some of the parents, have all signed up to help the students build the booths.

"I'm going to send an email out tomorrow with different times over the next few weeks." I nod in acknowledgement, letting out a breath. It feels like that took a few pounds off my chest. Even with two months left, it feels like we won't have enough time to get everything done. "How would you feel about getting lunch with me on Sunday? We can walk around and talk to the business owners after. I know some of them would want to donate."

I look at him over my shoulder, cursing myself for not thinking about that. Especially when my siblings, and best friend, are business owners down by the beach. Grady laughs at the scornful look on my face, but I nod in agreement anyway.

Maybe he deserves more of a reaction out of me, but he asked me so casually if I wanted to get lunch. I can't assume that he was asking me on a date.

You know he was.

Okay, fine. I know he meant it as a date but maybe I want a little bit more too. My nod feels appropriate. The small smile on Grady's face tells me that he isn't put off by it in the slightest.

That at least makes this next part a little easier.

"What are you doing Friday night?" I stick my head under the desk, pretending that this googly eye is really stuck.

"Nothing, why?" Grady answers without hesitation. The quiet squeak of his shoes tells me he turned toward me.

"I was wo–"

"Genevieve, turn around."

I stick my head further under the table in protest. "Why?"

I can hear his goofy smile from his voice. "When I asked you on a date, I looked you in the eye."

That makes me turn around. I swing my body around and give him a scowl. "No, you looked me in the eye when you asked how I felt about getting lunch on Sunday." He's about to respond, probably to say something like *semantics* or equally as infuriating. I cut him off, "So, *how do you feel* about going to Yellow Cab on Friday with us?"

"Us?" He raises his eyebrow, clearly not loving the idea of sharing me.

I hide my possessive delight. "Lexi's birthday is next Tuesday. We're celebrating on Friday."

"Okay, sure. I feel like going with you guys." He shrugs his shoulders, acting all too casual again. I roll my eyes and face the desk, bored of this game we're playing. "On one condition."

Slowly, I turn back toward him. I roll my hand in the air, indicating for him to go on.

"Okay, not a condition. I take that back." I chuckle at that; all of the tediously annoying tension easing between us. "Viv, will you go on a date with me before we go out with everyone? I'll pick you up at your door, we can go to Clear Horizons for a bite and a drink, then we'll go to the bar. Afterward, I'll take you home."

Two things I instantly notice: he called me Viv, which is somehow much more endearing at this moment, and he didn't specify whose home he'd be taking me to. The second one makes goosebumps pop up across my neck and back.

At this point, I'm almost positive that Grady and I both know that this is just a game of cat and mouse. I don't really know which one is which, though. It probably changes every day, maybe every minute, where we're concerned. As much as I enjoy it, there are a few things I would enjoy even more with him. Starting with the things he can do with his fingers.

"Yes, Grady. I'll go on a date with you," I say coyly, his eyes blazing at the innocent act. "We have to meet them at eight-thirty."

Grady gives me the happiest, most charming smile I've ever seen on him. "I'll get you at six then."

I nod and turn back toward the desk. Grady stays and helps me clean off the remaining ten, even though we don't have much more to discuss about the fundraiser today. He walks me to my car and places a soft, chaste kiss to my lips. It's perfect for this moment.

Chapter Twenty-Eight
Grady

Leaning back in my chair, I'm happily taking in the view around me. I brought Vivi to Clear Horizons Brewery for a quick dinner. She has a goofy smile as she sets our drinks and appetizers up for an Instagram story. Once she finally arranges the guacamole and bacon cheese fries in what she deems appropriate, she takes a quick snap as she moves the phone from her drink and the food up to the drink in my hand. I don't have social media, but it doesn't bother me at all if she wants to post about me. If anything, it brings a strong sense of satisfaction.

"Do you have a lot of followers?" I ask, her seriousness making me curious.

She snorts out a laugh. "No, I only have like fifty. I keep my account private. Nothing I post is serious. There's a lot of food, and sometimes things about books I'm reading. I post the worst photos of myself. Sometimes my siblings and Lexi as well. It's just for fun and only for me."

I smile, somehow loving the fact that she doesn't take things like that seriously. She sees it as another way for her to be goofy and enjoy herself. And it's not that I'm judgmental of people who do use Instagram, not at all. This is just a very *Vivi* thing, and I love it for that reason alone.

"Can I scroll through it?"

"Sure," she hands me her phone. Just like she said, there isn't anything serious on her page. The most recent post is from last Monday. I recognize the little bandana she wore because I thought it was freaking adorable. The one before that is of the doughnuts I brought her a few weeks ago. I didn't realize she took the picture. Clicking on it, I see a comments from Lexi and Calypso that make me laugh but keep scrolling. Right before that is from a couple of weeks ago when she went kayaking with Asher for the afternoon. She has an array of photos of her siblings that seem to be taken in surprise. Most of the ones of Lexi are of her laughing, head tipped back and smiling. I click on one of them and read the caption, *the only way I want to remember her.* I don't try to hide the grin as I look through some of the other photos. The beach. Books. Brighter Daze. Dinners and lunches. Flowers. Close ups of her eyes and random shots of the horizon while she's out on the water.

It's such an honest look into the life of Genevieve over the last few years and I don't want to give it back. I almost want to create an account for the first time in my life so I can analyze every single post.

Reluctantly, I hand her the phone back.

"You don't have any social media." She's stating the fact, not asking a question. I quirk a brow at her.

"Have you tried to search me?"

Giving me a noncommittal shrug, she says, "Maybe once or twice. For research purposes."

"What was the research?"

"You always want the guy who broke your teenage heart to turn out ugly." My head tips back in laughter. She says it so confidently that I actually question if that was the reason.

Holding out my arms to the side I ask, "And? Am I hideous?"

"No, Grady. Fortunately for you, you're definitely not hideous." She gives me a small smile, her cheeks turning the lightest shade of pink.

"Would it have been easier for you to ignore me if I was?"

She stabs another fry, holding it up to her mouth. "Oh yeah, it was what I was really hoping for."

I lean back in my chair and give her a cocky smirk. "You knew that I'd be hard to resist?"

"Ugh." She affectionately rolls her eyes. "More like I knew you would stop at nothing to get what you want."

"And you were just so sure that I'd want you?"

"Obviously. And clearly, I was right." She waves her hand in my direction. "You're like, obsessed with me," she teases.

I shake my head, chuckling at her exaggeration. Even if it really isn't too far off from the truth anymore.

I wanted to stay close to the beach, in hopes that we'll have some time to walk around before we have to meet everyone else. I hadn't had much time to take the girls down more than a couple of afternoons during the summer. But the beach has always been my place with Vivi more than anything.

And even though we both know we'll be cutting it close on time, she agreed to go anyway. So here we are, walking across the shore for the last ten minutes.

"This is definitely in the top three things I missed about living here," I admit.

"What would be the other two?" she asks quietly, just loud enough to hear over the waves. We've been walking in silence for a majority of our trek.

"Pfff." I let out a breath of air, thinking it over. "Top three would be walking on the beach, time with my family—especially holidays—and… and you." I link my pinky with hers, pulling her to a stop. The look on her face tells me enough. *She doesn't believe me.* "Viv, I missed you before I ever moved away. I missed you from the first birthday I didn't spend with you because I, selfishly, couldn't see you with Brody that day. Not on a day that had always been *ours.* It was your birthday, but that day felt like mine too somehow."

She inhales sharply in surprise. I slip my hand around the nape of her neck and lean down, our noses brushing, our lips only an inch apart. I continue, "I wasn't delusional. I never expected *this.* Nights like tonight, and the ones spent at your house, weren't something I would've ever allowed myself to wish for. I missed you though. You'll always be my best friend more than anything else. But I'm so lucky that you're giving me this chance to be everything to you."

"I missed you too," she whispers in a trembling voice. Her fingers find my belt loops, pulling our bodies flush to each other. "I never allowed myself to wish for this either. But I would be lucky to be something to you and to your daughters."

I nod, letting the way my lips brush against her convey the words I can't articulate. She's more than just someone to me. She's my first and best friend, my first crush, my first kiss. The girl who I grew up with, and who I spent countless nights and holidays with. She's so much more to me than what I can put into words, and these last couple of months have only solidified that fact.

She's the woman I was always supposed to end up with. And I'm not letting anything come in the way of that again.

She stands up on her toes, sinking further into the sand. Her annoyed *hmmpf* is adorable but I take pity on her. Both of my hands find their way to her jaw, tilting her mouth up to me as I lean down and deepen the kiss. I gently stroke her cheeks and relish in the feel of her hands on my hips. After a long moment, I ease away from her. She gives me a goofy, satisfied grin that begs for me to plant one more kiss there. So, I do.

There are a few reasons I've never been to Yellow Cab—one of which is that Harper said he was going to come here when Vivi ran into him at Spotlight at the beginning of the school year. I would do just about anything to avoid seeing him at all costs, especially when I'm trying to enjoy my night with Genevieve. But I can't lie, the place is freaking cool.

An array of disco balls are hung across the ceiling, lighting up the booths that look like actual taxi cabs. The DJ plays from the top of a miniature version of the Empire State Building. There are a few hot dog carts that serve what looks like Jell-O shots. You have to get on the subway to get to the bar. When we were walking back from the beach, Vivi told me that during Christmas they swap out the Empire State Building for the Rockefeller Tower and put a Christmas tree in here. I have no idea where they can fit it. And once a month, there's a drag night that includes go-go dancers that dress up like the Statue of Liberty.

Vivi grabs my hand and pulls us further into the crowd. She

makes a beeline for a booth toward the back near the pool tables in Central Park. This booth is a yellow SUV, allowing room for larger parties.

Lexi, Calypso, Asher, and Hudson are here already. Knox said he and Lucas are coming out but haven't arrived yet. There are two guys and a woman that I don't recognize. Two of them look vaguely familiar but I can't place them.

"Hey!" Lexi calls over the music. She's in the middle of everyone, but she stands up to give Vivi's arms a hug. She gives me an enthusiastic wave. I think she has a good buzz going. *Good for her.* It's her birthday after all.

Lexi points a finger at Vivi and shouts in an accusing tone, "You didn't tell me that Yaz was going to be in town!"

Yaz. *Yasmin Hernandez.* Lexi's childhood best friend. I never knew her very well. I don't remember her and Vivi ever having any problems between them either. When I look down at her, Vivi has a beautiful, bright smile as she takes in her best friend's shock. She happily waves to Yasmin before scooting into the booth next to Calypso. She let my hand go before we reached the table, but she calls me to sit down next to her.

I slide in, allowing my thigh to press against hers. I want to respect her need for privacy—I know how nosey everyone in this town can be—but I really just want to touch her all the time. It doesn't matter how innocent. I just want to know that she's really there, beside me.

She waves at the guys sitting across from us, and leans in to whisper, "That's Gavin from the bookstore, and his boyfriend." Her lips are right next to my ear, her breath is warm against my skin.

"I thought he looked familiar."

"Oh, I think I see Knox and Lucas." She tries to stand, peering over the crowd. She waves them over and plops back down in her spot, pushing her thigh into mine again.

A few seconds later, Knox slaps a hand on my shoulder. "Hey! I'm going to go buy the birthday girl a drink. Do you guys want anything?"

I look at Vivi who's nodding up at him. I chuckle and stand from the booth, gesturing for Lucas to sit down. "I'll go with you."

Knox and I are about to make our way toward the bar when I hear Vivi over the music. "Wait, Grady!"

I turn back around and lean toward her on the table, so she doesn't have to shout. "What?" I suppress the urge to call her *love* or *Genevieve*.

"You didn't ask what I want," she says with just enough snark to pull a smug grin across my face. I was planning on letting this be a quiet win, one that I didn't gloat about, but she would've known.

"I don't have to." I shrug. "A blood orange margarita. On the rocks with salt."

Calypso snorts into her drink, pretending like she isn't paying attention. Lucas looks like he has a front row seat to the Superbowl.

"Maybe I don't want that." She tilts her chin up like a brat.

My smile grows. "You do. But in case I'm wrong, what would you like to drink, Viv?"

She *barely* bites her lips in time to stop the smile, but I notice. I give her a few seconds to say something but her only response is an eye roll as she sits back.

I turn toward the bar with Knox, but I can hear Calypso laugh, "Wow."

"That was really hot," Lucas admits.

Once we're in line, Knox turns toward me, "What just happened? I couldn't hear anything."

I tilt my head back and laugh. "Your husband had a front-row seat. I'll let him have the honor of telling you."

When we get back to the table, I know immediately that something's up. Vivi and Lexi are leaning toward each other across the table. Vivi is nodding and Lexi looks way too superior.

"What's up?" I hand Vivi her drink.

Lexi is the one who answers, "I want to play pool. It's my birthday after all."

"Okay," I shrug. "Want to be my partner?" I ask Knox, already knowing that it's safer for everyone to let the two of them be on the same team. I don't doubt that their childhood hostility comes out quickly when they're in competition.

"Sure," Knox nods.

We look back at them and suddenly I feel like we made a grave mistake by agreeing to play. Vivi looks way too innocent. Lexi is smiling like she knows a secret—which is how she looks most of the time, but this is worse somehow. Calypso gives me a sympathetic smile, shaking her head. Hudson lets out a low whistle, and Asher tips his water glass toward me, in a silent *good luck.*

"I'm pretty good," Knox says. "It'll be a good game. Chill out."

Knowing Vivi *and* Lexi, I'm not so sure about that.

Chapter Twenty-Nine
Grady

It's a good game but not for Knox and me.

"What the fuck?" he mutters.

Lexi and Vivi are on their second turn and have already sunk half the solid balls.

The little troll is smiling at me from across the pool table, and I can't help but laugh and shake my head in return.

She's so beautiful. Especially in these moments of pure giddiness.

"How did you get so good at this?" I ask.

Vivi laughs, letting Lexi answer this one. "We used to hustle boys for drinks. Duh." She lines up the pool cue and shoots. Another clean shot. "We're also great at beer pong."

"We are going on an eight-year streak, and we don't plan on losing anytime soon. Definitely not tonight." Vivi's talking a lot of shit, but she looks so happy doing it, I don't want her to stop. I don't know why this is turning me on, but I love when she's snarky and a little bratty.

It gives me a few good reasons to tease the living hell out of her later.

"We could catch up." I don't even try to sound convincing. Lexi is already lining up to sink another ball.

Two games later, and Knox and I are only doing slightly better this round. Half of our striped balls have made it into a pocket, but Vivi is lining up to sink the last solid ball into a corner pocket—

Oh, there it goes. A perfect shot. Again.

She stands up and gives me a saccharine smile I've never seen before. It's probably a mix of the alcohol and winning streak, but she looks so fucking adorable I want to lose ten more games to her.

Knox has other ideas. "Okay, okay. Just make the fucking eight ball and put us out of our misery, thanks."

Lexi's laugh can be heard over the music but it's Vivi I'm staring at. I can't hear her, but I read her lips, "Left corner pocket." She points to the pocket directly in front of me before leaning forward. She lines up her last shot and… makes it. Not surprising at all.

Lexi whoops like they just won the gold medal and Vivi bounces on her heels, beaming at me. I simper at her, shaking my head.

"You really think you can beat anyone in this bar?" Knox asks, the exasperation is clear in his voice. He played college baseball too. He hates losing just as much as us.

Vivi's eyes move toward him, and I can't help but curse him silently for taking her attention away. She gives him her most cocky grin, but Lexi is the one who responds, "Yes. I'm confident enough to say that we can beat anyone in this bar right now. Pick our opponent." She sweeps her arm out toward the crowds.

I didn't have to see either one of their report cards to know that they both aced AP geometry *and* AP physics, and they've always been smart enough to apply that in any situation. I knew we never stood a chance but looking at how much fun Vivi and Lexi are having, was worth every shot to my ego. And the idea of her playing the shy, clueless girl only to hustle men is sexy as hell.

"Those guys," Knox points to a group of men on the other side of the room we're currently in.

"Okay," they say simultaneously with a little shrug.

They turn on their heels and walk toward the group. I give Knox a look like, *really, those freaking guys.*

They're a bit younger than us, maybe seniors in college or just graduated. They look like a mix of frat bros and athletes. In the last few months, I haven't seen Vivi show interest in anyone besides me. And from what people have said, she hasn't shown interest in anyone in a long time. But I can still admit that Knox picked a group of some of the most attractive men in the bar.

And I don't like the way they're looking at Vivi or Lexi, at all.

Do I think that either one of them cares about these men? No. They wouldn't give them the time of day, that much is obvious from where Knox and I are sitting.

Do I think the guys they're currently hustling seem to notice their indifference? No. From the looks in their eyes, they think they have a chance.

I know Vivi well enough—and am getting to know Lexi better—that I *know* this is part of their ploy. Every time one of them goes to line up a shot, they put all of their... assets on full display.

Lexi is thinner and less curvy than Vivi but she's tall and slender. She has a flat stomach that's peeking through her high-waisted mom jeans and white cut-off button down. Her chest may not be her attention grabber but the way her jeans hug her butt every time she leans forward is completely on purpose. At one point during the game, Lexi slowly slid off her oversized flannel to bring more attention to her backside. It's working the crowd how she intended.

Just like the group of men they're currently wrecking I can acknowledge when someone is attractive even if I'm not attracted to them. And Lexi is gorgeous. She always has been with her ivory skin and upturned onyx eyes matching her silky, long hair. She has high cheekbones and full lips that I don't doubt get the attention of any man or woman she wants.

Genevieve on the other hand… just like everything else she wears, it's modest enough. A high-waisted floral mini skirt that hugs her lush hips perfectly. Her yellow top has flared sleeves and ties in the front. Her brown wedges give her a couple extra inches of height but even in Converse, Lexi is taller.

When we were playing, I realized how Vivi's cleavage is amplified every time she bends forward. It's hard to miss, even for a blind man. What I didn't notice was how her skirt rides up just enough to tease without ever showing any of the goods. And I know that if I'm noticing that, so are the guys crowding around the table, waiting for the chance to get hustled by these two pretty little masterminds.

My eyes never stray from Vivi's body for longer than a few seconds and its torture. It accomplishes nothing except creating a slow simmer of jealousy to spread through my body with every smile she gives someone else. My grip on the glass gets tighter every time it's her turn to shoot. I can feel the way other men watch her as she walks slowly around the table, trailing her fingers across the wooden edge, as she decides her next shot. Knox even glances at me when one of the guys says something we can't hear but makes Vivi laugh. She playfully shoves his shoulder and moves in front of him to line up her shot.

"They're fucking good, I'll give them that," Knox chuckles and shakes his head in awe.

Yeah, they're too fucking good.

It's driving me crazy. Especially when I think about the endless college nights the two of them did just this, and exactly how a lot of those nights probably ended for Vivi. *Who* those nights ended with.

It should actually be illegal for two women who are this beautiful and smart to be friends. If only for my sanity.

They play another three games, beating all six of the guys in the group. The first pair they played wanted a rematch. The second game was even worse for them.

One of the guys leans down toward Vivi, pointing toward the bar. Probably offering her a drink. She grabs Lexi's hand and shakes her head. I can't read her lips from here, but she points toward us. For the first time in the last hour, the group notices us at the high-top table a few feet away from where they're playing. All at once, realization dawns on each of their faces. They just got hustled for the fun of it. They were nothing more than male egos to play with while Vivi and Lexi proved a point.

Walking hand in hand and stopping right in front of the high-top, the little troll happily states, "You guys *definitely* owe us some drinks."

As soon as the four of us get settled back into the booth, Calypso speaks up, "Fucking suckers."

"Any of you could have warned us," Knox retorts while looking for a server. He's sitting on the end across from me. I nod my agreement.

"Think of it as an initiation," Asher smirks.

"How many are there going to be? You guys' already

saran-wrapped my Jeep a month ago." They really did. And based on the current responses, my guess is Asher, Lexi and Vivi came in the middle of the night to relive her high school glory days and I was the target. It's a coincidence that the next morning I was already running almost thirty minutes late when I walked outside to find that. It was the last time I didn't park in the garage. "And will they all involve her?" I point toward Lexi.

"Don't make me chuck this at you," Lexi teases. Except I think she has been waiting a decade for any reason to throw another drink at a man.

I hold up my hands in surrender, chuckling.

Vivi places her hand high on my thigh and leans toward me. Tilting my face down to hers, she lightly squeezes and I almost groan. "I know we just sat but I really have to pee." She bounces in her seat a little, emphasizing her point… and her breasts.

It's less than two minutes later, after sitting back down, that I can't take it anymore. Telling no one in particular I say, "I'm going to get a drink from the bar."

Lexi's answering grin clues me in to the fact that not a single person at this table believes me. I choose to ignore all of them and make my way back toward the bathrooms.

The hallway is empty, so I lean against the wall across from the women's single restroom. *Perfect.*

In all honesty, I don't really know what I'm doing right now. I've never done anything like this.

But there's never been another woman who makes me feel this… wild, all-consuming possessiveness that I do with Genevieve.

Watching her reject that guy and walk back to me was *so* satisfying but not enough to fully calm the frustration pumping through my body.

She opens the door and takes a sharp inhale when she sees me. "Grady, what are—"

I place my hand on her stomach and push her backward before turning around just long enough to lock the door. Thankfully the bathrooms here are very clean so I don't hesitate to grip her ribs and push her against the counter.

"Grady," she breathes as she tilts her head up to me.

"Do you realize how crazy you made me out there?" I can smell the tequila on her breath. It took days to get the taste of her margarita out of my mouth after that night. Blood orange has been my new favorite flavor ever since, but I bet the faint taste of it on Vivi's tongue is even better.

She doesn't say anything, but a shiver runs through her entire body, and she gives me a small smirk that I want to kiss right off her beautiful face.

So that's exactly what I do.

This kiss is not sweet and tentative like the one from earlier tonight.

No, this one is as passionate and feral as I feel. Everything I'm putting into it, Vivi is giving right back. Driving me more and more wild.

Without thinking about it, the hand that's not holding her in place goes to the little bow at the front of her shirt. One light tug on the fabric has it falling open. I slowly push it off her breasts, leaving the sleeves right where they are. Vivi's chest rises and falls quickly, her breathing more shallow. My mouth waters as I take in her bare top half. Slowly, I move my hand up, rolling her puckered nipple in between my fingers, taking her mouth with mine again.

Without hesitation, she slips her hands up my shirt. Her hands run over the contours of my abs and pecs before she slips them to my back, feeling all of the muscles there next.

I suddenly realize that she hasn't seen me without a shirt yet. I had one on the entire weekend at her house and we haven't had any time like *this* since. After I tore my ACL, working out was still ingrained into my day-to-day routines. I'd been an athlete my entire life and had planned to stay one. It just felt natural to continue those habits after my recovery. I never put much thought into it.

Until right now. I'm silently thanking myself for every day that I've spent an hour in the gym because if Vivi's whimpers are any indication, she loves every part of my body I've given her so far.

She slides her palms lightly up my back, teasing me with the barest touches, before sinking her nails into my shoulders. I grab handfuls of each of her breasts in response. No matter how hard I try they spill out of my hands.

I alternate between squeezing her perfect tits and pinching her rosy buds, and it only takes about a minute before she's begging me for more.

"Grady," she moans into my mouth. I slip one of my hands to the back of her neck, pushing her mouth to mine again. She slips her hands down, toward my zipper, but I stop her before she can make work of it. "Please, Grady, *please.*" That word on her tongue is the sweetest thing I've ever heard but I won't let her have what she wants. Not like this, not for the first time. "More. I need *more.*"

I shake my head, telling myself I should cover her up and walk out of this bathroom with her. But no matter what my mind says, my body won't comply. "I'm not going to make love to you for the first time in the bathroom of a bar, Genevieve," I growl.

"Good thing I want you to *fuck me*, not make love to me." Her hands try to move back down, thinking she won.

I grab her wrists again, setting them around my neck. "There's no reason why that won't be the exact same thing for us."

"Grady," she whimpers, wrapping one of her legs around me. "Please. I need *something*."

I look down as her other leg snakes around my hips, pulling me closer to her. I get a peek of her dark green lace panties... the same pair I'm pretty sure short-circuited my brain when I was helping her with laundry.

Her eyes must drop down to where I'm staring. "I noticed that these were your favorite."

I drop my head to her forehead. "You're going to be the death of me." Her light chuckle pumps more heat into my veins. I can see the word *please* forming on her lips, but I've teased her enough. I've teased myself enough. "Your greedy pussy can have my fingers now, or nothing at all."

She responds with a deep moan and tugs on my hair. She pulls me down to her mouth as she nods. It's both an agreement and permission.

Without waiting another second, I push her panties to the side and slowly drag one finger from her soaked center to her clit. I give it a few light swipes, pulling back just enough to watch her writhe in front of me.

I slip two fingers into her, pumping at a pace I know is only getting her more worked up. "You're so needy for me. Aren't you, Genevieve?" She digs her nails into my skin again, and I revel in the feeling of it. I want her to leave scratches for me to find tomorrow. "That's not an answer."

"Yes, yes. You're right," she whimpers.

I let out a low hum of approval. "Has anyone ever made you as wet as I do?"

This time, she answers quickly, "No. No one else."

"Good." My hand starts to move faster. I curl my two fingers just enough to reach that spot I quickly learned she loves. My thumb moves to her clit, adding pressure until she screams out. "You have to be quiet, love."

"I can't, it's too—*oh god*—good. It's too fucking good. I want to be loud for you."

There is nothing I want more than that, but I want it in the privacy of my bedroom. I don't care about Vivi's past, I know I have one, but no one else will get to experience her like this again. From this point forward, this is all *mine.*

"I know, baby. Trust me, all I want is to hear how wild I can make you but not here." I slow my hand just enough to get her attention. "Do we need to stop?"

"Fuck you," she says with no bite at all. "No, don't fucking stop. I swear to whoever's holy up there. Gr—" Her head tilts back and my name turns into a moan as I fuck her with my fingers, harder and faster than before.

"You have to be quick though." The last thing I want is anyone coming to look for us right now.

Trying to catch her breath she says, "I'm right there. I promise, *right there.*"

She realizes she's being too loud before I have to remind her. Her head drops forward, and she claws at my shirt until it's high enough for her mouth to make contact with the skin just below my shoulder.

With each swipe at her clit, she digs her nails in deeper. Every pump of my fingers makes her bite down harder. Her moans grow louder, even as she leaves more than a couple love marks across my chest. Her hips start to buck, moving at the same pace as my fingers. Her chest is pressed against mine. And the flush painting her skin is the prettiest color I've ever seen.

She's everything I could wish for in a woman, but I've known that fact my entire life.

And just like she promised, she comes quick and hard on my fingers. I don't slow down until she has ridden out every second of pleasure. Not until her hands slip into my back pockets and she lays a soft kiss on each bite mark.

As I watch her worship my body that she just claimed as hers, I lift my fingers to my mouth. When I groan, she tilts her eyes up and watches as I lick her release off my fingers. I brush my wet thumb over her bottom lip before slipping it into her mouth.

I was wrong. *That's* my new favorite flavor and I can't wait until I can get my head in between her legs for a few hours.

Getting through the rest of the night was torture.

All I wanted was to be here. Leaning up against my dresser, as a very nosey and very pretty Vivi makes her way around the room. Taking in every single detail. She did the same thing with the foyer and kitchen before I practically shoved her up the stairs with a promise that she can spend as long as she wants looking through my home *tomorrow*. I can grant her a few minutes of this.

But next time I'm at her house, it's only fair if I finally get the full tour too. There's one room I haven't seen yet.

When she's ready, she turns back toward me. "Do you have clothes I can borrow?"

I swallow, suddenly nervous. "Yeah, I have some t-shirts and sweats you can borrow. You're more than welcome to whatever." She raises her eyebrows at me, picking up on my awkwardness.

When I spent the two nights at her house, I noticed that she likes those little silky pajama sets. Goddammit if I didn't love them too.

I haven't really seen her in sweats and things like that. I want her to be comfortable and I want her to know that tonight is only the first of many that I want her to spend here.

Clearing my throat, I mumble, "I actually bought you something. But you choose what's more comfortable."

She slowly sits on the edge of my bed, watching me as she unties the strings that wrap around her ankles. "What was that?" Her head tilts to the side.

I roll my eyes as my cheeks grow warmer. "I bought you something."

"Did you buy me lingerie?"

"Nooo. Should I have?"

She laughs and shrugs. "You have a pretty good idea of what I like now. Feel free to save me the money."

"Noted. It isn't lingerie." I open my top left drawer, where I keep my sleep shorts. I gently lift the folded gray set.

She grabs it, running her finger along the lace trimming. "You got me pajamas?"

I nod. "And a toothbrush."

The silvery hue of tears brims her eyes. "Grady…"

"You can wear my sweats if you want."

"Obviously I'm not wearing your old ass sweats. Don't be ridiculous." She holds the pajamas up to her chest as if I'd just snatch them from her.

"The toothbrush is in the top drawer." When she moves past me, I stand up straight and stop her with an arm around her waist. I place a soft kiss on her temple. "Is there anything else you need?"

She shakes her head. Bringing my hand up to kiss my knuckles, she untangles from me and goes into the bathroom.

Chapter Thirty

Vivi

Of course, I look through every one of Grady's bathroom drawers and cabinets while I brush my teeth. To no one's surprise, there isn't anything scandalous. Not unless you count a pair of briefs on the floor. Who is this man?

I spit out the toothpaste and rinse my mouth before taking one final look at myself in the mirror. The set that Grady picked out is perfect. There's no reason to deny that. It's a silky light gray tank top and shorts that fall around my upper thighs. It's something I'd pick out for myself.

And I *know* that this means something. You wouldn't pick up a pair of pajamas and a toothbrush for one night. You wouldn't even do that for a friend-with-benefits.

You do this for someone that you want to make comfortable. Someone that you want to take up a little space in your home. And that makes it so much better than stealing a pair of his sweats.

I'll probably steal a pair in the morning, let's just be honest.

I exit the bathroom and find Grady setting up what I assume is my side of the bed. There's a glass of water and an extra charger on the nightstand closest to the window, on the other side of the room from the door. It's a coincidence that he picked that side for me but it's the one I would've preferred. I take a few steps toward him, feeling shy and giddy all of a sudden.

"I'm going to just brush my teeth," he steps up next to me and places a soft kiss on my temple. Before he can walk away, I grab his arm and stand up on my toes, laying a sweet kiss on his lips.

"Thank you for everything tonight," I whisper against his lips. "It was more than I could have expected."

"Tonight's nothing compared to what I have planned." He closes the bathroom door, so I pull back the sheets and make myself comfortable. I text my siblings and Lexi to make sure they all made it home safely, then put my phone on the charger.

I'm working out the knots in my hair as Grady walks out. *Without a shirt*. I didn't have the mental capacity to fully take him in earlier. That moment was more about just feeling my hands on him. But now I get to *look* at him.

And of course, he's perfect. His abs aren't obnoxious but he's not rocking a dad bod either—they're just defined enough to see his six-pack with a delicious V pointing south. Accompanied by a broad chest and shoulders, he's everything I've imagined.

And *oh,* have I imagined.

"What are you doing?"

I don't bother pretending like I'm not completely ogling him. "What does it look like? Braiding my hair."

Chuckling, he asks, "Can I?"

I pause. "Can you what?"

"Can I braid your hair?"

My entire body stills. Looking up at him I ask, "You want to braid my hair? Do you even know how to braid hair?"

He walks toward the bed, rolling his eyes. "I have two daughters. Of course, I know how to braid hair. Who do you think helps them every morning?" He twists his finger telling me to turn around. I put my back to him and throw my hair over my shoulder. As he finishes untangling the knots he says, "I can admit that there are a few hairstyles that my mom and sister have to help me with. The braid crown thing is a hard one. And bubble braids. Blake does those the best. Mine are always a little too flat. But everything else, that's all me."

"Wow. Impressive," I say earnestly.

We fall into a comfortable silence while he puts my hair into one French braid down the middle. This moment feels more intimate than sex in a lot of ways—one I could live in forever.

Grady's fingers are soft, and he tugs gently, never causing any pain. He knots it perfectly, not too loose. And when he finishes, he rubs his fingers along my scalp, pulling out any too tight spots. I turn toward him, and he lays a gentle kiss on my cheek.

Pushing on his chest, I tease, "You are infuriating, do you know that?"

He chuckles playfully and climbs under the covers. "How so?"

I cross my legs and sit next to him. Waving my hand in front of me. "You can't just do things like that all the time. It's like you're perfect or something. Stop it."

His head tilts back in laughter, deep and rumbly. "I'm not perfect, Viv. But I'm really trying to be for you."

I jokingly grimace in response, but my blush gives me away. I contemplate if now is a good time to ask him the question I've been wondering for a while, knowing that only more will come from it.

He taps my forehead. "What are you thinking about?"

"You don't have to answer," I start, "but I've been curious about what happened with your knee."

"What do you mean? I assumed my parents told you or that you possibly saw an article. It wasn't a secret."

 He's right. As a top prospect it was a big deal in the sports world for a couple weeks. I've watched the clip when he's running the bases. The way his knee twists a little too far. You can't hear the pop in the video but it's like you can *see* it. He made it about halfway to third base before he collapsed onto his back. I've only watched the video once because it's one of those moments where you can feel the injury yourself, like a phantom pain. And the fact that it's *Grady* makes it so much worse.

 "I know what happened, yeah." I play with the edge of the comforter. "I guess I mean what happened after. That game was only a couple weeks after you came to visit. Your mom told us you were having a baby in June." I think she was waiting until after my birthday to break the news. "But it must have happened before that, knowing Stella's birthday." After a quiet second I add, "I'm not mad, obviously. This isn't a test or a game. I'm just curious how you're so okay with everything that's happened since then."

 He shrugs, looking unfazed. "We can talk about it. Arielle and I met at the beginning of our junior year. We both put off a humanities credit and were in Art History together."

 "I loved that class," I whisper to myself.

 He chuckles at my interruption. "It wasn't bad. But yeah, we met. We dated for a few months. We had broken up a few weeks before my parents' vow renewal." He grabs my hand, tugging gently until I look up at him. "I was not with anyone when I tried to talk to you that night. I don't know what I was expecting to happen, but I wouldn't have tried *anything*, not even a fight, if I was with someone else." I nod. I don't believe for a second Grady would ever hurt me or any woman in that way. "I mean, Arielle and I kind of knew that we weren't going to be together forever. I'd wanted to move back to San Diego and play for the Sharks, maybe play a few years for the farm team out in Vegas. But ultimately, I would've gone wherever I was drafted and that would've been fine. Arielle wanted to move back to the East coast. Neither one of us was ever willing to budge for the other. We knew that our relationship had a timeline, and we were okay with that for a while.

"A few weeks after my injury, I wasn't in a good place. Mentally or physically. I truthfully didn't know if I wanted to play baseball at a professional level anymore. I'd been questioning it for a while. But I was up for the draft that year, and it wasn't my decision at that point. I was eligible and there was a very good chance I would have been picked up. Anyway, early into my recovery, Arielle came to see me and told me that she was pregnant. We didn't get back together immediately but we were spending time together again and preparing for Stella. We just grew closer but neither one of us would budge. It kind of felt like if one of us couldn't move back to our hometown than neither of us was going to.

"The closer we got to Stella's due date, the more I realized *that* was what I wanted more than anything. I wanted to be a staple and present in Stella's life. I didn't want to miss out on moments because I was traveling or getting home hours after bedtime. I realized I wanted a normal life. And sure, I would have liked the opportunity to finish my college career differently but I'm happy with how it turned out. At this moment, I'm *really* happy with how it turned out."

I tangle our fingers together and let everything he just said process. I'm not sure if I really want this answer but I ask the other question that has been haunting my insecurities. "And Arielle... What happened after Daisy was born?"

Grady looks at me and runs his other hand along my thigh. "That started before Daisy was born. We didn't get married at first because we didn't want to force ourselves onto the other just because she was pregnant. And then Stella was born, and we were fighting while pretending to be a happy family. So, we got married with the delusion that it'd fix everything between us. It didn't. Daisy wasn't really an *accident*, but she wasn't really planned." He shrugs again. "Soon after she was born, things changed for the worse. I don't blame her—Daisy," he clarifies, "at all, *obviously*. Arielle and I were doing everything we could to save a dying marriage. A relationship that had died our junior year of college, honestly.

"I know it was hard for her to take care of both of them by herself during the day. I was the only one working. We both have an inheritance." Grady's cheeks turn pink. He has always been quiet about the money his paternal grandparents left him and Blake. "So, it wasn't like we were struggling but one of us had to work. We couldn't live off of that forever. We agreed just until Stella was in kindergarten, then she could do whatever she wanted, and I would support her. Teaching was more stable than theater work. Especially in Phoenix. But then Daisy was born…"

"And five years turned into eight years…" I finish for him.

He nods. "We went to couples counseling and saw therapists individually. We worked on our marriage for a few months, but it always came back to the same conclusion: neither one of us *wanted* to work on it anymore." He says it with such little emotion that a few more of those pesky insecurities quiet down. I know that he feels like he failed in some way because he's divorced and failed his daughters in some ways by extension. I can understand that. I don't agree with him, but I can understand. But there is no anger or longing in his voice when he talks about his marriage or Arielle. He's just giving me the information I'm asking for.

"She asked for the divorce," he continues. "I knew it was coming. Truthfully, I was just too lazy and jaded to do it myself.

Everything was as easy and amicable as possible. There were no big fights or arguments. We didn't even fight about who the girls would go with, not really. I mean, it was a conversation—a long one. But ultimately, we came to the same conclusion: Arielle needed a little more freedom for her career right now, and neither of us like the idea of nannies. My schedule's the same as their schedule. It just all worked out like it was probably always supposed to." He looks at me for a long moment. "Do you have any more questions?"

I shake my head and lean in to kiss him on the lips. His arm snakes around my waist, pulling me to straddle his lap.

"One more thing…" He kisses my nose and pulls away. "This is important." He runs his hand up my neck to grab my jaw. "I've never felt the way I do with you, with anyone else. And I don't just mean how I've felt in the last few months. No one's ever made me feel any of the things you have in my entire life. You're so many things to me—my first friend, my *best* friend, my first crush and kiss, the first girl I ever loved. But that still doesn't do it justice. You're so much more than all of that. And in the last few months, you have gone from the girl I always remembered to the woman I'm falling in love with."

I pull back just enough to look him in the eye. I don't say anything for a second, taking in this moment and his words. A piece of me has always been in love with Grady before I even understood what that meant. I guess I was in love with Brody at one point, but I never gave him pieces of myself in the way I did with Grady. He's all of those things to me too. Even if we haven't said *those* three words to each other. I don't know if I'm even ready for that, but that reassurance is everything I need right now.

I nod and lean forward, placing a feather-light kiss to his lips. "Me too. All of it." I'm done talking about our pasts, at least for tonight. Sure, we have more to talk about. Years and years' worth of things to rehash, but for the first time since Grady returned to Amada Beach, I'm letting myself believe that we'll figure it out. Maybe this will end… but maybe it won't.

I deepen the kiss, pulling him closer.

The one thing I know is that I don't want to go my entire life without knowing what it's like to have Grady and to be owned by him. Even if it's temporary. Even if it kills me when he's gone.

I lift up on my knees as my lips make their descent down his neck. My hands tug on the waistband of his shorts. He lifts his hips at my request and pushes them off. He does me the favor of not teasing me by keeping his briefs on.

No. When Grady kicks his shorts off, everything goes with them.

He's sitting there in front of me, naked as the day he was born, and I think I might start hyperventilating. My eyes drag along his body, going back to his half-hard cock that he lazily strokes as he watches me. He gets harder with each slow stroke up his length. When I place my hands on his thighs, his hips gently buck at the contact.

I replace his hand with mine, and we both watch as I slowly work him to his full length. My mouth practically starts to water at the sight of him. As amazing as his fingers have been, they're only a small appetizer to what I know he could do.

I'm not always a huge fan of giving head but there is no question about it—I've never wanted a man to come down my throat more than I do right now.

Leaning forward, I continue to stroke him when I whisper against his lips, "I want to show you that I can take care of you too." His deep, throaty groan sends a flash of heat to my core. But the rest of tonight isn't about me. He's already done so much for me, in more ways than just this. But right now, is about him. I open for him, reveling in the feel of his tongue tangling with mine. It's the neediest I've ever seen him. And I love it. I'll crave this power over him for the rest of my life.

I pull away and slowly make my way down his body, kissing and licking along the way. When I get to his gorgeous cock, I look up at him and marvel in the complete adoration I see in his eyes. "Without a doubt, you have the best dick in the entire world."

Grady chuckles, but it's deeper and more gravely than I've ever heard. It sends another wave of arousal through my body. My nipples pucker and I try to rub my thighs together in hopes of giving myself some form of relief. Grady's smug expression and dark eyes tell me that he's tracking everything that happens to my body. "You haven't even had it yet."

"It doesn't matter." I look back down at my hand pumping him. "I know you're not going to disappoint me."

He gives me an approving smile as he slips his hand under my braid and around my neck. He doesn't push me down. No, he just rubs his thumb around the nape of my neck. Not able to take it anymore, I lean down and run my tongue from the base upward. When I get to the tip and suck him into my mouth, we both let out deep, appreciating sounds.

I only take about half of him into my mouth at first, teasing him with the possibility of more. His hand tightens around my neck, but he never forces my actions. It makes me more excited to play with him. I release him from my mouth, instead pumping him with my hand again, paying attention to the tip in a way he seems to like. I lick my way down to his balls, sucking each one into my mouth. I moan at the feel of each one in my mouth—the vibrations causing an aftershock that shoots through him—and that's what finally breaks Grady's control.

"*Fuck,* Genevieve. If this is how good your mouth feels, I can't wait to be buried in your tight little pussy." I can't fight it anymore; his words alone almost send me over the edge. Just like he did the first time he finger-fucked me. One of my arms is bracing my weight over him, so the hand that has been pumping him moves down my body to my throbbing clit. "Yes, baby, I want you to come with me. Does sucking my cock turn you on?"

I nod right as my mouth descends down his length again. This time I take him as far back as I can. He's deep in my throat, only a couple inches of him that I can't fit. I bob my head, making fast and shallow strokes.

"Yes, fuck, just like that… such a good girl, knowing exactly how I like it." His words make me whimper around him, pushing me closer to the edge. In response, his hips buck up on accident, pushing him all the way to the back of my throat. "Fuck, I'm sorry." He tries to pull my head up, but I shake it in response. "Genevieve," he starts, in a warning.

I lift off of him slowly and look him directly in the eye. "You don't get to tell me what I can handle. I want you to fuck my mouth the way that *you* want. The way that I know I can, just like the good girl I am." His cock twitches in response. I can't hide my confident smirk. "I'm giving you what you need, and you're going to let me." Before he can say anything, I lower my head and slowly take him into my mouth once again. I don't stop until he's deep in my throat, showing him that I want this just as much as he does. His hand tightens around the braid at the base of my neck as my hand descends back down my body. I start to rub my clit at the same pace I suck him off. It takes less than a minute for Grady to lose all control.

Instead of moving my head, he holds me still by the grip he has in my hair. His hips lift off the bed, pushing him deeper before falling back down. He does this over and over, his speed starting slow but picking up with each thrust. His groans are guttural and primal and so fucking sexy. He says *'baby'* and *'so good'* and *'just like that'*, over and over, almost incoherently. The hand that's not holding my hair squeezes one of my breasts, focusing on the tight bud.

Grady is completely using me as his own personal fuck-toy to get himself off and I've never wanted to comply so badly. As my orgasm builds, my moans and whimpers get louder, making my throat vibrate around him. "I'm so close, baby," he groans. "I want to see you come before you taste me."

I try to nod my head around him, wanting the same thing. My pleasure builds and builds, pushing me toward the edge but never over. I press down on my clit, adding more pressure where my body's throbbing for it. He hums in approval when he pinches my nipple.

Fuck, I want to come for him so bad. But it's like I need something, I just don't know what.

As if Grady can read my mind, he pulls out until just my tongue is circling the tip. He tugs my hair, forcing my gaze up to him. "You look so pretty like this… like your mouth was made for my cock."

And that does it. I moan around his thick, perfect length as he pushes back into me, and Grady doesn't waste a single second. His hips start pumping to the same rhythm I rub my clit. This time, my body doesn't hesitate to give him what he wants. My vision goes black and all I know is the euphoria burning in my veins—so close to exploding. I have no control over my body, giving all of it over to Grady, who continues using me as he watches. That intense sensation shoots up my spine, making me see stars, while Grady pumps into my mouth relentlessly. He's doing most of the work so all I have to focus on is letting every last pulse of my orgasm move through me while this gorgeous, disciplined man comes undone under me.

"Fuck, baby, *yes*." Grady's thrusts turn shallower and more frantic until he pushes himself all the way down my throat one more time. His groan is a mix of pleasure and my name. The sound alone would be enough on lonely nights. He holds me in place with a tightened grip around the nape of my neck. A second later I feel the warm, salty taste of his arousal shoot down my throat, spurt after spurt coating the inside. His hips fall to the bed, and he pulls me down with his cock still buried in my mouth. My watery eyes meet his glazed pair. My gaze is curious, wanting to know exactly what he needs next. "Every last drop, love. Swallow all of it."

I pull my lips to his tip and place a kiss there before doing exactly what he says. I slowly take each of his balls into my mouth before moving back up his shaft. Starting at the base, I clean him off with my tongue, reveling in the predatory way he tracks my movements.

When I start kissing my way up his chest he murmurs into my hair, "My good girl. I'd do anything for you, Genevieve." His thumb brushes against my lower lip, reverently and so fucking possessive, as I'm sitting on my knees between his legs. He doesn't look inclined to put clothes on any time soon, and honestly, I hope he never does again. For the rest of my life, this is how I want Grady. Sleepy, satisfied, and naked.

He leans forward to kiss me, and I allow it for a few seconds. When his hands slip under my shorts, I push off of him, and get settled next to him. "It's my turn," he insists as he leans over me, caging my body against the mattress.

I place another quick kiss to his lips because I can't fucking help myself where he's concerned. "No, tonight was about taking care of *you*. That's what I did. And now we're going to bed."

I can tell he wants to argue, the lust in his eyes not cooling in the slightest. But I can also see the affection and gratitude peeking through, recognizing that this is about him.

Has anyone taken care of this man in the way he takes care of everyone else; in the way he so desperately needs?

No, I don't think anyone ever has. But I will.

He plops down on his back. He slips his arm under my neck, pulling me to his chest. I settle half on top of him, tangling our legs together and running one of my hands along his muscular stomach. He moves my braid over my shoulder and makes similar patterns along my back. We lay just like this, in quiet contentment, until we both drift off to sleep.

Chapter Thirty-One
Grady

This is the third time that I've had the immense pleasure of waking up to Vivi's soft curves wrapped around me and her berry vanilla scent overwhelming me in the most intoxicating way. I slide my hand up the leg she has around my waist in a vice grip. My hand settles at the top of her thigh, right where it meets her butt. Placing a soft kiss to the crown of her head, I settle my other arm behind my head. I have a few hours until Blake is going to bring the girls home, so I'm in no rush to end this moment with Vivi.

She stirs around me. Her hand moves to rub to sleep out of her eyes, but she stays exactly where she is. "Good morning," she murmurs. Somehow, she sounds even cuter waking up in my bed than she did the times on her floor.

"Good morning, love." She gives me the biggest, sleepiest smile I've ever seen. *She's so goddamn adorable.* It actually makes my heart hurt sometimes. "What're you so giddy about already?"

She gives me a small shrug, nuzzling closer to me. "That's the first time I've heard that in person."

I give her a kiss on the lips and her arms sneak around my neck pulling me close. I let her tease me with tugs to my hair and gentle rolls of her hips for a moment, then I take the control back.

Rolling her on top of me and scooting down the pillows, I ask, "How about breakfast in bed? I'm thinking I want something sweet today."

Her eyebrows raise in shock, but it's the pretty pink color warming her neck I can't take my eyes off of.

Answering her silent question, I tell her, "Yes, Genevieve, I mean you."

Her eyes flash in excitement and a small smile plays on her lips.

Laughing, I pull her down to me for another kiss. "I think I *am* actually obsessed with you."

She gives me a cheeky grin and sits back up. Booping my nose she says, "Good. Just how I want you." She lets her hand run through the light layer of scruff on my jaw and up to my messy curls.

"And I want you on my face." I give her butt a light smack. "Shorts. Off."

She gives me a fake exasperated look but the only heat in her eyes is due to her arousal. She stands over me on the bed, shimmies her shorts off and straddles my waist again. The entire time I have a perfect view of her body. My hands run up her thighs, stopping just below where we both want me. My thumbs skim just outside of her slit. Enjoying her growing frustration, the longer I tease her, my thumbs gently pull her open. She's exactly how I was hoping—soaked and needy.

One of my thumbs moves up through her trimmed curls. I start to rub light circles around her clit, and she immediately drops her hands to my chest. Her hips lightly roll against my covered pelvis and her breathing quickly grows shallower. My hands clamp down on her waist, stopping all movement.

"No. *Nope.*" She lets out a low whine in protest. "I'll get you off as many times as you want, baby. All morning if you beg me. But it's happening on my tongue or my cock."

My hands grab onto her ass as I pull her up my body. She hovers above me and settles her hands on the headboard. One hand grabs on tighter to the plush skin of her butt and the other snakes around the front of her hips, pulling her toward my tongue slowly.

She whimpers in anticipation the entire way. But as soon as I suck her clit between my lips, she lets out a deep, guttural moan. It's a new one and I revel in the sound, just like I have with every sound of pleasure she's made.

Very lightly I nibble on her throbbing bundle of nerves, and she drops a hand to my hair, holding me there. I give her what she asks for, only for a few seconds.

My mouth slides down to her dripping center and I suck on the warm skin, teasing her. With each little love bite I leave on her pussy, another rush of arousal coats my mouth in response. The hickeys are so light that they'll be gone within the hour, but I make a note to tease her inner thighs for hours next time so they mark her days afterward.

"*More,*" she begs with a breathy whisper.

Putting both of us out of our misery, I pull her down and take a slow, languid lick up her slit. Her breathy moan mixes perfectly with my satisfied groan.

This is all I need. Forever.

Working my tongue deeper into her, I marvel at the sweet taste of her. At the way her hips lightly roll over me. At the death grip she has on my hair. At her quiet whimpers mixed in with low *fucks* and *yeses* and *right theres.*

The sound of my name on her lips in these moments is the sexiest thing I've ever heard. I feel like a God when she chants my name over and over, so reverently you would think she was praying.

Slowly, I drag my mouth up to her clit again. Sucking and nibbling on her, the hand I've had on her ass moves to her entrance. I know she's wet enough for two fingers already, but I still work them into her slowly, letting her adjust to the stretch. As soon as my fingers crook just enough to hit her G-spot, her entire body shakes with need, coating my face in her delicious sweetness.

She's so pretty and responsive like this. Every little move I make causes her body to have some sort of reaction—each one better than the last.

Her hips start to gain more speed as she rides my face and my control snaps. The rest of the world doesn't matter. Right now, it's only me, Vivi and her soaking pussy. I stretch her with a third finger, and she groans in satisfaction.

"Fuck, Viv, you're perfect." The words are muffled against her but the way she clenches around my fingers tells me how much she loves to hear it. "Not only is your pussy needy, but greedy too. *Just how I want you.*" I repeat her words from earlier back to her and am immediately rewarded with deep moans and another wave of arousal coating my tongue.

"I'm coming… oh *fuck,*" she yells out, getting louder the closer she gets to her orgasm. It only fuels me more. I fuck her with my tongue and fingers at a relentless, punishing pace but her hips keep up with me the entire way.

Until her body goes stiff, a wild moan pulls from her throat at the same time her pussy squeezes my fingers so goddamn tight. I can't wait to be buried so deep in her—so soft and tight, I know I won't last long when I finally feel her warmth wrapped around me. "Grady, Grady, *Grady.*" She comes with my name on her lips.

Her hips lightly start to move on me again, wringing out every single second of the euphoric bliss she can. And I happily let her use me for her pleasure.

The truth is, I'm just as needy for her.

She slides down my body and collapses on my chest. I give her a few minutes to catch her breath, running my fingers up her back and playing with the hair that has fallen out of her braid. When she lightly starts to kiss my chest, I roll her onto her back and settle on top of her.

"What are you doing?" she asks with a cute little furrow in her brow. "How can you possibly be irritated with me right now?" I tease.

She rolls her eyes. With a faint blush she tells me, "I wanted to suck you off again."

I chuckle and place a sweet, possessive kiss on her lips. "You really are a greedy girl."

"Only with you." The look in her eyes is so vulnerable. The most open she has been with me in years.

"Me too, love." I lay kisses and nibbles along her breasts. "I'm going to clean you off then go get you breakfast."

"And after breakfast?" She perks up and it's so freaking adorable. I never want her to leave my bed.

"After I know you're fed and fully satiated, then you can have my cock again."

"Who knew you were so bossy?"

"Only with you," I wink.

She flops back on the pillows. "I wish I could say the same… but I'm bossy with everyone."

"It's one of my favorite things about you. Don't change." She gives me a sweet smile and I respond with a cocky smirk, the one I know she can't decide if she loves or hates. My head descends between her thighs, and we do it all over again.

Viv came on my face three times before she was begging me for a break. Not to stop, just a break. If anything, the last two rounds have made it clear how badly she wants my cock. Each orgasm came with the promise of how she was going to ride me so good, for hours.

I know Genevieve better than to ever doubt her when she's determined to do something. But it's cute that she thinks she's going to be in control. I'm pretty sure I've made it clear that she owns me, except in the bedroom. The roles change there. And with what I have planned, she's going to be *begging* me to take her for hours.

I'm lying on my back, in nothing but my briefs, while a very naked and very gorgeous Vivi is tangled up with my body. She draws soft shapes across my skin and lets out a deep, content sigh.

"What's going on in your pretty brain?"

"Just…" She chuckles and I can see the rueful smile from where I'm lying. "Imagine if we'd been doing that since high school."

I bark out a laugh, twisting her braid around my fingers. "I promise you; it would not have been like that in high school."

"Really?" She looks up at me, a playful glint in her eye. "I've been a pro since my very first time. Practically a porn star."

My chest shakes with a rumbly laugh. I pull her closer to me and lay a soft kiss on her head. "Yup, I'm sure, baby. There isn't a doubt in my mind that you would have ruined me just as much then as you have now. I don't think my dick could even get hard when it comes to someone else anymore." It's the truth. As pathetic as it may be.

She laughs and sets her chin on my chest, looking up at me. "You know, Grady... I'm kind of glad we didn't date in high school."

"I'm slightly offended, I think," I chuckle. "But go on."

She gives me a small, guilty smile. "No, it isn't because of how the sex may have been. I just... even before we fought, I didn't always really like myself when I was younger. I think that's normal when you're still figuring out *who* you are. But I like who I am now. I'm mostly happy with myself." She shrugs a little, making me think that there's still a little self-doubt there. I'll spend however long it takes to ease all of her fears. "I've always liked you," she admits, rolling her eyes at her confession, "but I like your daughters, and I like this black bedroom your mother hates, and I like watching you with my cats, and I like the man you've grown into. More than that, I like this *us* that we've grown into. I think it's my favorite version of us." She tilts her head and bites her bottom lip.

That's a big confession for her, and it makes me feel like the luckiest man in the entire world. Not only is Vivi starting to forgive and trust me again, but she's deciding to take this chance on me. After years of her independence and nursing her past hurts, she's decided that I'm worth the risk. I love her so goddamn much for it.

I've spent my life loving her in a lot of different ways. But this is different. This is a choice. And one I'll be making every day for the rest of my life if she allows me to.

My hand slips to the back of her neck and I pull her up to kiss me. "This is my favorite version of us too. It's only getting better this time around; do you understand me?"

She nods, her lips still a whisper on mine. "Yes, Grady. I understand. I want that with you."

"Good girl. Because I want everything with you." I want a happy marriage, more babies, and a house. Everything she's always dreamed of; I want to give to her. I want all of the good, bad, and boring that comes with that because all of it still looks so damn amazing with her by my side.

I deepen the kiss, about ready to ask her if we can get breakfast later, because right now I need to be inside of her. I'm ready to cross that line together, knowing that there's no coming back from it.

But my phone starts ringing on the nightstand. I look at the clock but it's only nine in the morning. Blake said she was going to take the kids to the aquarium before dropping them off for lunch. I decline the call without looking at the caller ID. "Ignore it," I murmur against her lips. It immediately starts ringing again. Vivi sits up and I groan in pathetic frustration.

Snickering, she says, "Check your phone. It could be an emergency."

Knowing she's right, I turn around and grab my ringing phone. My sister's name is flashing across the screen. "Hello? Blake? What's up?"

"Hey, I'm so sorry. I know you went out last night, but I have to drop Stella and Daisy off."

I sit up at the panic in her voice. "That's fine. What's going on?"

"Adrian's mom fell while she was watering the plants in her yard. Will already called the ambulance. Cami's been admitted but... it's bad, Grady. She's probably going to need surgery."

"How's Adrian doing?"

"He's worried. It's the same hip she fell on last year. She can't put it off anymore. I'm sorry about the change of pl–"

"Blake," I cut her off in my big brother voice, "don't you dare apologize. You and Adrian need to be there with them. Get your kids' overnight bags ready and I'll pick up all five of them. I'll need to borrow your Suburban for the night to fit all of them."

"That's fine, we can take Adrian's car." I can hear her growing panic. "Are you sure? I can take my three with me."

"No. You both should be there with no distractions. I'll take them to the aquarium, and you can pick them up from Mom's tomorrow."

"Okay, thank you."

"No problem. Blake, everything is going to be okay. Give me forty-five minutes and I'll be at your house."

We hang up with the promise to see each other soon. Vivi's starting to slide off the bed, still naked, as she texts on her phone.

"Who are you texting?" She's crazy if she thinks I'm going to let her take an Uber home after the last twenty-four hours.

"I'm seeing if Lexi's awake." She looks up and gives me a shy smile. "I figured it would be less awkward than any of my siblings coming to get me."

"No one is coming to get you. I'm taking you home." I turn toward my drawers and pull out a pair of sweats and a t-shirt for her. I throw them onto the bed before turning back to grab some clothes of my own. "Wouldn't Lexi be sleeping or doing her own trek home today?"

She pulls the shirt on and shakes her head. "Lexi never brings anyone to her birthday or any of our birthdays. Those days are special, you know? If she's seeing someone for at least a month around that time, then it's different. But never randoms."

I nod my head, only half-listening as she slips my sweats up her legs, all the way to her bare pussy. No bra, no panties. Just her body in my clothes. She's shorter than I am with soft curves. My clothes fit her for the most part, but they hug a little tight on some of my favorite places. I watch her walk to the mirror near my closet. She pulls the sweats up near her belly button before tying them in place. She grabs the hem of the shirt next, pulling it taut and into a knot where the sweats fall on her waist. After adjusting the shirt, she turns back toward me and smiles.

My old pair of sweats and ASU baseball tee have never looked so goddamn good.

"You can finish getting ready while I shower. Come on." I walk into the bathroom, Vivi tentatively following behind me. I grab her hand and lead her to the sink. I give her a kiss on the temple before I turn the shower on. Slipping out of my briefs, I tell her, "I'll be quick. We can stop at The Loop for something you can take home. I promised you breakfast."

She nods, giving me a beaming smile. I watch her turn toward the sink, grab her toothbrush from where she set it next to mine last night, and start her morning routine. It's all very domestic and intimate in a way I've never felt. Not even in my marriage. Everything is better with her than it ever would be with anyone else.

Chapter Thirty-Two
Grady

This morning I woke up, dropped all five of the kids off with my parents, and picked Vivi up so we could talk to some of the local business owners.

In only a couple short hours, we received more than a dozen items to raffle off throughout the evening, as well as different donations. All the restaurants are donating food for the concession stands, and Calypso had already agreed to baking the cakes for the cake walk.

It's also our first *real* date. Because that's what Vivi and I are doing now—dating. She said it herself yesterday morning. She more so said that she's glad we didn't date when we were younger and that she likes us now. I'm counting it.

I haven't been able to stop thinking about the entire night and morning with her but that conversation, when she opened herself up to me, was my favorite.

I brought her to a little Italian spot just outside of Amada Beach, a little closer to Aurora Hills. I wouldn't be surprised if she's been here before, but I didn't want anyone disturbing us throughout the meal. And despite the fact that she went to dinner with me at Clear

Horizons, I know she likes to pretend the rumor mill hasn't started around town.

She's wearing a white romper that ties around her waist and a deep V cut at her chest. Knowing she likes to wear her cute little outfits, that I absolutely adore, I wore a pair of green chino pants with a white and tan striped short-sleeved button down, putting a little more effort in what's normal for a walk around town and lunch. Maybe I'm completely biased, but I think we look really freaking great together.

She's giving me a sultry look that I can't totally decipher. Of course, it just drives me even more wild.

There is one thing that has been on my mind, but I've been worried that maybe I'll push her too far. Or that after Friday night, it will be redundant. But looking at her right now, I can't keep my mouth shut.

I clear my throat and lay my hand on the table. She gives me a funny look but takes it anyway. "There is one thing I wanted to clarify."

"Um. Okay? What is that?"

"I think this goes without saying but I don't want there to be any confusion for either of us. I'm not interested in seeing anyone else. Ever again, honestly, but we can work up to that at whatever pace you want." She snorts at that. "And I can't tell you what to do but I don't want you seeing anyone else either. All of this is at whatever pace you want to go, as long as it's just the two of us."

"I'm not planning on seeing anyone else either." *Ever again* is left unsaid but I can see the vulnerability in her eyes. It's enough for me. For now. She bites her lower lip, looking guilty. "It isn't that I'm embarrassed or anything like that. Lexi obviously knows about us, and my siblings aren't stupid. It's just something I would like as much privacy as possible right now. I'm not ready for people to think that they should have an opinion about us."

Not only would people at work talk about us dating, but people around town would as well. "Just us then."

She graces me with a sweet smile and goes back to her menu.

I watch Vivi read over the options. She crinkles her nose a few times, clearly unsure about what she wants.

All I can do is watch in complete adoration and contentment. In the last twenty-four hours, she's all I've been able to think about. I'm surprised she hasn't blocked my number from the amount of texts I sent her yesterday, just to check up on her. I even called her to say good night and hear her voice, but we still texted until one of us fell asleep. It's absolutely something we would have done as teenagers. And as innocent as it was, it's one of my new favorite things.

She peeks at me over her menu and it's so freaking adorable. "I kind of want the lobster dish," she says guiltily.

"Okay," I chuckle, leaning back in my own chair. "Get the lobster."

She shakes her head, "No. I'll get something else."

I push her menu down, so she looks at me. "Please don't be ridiculous. I'll be that guy who orders for you if you make me." She scowls at me, but I can see her resolve slipping. "I want you to get whatever you want. Plus, there is a bottle of a Pinot Grigio that would go well with that and the salmon I was looking at."

"You didn't have to bring me somewhere so expensive."

Maybe she hasn't ever been here.

I'm about to answer her when our server comes to the table. We get the whole spiel about the daily dishes and his recommendations. I order the bottle of wine and the coconut shrimp to start. At the last minute, Vivi chimes up to ask for an order of the calamari. When she looks back at me, she gives me a small little shrug. I respond with an approving smile and thank the server.

"Good. I knew there was something you wanted on the appetizer list. I was taking my best guess."

She laughs into her water glass. After taking a sip she says, "It was between the shrimp and the calamari."

"Why not get both, right?" I smile at her. Her back is turned a little more toward the ocean, and the way the sun creates a halo around her is ethereal. It's like the sun positioned itself perfectly, just to shine right over her. There's never been a person who deserves to glow as much as Genevieve.

She nods but continues her earlier point. "Yes, exactly. So, thank you. *But* you don't have to bring me to places like this... as much as I appreciate it."

"You're welcome. And I know I don't have to, but I want to. You deserve more than this but unfortunately you got stuck with the single father, not the billionaire or NHL player." It takes a second for realization to wash over her but once she remembers the moment from *the sunroom night*, as we've started to call it, she lets out one of her breathy cackles. They come so much more freely now, but they're still one of my favorites sounds in the world. Second only to the noises she makes when she orgasms.

With her cheekiest grin she says, "It's a good thing the single dads were always my favorite then."

The server fills our glasses and leaves the bottle on the table for us. Vivi's sitting forward with her chin on her hands, just looking at me with so much affection that my chest feels like it might burst open.

"Good thing," I agree with a small smirk. "But I promise you I can afford it. And before you argue about dipping into my inheritance—because I know that's what your cute, responsible butt would say—there's a good chunk of it left untouched. Arielle and

I got more for the house than we paid. Plus, I've gotten lucky with some random investments. One specifically."

"What is it?" she asks in disbelief. It doesn't even sound real, honestly. I was just trying to support some kids' dreams, not really understanding the appeal but the rest of the world seemed to.

"Have you heard of that game *Walking Through Books*? It's an app."

"Yeesss," she says slowly. I assumed she'd heard of it, even if she didn't play. It's basically an interactive game that allows you to play as the main character through the stories. Authors give the rights to include their novels. Sometimes they even help develop extra challenges that aren't a part of the main story—giving the players opportunities to make bigger mistakes and take greater risks. It's another way for authors to promote their books and give readers another platform to enjoy their favorite stories.

"Well," I chuckle awkwardly, fidgeting with my silverware, "the three kids who started that a few years ago were my students. They were in the first class I ever taught as an actual teacher, not an aide. A year after they graduated, I ran into them at an alumni thing at ASU. They told me about their app idea. I didn't totally understand it, but I was much more frivolous with my money back then." I laugh again. "I invested a couple thousand dollars. They were good kids, you know? I knew that they weren't trying to screw anyone over. When I finally got a financial advisor, he said it was a terrible investing move. A year later, the app blew up and they've developed a few smaller but still successful interactive games."

"Wow." She blinks at me.

"Yeah, I told you... it was mostly luck. I had no idea what I was doing. Now I let Gary—my financial advisor—help me with all those things so it has only gotten better in some ways."

"Wow," she says again, chuckling and looking a lot less guilty about our dinner.

"Plus," I add with a casual shrug, "It's really worked out for us in some ways."

"Us?" she asks in a skeptical voice.

"You and me, Viv." I cross my arms over my chest and give a small shrug. "One of their mom's happens to be my old principal…"

"The one who owed you a favor? And got us that information on the charities?"

Nodding, I reply, "That's the one."

"I guess that investment brought you more luck than just financial," she teases.

In a serious voice, looking her in the eye, I say, "It really did, Viv."

Later that evening, before needing to get the girls from my parents, Vivi's laughing freely and beautifully in my passenger seat—her belly laugh that tells me she's truly enjoying herself. I refuse to let her roll the windows up but she's being a good sport about her hair whipping us both.

This, the simple act of driving up the coast, was one of my favorite things to do in high school. My first car was an old blue Saturn Ion. It kind of sucked but I had the best memories in that car. There was a sunroof, so the twins and I used to drive up and down the coast in the middle of the night, taking turns sticking our heads out. Hudson typically preferred to drive but every once in a while, he'd get up there. Asher loved it though. He would spread his arms out, screaming at the top of his lungs.

"Where are we going?" She tries to hold back her hair out of her face but it's a fruitless effort.

Next time I'll braid it for her before we come out here.

"You'll see. Connect your music. It's another twenty minutes tops."

She puts on a playlist I think she made herself, and we roll up the windows just long enough to let her pull her hair up. My hand rests on her bare thigh, her fingers interlaced with mine. We don't talk much the rest of the drive, but I can hear her quietly singing and humming along to the music.

When we get to my favorite set of cliffs, I back in toward the edge so we can watch the sunset from the back of my car.

She walks around the back and pulls open the doors, jumping up to sit in the back of the Jeep. "Romantic," she says with a cheeky grin.

I pull out a bag with some of her favorite snacks—diet Cokes, Goldfish and Chips Ahoy—creating the perfect smorgasbord for Vivi. "Damn right it's romantic. Nothing says romance like Goldfish, especially where you're concerned." During one of our meetings, I noticed she keeps a box in her classroom to munch on. "Plus, this is something I definitely would have done with you in high school. I would've looked for any reason to get some privacy with you." We both know it would have been nonexistent at the time.

"Grady Miller," she starts in a fake appalled voice. "Did you bring me all the way out here so we could," she puts her hand up to her mouth as she whispers, "*fool around*?"

I step up to her and situate myself in between her legs. My hands find her waist and her legs instinctually wrap around mine. "Obviously that's exactly why I brought you out here." She gives me a heated look that only burns brighter as my hand runs up her neck to cup her jaw. "But I'm not getting arrested for public indecency or whatever, so you need to have some control tonight."

The smile she gives me tells me that she's going to love testing *my* control the rest of the evening.

Chapter Thirty-Three
Grady

"Wow," I sit back in the tandem kayak we borrowed from The Shack, the small surf shop her brothers own. Vivi sits in the front as she guides us through the caves in La Jolla.

She looks over her shoulder at me, giving me one of her pretty smiles. "You've really never been kayaking before?"

"No," I laugh," I promise.

A week after she woke up in my bed, I finally convinced her to bring me out here. She asked three times on the way here while she was explaining to me the best times of the year to go out on the water. It's pretty late in the season, so she was iffy about wanting to take me for the first time. I was insistent though. She's mentioned a few times that she hasn't gotten to go as often as she likes this year, but every time she talks about it, her entire being brightens.

"This was definitely one of the last good days to be out here for a few months. Thanks for bringing me," she whispers over her shoulder.

I lean forward so I'm right against her ear. "Thank *you* for bringing me, Viv. This is incredible."

And now, as we're floating idly outside of some caves and I twist her braid around my fingers, adding this to my growing collection of new favorite memories.

Eventually, we make our way back to my Jeep and pack everything up. We didn't get into the water, but the waves started to get a bit choppier on our way back to shore. Vivi's been shivering for fifteen minutes now and the sight of her being uncomfortable brings out something primal in me now.

Before she can climb into the passenger seat, I grab a hoodie from the back and wrap an arm around her waist. "Here, baby," I murmur into her hair before placing a soft kiss there. She turns around slowly in my arms and graces me with one of her pretty soft smiles—one that I'm almost positive she saves for only me now.

She lifts the sweater to her nose and takes a big whiff. "It smells like you."

As I watch her slip it over her head and crawl into the car, my phone starts ringing.

When I see Blake's name across the screen, I immediately go into panicking parent mode. Taking a deep breath, I answer. "Hello?"

"Hiii, Dad!" Stella and Daisy's voices ring through the speaker simultaneously.

"Hi, little ladies," I greet them as I get into the driver's seat and start the heater for Vivi. I can't stop the smile that pulls against my lips as she scooches down in her seat and lifts her feet to the heater. I lean across the console and wrap both in one of my hands, hoping to help warm them. "I'm going to be there to get you soon. Is everything okay?"

"Yesss," Daisy giggles.

"Can we stay the night with Auntie Blake and Uncle Adrian?" Stella cuts to the chase. "They're having pizza and carving pumpkins."

"Pleeease, Daddy! Auntie Blake said it was okay, *more* than okay actually!"

Laughing, I nod even though they can't see me. "Yes, darling. You guys can stay with your aunt. Let me talk to her really quickly though. I love you."

"Love you too!" They say at the same time before handing the phone to my chuckling sister. After a quick confirmation that she did in fact invite them to carve pumpkins, I make plans to pick them up in the morning and turn toward, who I hope, my plans now involve for the night.

I hang up the phone and give her feet one more squeeze before she drops them to the floor. Leaning my elbow on the console, I crowd her space until her breathing grows shallower and my lips are only a centimeter away from hers. "Stay the night with me, Genevieve."

My lips find Vivi's neck, and her head falls back with a moan. She insisted on getting to look around my house since we were in a rush the other night. I know she didn't really need forty-five minutes to take everything in. Now she's standing in front of the sliding glass doors, looking into my backyard. She's playing a game—seeing how crazy she can drive me.

Congratulations, you won.

Not able to take it anymore, I realize there is no reason we have to wait until we make it upstairs. The more I think about it... the more I like all the ways I could take her on this brand-new couch.

With her back to me, my hands start work on the little buttons that run down the front of her shirt. She leans her head against my shoulder, turning toward my mouth. My lips find hers, but I don't open for her until she's practically begging for it. As soon as I unbutton her top and slide it down her body, I make quick work of sliding her leggings down her legs before she turns around and laces her fingers through my hair. I grab onto her hips, guiding her around the front of the couch. I push her down to a sitting position and drop to my knees in front of her.

Her sharp inhale turns into shallow breaths and a hazy gaze. "You like me on my knees, don't you love?" I murmur into her neck.

Nodding, she rasps, "Yeah... I really fucking like it."

I place a soft kiss on her mouth. "Lean back, baby." Her hands are still tangled in my hair, pulling me with her. One of my arms slips around her, the other guiding her leg around my waist before settling on her plush ass. She licks against the seam of my lips, always needing more. I nip at her bottom lip before slipping my tongue into her mouth. She catches it between her teeth and lightly sucks it into her mouth. Thinking isn't possible at this point. The only thing I can manage is a groan saturated with need and slip my hand into her loose waves.

Her tongue slides against mine, and she makes the cutest little mewling sounds every time she thinks I'm about to pull away from her. I don't want to, but I know there is a good chance that I'll come far too quickly after sliding inside of her. Just the feel of her clenching my fingers and rubbing her ass against me was enough. And I *know* she will feel better than anything I could ever imagine.

Wanting to make sure that she finds as much pleasure as possible tonight, I slip out of her hold and slide my arms under her thighs. With her leaning back into the couch pillows and her legs over my shoulders, I have the world's most perfect view.

My hands run up her thighs, stopping right below her center. Under her little lacy thong, she's dripping for me. The sweet, slick sight of her makes my mouth water.

My eyes drag up to hers, and I watch her the entire time my mouth descends on her wet heat. She bites her lips, holding back a moan I can perfectly imagine in my mind. The same moan that's been the beginning of all of my nightly fantasies. My tongue makes contact with her clit, and she can't fight it anymore. A deep, guttural groan breaks out of her. Her fingers grip my hair, and her legs tighten around my head. She's so close already.

"Fuck, Grady," she moans as her head falls back. "So good, *so fucking good.*"

"I've been thinking about this nonstop." I slowly slip a finger into her. She's so wet and ready for me, I easily slip a second finger into her as I pump my hand at a leisurely pace. She whimpers and drops her hands to my shoulders, clawing at my skin. "Tell me you've been thinking about me too."

"Fuck, yes. Yes, I've been thinking about you." She can barely get a word out in between her needy gasps. "Every night for weeks. *Oh, yes,* yes, yes. Even most—oh fuck, Grady."

She's clenching my fingers so tightly I know she's close to the edge. I stop, leaving my fingers inside of her. "Even most what?"

"You're such a jackass," she huffs. Sitting up on her elbows, she looks me dead in the eye. "Even most mornings, I wake up to the thought of you between my thighs just like this. Happy?"

"To learn that you wake up already soaked thinking about me?" I slide the small scrap of lace off, marveling at the sight of her pretty pink pussy. "Yeah. That makes me extremely happy, Viv."

This time when I lower my mouth to her center, my tongue moves in slow circles, gaining speed with each pass of my fingers against her G-spot. When I find the rhythm she likes, her hips begin to buck against my face in time with me. "Good girl," I murmur against her. "You love coming on my tongue, don't you?" She nods, at a loss for words. Even her cries have gone silent as her orgasm builds. "Me too, baby. I love when you drench my face."

A strangled cry breaks out of her at my words. I take her throbbing clit back into my mouth and suck hard. My teeth nibble down lightly, adding the pressure I now know drives her wild. Her hands grip my hair tighter and my fingers pump inside her faster. I work her tight pussy as she fucks my face, pushing herself over the edge. It's the most beautiful sight I've ever seen—the way the flush warms her entire body, the way she bites down on her bottom lip as she comes down from the high, the way her gaze always comes back to me licking her arousal off her when she's done seeing stars.

"Grady," she murmurs, satiated and sleepy.

Keeping my arms under her thighs, I push up to her eye level. "I'm not done with you yet." Her eyes snap up to mine, and all the satisfaction from a few seconds ago is gone, replaced with a new round of lust and heat and need. "I need you, baby." *In more ways than just physical.*

With a soft smile, she runs her thumb along my bottom lip. "Me too."

I kiss the pad of her finger and catch her gaze. "I can go upstairs and get a condom. It's your choice. But I'm clean. There hasn't been anyone else, and I don't want there to be anyone else. Ever again."

She nods in agreement. "I'm clean. No one else... ever again." I lean forward, still holding her legs hostage, and lay a passionate, possessive kiss on her lips. "I want all of you. I... I want you to be the first, and *only* man, that comes inside of me, who gets to claim that part of me." She looks at me a little sheepishly, surprised by her own filthy demand. One that I'm happy and ready to comply with. I wouldn't have been angry if another man had this privilege but now that I know I'm the first? It stirs up that possessive beast inside of me—the one that only seems to awaken whenever she's concerned.

A primal, satisfied sound breaks out of my chest in response, only a moment before my mouth crashes down on hers, demanding entrance. She grants me what I want and takes just as much from me in return. "By the end of the night, there'll be no question about who your pussy belongs to. Understand?"

With a sharp inhale and an excited glint in her eye, she nods. "Ruin me, Grady. I'm already yours."

My control snaps. One of my hands drops to undo my pants. I slip them down to my knees, not bothering to spend the time taking them fully off. My other hand works its way to her back, unsnapping the clasp of her bra. She slides it off and throws it over the couch.

She's so pretty and flushed and *mine.*

I line the tip of my cock up to her entrance, but I tease her with the possibility of pushing inside of her. Quickly, I slip my arms under her legs again, holding her body in my control. Holding my palms to her, fingers outstretched, I tell her, "Let me see your hands."

She gives me a curious look before lifting her hands into mine. As soon as my fingers lace around hers, I push our hands to the cushions, right next to her head.

Her chest heaves in anticipation. Her submission to me sends another wave of heat to her pussy at the same moment I slowly push into her. She's so tight, *so goddamn tight.* I've never felt anything better, but I hold myself together, not wanting to hurt her. "I should have gotten you ready with another finger, baby.

I'm sorry." My forehead drops to hers, and we share breaths as my length stretches her.

Shaking her head back and forth, she whispers, "No, you feel so good. So big. You make me feel so fucking full, Grady."

"I'm not all the way in yet, baby." I pull out a little, not wanting to overwhelm her. But her whimper tells me otherwise.

"More, *more*," she begs for me, and I don't ever want to tell this woman no. I slowly slide myself all the way inside as she chants *yes* in my ear.

I kiss her roughly, needing more contact with her. I almost can't believe this is real, that I'm fully seated in Vivi's soft heat as she clenches so tightly around my cock. This is what all my wet dreams are about and now that I'm experiencing it, I never want to go another day without it.

"Are you okay, love?" My lips are still against hers, but her breathing has turned shallower.

"Yes, I want more. Fuck me, Grady. *Please*, Grady… oh god, please…"

"I love when you beg," I chuckle. With our hands interlaced next to her head and her legs wrapped around my arms, I pull out of her to the tip before slamming back home. Her moan is feral and needy and addictive. I do the same thing a few more times, each pull out just as slow and tortuous only to thrust into her harder and harder. She makes that sexy throaty noise every single time.

"Faster and harder," she groans. "I told you to *fuck me*, Grady." She tries to sound firm and in control but there's only so much bravado she can muster when her pussy is milking my cock so goddamn perfectly.

A dark chuckle rumbles out of my chest. "I'm just getting you ready, love."

"I'm ready. *Fuck,* I'm ready, Grady." Her fingers tighten around mine as she clenches around me.

I place a kiss on her temple and whisper in her ear, "Greedy girls get fucked until their pussy is dripping with my cum. Is that what you want, Genevieve? Are you greedy for my cock?"

She's writhing below me and the wetter she gets, the more I want to tease her. "Yes. Fuck yes, I am. All I want is to be used for your pleasure."

Pulling her further down, I place a knee on the couch to change the angle. Like this, I can push even deeper into her. My hips snap forward at a quicker pace, giving her no warning. Her perfect tits bounce as I thrust in and out of her relentlessly. I drop my mouth to one of her pinched buds, rolling it between my teeth and lips. Her moans turn into desperate cries. Her nails dig into my hands as she tries to get any sort of grip on me, but she said she wanted to be used for my pleasure. So, I'm giving her exactly what she asked for.

"You're mine," I growl against her breast. "*Mine.* I don't care about our pasts. As far as I'm concerned, you've always been mine and no one else." She nods and moans in agreement, tightening around me with each word. "But more importantly, Genevieve," I lift my head to look at her beautiful hazel eyes—the heat in them bringing out the golden brown, "*I'm yours.* I've always been yours." A deep satisfied moan claws out of her chest at my promise. I've never heard anything so possessive and desperate from her. It urges me on, faster and harder.

I hold her body in my control, pumping my thick length in and out of her. She watches as I work myself with quick strokes. Her eyes are glazed over and hooded. Her pussy is gripping onto my cock harder with each thrust. I watch Vivi's desperate cries turn to wild moans. Biting my lip to hold my own orgasm at bay, I buck my hips frantically, making sure that she reaches her release first.

Her body goes loose around me, melting back into the couch, and she gives me satisfied, light moans as I continue to fuck her. One of my hands drops hers and finds its way to the nape of her neck. I tilt her head down so she's watching where we are connected. "You're going to watch me claim this pretty little pussy as mine." She nods, never breaking her gaze from where we're connected. The reverent look in her eyes causes the tingling in my spine to intensify, my balls growing impossibly tight. Her free hand drops to her clit, working herself to another orgasm.

"I want to come with you," she whispers in between breathy moans.

I nod, wanting the same thing so goddamn bad. But the sight of her taking my cock and touching herself at the same time is too much. My hips start to slow, and my movements turn more rigid. "Genevieve, baby," I groan. "I'm—baby, I'm coming."

Both of my hands drop to her hips, and her newly free hand immediately goes to her left breast. She squeezes the soft skin, rolls her nipple between her fingers, and repeats the movements. "Me too, Grady. Fuck, I'm right there with yo—" she moans at the same time I spill inside of her. She convulses around me while I fill her up for the first time, claiming her in another way as mine.

Without breaking our connection, I grab both sides of her face and pull her in for a deep kiss.

"Again," she mutters as my mouth makes its way along the column of her neck.

Laughing, I pull out of her and use my fingers to push my cum back inside of her. I watch as she tightens around my fingers, begging for more. When I'm satisfied that not a single drop was wasted, I lean over her. She's already flushed from the few pumps of my fingers.

"I told you that my cum would be dripping down your thighs by the time I fully claimed you as mine. We aren't anywhere close to that."

A shudder works its way up her body, and I take her rosy nipple into my mouth again, getting us both ready for the next round.

Chapter Thirty-Four
Grady

Mon, Oct 31 at 6:09 PM

Arielle

God they're adorable! Thanks for FTing me before taking them trick or treating

Of course. They were excited to see you. And tell your friend in the props department thanks again. They love their headbands.

I've already sent her pictures and she's dying over how cute they are

Call me when you get home. I want to talk to you, Grady

One of my favorite traditions growing up was trick-or-treating around town on Halloween. Each of the businesses hold booths to give out candy, some even include fun activities. Maddon Hardware always does a haunted house. It has gotten a reputation over the years and kids younger than twelve aren't allowed anymore because Stanley always goes all out for it. Hopefully his nephew will keep the tradition alive.

This year is the girls' first time. Blake, Adrian and their three kids are joining us. Stella and Daisy dressed up as a moon and sun respectfully. Millie wanted to dress up as Mirabel from Encanto, forcing her brothers to be Bruno and Camilo. They all look adorable, and I hope this is something we can enjoy for as many years as possible.

We've made it around the block, with only a few businesses left. The next one coming up is Brighter Daze. Daisy has been asking all night when we would get to the bookstore. None of us said anything but I know we're all trying to push it off until the end—not because I don't want to see Vivi, but because I know Blake is uncomfortable. I'm always excited to see her but even more so today. She refused to tell me what she'd be wearing. She claims I won't have any idea but wants me to guess anyway.

Daisy tugs on my hand, trying to skip forward. "Daddy! Look! It's the bookstore!"

Blake keeps her face neutral, but I can't help but wonder what she's thinking. She's been on better terms with Calypso, at least she was the last time I saw them. They'd even made plans for Calypso to bake the next years' worth of birthday cakes. She's never really known Lexi, so they just ignore each other. It doesn't appear to be from animosity, just awkward circumstances, I guess. So that just leaves my sister and Vivi. They were close growing up. Blake looked up to Vivi like the older sister she never had, and

Vivi treated Blake like she did all of her other friends—as someone important to her. I'm not totally sure about what happened but I think it was around the same time that my friendship with Vivi started to come to an unwelcome end.

We don't really talk about Blake ever, but I think she's the biggest reason we're keeping our relationship so quiet—or pretending to.

We walk up to the storefront, and I open the door, heading inside as everyone follows Daisy, still walking beside me.

As soon as we walk in, I see the three of them behind the counter. They're in identical skintight latex-looking jumpsuits. Calypso's in red, Vivi's in green, and Lexi's in yellow.

I know that I would love nothing more than to peel that little outfit off of her body and I know I'm going to *love* the way it hugs every curve once I get a full view of her. What I don't know is who she's supposed to be.

Daisy runs to the back, jumping up and down to show off her sun costume. Stella and Millie follow behind at a more timid pace. Calypso, Lexi and Vivi make a big show of complimenting and fawning over each of the kids' costumes. The girls are buzzing by the end of it.

"You three look great... as... um." I tilt my head, letting my eyes rove over Vivi as I try to figure it out. She gives me a smug grin that says *I won.* I don't really care who won this round. I'm just thankful we played the game because she looks so sexy with her hip against the counter, her arms crossed in front of her chest, channeling the brat I know she can be.

"They're the *Totally Spies!*" Blake swats my chest like it should be obvious. Adrian nods over her head with a fake look of disapproval. There's no way he knew who they were supposed to be either. Standing with Kayson on her hip, she gives each of them a small smile. "You guys look cute."

A comment like that from Blake is more than an olive branch. It's an entire grove.

Lexi and Calypso give her a quick thanks. Vivi smiles cautiously at Blake. "Thanks. I love their costumes." She points to Blake's three kids. "Did you sew them?"

Blake nods and tells Vivi about the other costumes she's crafted for them over the years. We spend about twenty minutes making small talk and looking around the store before we wander off to finish the evening. Blake was friendly, if a little quiet. She agreed to let Millie tag along on the tea party that they're planning for Bonnie in December. It was the longest we spent in any other store, and it leaves me feeling hopeful that Blake and Vivi can make amends too.

Mon, Oct 31 at 8:13 PM

Arielle

We promised to stay friends but you refuse to talk to me. Come on Grady

> I'm not. I've been busy and I'm trying to start my life in here. Of course that'll always include you, because of the girls, but how that looks in MY life is different. It's normal, Arielle.

I don't know if I like that

> It's the way it is.

Vivi

"Sooo," Calypso starts, pausing to make sure the store is empty after Grady and his family left, "how are things with him?"

I look up from my phone, about to immediately text him like a lovesick fool.

Obviously, we aren't doing a good job of hiding things—I don't know if I even want to anymore.

"Um." I don't really know where to start.

"You don't have to tell me anything," Lyp resigns, a flash of hurt in her eyes. "But if you wanted to talk to me about it, you could. I won't say anything."

Guilt washes over me. Calypso and I have *always* been close. She, Lexi, and I are a trio by now, especially since her childhood best friend moved away a few years ago. They hardly talk and it only makes me feel worse for hiding things from her but... "It isn't that I don't want to talk to you about it and I know that we have talked about," I whisper, "sex," then speak normally, "before, but this is about *Grady.* Is that okay?"

Calypso looks really confused for a second before snickering at my modesty, Lexi joining in. Calypso is as comfortable with the topic of sex, and almost as open about her own life, as Lexi.

"Shut up, I don't care. I mean... honestly... I've just kind of wondered if Grady has a big dick or not," she laughs but doesn't bat an eye at her own brazen curiosity.

"Wait," Lexi leans forward pointing at Calypso across the counter. "She can ask if Grady has a big dick, but I can't call him Daddy?"

"Ew, no," I laugh. "That's what *Daisy* calls him. You can't call him that *ever*, got it?"

"I'm asking as an older sister, Lexi." She gives her a fake scolding look. With a small tilt of her lips, her eyes cut to me, and she says, "I have to make sure my baby sister is getting dicked down good, right?"

I cackle and push past my embarrassment, saying, "You don't have to worry about that, okay? He's... more than enough to keep me happy. I promise." I widen my eyes in emphasis.

Lexi and Calypso fake whoop and high-five.

"You're so embarrassing, *stop*." I cover my face.

They settle down and Calypso gives me a genuine look. "This just feels right, you know? I'm happy for you, Viv, and I want you to let me be a part of your happiness."

I nod at her. In between trick-or-treaters, I tell her all about mine and Grady's time together. Starting all the way back to our first meeting in his classroom. She listens the entire time, smiling in an encouraging way.

"It may have taken him a while to develop it, but that man has big dick energy, and I love that for you." Calypso nods in approval.

Laughing, I finally decide to bite the bullet and ask Calypso the question that has been burning my tongue for a while. "Lyp? Not to sound like an asshole or anything, but why are you so nice to Stella and Daisy?"

Lexi barks out a laugh and Calypso does too after a second. "Excuse me?" She looks between us. "Do I typically go around stealing candy from babies and kicking children?"

Snickering, I shake my head. "You just don't typically take an interest in kids, but you have with them. It's sweet. It's almost like... I don't know..." I don't want to say it because it sounds silly and presumptuous.

She gives me a soft, unfamiliar smile—nothing about Calypso

can really be described as soft. "It's almost like maybe, possibly, I could be an aunt to those two little girls, right?" I nod, not saying anything. "I'm going to take an interest in *your* kids. And Hudson's. If Asher ever changes his mind, his kids too. And I guess I just figured that sometime in the future, I might be their father's sister-in-law. Which would make me their aunt." She gives me a small shrug.

"Yeah, maybe," I agree. And for the first time, I allow myself to share that hope with someone other than Grady.

Mon, Oct 31 at 10:04 PM

Grady

I'll be honest… I've absolutely no idea what you were supposed to be but I would pay good money to see you in that costume again.

> I didn't realize that role playing was a kink of yours

I would try just about anything with you.

> There are definitely a few things I can think of that I haven't tried yet

Make me one of your pretty little lists and we can start work on it as soon as possible.

> That's probably the sexiest thing anyone has EVER said to me

> I'm going to spend some quality time with myself and think about you now

> Good night Grady ☾

Call me before bed so I can tell you good night properly.

Chapter Thirty-Five
Grady

The evening after Halloween, I push Vivi up against her car with one hand on her hip, the other braced behind her on the car. "Thanks for coming to dinner," I whisper only inches from her lips.

"Thanks for having me. It was really nice." Her voice is just as soft as mine.

Tonight was the first time that Vivi came over for dinner with the girls. I told them that Vivi was my childhood best friend, and that I've been hanging out with her and her family more. It isn't a total shock to them. They see Vivi at school—even seeking her out sometime—and at our parents' monthly dinners. Not to mention they both are excited to attend the fair at the end of the semester.

They took the initial news about our dinner guest as I had anticipated. Daisy was practically bouncing in her chair, asking if the entire Davies family would be there. When I told her it would only be Vivi, she said that was perfectly fine. It gave them more time to show Vivi all of their toys and their new bedrooms. Everyone else could come see it another day, according to her. Stella sat there quietly, taking in the news, and not having much of a reaction. When I asked if it was okay with her, she shrugged and said it was fine.

I knew it wasn't that simple, but I also know she likes Vivi. This whole situation is just harder for her than it is for Daisy. Which is understandable. I never expected me starting to date to be easy on either one of them. I also didn't think I'd even be interested in a relationship for a long, long time.

Clearly, I was underestimating my feelings for Vivi. I don't want anything to be halfway with her. She deserves everything, and I want to give that to her. My life has been better, and brighter, with her back in it these last few months. She would never replace their mom and I don't want her to, but she could be that same light in my daughters' lives too.

"I should get going," she whispers, her breath warming my lips.

"I wish you could stay." My hand squeezes her hip, not wanting to let her go.

"Me too but tonight was probably a lot for them already."

Vivi's understanding and commitment to my daughters makes me love her more. I've stopped denying that fact to myself but as always, I'm giving her the time she needs before we take that step. Her showing up to dinner tonight tells me more than enough.

"You're right. Let me know when you get home though." I place a soft kiss on her lips.

"Okay." I can feel her smiling against my mouth.

"And call me before bed. I'm going to go get them ready now." I give her another soft brush of my lips.

She nods. "Okay." Her hands slip around my waist to my back, holding me close. I take a step into her and push her against her car. I wrap her hair around my fist and hold her head at the perfect angle. Teasing her for a few seconds with the promise of a kiss, I lean down and place my mouth on hers. Like how most of our kisses start now, it's sweet and affectionate and unhurried. It isn't until I feel Vivi's fingers lightly tighten on my back that I deepen the kiss. I nip at her lips, and she opens for me, slipping her tongue along mine. I allow myself a few minutes of holding her against me before I buckle her into her car and watch her pullout of my driveway.

It has been two days since Vivi came over for dinner and things have... taken a turn for the worst at my house. Daisy's been cheerful as usual but has FaceTimed with Arielle four times in the last forty-eight hours. I don't mind at all that she misses her mom and wants to talk to her, *obviously*, but it's hard for Arielle and me to make it happen every time she wants to. Arielle's getting into a string of more frequent shows and longer road trips in between.

Stella has been bordering disrespectful, crossing the line in small ways she never has before. She's been *forgetting* her most basic manners. She slammed her door in Daisy's face and refused to play with her last night. I know they're going to have fights, but this isn't about Daisy. Even her teacher pulled me aside this afternoon. She rolled her eyes when she was called to work on the whiteboard, and flat out refused to help her classmate when asked.

I haven't told Arielle I'm dating someone yet. I don't really know how to handle that conversation and I hate that I have to tell my ex-wife at all.

This all is just much more complicated than I'd really anticipated. I think I just got so wrapped up in Vivi and having her back in my life that I didn't stop to really think about how it would play out with so many people involved. It's completely unfair to her; all these extra people to consider come from my side of our relationship. She doesn't have any baggage that'll be around for the rest of her life. I don't mean the girls, and I know Vivi is almost as obsessed with them as I am, despite Stella's newfound attitude. But Brody isn't a part of Vivi's life anymore and he never will be. I can't say the same about Arielle. She's always going to be a part of my life in some way. I can't find it in me to regret my marriage to Arielle because I wouldn't have Stella and Daisy otherwise. The same way I can't totally hate my younger self for everything that happened. I wouldn't have my daughters if Vivi and I had been together our entire lives. It's all just so complicated and none of it's fair to Vivi.

It's one of the thoughts that plague my insecurities the most these days.

I had promised to take Vivi to dinner tonight since the girls had asked to spend time with Blake, but I sent her a text earlier asking if we could reschedule. I didn't go into details about it, just saying that I feel like it's important to spend time with the girls right now. Vivi sent back a quick *okay*, not giving me any indication where her head was.

Until she found me in my classroom at lunch. Already having plans to eat with Knox in his room today, Vivi just stopped in for a couple minutes.

When she asked if everything was okay, I was honest with her about the change in behaviors with my daughters the last few days. She nodded in understanding and was quiet for a moment. She eventually told me that she saw Stella in the hallway yesterday. Vivi waved and said hello, but Stella just kept walking. Her little friend Mary asked if she was going to say hi and Stella apparently said '*no, I don't know her*'. Mary was in Vivi's class last year, so she turned and gave her a shy greeting.

She wasn't mad at Stella. She didn't even appear to be hurt by Stella's cold shoulder but, her words have been playing through my head all afternoon.

"We can reschedule dinner." Vivi lifted off the desk she was leaning on and took a step toward me. "You should talk to your daughters. I... I didn't think about how keeping us a secret would start to cause problems. If anything, I was trying to avoid that from happening. Spend time with them tonight, talk to them and figure out what they're okay with. You've been patient with me. I can be patient with them."

My heart expanded ten sizes at the sincerity and promise in her words. "Thank you. I don't think I'll ever be able to fully express my appreciation for you."

She gave me a cute smile. "You do all the time."

Before she could walk out, I caught her wrist and took a quick peek down the hallway. When it was all clear, I pressed a chaste kiss on her lips. "Tell Knox I said hi."

"You two are adorable attached at the hip like this." She laughed but she wasn't wrong. I'd gotten really close with Knox and Lucas over the last couple of months. Asher and Hudson have joined us for drinks more than a couple times. "Call me later. If you want. It's okay if not."

"I'll call you."

A few hours later, I'm getting three bowls of ice cream ready. Complete with all the toppings—chocolate, sprinkles, whipped cream and banana slices. I'll probably regret this tactic in two hours but right now, I'm not above sweetening my daughters up with sugar. It's going to be a hard conversation for all of us.

I set the bowls in front of the girls as they sit on the stools at the island while I stand on the other side, looking at them.

Stella gives me a questioning look before picking up her spoon but makes no move to take a scoop. Daisy digs right in, so innocent and naïve of what's about to come.

"So," I start slowly, catching how Stella's entire body goes stiff, "I've been meaning to ask you how you felt about Vivi coming to dinner the other night." Neither of them says anything. Stella stares at me but Daisy's eyes are glued to her bowl. "Was it bad?"

They both shrug.

"Did something happen to make it a bad time?"

They shake their heads.

"Would you be okay with Vivi coming over for dinner more often?"

They both shrug again.

I take a deep breath, knowing my frustration will not help the situation. Sometimes it feels like a mutiny now that they outnumber me.

"Can either of you please use your words to tell me what you're thinking?"

Stella twists her lips to the side and looks away. After a few seconds, Daisy says, "I like Vivi coming over. She's fun. But is she going to be our new mom?"

I shake my head. "No," I answer quickly. Stella looks back at me. "No one is replacing your mom. Vivi wants to be... your friend." That seems like a good place to start. "You have a really good mom, who loves you. You don't need a new one." Daisy nods but she looks sad swirling her ice cream in the bowl. "Stell?" I try to prompt her to speak.

"Are *you* replacing our mom?" The question guts me because the honest answer is *yes, I am*. But is Vivi the replacement? Or were Arielle and I like fitting a round block into a square hole? It fits but that doesn't mean it matches. All of that's too complicated for them to understand though, and none of it's going to make them feel better.

I lean forward on my hands and give them both long looks. "Your mom is very important to me, and she's always going to be very important to me. We share the two most precious gifts in this world, and I'll always be grateful for her. She'll always have a place in my heart and my life.' That's true. "But it's... different. Your mom and I are friends now. That means we don't live together, and we don't kiss each other anymore. One day we'll do those things with someone else."

"You already do that with Vivi," Stella states so plainly. I flinch at her blunt honesty, but the last few days suddenly make more sense.

Nodding I admit, "You're right. Vivi and I kiss now. One day, in the future, maybe she will live with us but not until you both are okay with that. This is *your* home. *Our* home. Understood?" They both nod. "Stell, how do you know Vivi and I kiss?"

"Was it a secret?" she retorts.

"Nooo," I say slowly. I don't want to teach my daughters to keep secrets. It'll happen someday, but right now I want them to know they can talk to me about anything. "But I wanted to tell you both myself. Obviously, I was careless. I'm sorry that you didn't find out from me."

She looks down and I can see the tears gathering in her eyes. "When you walked her outside after dinner. I was watching through the front window."

I nod. There's no point in being mad. I should have thought about that. It *was* careless of me. "Do you want me and Vivi to stop?"

Stella and Daisy both look up at me, conflicted. I continue, "You two are the most important people in my life. You come first.

Always. And… if you need more time, then I can tell Vivi that we need to be non-kissing friends right now." The thought of having that conversation guts me. I can't imagine being just her friend after the last couple months of slowly gaining every part of her. I know she would understand but it doesn't stop the ache.

Stella shakes her head, a tear slipping over her cheek. "No. You've seemed really happy. You smile a lot more here than you ever did in Phoenix. I don't want you to stop smiling."

"Me neither, Daddy." Tears start falling down Daisy's cheeks too. "I like when you're happy and I… I want Vivi to be my friend."

My eyes start to burn but I blink back my tears, trying to hold it together for them. I cried in front of them once when their mom moved out, and it was a mistake. My tears only made them even more sad. I look at Stella and she nods in agreement, more tears falling.

I walk around the island and scoop them both up into my arms. They each wrap their arms around my neck as I walk to the couch and get settled. "I've only felt overflowing love and happiness since you two were born, but I want to be a dad who smiles more. And you're right, Vivi makes me smile."

"She makes me smile too," Daisy says in a small voice as she wipes her eyes.

"Stell? What do you think? Could Vivi be someone who makes you smile one day?"

She looks at me for a long time and I use my thumb to wipe the lingering tears on her cheeks. She places her head back on my shoulder and gives me one quick bob of her head. "Can we watch a movie before bed?"

"Sure, sweetheart." I grab the remote and open the Disney Plus app. Stella and Daisy snuggle into each side of me and we lay like that for the entirety of the film.

After Daisy's in bed, I stop by Stella's room and sit on the edge of her bed. I push her hair out of her face while she gives me a contemplative look. "I'm sorry I haven't been very nice," she adds after a second. "I promise I'll help Patrick with his math tomorrow."

I lean down and place a kiss on her forehead. "It's okay to have big feelings and not know how to handle them. You're still learning, and you will be for the rest of your life. It doesn't stop but thank you for talking to me tonight."

She nods, her hands tucked in between her head and pillow. "I know I don't act like it sometimes, but I do like Vivi... I just miss mom too."

"I know, Stell. Neither trumps the other, okay? You get to feel both of those things."

She nods again and gives me a small smile. I sit with her for a while longer, until her breathing slows, and she looks like she's in a peaceful dream.

I go downstairs to clean up the bowls of ice cream that were forgotten earlier. Pulling my phone out of my back pocket, I go straight to Vivi's contact and call her. Even just hearing her voice while I tidy up sends a rush of relief and domesticity through me.

Chapter Thirty-Six
Grady

Mine and Vivi's eyes immediately snap to each other. We aren't sitting directly across from each other tonight so we both have to turn our heads to the right a little. Everyone is quiet, and for some reason Lexi looks the most surprised out of anyone.

Daisy's words still ring through the air like an anvil.

Yeah, Daddy and Vivi kiss now. Right, Dad?

She's so innocent and sweet. She has no idea that she just dropped a bomb. One that's about twenty-five years in the making.

It has been exactly three days since I sat my daughters down and talked to them about Vivi. Daisy snapped back to herself like a rubber band after that. I even found her hanging out in Vivi's classroom on Friday. Stella's adjusting at a slower rate, but Vivi and I are patient, giving Stella the time she needs.

Her little sister obviously has other plans for all of us.

No one mentioned kissing, or even Vivi. My mom asked how Daisy's week was and if we did anything exciting. She has no idea how *exciting* that nugget of information is to my mom and Bonnie. I slowly drag my eyes away from Vivi's mortified expression and look around the table.

I'm pretty sure that everyone was just letting Vivi believe that it was a secret even if they all had some idea about what was going on. We've been seen around Amada Beach with each other more than once in the last few weeks, first of all. Not to mention that her siblings were all at Yellow Cab—where we showed up together, disappeared for twenty minutes together, and left together.

We haven't been doing a very good job at hiding anything, not that *I* ever wanted to.

I roll my eyes at Lexi and her fake shock. Her eyes are wide, one hand clutching the chair's arm and the other covering a gasp. Asher and Calypso are both leaning back in their chairs with huge grins, looking like they're tucked in for the show. Hudson's expression is indiscernible—flat lips and raised eyebrows—but he doesn't look angry. It's pretty much what I would've expected from him. Even Blake has a small smile playing on her lips, but her husband has his arm draped around her shoulders, beaming next to her.

At the same time, Bonnie and my mom *squeal*—it's a sound I've never heard from either of them, but one Daisy makes daily—and jump out of their chairs. My dad chuckles at the end of the table.

Look, I'm happier than anyone about me and Vivi. Probably more than even her. I know there was a part of her that feels like she lost some game between us and it's a win I'll never brag about. But their reaction feels *a little* dramatic. Especially once we get yanked out of our chairs for a group hug.

Each of our mom's grip onto our elbows, dragging us out of our seats and to one end of the table. They use their super-mom strength to shove us together. Vivi's face smacks into my chest. *Hard.* Before I can lift a hand to soothe the spot, their arms wrap around us like a vice. Someone—probably Lexi—starts a slow clap that overtakes the table within seconds. Vivi is stuck facing the backyard but when I turn, I see even Stella clapping along. I share a small smile with her and mouth *love you.* She drops her hands but mouths back, "I love you too, dad."

When our mom's break apart, Vivi awkwardly turns toward the table. She glances around before clearing her throat. "I know this *must* come as a surprise to you—"

Lexi practically squawks, throwing her head back. Her comment even pulls a few chuckles from Blake and Hudson.

"This is… this is the best day of my life," my mom exaggerates, wiping her non-existent tears.

Blake raises a hand in the air. "Uh. How about the days we were born? Or even your grandchildren?"

"*Morrita,* I am hoping to get *more* grandchildren. And we all know that Adrian got a vasectomy."

He coughs into Blake's shoulder. Blake narrows her eyes at our mom. "*No ellos no,*" Blake snaps back. I never learned Spanish, but Blake took to the language easily from a young age and has been teaching Stella with my mom. I know enough to translate though—no, not everyone at the table knew that piece of information.

My mom waves her hand in Blake's direction. "*No importante.*" *That's not important.*

Blake's eyes flash to mine, her expression is screaming *is this woman fucking serious?* The miniscule smile on her face tells me she's joking though. I don't expect any congratulations from her. I know she's giving me, *us,* as much as she can right now. And it means everything to me.

"Let's slow down." I don't have to look at Vivi to feel the panic radiating off of her. It doesn't matter how much she wants children—this isn't a conversation she wants to have in front of our families.

I see the reluctancy in Bonnie's eyes but, knowing her daughter, she relents. "I can wait a few more years for a wedding. I'm just so happy you two have finally figured it out."

Vivi rolls her eyes on her way back to her seat, but she doesn't try to hide her beautiful smile or flushed cheeks. When she sits back down next to my dad, she gives him a small smile. He slips his arm around her shoulder, whispers something in her ear that makes Vivi's eyes tear up. He leans over to give her a kiss on the top of her head before making a toast to the happy news.

*This is right. This *is* my family.*

Chapter Thirty-Seven
Vivi

I'm finishing getting dressed when Lexi storms into my bedroom. It isn't the first time she's seen my boobs, considering we shared a small studio apartment for an entire semester. She doesn't even blink an eye at my topless chest or the fact that my nipples are pointed straight toward her.

"I need your brown boots." She walks into my closet, rummaging around for whatever pair of shoes she's looking for.

Shoes are the only things Lexi and I can really share—but even then, it's rare. Our styles are so different I have no idea what boots she could be looking for.

"What time are we leaving?" she yells from the closet. I can hear her huffing and puffing, so she must be putting on whatever pair of shoes she was looking for.

"Oh, uh. You wanted to drive together?" I ask nervously.

She hobbles out with one boot on, the other in her hand. The light brown booties actually go perfect with her wide leg jeans and dark cropped glen plaid sweater and turtleneck combo. "What do you mean? We always drive together?"

"You look really cute, by the way."

"I know. You too." She points toward my white mini sweater dress I slipped over my head and knee high dark brown boots. "But don't change the subject."

I sit on the edge of my bed, putting my earrings on. "Grady's going to pick me up. He will be with both of his daughters."

"Okaaay..." she says slowly. "So what time is he getting us?"

The only option I really have is to laugh at her abrasive personality. "Let me check."

Thurs, Nov. 24 at 4:23 P.M.

> Lexi is wondering what time you're picking us up.

Grady

> I'll be there in 15. Let Lexi know she's going to have to squeeze between the car seats in the backseat.

> She doesn't care

> She's just offended that we would even consider making her show up to Thanksgiving dinner alone.

> Not that I don't love having her as our shadow but is she not spending today with her family?

> Her family started to spend the day with us

> Knox & Lucas are coming too it's going to be the biggest one yet

> Can't wait. I am getting the girls buckled now. They want to spend the night with Millie. Bring a bag. We can drop Lexi off on the way home.

> Yes sir

> You have no idea what you started.

Lexi swings the front door open, "Took you lo–" She clears her throat. "Hello, there."

I grab my purse off the counter and walk toward her. When I see Daisy and Stella standing at the door with Grady, I know immediately what they're looking for. Or, I should say *who* they're looking for. "Hi, Cinnamon and Vanilla are probably hiding in the bathroom. You can go check the bathtub really quickly."

Our sleepovers have been minimal with how busy we both have been lately, even if the cat's been out of the bag for about three weeks now. Daisy may be excited that we're together, and Stella is quickly warming up to the idea, but it doesn't mean that either has been ready to wake up to me in the kitchen or at their breakfast table. So, we take advantage of the nights the girls go with their grandparents or Blake.

But that doesn't mean we haven't shared a few dinners, mostly at their house. Except last week, the girls *begged* to have dinner at my house when they learned I have two cats. It was love at first sight for all four of them.

And there aren't enough words in the English dictionary to describe the surreal feeling of having the three of them here, in my home, so happy and *excited*. Even if it was more for my cats than me, I don't give a fuck.

Stella and Daisy can have all the time in the world to come around to the idea of Grady and I, if it means that's what I have to look forward to for a lifetime.

The sounds of their sweet little laughs as they run down the hallway brings a huge smile to my face. Grady steps inside and immediately slips his arm around my waist and pulls me in for a kiss. I melt into him, letting the happiness of the last few weeks warm my bones.

"Excuse me, I'm standing right here."

Grady and I pull apart, and he gives Lexi a smug smirk that's so fucking sexy it isn't fair we aren't alone right now. "All of a sudden you hate PDA?"

"Only when I am going through a dry streak," Lexi mutters. I supportively pat her back, giving her a fake sympathetic look. "Fuck off." She pushes my hand away.

"Swear jar!" Stella yells from the bathroom. My head falls back with laughter, so much freer and brighter than it's been in years.

When we get to my mom's house, we run into Lexi's family in the driveway. Her parents, Mark and Nathalie, pull each of us into a hug. After a moment of Lexi explaining how she knows Grady, they remembered him as the *very respectful and responsible boy* who took their daughter to homecoming. At this point, I can't do anything but try not to laugh at their confusion when Lexi tells them that Grady's here with me tonight. Maybe confusion isn't the right word—more like *concern* that Lexi and I will start to brawl right here, right now, at the mention of our high school days.

Johnny looks unsure of how to greet Grady—his baseball coach—but Grady takes the initiative by patting him on the shoulder and telling him how great he was at the last practice while they walk inside.

Leaning in toward me, Lexi whispers, "Do you think G knows that Johnny has a thing for his woman?"

Nathalie snickers at her daughter and I bark out a laugh. "Shut up, Alexandra."

Except she's not wrong. Johnny declared he was in love with me the first time Lexi brought me over to her house, during Christmas break our freshman year of college. It was awkward and adorable, and no matter how much he tries to say he's over the crush, the boy wears his heart on his sleeve.

Lexi flicks my forehead at the use of her full name, but her mom lovingly wraps an arm around my shoulders, chastising her daughter, "Leave your brother alone, Alexandra. It's not his fault he succumbs to beautiful women."

"Ugh, don't we all," Lexi teases and bumps my hip. I grab her arm, locking it around mine. She bends down enough to lean her head on my shoulder and says gently, "Have I told you lately that I'm thankful for you?"

Placing a soft kiss on the crown of her head, I tell her, "You don't have to, Lex. I'm thankful for you too."

Standing straight but pulling my arm closer to her, she says quiet enough for only me to hear, "I'm thankful for him too. For the fact that it feels like he's breathing life back into you."

I nod, not knowing what else to say and not wanting to cry seconds before we walk into the Miller's yard.

And even though Lexi's words will stick with me for a long time, as soon as I cross the gate, the mood immediately changes.

Yes, I'm thankful. More importantly, I'm *happy*.

Calypso and Hudson are sitting on the love seat together, looking through photo albums that have just as many pictures of us as there are of Grady and Blake. Asher is picking Daisy up and setting her on his shoulders as Stella walks beside them, showing him all the words she learned to spell for the upcoming competition. My mom and Grady's parents are greeting Mark and Nathalie with hugs and a glass of wine. Lexi doesn't slip out of my hold until Grady makes his way back to me, sliding his arm around my waist and pulling me in close for the first time in front of our families. We're only missing Blake's bunch but they're on their way from Adrian's parents' house and Knox is stopping here for dessert. So, in a few hours, all of our people will be under one roof.

And maybe we have a lot to work out still—conversations to have and boundaries to set—but none of that matters right now.

All that matters is that for the first time in way too fucking long, I'm so incredibly happy and full of love. Nothing could pop this bubble.

Grady

"Okay but he's kind of gorgeous," Lexi muses from the backseat of my Jeep.

"You found him?" Vivi whirls around in her seat.

"Yeah, it was so easy. He doesn't post often but he has a few new posts within the last year. So that's not a bad sign." I watch from the rearview mirror as she scrolls through her phone.

"Give me, give me!" Vivi enthusiastically reaches for the phone.

My eyes cut to her in the passenger seat next to me. I can feel the scowl creeping across my features. "Holy shit, *yes*. He's perfect for her. Am I looking at Thor with *tattoos*? Please."

I clear my throat. "Excuse me, I'm sitting *right here.*"

Vivi laughs, handing the phone back to Lexi and places a kiss on my cheek.

"We aren't looking at Lucas's cousin with the perspective of wanting him for ourselves," Lexi explains. "We are looking at him as potential for Lyp, and I really think we just found her kryptonite."

"That's Superman," I tell her.

"Please shut the fuck up and look at him. Remember, *for* Calypso."

I roll to a stop sign, and after checking that all the roads are clear, I turn toward the two matchmakers. I raise my eyebrows, waiting to see what all this fuss is about. Lexi pushes her phone between Vivi and I, placing it so we can all scroll through his Instagram together.

Stanley has started to let people know that come next fall, he'll be retiring and handing over the two businesses to his nephew Liam. I already knew about this, so I wasn't shocked when Lucas casually let it slip during dinner. Calypso showed no interest in the news or the man but that isn't going to stop anyone in this town from making their own decisions. Just take Lexi for example.

The most recent photo is a Chris Hemsworth look-alike but with tattoos, exactly as Vivi said. One of his sleeves looks like a random array of traditional tattoos. They're all black and grey, and there doesn't appear to be a rhyme or reason to them. It's too small to see what each one is but you can see that the quality is good. His other arm is an array of colors that are perfectly blended and arranged into a series of different plants and flowers. It's mostly made up of shades of green but there are all the colors of the rainbow displayed as variations of flowers throughout. He's broad and muscular with an easy smile. His blonde hair is short on the sides and nicely styled. He looks like the type of guy who enjoys looking good but doesn't have to put a lot of effort into it.

One thing I remember about Calypso's ex-husband was that he was a pretty boy. I guess there isn't anything necessarily wrong with that, but he put more effort into his own appearances than he probably spent showering Calypso in the attention she's always demanded from her boyfriends. And if she didn't get it, she didn't keep them around. It's clear that as an adult, she's independent and doesn't reply on anyone to supply her with her lowkey, but lavish, lifestyle. And I don't think she would make the same mistake twice by wasting time on a man who doesn't want to spoil her the way she does herself.

They look up at me expectantly at the same time. I clear my throat and nod, "Yeah, that's an attractive man. Calypso doesn't stand a chance if he sets his sights on her."

"Oh, he will. Don't you worry," Lexi promises in an evil genius voice. She scrolls through the four other recent photos—his long-haired dachshund apparently named Rosie, the skeleton of the house he built for his mom this year, him cuddling up with Rosie in bed, him and his sister on a road trip, and him with his niece.

"She's fucked," Vivi chuckles.

Chapter Thirty-Eight
Vivi

Grady pulls into my driveway, but instead of waiting for Lexi to get out, he puts the car in park and unbuckles. Confused, I start to do the same, but he stops me with a hand over my seatbelt.

"I forgot something here. I am just going to grab it and I'll be right back." He gives me a sultry look that sends a hot pulse directly between my legs. But the uncertainty tamps that down a little.

Grady has stayed the night a couple times in the last few weeks, but we usually stay at his place when we get the chance. Last time he was here, Lexi walked in looking for half the ingredients she needed for her dinner. I was tucked under a throw blanket on the couch, satiated from a round of mind-blowing sex we had just finished. Grady barely pulled his briefs up to his waist when she walked in, gave his crotch one quick glance and a brisk *I like what you're working with* before grabbing the eggs, breadcrumbs and marinara sauce and leaving.

After that, Grady has pushed for our sleepovers to be at his house. Understandably.

"Come on, I'll let you in," Lexi says. He gives me a quick kiss before he walks toward the garage with Lexi. She says something that makes his head tip back in laughter before opening the door, waves bye and I watch as he makes his way into my place.

I scroll through my phone, sending thank you texts to my mom and Selena. A few minutes pass, and I start to wonder if Grady really did leave something at my place. I'm starting to get worried when he finally makes his way outside. He pulls out his phone, his thumbs moving rapidly over the screen, before walking to the side of the house where the trash cans are. I can't see what he has but he tosses a shopping bag in one of the cans and heads back to the car.

As he's getting in the Jeep, Lexi's head pokes out and with one final wave, she presses the button for the garage door. I turn my head toward Grady, "I could've just given you the code."

"Lexi said she was worried about me coming to stalk you two, so I wasn't allowed to have it."

Chuckling I mutter, "She's so fucking weird."

Nodding, he starts the car. "I have everything I need."

"What *did* you need?"

"You'll see," he teases with that sexy grin again. His eyes are dark and heated. It makes my skin tingle even if I have no idea what he's planning.

I settle back in my seat as he pulls back onto the road. "What were you throwing away?"

This time, his smile is so shy and cute and dare I say *nervous*. "I figured I would check on the pussies." That makes me laugh as I watch him from the passenger seat. "I gave them some food, filled their water bowl and cleaned the litter box for them." He shrugs and says it so casually, as if it isn't a big deal. He has *no* reason to take that responsibility upon himself, but it makes my heart grow ten sizes anyway.

I grab the hand he has resting on the gear shift and set our interlaced fingers on my thigh. "You're too good to me."

"No, baby. This is only the bare minimum of what you deserve."

I squeeze his hand, giving him a small smile even though he's looking at the road. "And what do you deserve?"

He gives me a side-eye look; from my seat I can see the affection in his expression. "Whatever you'll give me."

"Everything then."

Lifting my hand to his lips, he places a kiss on each of my knuckles. "Do you need anything before we go home?"

Home.

I love the sound of that. It doesn't matter that we are going to Grady's house after just leaving mine. Wherever Grady is, my home is there now.

I shake my head. "No, take me home."

When I walk out of the bathroom, I find Grady sitting on the edge of the bed, waiting for me. He already got my side ready—a glass of water and an extra charger. Sometimes he leaves a hair tie on the nightstand so he can braid my hair before bed, but he did that while I was brushing my teeth tonight.

"What's going on?" I ask cautiously, choosing to lean against the dresser. He casually stands up and walks toward me. He lets one hand fall to the dresser next to my hip, the other plays with the hem of my silky shorts. He bought me another pair—this one white with a dainty wildflower print.

In his husky bedroom voice, that could make me do just about anything, he says, "I want to try something with you tonight."

"Uh, what—" When I see him grab the silky tie off his dresser, an electric current zaps through my body. "What are you doing with that?"

He chuckles quietly, slowly walking closer toward me. He's looking at me like a starved lion. And I am the lonely gazelle he's about to devour.

Subconsciously I take a step back. The deep, rumbly sound rolls out of him again as he takes one large step. He's right in front of me now, his arm wrapping around my waist. "Do you trust me?" There's a slight panicked edge to his voice.

I tilt my head, giving him a serious look. "Of course, Grady. I trust you more than anyone else, especially now."

"I want to tie you up."

My mouth twists to the side. The idea mostly arouses me but there is a part of me that's nervous. I don't like the idea of not being able to touch *him*. But I've never done this with anyone. Grady looks so confident in his desires that it makes me wonder where this is coming from. "Have you ever done this before?"

"No," he answers immediately. "But I want to try this with you. If you want to. If you're uncomfortable then we won't."

I scan his face, looking for answers even though I know mine is going to be yes. I look down at the light blue tie again. "I've never seen you wear a tie before... is that from your wedding?"

He scowls at me but the gentle, yet firm hold he takes on my chin says otherwise. "No, Genevieve. I would *never*." He actually sounds annoyed with me and that's uncommon for Grady. It startles me back a little.

If I'm being honest, I know it's an unfair assumption. Grady hasn't ever blurred the lines of his previous marriage and our relationship. But my insecurities are still so loud sometimes. I bite my lip, hoping I didn't ruin the night.

He pulls me closer to him again and his eyes soften. "I own very few things from when I was married. And all of it is because it was something that was *mine*, like my Jeep, not ever ours. This tie…" He clears his voice, looking nervous again. "This isn't from my wedding."

I glance down again, doing a double take. *It can't be.* That would be… crazy. Right?

"Is that the tie from your senior prom?" He doesn't say anything, but I find him nodding when I look up at him.

He takes a deep breath, looking adorably shy. "I kept it because it was the last good memory we had together. Even if the reason it happened wasn't. I needed something to remind me that it was real."

My hands run up his chest, settling on the back of his neck. "I want to do this with you." Maybe it's stupid, maybe it shouldn't matter. But the fact that Grady saved that tie from one of the last nights we talked before he left for college means more than a little to me. And it makes *this* mean a hell of a lot more.

He looks for any sign of apprehension on my face. "Really?"

I nod and pull him down to my lips. "I trust you, Grady. I want this with you." He groans just as our lips clash. My hands grip onto his hair, his slip up the silky tank top. He runs his tongue along the seam of my mouth but even when I open for him, the kiss stays soft; passionate but languid.

I have a feeling this isn't how Grady is going to be in a few minutes, so I decide to soak in the moment. I melt into him, letting him ravish me at whatever pace he wants.

It isn't until I start to feel his growing length against my stomach. My hips buck in response, too short to get him where I suddenly need him. He doesn't oblige me. In fact, he does the complete opposite. He tightens his grip on my waist, pulling me closer to him so I can barely move at all.

His tongue plunges deeper into my mouth, taking back control. I get lost in the moment, needing nothing else except for the taste of him. We get lost in each other for a few minutes before Grady slowly breaks the kiss.

With his hands on my hips, he guides me backwards. "Sit on the bed, baby." I drop down and watch as Grady lifts his shirt off him. Next, he unbuckles his belt and pulls it off. His eyes move over me as he unbuttons his pants but doesn't push them off. My eyes shoot up to his and I can feel the pout on my lips.

He lightly rubs his thumb along my cheek, laughing quietly. "Soon. You're not even tied up yet."

"I'm impatient." I rub my legs together for emphasis. Grady's eyes darken with an alluring tilt of his lips.

He grabs the hem of my shirt. "Arms." I lift them over my head, and he slips the top off of me. Instinctually, I raise my hips off the bed and watch as he drags the shorts to the floor. "Lay back."

I do as I'm told, scooting toward the headrest.

"Are you comfortable?" His voice is silky and soothing against my lingering nerves. I push some of the pillows off the bed, lying flat on my back, I nod up at him. He smiles down at me—one so full of love and adoration that it brings tears to my eyes. He straddles my waist and leans down to tell me how beautiful I am before gently grabbing my wrists and pulling them over my head. He uses the tie to secure me in place. I give a cautious pull on the knot, realizing that it is looser than I expected. I could slip my hands out if I needed to. But Grady's trusting me to give myself over to him. And I trust him to take care of me. "Are you okay, love?"

"Yes." It is a breathy whisper I'm not sure he can even hear. But he leans down and places a soft kiss on my nose.

"Good."

He crawls off of me, and I am suddenly aware that I'm *naked*. Obviously, I remember how this happened but now as I am laid out bare for him, I become more self-conscious. Grady sticks his right hand into his front pocket, looking for something. When he looks up, catching me subconsciously pulling my knees up, he places a hand on my leg pushing it back down. With a firm shake of his head, he *finally* moves to push the rest of his clothes down.

I think watching Grady undress is my favorite thing ever. It might as well be primetime TV in my world.

Slowly, he drags the fabric down his muscular legs and drops them to the floor. He crawls in between my legs, giving me a perfect view of his body. His broad chest and tight abs, down to his thick length and brawny thighs. I am so focused on his miraculous body that I don't notice right away that he's holding something.

He opens his hand, and a small cotton bag hangs from his finger. I would recognize that smiley face embroidery anywhere… especially because I keep *that* in my bedside table.

"And to think I believed you just cared so much about my cats," I tease.

"Excuse me." He places a hand on each of my thighs. "I take the care of Cinnamon and Vanilla *very* seriously. They come second only to one other pussy." My chest shakes with silent laughter, trying to give Grady a stern look. Before I have a chance to reply he admits, "I was going to get your pink dildo. You know the one you love to talk about."

Chuckling, I shake my head. "You mean the one *you* like me to use while on the phone with you."

"Semantics. Except that thing is *huge*," he teases with a cheeky grin and fake horrified look. "No way I would want you to have a side-by-side comparison."

My incredulous scoff quickly turns into a fit of giggles. With my hands still tied up, my own option is to kick his chest. "Oh my god, *shut up.*" His laugh is deep and reverberates throughout my entire body. Most specifically it sends a wave of wet heat straight to my core. "Are you going to do something, or am I just your own personal show right now?"

His eyes rake up my body before a sexy smirk pulls on his lips. "I kind of like the idea of that. Let's see how wet I can get you with my words alone."

I groan, a mix of desire and torture. "Please don't tease me like this. I want you so bad right now, Grady."

"Just right now?" He tsks, his knuckle ever so lightly, running up and down my seam. "You're not always this soaked for me?"

"Grady," I try to scold, but the desperation is thick in my voice. There's no hiding it.

"Just be a good girl and let me look a little longer, baby." I feel the arousal hit my center at the same time he growls, primal and possessive. "You know... it doesn't surprise me that you have a praise kink, but I am so lucky that I get to be the one making you feel good."

I whimper as he slowly pushes his middle finger into me. "I don't feel good right now. I just feel... I feel needy and frustrated. Please, Grady."

His dark chuckle deliciously scrapes against my skin. "That's exactly how I want you. You're going to come on my fingers, then my tongue. And if you prove to me that you deserve it, then you can come on my cock."

"Deserve it?" My outrage is drowned out by the moan of pleasure as he slips his finger deeper inside me and starts fucking me, quickening his pace at his own leisure.

"That's right. You can have my cock when I decide you've earned it."

"Oh, *fuck me*," I keen, wanting to give Grady what he wants but also so fucking ready to feel him in me. As much as I love his fingers and mouth, those aren't what I want right now.

Amused, he leans over me. "I already told you I would… but you have to let me have my fun first. Okay?"

I nod, whimpering at his promises.

Still leaning over me on one arm, he continues to work his finger in and out. His pace is faster, more frantic as I clench around him. He hits a particularly sensitive spot and slips another finger in as my body arches up. "You're so goddamn beautiful, Viv… just like that, baby. I love watching you come for me."

My hips buck, looking for just a little more sensation than what I'm currently getting. In a whiny voice, I prepare to beg. "Grady, please… I just… oh *fuck,* I need—" A feral moan is ripped out of me, cutting off my demands.

Grady continues to massage my G-spot—something I'm certain only he has ever been able to find every single time—but his lips are only inches from mine. "What do you need, baby? Use your words."

"I need… you." My breathing grows more labored. I'm so close, but I just need *more.*

"You have me, pretty girl. Tell me what else you need."

"Clit," I mumble. "I need you to massage my clit. And kiss me. Please, for the love of all that's holy, fucking *kiss me*."

"Look at you, telling me exactly what you want… but I can do one better for you." I feel his approving smile against my lips as they press down on mine. I waste no time slipping my tongue into his mouth, sucking on his when I catch it between my teeth. The soft buzzing of the small toy catches my attention only a second before I feel the familiar stimulation.

I don't know how long I can handle not being able to touch

him but right now, it is making everything else so much more overwhelming. Usually, I grip his hair or dig my nails into him to keep me grounded. But without that, I feel like I am standing on the edge of the cliff without anything to catch me.

The rough passion in his kiss mixed with the way his fingers rub and scissor inside of me is perfect. But it's all of that, plus the continuous vibration, that pushes me off the edge. One of my legs wrap around his waist, finding the only security I can right now, wanting to keep him as close as possible. His tongue fucks my mouth just as relentlessly and possessively as his fingers fuck my pussy.

He whispers '*good girl*' and '*you're so fucking beautiful*' and the sweetest nothings I've ever heard in my entire life. There's not one second where Grady isn't showering me in affection.

My moans die off and my body melts into the mattress. I keep my leg wrapped around him, not wanting him to get too far.

"You're doing so good for me, love. But I want one more before you get my cock."

I nod, frantically. It isn't a want anymore, it's a *need*. And I'll do just about anything Grady wants right now. Shyly, I look up at him. "But..." He quirks an eyebrow at me, a silent urge to go on. I try to catch my breath. "But I want to ride you." It's one of the only positions we haven't tried yet and the thought of sinking down on his thick shaft has been the star of my fantasies for the last week.

Grady gives me a deep kiss, one that takes me to another dimension. One where it's only us, forever, tangled up and tasting each other. One I never want to leave.

"Let me have you like this a little longer and I promise you can ride my cock to your little heart's desire."

I whimper at the image, making me even needier. "Hurry and make me come then."

His lips finally dip down to my breasts, sucking one peaked nipple into his warm mouth. "You're not in control right now," he murmurs against my skin.

"Don't you want to fuck m—*I'm sorry*," I say sarcastically. "Don't you want to *make love* to me?"

Lifting his head, he gives me a dark look that tells me exactly how much he wants to devour me right now. "Trust me, it's painful how badly I wish I was buried in your tight pussy right now, but I'm going to take my time with you."

I glance down at his erection, long and thick, when I notice the pre-cum dripping from the tip. My mouth waters wishing I could lick that up for him. "You're a masochist," I breathe.

Chuckling darkly, he makes his way down my body—kissing, licking, and sucking all along my breasts and tummy. Stopping right above the apex of my thighs, he says thickly, "Only when it comes to your pleasure."

And with that, his head dips down as he licks all the way up to my clit. The sound that pulls out of me is deep and guttural and primal in a way that only happens for him. The fire burning in his dark brown eyes tells me exactly how much he would love to consume me whole right now. And I swear, there is nothing I want more.

He alternates between teasing up my slit and nibbling on my sensitive bundle of nerves. If I had my way, I would keep him right at that spot with my hands in hair. But I'm still completely at his mercy and the teasing is relentless.

"I thought you wanted to come... what's taking so long?" He looks up at me with a challenging look.

"*You.* You're working me up for nothing," I pout.

"Am I?" He asks quietly, at the same time I hear the light buzzing again, this time on a faster setting. "I just wanted to make sure you were ready."

"You know I am." I moan as he runs the toy up my center ever so slightly. "I am so fucking wet for you, Grady, don't pretend like you aren't knuckle deep in me right this second."

He bites the inside of my thigh at my sass, and we both let out the same noise coated in need.

With that, he gives me exactly what I asked for. His mouth stays on my center, fucking me relentlessly with his tongue. The moment he drops the vibrator to my clit, pushing the toy against my sensitive flesh and giving it a swirl, I know I am at the precipice again. It's quick and overwhelming this time. With such little build up, it feels even more euphoric, but doesn't last nearly as long as the first.

Leaning his head on my thigh—the other leg still hanging over his shoulder—he watches me with a lazy grin as I come down from the high. Our eyes lock as my breaths even out and he places light kisses on the soft skin along my inner thighs.

And then so fucking slowly, he crawls up my body again. His hands go to mine, but instead of untying me, he interlaces our fingers together. With a heated kiss, he rocks his hard cock against me. We groan in unison, his grip on my hips growing tighter with each thrust against my slick center.

I know after one more, I'll be done for a while. Too overstimulated and satiated to go on. And I don't want that, not like this.

I turn my head, breaking the kiss. *"Please, Grady."* The high-pitched tone in my voice is so apparent now, I know he's taking pity on me.

With his lips against my neck, he tells me, "You did so good, baby."

The light pressure around my wrists eases and they fall to the bed. Before I can grab onto him, Grady takes them in his hands, examining each one. It wasn't tight enough to hurt but my ivory skin reddens easily. "I am okay," I reassure him. "I just want you. Now."

His eyes darken completely as he slips his arms behind my back, flipping us over until I am on top of him.

Out of patience and overflowing with lust, I don't waste any time. I grab his hardness with one hand, giving him two rough strokes, before lining him up with my center.

"I want you to take me all at once." I revel in the sensation of his tip stretching me to fit him. "You're fucking drenched, baby, so I know you can. I want to watch you slide down my cock."

I nod desperately wanting the same thing. I slide down another inch and my mouth opens in a silent scream. Usually, Grady slowly works his thickness into me with shallow thrusts, but this is something different. I feel like I'm going at a glacial pace, but it is the fullest I've ever felt. I take my time sinking down, taking his full length inside me. He's patient the entire time, letting me adjust to his size inch by inch. And no matter how badly my hips want to buck up, I don't let myself. I take him all at once, just like he asked.

"Good girl. *Good fucking girl,* Genevieve." A whimper breaks out of me, my hands drop to his chest, and I dig my nails into his pecs looking for anything to ground me to him.

"Fuck, Grady... You're so big." My head rolls back as his cock twitches inside of me. "This position is something else."

"I could watch you feed my cock into your pretty pink pussy for the rest of my life." It sounds more like a promise than an observation. He runs his hands up to my breasts, gripping each one hard. "You take me so well, baby. You really were made for me."

I let out an incoherent agreement, wanting him to know that in the very depth of my soul, I believe the same thing. *We were made for each other.* Nothing has ever made me feel as complete as Grady does, especially when he's buried so deep in me it feels like we'll never unravel ourselves again.

Grady and I are one being—connected in so many more ways than just our bodies.

I lift my hips up, almost slipping off of him totally, but instead slamming back down when I get to the tip. His breath hitches, and it only urges me on further.

Taking a page out of his book, I start with a slow rhythm. Each roll of my hips turning rougher, harder, faster. "I am so close, Grady." It comes out so garbled I'm surprised he can understand.

"Me too, baby." He lifts his hips to meet mine, matching my pace thrust for thrust. "I'm going to fill you up but not until you're coming with me."

"Touch me. I want to feel you everywhere."

His hands drop from my breasts, replaced with the wet sucking of his mouth. One of his hands grips my ass cheek tight and the other falls to my clit, rubbing tight little circles—the way he knows will bring me to orgasm the quickest. He's over the teasing, not liking it so much when he's on the other side. He's impossibly hard, ready to come in me but not until he's positive that I've gotten there first.

"You're everything to me, Vivi." He nuzzles his face between my breasts, holding me close to him. "I need you to come for me n—oh *goddammit*, you're choking my cock."

My hips move frantically but Grady's still right there with me, matching my pace and fucking me so hard I swear I can feel him in my throat. "So fucking *goo*—" I start at the same moment he hits the front wall perfectly, over and over. The euphoric wave breaks around me, pulling me down with only the sound of my needy, feral moans as warning.

Grady holds my hips still, pumping into me as I ride out my orgasm and he reaches his. It feels like I am drowning in my desire endlessly, before Grady holds me against him by my ass, as deep in me as he can go. I fall forward, nipping and kissing his chest as he spills inside of me.

After we are both spent and so fucking satisfied, I stay on top of him. Catching my breath, I can still feel him twitching inside of me and my walls fluttering in response. I'm not ready for the empty feeling of him pulling out yet.

So, we lay there for who knows how long. Time doesn't exist when I'm naked in Grady's bed, his body wrapped up with mine. After several minutes that end entirely too quickly, Grady brushes the hair off my face and demands that I meet him in his shower to do it all again.

Chapter Thirty-Nine
Grady

My eyes crack open at the banging on the front door. It's muted but loud enough to hear upstairs. Silky red strands are sprawled across my chest, and I consider ignoring the door.

If I stay here, wrapped up in the sweet vanilla berry scent of Vivi, maybe they'll go away.

That's until her hazel eyes flutter open. She's the lightest sleeper in the world I've quickly learned, I'm surprised it took this long to wake.

Vivi sits up, wiping the sleep out of her eyes with one hand and playfully shoving my shoulder with the other. "You need to get that."

"Stay here," I mumble.

Grabbing a pair of sweats from the dresser, I slide them up my legs before making my way downstairs. My exhaustion and frustration dissipate when I open the door.

Blake is standing on the porch with a miserable looking Daisy in her arms and Stella silently crying next to her.

I scoop Stella up and reach for Daisy immediately. "What happened?"

"They all woke up about an hour ago, one getting sick after the other."

I feel their foreheads. *Definitely a fever.* "All five of them?"

She nods and looks over my shoulder. Vivi put on a pair of leggings and a sweater she must have brought with her. She stops a few feet behind me, giving a sympathetic smile to my sick daughters. Her and my sister give each other an awkward but polite wave. "Sorry to interrupt. But they wanted to be with you."

"Thank you for bringing them home. I've got this. Go be with your kids, and I'll call to check on Knox."

Blake quickly makes her way to her car, not looking back. I take a mental note to call her later.

When I face Vivi, I don't know what to say. This isn't how I want to end our morning, but I don't have the capacity to give her anything more right now. Not when my daughters need my full attention.

"Viv, I—I need to get them into a bath." My thoughts are jumbled. This isn't the first time the girls are sick at the same time but it's the first time that I have to do it all alone. "Can I call you a car? I'm so sorry but I just…" I trail off, shaking my head. Daisy is gripping tightly to my shirt, and I can feel her cool sweat through her pajamas.

She recovers quickly from the shock of my dismissal. "I'll text Calypso. Go take care of them."

Stella's tears wet my shoulder. "I don't feel good," she says in the smallest voice I have ever heard. Daisy nods on my other side.

When I don't move, she waves her hands toward the stairs. "Go, Grady. I'll be okay. They need you."

I nod, taking the first step. Then another and another. I look back only once to give her a grateful smile. Hers is sad but understanding. I know it isn't fair but even though I gave her a blatant dismissal, I wish she would push her feet into the ground and stay.

It just doesn't feel fair to ask her to stay. This isn't her responsibility even if I desperately wish it was.

I feel in over my head for the first time since I became a single parent, and I don't want to be alone again.

An hour and a half later, I'm making my way downstairs. Both girls are bathed and sleeping in their beds. Neither one has thrown up in the last thirty minutes—it feels like a small victory. One I'll happily take right now.

I hear the noise before I get to the kitchen. It sounds like someone is tinkering around in the drawers before I hear the faint *click click click* of the stove turning on.

A sigh of relief escapes me realizing it's probably my mom coming to check on us. Blake definitely saw my panic, even if she was avoiding eye contact. It's like her to call for help—she's stronger than me in that way. And as pathetic as it is, the thought of my mom coming to help is so comf—

Not my mom.

Vivi.

Her beautiful red hair is pulled half up, and she's in her green sweater and shorts outfit again matched with a pair of white fuzzy socks. She turns when she hears me shuffle in. With a shy smile, she gives me an awkward wave. "Hi. I—uh. I know you asked me to leave," she mumbles, her brows furrowing, "but it didn't feel right." I take a small step toward her. "I stopped at the store on my way back. I was going to make some chicken noodle soup for the girls, and I brought crackers and Gatorade. I, uh, also brought you lunch… I figured if they were asleep, we could eat really quick then I'll leave. But if I'm overstepping then I'll go now." She takes a step back; I take a larger one coming in front of her.

"Don't leave." Brushing a stand of hair behind her ear, I give her a grateful smile. "Stay and eat with me."

"Are you sure?"

"Yes." I give her a soft kiss on the lips and rest my forehead on hers. "I'm so glad you're here. I didn't want to be alone… I'm so tired of being alone, Viv." My voice is raw in a way I've never heard before.

Cupping my jaw, she pulls back to look me in the eye. "I don't want to be alone anymore either, Grady. I want to be with you. Let me be here for you." There is so much vulnerability in her eyes it hurts, but I don't let myself look away.

I place another kiss on her lips but before I can deepen it in the way I am craving, my stomach grumbles. Laughing, she pulls out of my hold and grabs the to-go bag off the counter.

"I figured your stomach must be in a similar state to mine after last night," she shamelessly gives me a long once over before turning back toward the counter. "I got breakfast sandwiches from Morning Munch and some coffee from Daily Drips… Don't tell Calypso." She shoots me a sly smile on her way to the small dining table.

"As long as you got me the sausage and hashbrown sandwich, your secret is safe with me," I tease.

She plops down in the seat, rolling her eyes. "I know you. Of course, it's the sausage and hashbrown."

And isn't that the goddamn truth? This woman knows me, *sees* me, even when I try my best to hide.

Two hours later, Vivi and I are playing our second round of Skip-Bo. It was one of our favorites growing up. In between checking on the girls—still sleeping, thankfully—I pulled this out of the game cabinet. Most of what's in there are board games but I've kept this one over the years because it reminds me of her. The spark of competition in her eye is nostalgic and sexy, all at once.

Vivi's on a roll, working through her stockpile and kicking my ass again, when we hear shuffling down the stairs. She turns in her seat to peer around the corner as I stand up, walking to find Daisy in her pajamas with her blankie wrapped around her shoulders and Princess Pumpkin Pie tucked under her arm.

"Hi, darling." I scoop her into my arms. She nuzzles closer into my neck. "How are you feeling?"

She's still too hot but some of the clamminess has subsided. "Better," she whispers. "I'm hungry but I'm scared."

"Let me go check on your sister and I can heat up some soup, okay?" She nods against my shoulder. "Vivi's in the kitchen. She didn't want to leave you guys without making sure you're okay."

Her head lifts up as she tries to see Vivi from here. "Really? Is she going to stay? I just woke up. She can't leave yet." Her lip starts to tremble—she's always more emotional when she isn't feeling well.

"Why don't you go ask her if she wants to watch a movie? I can make you and Stell a bed in the living room, and you can eat your soup in there today." Setting her down, I watch as she makes her way into the kitchen. I hear Vivi's chair scoot back and her quiet words to Daisy I can't make out.

Upstairs, I find Stella awake in her bed, dazedly staring at the wall. "Hi, sweetheart." I brush some hair out of her face. "Do you want to go downstairs? I have soup and I'm going to make a bed for you and Daisy in the living room." She nods, looking worse than Daisy. Tentatively I add, "And a special visitor's here to see you."

Her eyes cut to mine, filled to the brim with tears. "Is it Vivi?"

Nodding, I start to pull the blankets off of her. She's still too warm and sweaty. Her fever isn't breaking like Daisy's yet. "How about another quick bath and then we can meet them downstairs?"

She sits up on the mattress but doesn't get out of bed. She looks up at me with fresh tears running down her cheeks. "Can you carry me?" Where Daisy gets emotional, Stella gets needier. I would do anything to take her discomfort away, but I live for those few moments where she still needs me the most.

After Stella is bathed and in a new pair of pajamas, we make our way downstairs—her little arms still wrapped around my neck as I rub her back. We can hear quiet giggles that have her lifting her head in curiosity.

When we round the corner into the living room, my large body suddenly feels too small for the amount of love it's trying to hold.

Vivi made herself at home—as she *always* should—and set up the bed on the floor. It's one of her best blanket forts to date, actually. It's just large enough for the four of us if we squeeze in and there'll be plenty of room for the girls to stay in there as long as they want. Just to the side of the pillows I can see a small trash can she took from the bathroom.

But it's the sight of Vivi kneeling beside Daisy, helping to fluff her pillows just right, before tucking her in the same way Bonnie used to when we were really little.

"Arms—in or out?" Vivi asks.

"Out," Daisy says quietly with a small smile on her lips. She holds her arms up so Vivi can get the blanket situated.

Tucking it in extra tight around her body, Vivi singsongs, "Snug as a bug in a rug."

"In a rug?" Daisy giggles.

"Some people say mug, I like rug better."

"Who's going to tuck you in?"

Vivi sits back and rubs her hand down Daisy's head. "I'm here to take care of you, little lady."

Daisy nods but doesn't look convinced. "Next time you're sick, we'll take care of you. You'll need to be snug as a bug too."

"Deal."

Stella watches the entire exchange from my arms with me. She lightly taps my cheek to get my attention and whispers, "I want to go lay down with Dais."

Vivi turns around at the sound of my feet moving across the hardwood floor. "Hi, Stella girl, do you want to be a bug too?"

Stella climbs out of my arms and goes to Vivi. Without thinking about it she throws her arms around her neck and whispers so quiet I almost can't hear it, "Can I be in a rug too?"

I can see Vivi's arms tighten around her back, and she closes her eyes, trying to hold the tears at bay. "Of course, you can. Let's get you comfy so we can watch the all-time feel better movie."

She doesn't have to say it for me to know for certain—*The Princess Diaries*. She got the flu in elementary school, and I wasn't allowed to see her for days so I wouldn't get sick too. At that point in my life, I'd never gone more than maybe two days without seeing her so after four, I couldn't handle it anymore. I snuck into her room with one of those old portable DVD players that were popular in the early 2000's and we stayed up all night watching the movie three times in a row.

Not saying that's what cured her but the next day, she was feeling well enough to at least move to the couch and be around people.

I leave my three favorite girls in the living room while Vivi helps to get them settled and I go warm up the soup Vivi made.

When I return, Vivi's lying next to Stella—who is holding her hand—but there's just enough room on the other side of Daisy for me. I crawl in and get settled with one bowl of soup for Daisy while Vivi helps Stella hold hers.

And the rest of the afternoon goes much the same way.

The girls only get sick once or twice more before their stomachs settle, but don't feel well enough to do much else. So, we stay in the fort Vivi built, taking turns picking movies in between soup breaks and naps well into the evening.

I hope my girls are feeling better, but I know *I* am.

Chapter Forty
Grady

Vivi and I were standing in the kitchen, talking about when she should leave for the night and if she'd come back in the morning. We haven't crossed the line of sleepovers when the girls are home, but a timid Stella walked in with Daisy's hand in hers and, confidently asked Vivi if she would be staying for breakfast.

There was a mutual relief that flowed between the two of us. Just the thought of being away from her after everything she did for us today feels wrong.

Most days I can find comfort in knowing Vivi's only five miles from me and a phone call away whenever I miss her, but tonight's different. I *need* all three of them under one roof with me more than ever.

That's how Vivi ended up taking a bath while I got the girls ready for bed.

When I make my way back into the master bathroom, I find Vivi lounging in the tub just like I left her. A couple weeks ago I had her order extra of her berry hair products so she could keep them here, but I also stopped by Lush for some of the different bath products I know she loves. Tonight, she chose the bubbles.

Her hair is dry and piled on top of her head—she's probably too tired to deal with it tonight. When she notices me through the light wall of steam and the quiet music of her nighttime playlist, she turns on her side to get a better look at me. She doesn't say anything. Instead, she gives me a small grin. I strip off my shirt as she watches, her lips spreading further across her face.

I stop on the side of the clawfoot tub and brace my hands on each side. "Stay right here while I shower." She nods and I reward her with a possessive kiss.

I start the shower before stepping out of my pants and briefs. Vivi's eyes are on me throughout the process but every time I take a peek at her, I see nothing but affection and a hint of heat. I let her look, never shying away from her. If anything, it's these moments that I love the most. These quiet, intimate moments that in some ways mean so much more than sex. I wouldn't trade the feeling of her wrapped around me, moaning my name, and scratching down my back for anything in the world. But this isn't something you would share with just anyone, in the way you might share your body with a stranger. These moments are saved for the person who makes you feel like they are your home.

And Vivi makes me feel like that. I'm home when I'm with her.

I let the steaming water run over me for a couple minutes before working through my shower routine. I turn the water off and wrap a towel around me when I step out. Vivi's eyes slowly crack open, and she watches me with a lazy smile again. I dry off enough to slip a clean pair of briefs on. She sits up, preparing to stand up but I stop her with a hand to her shoulder.

"Not yet."

She gives me a confused look but leans back in the tub, watching as I pull a stool over. I'm sitting behind her, so she has to turn her head to track my movements.

"May I?" I tap her head. She knows I mean her hair, so she pulls the hair tie out and drapes it over the outside of the tub. I use my fingers to work out the knots and she sinks a little deeper into the water. I take longer than what is necessary, reveling in the feel of her silky auburn strands sliding along my hands.

She's silent for a few minutes, but I can practically hear her mind whirling with too many thoughts. "What are you thinking about, love?"

She rests her hand on top of the water, trying to flatten out the small tremors. Right as I start to resign myself to the fact she's too lost in her own thoughts, she asks quietly, "Do you ever think about your parents vow renewal?"

The question makes me pause, scoffing at the memory. "I try not to."

From this angle, I can see her nibbling on her bottom lip. "Why not?"

"You were there, Viv... I mean, you were *kind of* there... Right?"

"I wish I could say I was but no. My head was pretty much in another dimension that entire night... except for when I said I hated you." She looks at me with a guilty expression. "Which was a lie," she adds quickly.

I give her a small smile. "Thanks for the clarification, love. But do you not remember anything about that night?"

She shakes her head. "Tell me what happened," she replies a little too meek for my liking.

"It isn't a big deal." I shrug, trying to brush off the bad memory. Neither one of us held back that night. She's lucky she doesn't remember it.

"Please, Grady. It has bothered me for years. I feel like such an asshole anytime I think about it."

I take a deep breath. "I was the ass, Viv."

I walked to the front porch and saw Vivi sprawled out on the stairs, staring up at the sky. I couldn't tell if she was laughing or crying or a weird mix of both.

Bonnie had demanded Vivi try to sober up or go home after she knocked over one of the flower arrangements.

Drunk had not been a good look on any of them that night but most specifically Vivi. It was obvious she was drinking to solve a problem and I don't know why I needed to talk to her then. I knew it wasn't a good idea, but I had to say something to her. I didn't know when I would see her again.

I stopped in front of her and cleared my throat.

She slowly cracked open one eye and let out the loudest, most dramatic groan when she saw it was me.

"Oh, just the person I've been waiting for."

"Excuse me?"

"You talked to my brothers… and my sister… and my mom… Hell, you even talked to your junior year homecoming date—"

"Funny she came with *you* tonight."

"But you don't talk to me." *She sits up on her elbows, barely able to hold her head up.* "Nope. Not pathetic, little Vivi. Not that annoying girl next door, right?"

"I have no idea what you're talking about right now, but you sound like an idiot." *I regretted the words as soon as I said them, but I stuffed my hands in my pockets, waiting for the volcano to erupt.*

She huffs out an annoyed breath. "Yeah, of course you don't. Because I'm nothing. Nothing to anyone. Not even myself." *She falls backwards and stares up at the sky again.* "You can go now. Thanks for* nothing."

I don't know why that grated me so much, but it did. She isn't nothing. This fiery woman I've known my entire life is everything.

"Just because *he* made you feel like that, doesn't mean it's true.

Now sit up," I snapped at her in a way I never had before. *"I'm trying to have a goddamn conversation with you."*

I was trying to apologize to her, to get on my knees and beg for her forgiveness if that's what it took. But she wouldn't let me. And that made me unfairly angry.

"Well, Grady Miller," sneering my name like a slur, *"I don't want to talk to you."*

I started to turn away before my growing temper got the best of me. "I'm sorry you dated a jackass," I spit out, *"and I'm sorry you don't have any friends left so that you're forced to hang out with your lifelong arch nemesis."*

"You don't know what you're talking about," she replied in a deceptively quiet voice.

"I'm sorry that no one can live up to your standards," I continue on. *"It must be a pretty lonely life."*

"Yeah, it kind of is," she agrees, suddenly more awake. *"But it has to be better than the nice guy bullshit you like to live by. You know, like how you don't have a fucking backbone and couldn't keep a promise to save your life."*

"I only keep the promises that matter."

I had to bite my lip to fight back the apology. It took everything in me not to let the instant remorse bring me to my knees.

All of the most important promises I had ever made, and broken, were to the girl sitting in front of me.

"I hate you."

Vivi doesn't say anything to me for a while after the recap of that night and I really don't have anything to say either. It wasn't one of our best moments by far.

"Wow, Grady..." I prepare for her to lash out at me for the horrible things I said. *I deserve it.* "That... I'm so sorry." She turns toward me and places her hands on my chest. "You need to know

I didn't mean any of that."

Tying her braid at the end, I slip off the stool and kneel next to her. "I know that Viv. I didn't mean anything I said either, but it's eaten me alive for years." Her eyes start to well with tears. "Baby…" I say quietly. The green in her eyes is brighter than usual—her tears bringing out the mossy color. It's my favorite shade of green but I hate that it means she's upset in order for me to see it. "You have no idea how much I wish I could go back and take away all of the hurt that people caused you. And not just what I did but that's definitely at the top of my list. And it's not because I pity you, Genevieve." I gently place both hands on either side of her face. "It's because *I love you.* I love you so much that the idea of anyone causing you pain, even myself, makes me irrationally angry. I love you so much that I wish I could just wrap you up and keep you in my bed forever, never having to share you again. But I love you so much that I know you deserve to shine for the entire world, and I don't want to take that away from you."

Her bottom lip trembles and I'm about to tell her that she doesn't have to say it back. I didn't say it with any expectations. I said it because it has been sitting on my tongue my entire life, but it's been harder to hide the last couple months. Right as I open my mouth, she whispers the most beautiful words I've ever heard.

"I love you, too, Grady. I've loved you my entire life and I don't think I could stop even if I wanted to. I love you so much it hurts sometimes."

I lean forward, planting my mouth on hers. Her wet hands lay over mine, still cradling her head. I swipe my tongue along her lips, asking for entrance, for more. She opens for me at the same time I feel another of her tears roll down her cheek. I pull back, resting my forehead on hers, as I swipe the lingering tears with my thumb. "I'm going to spend my entire life making sure you never hurt again." I place a soft kiss on her nose. "Let's get ready for bed, love."

Chapter Forty-One
Vivi

As soon as I stand from the tub, Grady's right in front of me with a towel. I go to grab it from him but instead he wraps it around me with such gentleness and adoration that it makes my eyes burn again.

Grady loves me.

Three simple words that mean more to me than he'll ever understand. Three little words that I feel like I've been waiting my entire life to hear from him and they're sweeter than I could have ever imagined. And trust me, I imagined it so many times it's embarrassing.

Grady tucks the towel in around my breasts to hold it up and grabs another from the cabinet. He slowly pulls me toward the counter, turning me around so my butt is leaning against the edge. With the spare towel, he starts to dry off my arms and shoulders. When he's done with the top half, he kneels down and wipes off the droplets from my legs. The entire time, I watch him in silence.

Grady on his knees before me is a sight to see no matter what he's doing, but the affection and love radiating off of him is overwhelming in the best way. This simple gesture is the most worshiped my body has ever felt outside of sex with him.

I've let that broken memory play through my head for years, trying to remember why Grady and I went for blood the night of the vow renewal. I knew that it started with me—there wasn't a doubt in my mind about that. I was drunk and still reeling from the fallout freshman year and scared to see him for the first time in almost three years. I never allowed myself to believe that Grady truly cared about me, definitely not anywhere near as much as I care about him.

But now? As I watch him taking the time to wipe off each individual droplet before he grabs the vanilla lotion from his cabinet, I don't question it at all. For the first time in my entire life, I have no doubts that the man in front of me loves me as much as I love him.

Grady pushes down on the pump a few times before placing my hands on his shoulders and rubbing the lotions into my skin. It smells exactly like the vanilla perfume I use. When he finishes with my arms, he drops back down to his knees. Lifting my left leg to his shoulder, he continues to process before gently setting me back on the floor and grabbing for my right leg.

When he stands up, his eyes drop to the towel tied around me. His hand slowly reaches toward the knot around my breasts, and when I don't make a complaint, he tugs on the towel. We both watch it fall to the floor then I watch Grady's eyes eat up every inch of me. He puts more lotion in his hands and warms it before lathering the rest of my body, starting with my tummy and chest. Part of me thinks it should be awkward, but it isn't. Not even for a second. It's another one of those moments that feel so fucking intimate I almost can't believe that this is my life now.

He's standing behind me, but we make eye contact through the mirror. "You're so goddamn beautiful, Viv." His voice is low and husky. There is heat in his eyes, and he's standing so close I can feel his growing hardness. But it's the unconditional devotion I see in his gaze that almost sends me to my knees.

I turn around, pulling him closer by his hips. "So are you," I whisper with a small, teasing smile. He huffs out a laugh and brushes my braid over my shoulder.

"Thanks, baby," he murmurs against my lips. That pulls a happy grin across my face. Grady lets out a sigh of relief. "You have no idea how much peace seeing your smile has brought me today."

I place a soft kiss on his jaw in response. "I need you," my hands tighten, pulling him even closer despite the fact that his body is already flush against mine.

He runs his hands up my back, one of them gripping onto the nape of my neck. "You have me. I'm yours."

"Show me you're mine."

Tilting my head back, he lets out a low groan as I slip onto the counter and open my legs so he can step between them. His free hand goes to one of my thighs, tickling my skin in the most delicious and agonizing way. *Finally,* Grady drops his lips to mine. It doesn't matter how many times I kiss him, or how chaste it is sometimes. Each kiss never fails to release a million butterflies in my stomach.

Thankfully he doesn't tease me with a soft kiss for too long. Within a couple of seconds, he's nipping at my bottom lip—his possessive and demanding way of asking for me to open for him.

My tongue slips into his mouth but we both know that this is his show to direct. His fingers lightly trail up to the apex of my thighs, right where I'm soaked and warm and so fucking needy for him. His featherlight touch across my slit is more tortuous than it is relieving. My hips buck in response, looking for more pressure but the only thing that comes from that is him pulling his hand back to my thigh and a frustrated whimper from me.

A rumble of laughter leaves him as he pulls my hair back and drops his mouth to my neck. He kisses and licks his way down to my nipples, sucking one between his teeth and using the hand that was between my legs to roll the hardened peak of the other one between his fingers. He knows exactly how I like him to touch me here—soft nibbles and harder pinches–but it isn't where I want him. Where I *need* him.

With my head still tilted back, I beg, "I need more. Please, Grady. Not your fingers, not your mouth." He lifts off my breast and stands up. At his full height like this, he towers over me.

Tightening his grip on my hair a little more, always hovering that line between pleasure and pain, he purrs, "Say it."

My entire body flushes at his demand. It's nowhere near the dirtiest thing he's ever said but I've never seen Grady like this... so possessive in this way. Like instead of wanting to claim me, he wants to protect me. It makes me feel precious and treasured and *loved*.

"I want your cock. I want you to come in me." My hands move down to the waistband of his briefs, pushing them down to his ankles. He kicks them to the side and pulls me closer to the edge of the counter, wrapping my legs around his waist. "I want to feel how much you love me."

I brace my hands on the counter behind me but one of his arms moves to my waist, keeping me close. His other hand moves down to his thick length as he lines himself up with my slick center. "So much, baby."

He kisses me as he slowly pushes all the way inside of me. His lips are soft but controlling. He lightly sucks on my tongue and nips at my lips. His hand moves from where we're connected up to palm my breast. When he's fully seated, we both groan out each other's name. He moves his hips in languid strokes, not appearing to be in any rush to end this moment.

"You're so perfect, baby." He barely lifts his lips off mine. It comes out mumbled, but I understand him as clearly as if he was yelling through a megaphone. "In every single way, you're perfect for me."

My hands run up to his shoulders and I dig my nails in, holding him close. "That's all I've ever wanted to be, Grady." He lets out a strangled breath and speeds up his thrusts.

The friction is closer to where I need it, so I push my hips forward, seeking more. When I feel the pressure against my clit, my hands immediately fall back to the counter. With my weight held behind me, it allows me to get even closer to him, adding more pressure where I'm throbbing.

"Does my needy girl's clit want some attention?" His voice is teasing but his eyes are dark and full of heat.

"Yes, *please*," I breathe. The desperation in my voice makes his cock twitch deep inside of me. I'm already gasping his name when his thumb starts working my sensitive nub. It's *exactly* what I need. His deep strokes mixed with the feel of his hands worshiping my breast and clit is pure heaven. One so good that not even a god could bring me here, only Grady.

"You're so beautiful like this, love. Spread out and bare for me." His possessive words push me closer to the edge, my entire body pulling tight but not quite there yet. I watch him watch his cock slide in and out of me. "You have the prettiest pussy and it's all *mine.*"

"*Yours,*" I confirm on a deep moan. He rewards me by quickening his pace even more.

Grady has made it clear that whether he's pounding into me from behind or sensually moving inside of me, he's *always* making love to me. After one round last weekend, he left my ass red and raw. Only to soothe and kiss it, while telling me everything he promises to do with me, both dirty and not.

But tonight's different. Just like his earlier protective behavior, it feels like Grady refuses to cause me any pain tonight, even if it's enjoyable. Tonight, there is no biting or spanking.

I wanted him to show me how much he loves me, and that's exactly what he's doing.

The fact alone brings me so close to the edge. And I know from his shallow breathes and the raspy way he's saying my name that he's right there with me.

"Just a little faster," I quietly plead.

One of his hands drops to the counter, interlacing his fingers over mine and dropping his mouth back to my breasts, as his thrusts pick up speed. The hard, fast pace of his hips amplifies the intensity so quickly. Within seconds, I'm clenching so tightly around Grady. He lifts his mouth letting out a primal, guttural sound but one of my hands immediately finds his head. I grip his hair and push his mouth back to my nipple.

"Right there... *oh fuck*... I'm so cl—" A strained cry falls out of me right as I see stars. My body goes rigid, the feeling of pure unadulterated bliss flowing through me.

"Fuck, Genevieve. You feel so good... So warm and soft and tight. So, fucking tight." He bites down right above my nipple, licking and sucking that spot as he lets go. My pussy is still pulsing around him, sensitive from my own orgasm, when his hips snap forward one final time. He pulls my thighs further apart, burying himself as deep in me as he can. "I love you. I'm so goddamn in love with you."

I drop my lips to the crown of his head, murmuring into his hair. "I'm so fucking in love with you, Grady."

He tells me it over and over, in between his licks and kisses on my other breast in the exact same spot. He tells me how much he loves me until he's completely spent, filling me with every last drop of his release.

We stay connected for a while afterward, kissing every inch we can reach from our position. Eventually he slowly pulls out, but the reluctance is written all over his face. I exhale a breathy laugh, pure satisfaction coursing through my veins. He gives me a sexy smirk and reaches for one of the towels on the counter. He wets a corner of it and cleans me off before giving me a moment of privacy while going to get the pair of gray pajamas and a new pair of briefs. We brush our teeth with his arm wrapped around my waist the entire time. He holds my hand while we walk to the bed before he snuggles under the covers and pulls me close to his chest. We share kisses and *I love yous* for a while after. I don't know who falls asleep first but I'm so fucking happy when I do.

Chapter Forty-Two
Grady

Vivi and I woke up by seven o'clock, followed by Stella and Daisy less than thirty minutes later. Vivi changed back into her clothes from the night before. We decided it was better to play it on the safer side, not knowing what might upset them. Their feelings very easily could have changed in the last ten hours.

They sleepily trudged their way down the stairs and are now pulling themselves into a stool at the island.

"Good morning," I say easily. I walk around the counter to give each one a kiss on the head. They mutter a greeting back.

Vivi pushes off the counter across from the island and walks forward. "Good morning." She gives them a soft smile and takes another sip of her coffee. Daisy replies quietly but Stella gives a small wave. My eyes meet hers, preparing for a change of heart. She looks back down to them. "Do you still want to have breakfast?"

Stella and Daisy's heads slowly turn toward each other. Sometimes they do this when they've already talked through their plans of attack but want to make sure neither has changed their mind. I tense, not knowing what they've agreed to.

Turning back to Vivi, Stella takes a deep breath and nods her head. "Yeah, we were hoping you like strawberry pancakes. Dad makes the best ones." My shoulders drop with relief. Vivi looks surprised but gives them her prettiest smile anyway.

"I *love* strawberry pancakes." She crosses her arms and leans forward on the island. "I was just telling your dad I was in the mood for bacon too. What do you think?"

"Oooh, yes!" Daisy exclaims, wiggling in her seat. "Can I have juice?"

"Sure," I rub her head. "What kind would you like?"

"Apple, please."

"Can I have pineapple?" Stella asks.

Nodding, I move toward the fridge, but Vivi beats me to it. She grabs each bottle, two small cups and straws. The way she so naturally inserts herself into our morning makes my heart ache. She sets them on the counter and points toward the wall of shelves. "Is that another speaker? Can I play music?"

"Go ahead. I'll start the food." She nods and pulls her phone out. As I'm setting everything up on the counter, I glance over at her. She's biting her bottom lip with furrowed brows. She looks like choosing the right music for this moment is the most important decision of her day.

"You may have heard some of this at your grandma's. She and my mom have always listened to music when they're cooking." Elton John's familiar voice pours from the speakers. She turns back to me. "How can I help?"

"Do you want to cut the strawberries? I can start on the bacon."

She nods and sets up the cutting board on the counter.

Vivi is a morning person if I've ever seen one. She's humming along to the music, slightly swaying back and forth to the tune. I'm behind her at the stove, so I can't be sure, but I would bet my entire baseball card collection that she has a small smile on her face. And when I glance back, Stella and Daisy are watching her with a quiet curiosity.

With my focus on the bacon, I ask, "Is this still one of your mom's favorite songs?"

"Yeah," Vivi answers. This time I *know* she's smiling. "I don't remember but my dad used to listen to "Your Song" every weekend while cooking for us, just like this." She chuckles.

"We've never met your dad," Daisy says.

I turn my head, trying to gauge Vivi's reaction from the back.

"Oh, no. Uhm. You haven't." She looks back to me, a silent question in her eyes. I know some parents try to shield their kids from death, and I respect their decisions, but I think it's okay for mine to understand the reality of life. I nod and face the stove again. "My dad passed away when I was only four."

"What happened?" Stella asks.

"He was in a car accident coming home from work."

Daisy speaks after a few seconds. "Do you miss him?"

I hear Vivi set the knife down. Peeking at her, I see her lean forward on the counter again. "Yeah," she says quietly. "I do miss him. I don't have a lot of memories of him. He used to drive me around at night when I couldn't sleep and he always smelled like the ocean, even though he worked in a hospital. And any morning he didn't have to be there until a little bit later, he would hold me on his lap and watch The Wiggles with me."

"I love The Wiggles!"

Vivi laughs, probably startled by the sudden excitement. "I used to love them too. But the people were different when I was younger."

"Well, you can come watch The Wiggles with me anytime you want. Daddy will even cook for you and listen to music. Right,

Dad?"

Smiling at her over my shoulder, "That's right, Dais."

The sound of chopping starts up again. "Thanks, little lady. I'll definitely take you up on that offer."

The girls ramble on while they sit at the island while we cook, requesting songs that now remind them of their grandma and Bonnie like "Dancing Queen" or "Come On Eileen." When the latter comes on, Daisy jumps out of her stool and rounds the island to grab Vivi's hand. She twirls herself under her arm and goofily shakes her hips, giving Vivi questioning, unsure eyes the entire time. Within seconds Vivi to start moving her hips along with the music and singing with her head thrown back.

Stella watches from her seat, and even though I can see the longing in her eyes, she doesn't get out of her seat. I wink at her before turning back to the pancakes cooking.

"Stellaaa!" Daisy giggles a few seconds later, and when I turn back around, my oldest daughter is holding Vivi's other hand. She uses the support to practice her pirouettes. She's *sure* she wants to be a ballerina after learning that her favorite person Calypso was in dance her entire childhood. I signed her up to start classes in the new year.

Vivi just stands between them, beaming down at each of my girls and reciting the words while she sways in place. They use her as balance as they twirl, bounce and shake. When the bridge starts, Vivi takes their hands to pull in a sort of marching line, leading them to the dining room table. My cheeks hurt from smiling so wide by the time I plate all of the food and carry it over to the table.

Vivi's getting the table set with their glasses of juice, plates, and silverware. She grabs her coffee cup and my small, handmade one from the counter.

With an endearing quirk to her lips, she bites back a laugh. "So I've been meaning to ask… Who made this masterpiece for your dad?"

Daisy shrinks in her seat a little, hardly ever shy, and lets out a sweet little giggle. "Me. But I'm going to make him a new one," she adds quickly.

"I love my mug." Truthfully, it works because I like my brewed coffee black. If I needed to mix in creamer and sugar, it'd be a bit harder to use it so often with the add-ins taking up half the small capacity.

"Daaaddy," Daisy rolls her eyes dramatically. "I know there's a hole in it."

Stella and Vivi laugh. "So?" I ask.

"It's too small for you!"

"Do you enjoy pottery?" Vivi cuts in.

Sitting up on her knees, Daisy nods emphatically. "Yes! Stella's starting ballet after Christmas, and Daddy said he'll find a pottery class for me." With a giddy smile, she tells Vivi, "Matty's going to do pottery *and* surfing with me."

"Matty's a good one," she winks at Daisy.

"He's the *best* friend I could ever want." She's saying it like confirmation, like a secret between the two of them. "But I wanna make you a mug soon too."

"I'd love that, Daisy."

Daisy's shimmying her shoulders in the chair, happy as can be, when Stella asks reluctantly, "Will you come to my recitals? I mean… it might not be for a while…"

Reaching across the table, Vivi gently sets her hand on Stella's and promises, "Doesn't matter when it is. I wouldn't miss it for the world, Stella girl."

Stella grips her hand and smiles wider than I've seen in months.

Daisy, needing in on the lovefest, jumps off her seat to take the free one on the other side of Vivi and grips her other hand. "I'm happy you're here." Stella nods lightly in confirmation.

Chapter Forty-Three
Vivi

About two weeks after all the kids got sick, things started to change quickly. Grady and I are almost done with the fair. Last week, we met with each of the groups to get an idea of where they are with their booths. Not surprising, Harper and some of the coaches haven't started any sort of preparation. I think Grady noticed my eye twitching because he took over the conversation without a second thought. The flippant shrug he gave Harper mixed with his commanding demeanor as he told Harper exactly what to expect over the next few weeks was sexy as hell. I may have invited him back to my house that night just to give him head—as if it's any sort of hardship.

We haven't had any more sleepovers with all four of us, not wanting to put too much pressure on the girls. I'm taking each day at a time with them and enjoying every moment for what it is. That isn't something I've done in a long time.

At the last family dinner, Calypso and I finally told my mom how we planned a late birthday celebration for her. A girls' day at the new tearoom, Spilled Honey. Daisy, Stella, and Millie have been giddy about it for the last two weeks, especially after my mom chose the Alice in Wonderland themed room when she heard the options.

To all of our surprise, and Selena's motherly delight, Blake not only sewed each of the girls their own Alice-inspired dresses, but she joined us. She kept mostly to the kids and our moms, but the fact she showed up at all is a good sign for the future. Lexi even went out of her way to get to know Blake better.

It was such a great day, and the first time I've gotten to spend time with Stella and Daisy without Grady outside of the school. I can only hope that it'll push our relationships forward even more. Even on the harder days, I find myself falling more and more in love with these little girls just like I am with their dad.

Now they're sleepy and buckled up in the backseat with the quiet tunes of Calypso's playlist coming through the speakers. They were so excited to see her in the car when I picked them up, especially Stella. It was adorable. But watching Calypso open her heart to them fills me with so much love I can't express it.

"Who is that?" Calypso sits up straighter in her seat. As we pull down the street, I can see who she's talking about, but I don't know her. She's tall and thin, similar to Lyp, but her hair is dark, and her skin is even fairer than mine. Her and Grady are standing a few feet apart, but they look comfortable with each other. That's until Grady sees my car approaching. His smile drops a fraction, and even from a distance I can see his shoulders tense.

I know who is standing on his driveway before Daisy says anything.

"Mommy! She's here already!"

"What?" Calypso and Stella ask at the same time. Both sounding confused but the latter's is mixed with excitement too.

I can feel Calypso's eyes boring into me. "I didn't know your mom was visiting," she tells the girls without looking away.

"It's for my birthday." Stella is slower to unbuckle than usual, but Daisy is squirming in her seat, trying to get out as soon as possible.

There's a ringing in my ears, but I push past it, knowing Calypso is expecting a different answer. "Her show is on a break until they pick up in New York closer to Christmas. So, she's spending a week here. She wasn't supposed to be here until tomorrow..."

Grady opens the back door to help Daisy at the same moment Calypso asks, "Here?" She gives Grady a sharp look, her voice dripping with indignation. He gives me a confused look through the rearview mirror, but I just give him a quick head shake in response. The sound of him closing the door makes me flinch as I watch Daisy run into her mom's arms. Well aware that Stella's in the backseat, I try to keep my breathing calm.

"Are you coming to meet her?"

I turn toward her. "Would you like me to?"

Please say no, please say no, please say no.

She looks between her mom and I, nods once and jumps out of the car.

"*Fuck.* Fuck me," I whisper.

"She's staying here?" She points toward the house but making sure no one out of the car can see.

"Not *here*, but in an AirBNB somewhere nearby."

Grady lightly knocks on my window, making me flinch again. He gives me a questioning look, one that asks *are you coming out or leaving?*

Fuck, would I love to leave right now—and I know he'd grant me this out if I wanted it. But I can't do that to Stella. She seemed hesitant to see her mom and I don't want to add any weirdness to the situation. I know she feels guilty about liking me and loving her.

"We're going to meet her," I say it more to myself but Calypso nods, not bothering to put on her friendly face.

I reach to open my door, but Grady beats me to it. "Hey," he says lowering his voice for only me to hear. "Are you okay? It was a surprise she came in a day early. I would have told you."

I glance back toward Arielle, who is kneeling on the driveway talking to her daughters. She's fucking gorgeous. It shouldn't be a surprise considering Grady is an Adonis and they made the two most beautiful little girls I've ever seen. Her cool elegance and natural confidence are so different from me. I don't need to talk to her to pick up on it. She's just one of those women who emits that energy.

"What does she think I am to you?" The question comes out with more of an edge than I intend, but it occurs to me we haven't had this conversation.

"What?"

"Does she know about us?" His eyes shudder but he tries to recover quickly. I know him too well though. I bite the inside of my cheek, nodding. "Got it. Childhood friend."

"Viv—" I push past him, putting on a brave face for Stella and Daisy.

I am a little shocked when it's Stella who grabs mine and Lyp's hands, pulling us forward. Calypso's smile drops from her face the moment the girls aren't looking. Grady is shuffling behind us; the tension radiating off of him.

Stella stops, keeping her fingers interlaced with ours. Arielle glances down at the connection but doesn't say anything. "Mom, this is Vivi and Calypso. They're our new friends out here."

"Oh, *your* new friends?" Her eyes cut to Grady, accusingly. I want to crawl under a rock and die but I force myself to keep my head high.

Yes, Grady should have told her about me. That's on him, without a single doubt. But the look she's giving Grady doesn't sit right with me either. From the wrath I can *feel* coming off of Calypso, I know she thinks the same.

Arielle's looking at him as if he had an affair, as if he betrayed her. And that simply isn't true.

She finally looks toward us. "Hi, I'm Arielle." Her voice is friendly but tense.

I give her an awkward wave with my free hand. "Vivi."

She slowly nods. "I got that."

Next to me, my sister cocks her head, preparing for confrontation. "I'm her sister, Calypso." It's the only clue Arielle needs to figure out which one of us is *with* her ex-husband.

Arielle tries to pick up Daisy, but she wiggles out of her hold. "They took us to a tea party today! It was in Wonderland." She does her typical twirls around all our legs. I smile down at her, making Arielle stiffen.

"That's great." Her smile says otherwise. "How do you know Grady?"

The question is directed toward me, but Calypso takes the metaphorical mic. "Oh, we've known Grady forever. Basically, their entire lives," she points between Grady and me. "Our moms are best friends. We practically grew up in one household."

Arielle's eyes cut to Calypso's, slightly unsure but not backing down. I, however, am frozen in place.

In a saccharine voice Arielle says, "So… that would make you, what?" She points between the three of us. "Siblings?"

"No." Grady's voice is sudden and firm, but he doesn't elaborate. He still doesn't tell her who I am to him besides a family friend. I can feel myself shrink five feet and color blooms on my cheeks. Arielle turns her attention back to me. She gives me a slow once over, a mocking grin pulling across her face as she focuses on my bright auburn hair.

Realization washes over her, followed by a syrupy laugh that I immediately hate. "*Oh.* You're the little girl next door. The one who had a crush on Grady. Blake mentioned you a few times. That's cute."

Whether she knows it or not, she hit a nerve. Not only did she belittle my relationship with Grady, but she played into my biggest insecurity: that I've always wanted Grady more than he wants me... and the fact that he didn't tell her about me, after all of our plans and promises, hurts.

It's a fucking punch to the soul if I'm being honest.

"Actually—"

"Actually," I cut Calypso off, "we were just leaving. Have a good week together." I gently pull my hand from Stella's, but she wraps both of her arms around my tummy.

"Thanks for today." She squeezes me and I squeeze back.

"You're very welcome, little lady." Arielle's head snaps toward Grady, probably wondering why I feel comfortable enough to call their daughters the same endearment he uses. Daisy follows her sister, both stopping to hug Calypso on the way inside.

Lyp throws one more scathing look at Arielle, who pretends to miss it as she follows her daughters into Grady's house. The sight makes me sick to my stomach. I slip my key into my sister's hand and turn toward the car, walking back in a daze.

Grady grabs my wrist. "Viv, I *never* spoke about you like that. Blake wouldn't either. I don't know what she's talking about." I nod, wanting to believe him but not being able to rationalize it. "I'm going to make it clear who you are to me. To us."

I slip my hand out of his, giving his chest a gentle but firm pat. "You do whatever you think you need to." With that, I walk to my car—not kissing Grady goodbye for the first time in months—and do my best to not lose my head until I'm in the comfort of my own home.

Chapter Forty-Four

Vivi

My eyes burn from staring out my classroom window but it's better than the burn from crying last night. Again.

I *should* be focusing on this goddamn admissions essay. It's the last thing I need to finish before I can submit my application in January but every time I look at the Word document, fresh tears start to form.

Describe someone who has changed your life, and how.

I'd been planning to write about Grady, because he has, without a single doubt in my mind, changed my life more than anyone else ever has. But right now, it feels like someone is stabbing me in the heart when I think about him right now.

It's been three days since I've seen Grady. That includes at work. Mostly because I've been doing everything I can to avoid him. He's called but I'm *busy* every time. He texted me last night, not for the first time, to tell me the girls were staying with Arielle, wondering if I wanted to go over. I told him I was with Lexi and Calypso. It wasn't a total lie—we always have dinner at my house at least once a week. But it hasn't ever stopped me before when the girls were staying somewhere else.

And as much as I crave his weight wrapped around me, I'm just too… confused. Disappointed. *Hurt.* The thought of getting one secret night with him while he spends the week with her makes me nauseous.

I thought I was ready for this, that I was strong enough to be with Grady knowing his ex-wife would *always* be in his life. I thought that maybe my love for him and his daughters would outweigh all of my soul-deep insecurities.

But from the moment I saw them standing together, I've been drowning in all my self-doubt.

I need some time to lick my wounds privately. Grady knows that. It's why he sent Knox down to the elementary wing of the school today. He was casually coming to check up on me, concern clear in his eyes. I shouldn't have hated it as much as I did.

It wasn't just the look though. I hate how much I wish it was Grady who came to my classroom. So, I could yell at him and fight with him and *push him away*. But no, Grady knows me as well as I know him. He knows I need time alone even if it feels like my entire heart is bleeding out of my chest.

Mr. Sparks wanted to meet today to talk about the fair. The STEM club is using some of the robots from previous years to have battles and races. It sounds pretty cool, and if it weren't for him, I'd be back at home under my covers already. I've even locked Lexi out the last few nights—something we've *never* done since sharing the studio apartment.

I turn toward the quiet knock on the door, expecting to find my coworker.

A sad looking Stella is one of the last people I expected to be here though.

"Hi, little lady. Want to come in?" She nods, taking a tentative step inside. "Pull up a seat."

She settles in her chair next to my desk. "Hi."

"Hi." I give her a small smile. "Want to split that with me?" I point toward the chocolate on my desk.

Her smile grows a fraction, but she stays quiet.

I break it in half, hand her one, and lean back in my chair. She nibbles on her piece, glancing toward the door more than once.

"What's up? Did you get in trouble or something?"

With wide eyes she shakes her head and blurts out, "I was listening to my dad's conversation again…" My gut is screaming at me that it won't be as funny as the first time.

"Okay… Do you want to talk about it?"

"Will you be mad at me?" My brow furrows and I shake my head. "My mom said she misses us… She wants Dad to move us to New York. Closer to her and our other grandparents."

"Oh," I breathe. I can feel the anxiety take over my body. Trying to hide my shaking legs from Stella, I place my hands firmly on my knees.

"I don't want to move again. I like it here… I like my Abuela and Grampa. I like Millie and my new friends." Her lower lip starts to inch out a little. "I even like *you*."

A chuckle falls out of me, but it isn't enough to totally keep the tears at bay. I quickly wipe one away. "I don't see your dad going anywhere." That isn't totally true. If Stella and Daisy *wanted* to be closer to Arielle, I know he'd be on the next plane. I love him for it but I also really fucking hate him for it. But I am praying to whoever's holy up there that he won't.

"He didn't say no. He just said he wants to do what's right for Daisy and me."

I can perfectly imagine him saying that since I've heard him mention it more than once. He's such a good dad, and I'm the asshole who's angry about it.

"What do you and Daisy want?"

I don't mean to claim Stella as my child in anyway but *holy fuck*, this parenting thing is harder than I would've ever imagined. How do parents constantly push themselves to the side for their kids?

I mean... I get it. Because if it would heal their little innocent hearts, I'd *help* Grady pack up and move, no matter what it did to me. But I don't think it's what's best for them. I just don't know if that's ultimately coming from a selfish place or if my opinion matters at all right now.

Her hands twist in her lap, and she refuses to make eye contact. "She doesn't know. I didn't want to tell her... I know she was having a hard time making friends, but she has Matty now. And she loves you and your mom and everyone else. She wants to learn how to surf, and I just want Daisy to be happy," her voice wavering, lips starting to tremble.

"Oh, Stella, honey... What's going to make *you* happy? Because I know that your dad would give up everything in the world for you two."

She thinks it over, wiping away tears. "I want to stay here. And I don't want my dad to give up anything." Her words are broken sobs but thankfully, I have a lot of experience with emotional children. "He's *smiling*. He barely smiled for years and now he does all the time. I don't want him to stop."

My hands come up to my mouth, taking a deep breath and trying to hold myself together. This is so much more than any kid should have to deal with.

"Can I give you a hug?"

She looks up at me, unsure for only a second, before nodding. I wrap my arms around her and let her just lay in my comfort for a second. Brushing some of the hair off her shoulder I tell her, "I trust your dad to do what's right for all three of you." It's not a lie—but I don't know if I trust him to do right by *me*. "You need to trust him too. And tell him what you want. His full honesty rules don't only apply to him… that includes you girls as well, okay?"

She nods against my chest, not moving from my embrace. I sit with her for a while longer, my head resting on hers. Despite the terrible, sinking feeling in my stomach, this moment with Stella is so much bigger than my feelings. She came to *me,* she trusted *me,* she let *me* comfort her.

It's so much more than just losing Grady now. If he decides to take his daughters and leave, I'm losing the only future that brought me any sense of happiness.

Another light knock on the door pulls my attention that way. Mr. Sparks is standing in his typical trousers and blazer combination. "I didn't mean to interrupt. Do you want to reschedule?" His tone is light and understanding. He may be a shy man but, he's also one of the sweetest when you get him talking.

I look down at Stella, who shakes her head. "No, I don't want my dad finding me here…"

Me either.

"Maybe you should go wait for him on the playground. Where's Daisy?"

"She's waiting for me out there." She slides off her chair, pulling it back to the desk.

"I'll take care of that," Mr. Sparks says. Stella nods and walks out of the room. When he sits down, he gives me a concerned look. "Are you ready to start, or do we need a minute?"

"No, no. Let's start. I'm really excited for your booth." I plaster on my biggest smile, knowing how fake it probably looks right now. Mr. Sparks pats my shoulder but takes pity on me, opening his folder and laying out his booth plans.

Chapter Forty-Five
Grady

"This place is cute," Arielle muses from across the table. Stella wanted to have her birthday at Tossin' Tomatoes, and I am pretty sure Carlo cried when I called to tell him. "I remember seeing it in your photo albums."

I nod, not bothering to carry a conversation. Thankfully, my ever-polite mother entertains my ex-wife while I try not to stare at the entrance. Almost everyone is here. My parents, Blake's family, Bonnie, Knox, and his boys. Not only did Vivi not show up, but none of her siblings are here either. Calypso doesn't surprise me—it's probably better Arielle and her stay far away from each other—but Asher and Hudson do.

I want to be angry with them, but I'm mostly confused. I knew that it'd be weird for Arielle to be here, but I didn't expect it to cause such a strain between us.

The moment Vivi asked what Arielle knew about us, I knew I messed up. Really bad. Pretty fucking horribly actually.

I was trying to protect what we have. I don't want to share my new life with Arielle. I've been trying to keep space between her and I. It's for the best at this point. But I knew she wanted to talk, and I just kept blowing her off because I had an inkling about what she wanted to discuss. Arielle's always had a hard time with change. It's partly why I stayed in the marriage so long; I was worried about her. Truthfully, I was surprised when she asked for the divorce. In a weird way, I was even *proud* of her.

I may not be in love with Arielle, but I know her. She doesn't want to get back together, not really. She misses the girls—understandably so—and she's lonely. I think in Arielle's mind, it's better to be together and unhappy, than to be alone.

I get it. I had the same thoughts for a while. Then she left, and it wasn't as hard as I had anticipated. Maybe because I had the girls, but I was okay. And now? After having Vivi? No one else will ever compare. I couldn't even convince myself that I *liked* someone else enough to want them as anything more than a friend.

My entire soul belongs to her, it always has. I'm not a spiritual man, at all, but she makes me wish I was. Vivi makes me want to believe in so much more. Things like past lives and future lives and all of that crap. Because *if* it is true, I know that we would find each other in every single one. And an eternity with her is only scratching the surface of what I want with her.

The longer I wait for her to show up, losing hope by the second, a sick feeling in the pit of my stomach starts to grow. I've tried to deny it, but I had a feeling this was going to happen when Stella came home from school with her gift—Vivi had given it to her early.

Then the entrance swings open and I see Asher and Hudson and…

No one else.

I leave my heart on the floor and walk over to them. Hudson gives me a long look, but Asher looks slightly awkward. "Hey, G. Sorry we're late."

"You're good. Stella will be happy to see you both."

Knox shuffles over, following Arielle who glides across the room as if it's her own personal stage. All it does is make me miss the way Vivi breezes through a space, bringing life to everyone around her.

"Are these more of your friends?" Arielle asks with a hand on my arm. I close my eyes, releasing a breath before looking at the twins.

There are simultaneous looks of brotherly disappointment that pop up on their faces. I've only seen this look once before—when Asher asked me straight to my face if I liked Vivi in high school, but I was too much of a coward to admit it. Somehow it feels even more scathing.

Nodding, I step out of Arielle's touch. "Yeah, two of my childhood best friends. Asher and Hudson, this is Arielle, my ex-wife." We all know who she is, but it still feels necessary.

The tension is thick but if Arielle notices, she doesn't let on. She sticks her hand out, never missing a beat. "It's so good to meet you. Grady's told me a lot about you over the years." She playfully nudges me with her shoulder. I take another step to the side, ignoring the puzzled look she gives me.

Whether it's a blessing or a curse is to be determined, but Carlo makes his way to our small group as his servers drop off a variety of pizzas. "Good to see you boys." He clasps Knox on the shoulder, letting him know that he's included even as a newcomer. "Where're the girls?"

I open my mouth, fumbling for words. Instead, Hudson mutters, "They were busy. Some stuff at the bookstore came up." No one acknowledges the fact that only two of them work there.

"Too bad," Carlo says, ignoring Arielle. They've never met but I would bet my 1952 Topps Mickey Mantle card that my parents have shown him photos over the years. "I was looking forward to seeing the whole group here again. Especially you and the little firecracker." He smiles fondly thinking about Vivi. My chest aches, not able to handle even a few days away from her anymore.

"I'm gonna say hi to your folks and have a slice or two." He pats my shoulder, stopping next to me. "Grady, I'm proud of the man you've become and for bringing your family home. But don't waste any more time, son."

He says it low for only me to hear but when I look to my side, I know Arielle is questioning what he meant.

Arielle set up a mini-DIY spa at her AirBNB for the girls and Millie. It was always the plan but she's doing me a solid tonight without realizing it.

I pull into Vivi's driveway, and it's exactly as I suspected. Calypso's red convertible is parked out front and the lights on Vivi's side of the duplex are on. It's Wine Wednesday, and the only thing they would've skipped that for, they didn't attend either. Maybe I should be madder than I am but all I feel is dread and guilt.

I walk up to the door, knocking softly. I can hear Lexi's boisterous laugh, so they have to be close. Next comes her muffled words about thanking Asher and Hudson for the di–

"You're not delivery from Max's." She tilts her head, giving me a hard look.

"Uh. No, I'm not. I'm sure you know why I'm here."

"Wait there." She slams the door in my face, probably asking Vivi how she wants to handle this *situation*. It's weird how normal it is to see Lexi as her protector now.

A minute later, the door slowly cracks open and Vivi slips out, shutting it firmly behind her.

And *fuck me*, of course she's in her little green sweater set that just about brings me to my knees every time. It's the perfect mix of sexy and adorable, just like her. Her hair is half up in two little buns and her feet are covered by knee high white socks. Maybe it's weird but this is quite literally my wet dream—especially knowing the sexy little lingerie set she no doubt has on underneath. It just makes this conversation that much harder.

"Hey." My voice sounds raw, even to my own ears.

In the smallest voice I've ever heard from her, she says, "Hi. What're you doing here?"

"I wanted to check on you... Stella and Daisy were wondering where you were tonight." She lifts her hand to her mouth, trying to hold in her strangled sob. "Vivi..." I take a tentative step toward her only to be let down when she presses herself against the door.

"Grady." She holds her hand up to stop me. "I know you're considering moving to New York with the girls."

My mouth opens and closes, trying to figure out how she knows that when it suddenly hits me. "Stella..."

"Quite the eavesdropper. Don't be mad at her, Grady. She didn't tell me to be mean. She was just confused, and looking for an adult she trusts." She wipes under her eye, holding herself around the waist with her other arm. "She said she even likes me, actually." A sad huff escapes out of her.

"I'm... I'm not mad at her. I'm just confused. I am not moving to New York, Viv."

Her eyes flash to mine now. "Does Arielle know that?"

"She—no. She doesn't know. *Yet*. You have to believe me."

She nods looking away from me. "I do believe you, but it just... it isn't enough, Grady."

The air rushes out of my lungs, leaving me feeling even more disoriented than the last few days. "What do you mean?"

"I can handle being second to your daughters. I *expect* to be second to them, always. Bu—" Another sob crawls up her throat. Taking a deep breath, she looks at me, stiffening her shoulders. "But I can't be second to your ex-wife."

"You aren't." I shake my head frantically, wanting more than anything to reach for her.

She shakes her head back. "You didn't tell her about me, Grady. You've been promising me your entire future for two months now, but you haven't told *her*. Whether she knew what she was doing or not, you sat there while she picked at one of my biggest insecurities." The little girl next door comment. I was an idiot to pretend it wouldn't affect her much. "You were either… unsure about us or scared to let that part of your life go or…" She can't hold back the sobs anymore. Pushing through her tears, she finishes, "Or you were embarrassed of me. And I can't live with that, Grady. I don't deserve to live with that."

"No, fuck. *No*." I tug on my short hair. "I am not embarrassed by you Vivi. I just… I had a feeling Arielle wanted to talk about us, about getting back together. I didn't want that. So, I avoided her, only talking about the girls and answering calls when the girls were around. She doesn't want *me*; she just doesn't like change. And I don't want her. I want *you*. I only want you, Vivi. I was trying to protect what we have because that's what matters to me. *You* matter to me." She just shakes her head, holding her hand up to stop me again. I didn't realize I took a step toward her, but I take one back, even though it kills me.

"You *avoided* the situation. Just like you avoided me," she shakes with another sob, "and Amada Beach and your family and everything else. When are you going to learn, Grady?" The tears are really flowing now, her arms thrown out to her side. "You can't avoid these conversations. Arielle is going to be in your life *forever*, regardless of if I am or not."

"You don't mean that."

"It's the truth, Grady. And you need to realize that. Sure, some people can go the rest of their lives without seeing their ex-spouse, but you have two kids together. That's not your reality, Grady. You *avoided* Arielle but did you set those boundaries with her? Did you tell her that you don't want to get back together? That you think being separated and raising the girls in Amada Beach is the best choice for them? Did you tell her that you think *I'm* the best choice for *you*?"

Goddammit.

My heart practically stops in my chest.

She's right. Of course, she's right. I told Genevieve that I would choose her, choose this life, here. But I didn't talk to the one person who needs to know that. I wanted to believe that Arielle didn't have a place in our life here but that was naïve and selfish. Not only to Vivi, but to my daughters.

I should've told Arielle who Vivi is to me, and I should have prepared Vivi better. I shouldn't have let them run into each other that way.

Fuck.

"I am going to tell her. Tomorrow… she's with the girls, celebrating Stella's birthday. But I am going to tell her. There will be no room for confusion. I am staying here. With *you*."

"You do what you need to do, Grady, but…" She shakes her head. I could go my entire life without seeing her do that again. "I need time. All of this… it brings up a lot that isn't fair to put on you. I thought I was able to be the happy, easygoing stepmom but now I'm not so sure. I need some time to think."

"Think about what, Genevieve?" The crack in my voice is apparent, and it only makes her cry harder.

"Us. This. I got so fucking caught up in you I never considered the reality of what it all meant. Not outside the borders of this town, at least."

I take a step forward now. Not touching her but standing only inches from her. Close enough to feel her warmth and get a whiff of her berry vanilla scent I need like oxygen now. "Don't do this. I can make it right."

She puts her hand on my chest, but instead of pushing me away she grips onto my t-shirt. "You need time to figure this out on your own. And I… I need space to work through these insecurities alone. They have nothing to do with you, not really."

My hands press into the door next to her, my head hanging between us. "How long?" It comes out strangled.

With a weak shrug she says, "I do… don't know. Everything for the fair is pretty much squared away. Let's just get through that first. Please?"

I resign myself to this *reality* and nod. "Fine. A week and a half. It's going to be the worst time of my life. So much worse than anything before." I gently hold her chin, marveling in the way she melts into the touch. "Because now that I've had you, *really* had you, Vivi, I won't accept anything else. You're it for me, and I know I am for you too. So, take these few days and do whatever you think you need to do to be ready to spend our lives together, baby. But just so you know what I'll be doing over the next week… I'm going to set my boundaries with Arielle tomorrow, I'm going to talk to my daughters about what they want our life to look like in Amada Beach and I'm going to think of all the ways I'll spend every second of my life loving you."

She turns her head further into my palm. "I want that, Grady," she whispers. "I want that so badly."

I cup the other side of her face. "It's the only reality I believe in, Viv." I place a lingering kiss on her forehead, wanting so much more, before walking to my Jeep.

Chapter Forty-Six
Grady

I'm sitting on the couch, my hands folded between my thighs, as I wait for Arielle to tuck the girls in for the last time before she leaves for New York.

I wouldn't say I've been dreading this conversation, but I haven't been sure how to start it either. My relationship with Arielle has always been so different than the one I have with Vivi.

With Genevieve, I've *always* wanted to give her all of me—every last piece, even the ones I hate or am embarrassed of.

But with Arielle, we've always held our best *and* darkest parts close to our chests. We don't communicate directly. We tiptoe around the topic and drop passive-aggressive comments to each other. We couldn't even admit we wanted a divorce without a therapist guiding the conversation. I have no idea how tonight is going to go.

Ready or not, I hear her make her way down the stairs. When she sees me on the couch, she pauses before tentatively walking closer.

"Grady?" she asks in her soft, melodic voice.

"We need to talk."

"It sounds like you're breaking up with me," she quips in a teasing tone. I don't say anything, I just look up at her with somber eyes. "Okay, bad joke... What's up?" she responds casually, falling into the armchair across from me.

"Arielle... we aren't together anymore," I state bluntly.

Her brows furrow and she leans back like she's avoiding a physical blow. "I know that. I asked for the divorce."

"But you regret it, don't you?"

We stare at each other for a long time but finally she nods. "Do you?"

I take a deep breath and run my hands down my jean covered thighs. "No," I say honestly. "Not even for a second."

Her eyes widen slightly and her body tenses, but she doesn't say anything. We just sit there, staring at each other for a few seconds.

Finally, I decide to continue, "We never really... wanted to get married." She masks her expression into cool indifference, but I know her better than that. It doesn't matter what we *wanted*. It's about what we chose to do and then failed at it. "Stella and Daisy were always the best parts of us. If it wasn't for them, we wouldn't have gotten back together. We would've graduated, you would've moved to New York and me... well, I woul—"

"You'd still be living in Amada Beach and dating *Vivi*." The way she says her name raises my hackles.

I nod. "I can only hope that she and I would've reconnected even if the girls hadn't wandered into her classroom."

She purses her lips and crosses her arms, giving me an assessing look. "Tell me about her."

"Excuse me?" I'm stunned by her demand. It wasn't what I was expecting.

"If she's going to be a part of *our* daughters' lives, then I have a right to know somethings about her."

"You trusted me to take care of them, so you need to trust me to bring good people into their lives," I counter.

"I do, Grady," she says with so much sincerity. "But they're still *mine.*" Arielle isn't an emotional woman but the tremble of her lip clues me into how hard this is for her. Being away from the girls, feeling like she lost something—a family.

I sigh, knowing she's right. If the girls were with her and she was seeing a new man, I'd want to know who was going to be in their lives. "Okay, what do you want to know?"

"She's the girl from the photo albums, isn't she? I remember the red hair."

Nodding, I don't break eye contact as I explain to Arielle my complex history with Vivi. "Yes, she was my childhood best friend. Her brothers, Asher and Hudson, were, too. And Bonnie is my parents' best friend. I was close with her entire family—"

"Even the sister?" she questions with a raised brow.

Chuckling, I nod. "Yes, even Calypso. She's like an older sister to me. When I was in high school, Vivi and I had a falling out. She never forgave me for it." I don't go into detail about it. She doesn't need them. "We talked a few times after, but it was few and far between. By the time I met you, I hadn't spoken to her or any of her siblings in almost three years. I don't want you to think I was holding onto something while we were together. That wasn't the case… I wanted things to work out with us, Arielle. I did."

"For the girls?"

"Mostly, yes. But because I loved you. I *love* you. I always will. But I'm not *in love* with you." We're both quiet but I can tell she's working through what I'm saying. With a gentler tone I add, "And you aren't in love with me."

"Were we ever in love?" she whispers, looking away.

"I don't know, Arielle. I really don't." I feel like a cretin saying that to her, but I never felt half of what I do for Vivi when I was with Arielle. And I *know* it wasn't one-sided... So badly, I want Arielle to find the same for herself.

"You're in love with her? Vivi?" The ice in her tone has thawed when she says her name this time.

"Yes, I am. And I haven't been very fair to either of you about it." Her face crinkles in confusion. "I should've told you that I was planning on bringing someone new into the girls' lives. You deserved a warning so maybe you and her could have met... differently."

She sucks her lips into her mouth, thinking it over. Finally, she says, "And Vivi deserves better than being a secret from your ex-wife." I look down again, nodding, and ashamed. "The girls haven't been able to stop talking about her," she laughs ruefully.

"They like her a lot. She's good to them." I pause thinking my next words carefully. "She's patient. Daisy was an easy egg to crack." That makes her actually laugh, the smile reaching her eyes. "But Stella... it was harder for her. They both miss you, and Stella felt guilty about liking Vivi. She didn't want to upset you."

One single tear slips down her cheek. It's in my nature to comfort, but I hold myself back, not wanting to cause any more confusion. "I don't want them to be scared of loving someone new because of *me*."

"I know, Arielle. But you're their mom. They'll never want to do anything that might hurt you, even accidentally." She nods but stays quiet for a long time. I take in her fair skin and dark brown hair that's the same shade as her eyes... and I feel nothing. I just miss Genevieve.

"I should apologize to her," she says quietly, more to herself than anything. I shake my head, but she cuts me off before I can speak. "No, Grady. I should. I just felt... scared to see my people with someone new. But *you* aren't *mine* anymore."

"No, I'm not. But Stella and Daisy will *always* be yours. Vivi doesn't change that. And she doesn't want to."

Another tear slips down but she bats it away quickly. She takes a deep breath and sits up straighter. "You need to fix things with this woman, if only so I can say sorry... and hopefully prove I'm not a total twat."

Laughing, I finally lean over and grab Arielle's hand. She slips hers into mine, but we don't interlace fingers like we used. We just give each other a small squeeze and stare at each other.

"I don't know how to move on, Grady... I don't just mean from you because you're right—we weren't happy. I'm just so scared to be alone. And I hate being away from the girls I don't want them to grow up thinking I don't love them. I just..."

I cover her hand with my other one, pulling gently until she looks at me. "Yes, you do. You're so strong, Arielle. You were right to ask for the divorce." She doesn't try to wipe the tears running down her cheeks. "We couldn't live like that forever. We didn't *deserve* to." So unhappy, half-loved and alone in a relationship. "You deserve to be happy and to accomplish your dreams. You deserve to be a little selfish for the first time in your adult life." She starts crying hard, covering her face with her free hand. "And you and I—*together*—will make sure the girls know you love them so much. You're setting an example for them. One I am so proud of."

"Do you mean that?" She looks up at me. Her nose is red, and her cheeks have tear streaks running down them. I've never seen her look so young and vulnerable.

"Yes, Arielle. I do. I'm so thankful you're their mom."

She nods and tries to catch her breath. "I feel the same way about you. Even though we weren't meant to be together, you were so good to me for years. And I'll never forget that."

"Me neither," I say softly with a shake of my head. "But... the girls and I are staying here. We can't uproot their lives again. Stella's doing phenomenal in school, and Daisy has her first friend."

She nods again. "And this is *your* home."

"It is. But any place that Stella and Daisy are, is your home too. You're welcome to come visit anytime you want—with some warning," I offer her a small smile and she huffs out a laugh. "And the girls will take trips to see you in New York or wherever you're touring. I want them to see that part of your life because you're incredible on a stage." It's true. I saw a few plays she was in at ASU. She's talented and captivating. It's partly why I knew this was the right choice for us.

"I want them to be a part of everything, even if we're apart."

"They will be. We'll make sure of it."

"Can we plan? For the next few months? I have my next tour dates already... I just need to know when I can see them."

"Yes, Arielle. I think that's a great idea." Holding her hand, I lift her off the chair and wrap my arms around her shoulders. Hers tentatively wraps hers around my chest as she cries into my shirt.

"I just miss them so much, Grady. It *physically* hurts."

Rubbing her back, I nod not knowing what to say. I was going crazy when they were gone for less than a week—I can't imagine what Arielle deals with on a daily basis, but I see what the girls feel every day. And I don't want any of them to hurt. So, I unwrap myself from Arielle and guide her to the island where we sit for the next two hours—planning out the next six months of visits, coming up with weekly FaceTime schedules and trying to figure out how to better co-parent despite the distance.

The hollow feeling in my chest doesn't leave but the hundred-pound weight on my shoulders finally feels like it's been lifted.

Chapter Forty-Seven
Grady

"You know, I've never seen you act like such a surly fuck before." Knox takes a seat next to me in the cafeteria. It's become the pseudo-warehouse for all the fundraiser materials and booths. Ours is one of the last that need to be built but I wanted to wait until Hudson had an afternoon free. Not only is he the most talented out of the three of us, but I wanted the guys to get to know their infield assistant coach.

Johnny, Lexi's little brother, came up with the idea to do darts but instead of a board, we're using balloons filled with paint. He said he got the idea from all the times Lexi has made him watch *The Princess Diaries*, which made me laugh at the time.

In the last week I haven't wanted to laugh at anything though. I feel numb without talking to Vivi. I don't know how I did this for a decade, but it feels impossible now. The only thing that brings me any peace is my daughters, so I've spent the last hour watching them fill up balloons with Jeremy and some of the other guys.

Not having anything to say to Knox, I just shrug. He's right. I'm not usually this prickly. I'm acting like Hudson, and even he's put his grumpy attitude on hold while he works with the kids. I'd be lying if I said I haven't noticed how most of them are trying to ignore me as much as possible. Nor do I blame them.

He punches me on the arm. Actually, punches me, not playfully. He means it. Rubbing my arm, I look at him. "What the fuck?"

His eyes widen in surprise. "I've never heard you cuss before. You must be upset."

"Shut up, Knox. Just get whatever you want to say off your chest. I don't have the mental capacity for your typical repertoire today."

He covers the hurt on his face quickly but not before I see it.

Goddammit. I really am acting like a douche, but I can't help it. I only have enough niceness to extend toward my daughters right now, and even that leaves me exhausted in a different way every night. It isn't fair to them.

And that's what it really comes down to; it isn't fair to *them*.

Things don't work out with their mom, they get stuck with me, I move them to a new city, I bring all of these people into their lives only to mess it up with the most important one.

They're still on the high from seeing their mom but I know it's coming to an end soon. They're going to ask about Vivi, and I have no idea what to tell them.

Knox doesn't bother responding, he just sits back watching Hudson wander over. This is a worse option.

"What's up?" He grumbles as he drops into the seat next to me.

"I was just letting G know that he's acting like a surly fuck."

I roll my eyes and lean back in my chair.

"He used to get like this sometimes, on the rare occasions that Vivi was mad at him, or when she'd bring her ex around the families."

Dropping my head into my hands, I ask, "Can we not mention *him* right now?"

Hudson chuckles, always finding humor in other people's misery. "You're lucky I'm here, or that we showed up to the party the other day. Calypso's threatened to castrate both of us more than once."

"That's just great," I mumble. "And Viv? Is she also threatening bodily harm?"

He gives me a long look, probably not sure how much he wants to tell me. "No, that's not her style and you know it. She hasn't really been talking to anyone, though. Lexi told Asher she's started to lock the garage door. They never do that."

Considering the time Lexi walked in and almost saw me butt naked, I know that they don't ever lock the doors to their shared garage.

Vivi's always hid herself away when she was upset so it's nothing new, but I can't help the guilt crawling up my throat. I don't want to be the reason she's retreating into herself, *again.* She's come so far in the last few months, opening herself up to new connections and I don't mean just me. Knox and Lucas, too. I don't want her to fall into old, lonely habits because of me.

"Dude," Knox starts, all the patience in his voice suddenly gone, "what are you going to do?"

Gripping my hair, I squeeze my eyes shut. "What do you mean?"

"What the *fuck* are you going to do to get my sister back?" Hudson is a surly fuck all the time, but he isn't an *angry* person. It only makes things worse that his anger is now directed at me.

"I don't know." And that's the truth. I've been trying to think of things all week to make this up to Vivi.

"Are you fucking kidding me, Grady? This bullshit again? Are you going to look me in the eye and swear you don't have a crush on her too? Let me get Asher here, so you can lie to both of us again."

Next to me, Knox leans forward. "That's the most words I've ever heard from you at once. Keep going."

Hudson chuckles but it dies off quickly. "That girl has been in love with you her entire fucking life, G. You know it, we all know it. All it would have taken was one simple *I like you* and she would've broken up with Brody in a second. But you were too much of a coward. I love you, man, but you were one then and you're one now. I don't blame you for what Brody did. That's on him and Molly, no one else. But I'll blame you if you break my sister's heart now." He shrugs in a jerky, frustrated way. "And we all knew that you loved her too. I don't give a fuck if you were married and had two beautiful little girls. You've always loved *her*. Stop hurting yourself."

Knox slow claps next to me, "Couldn't have said it better myself."

"The thought of her heart being broken again makes me want to projectile vomit, okay? Yeah, I love her. It's Vivi. *My* Viv. But I don't know how to make it up to her... You didn't see her when I tried to talk to her." She thinks I'm embarrassed to be with her, and I know at least a little bit of that comes from Arielle's off-handed comment about her being the little girl next door. It's a horrible coincidence the insult hit the bullseye.

Hudson glowers at me. "She's *my* sister. I don't need to be there to have a pretty good idea of how she reacted. She told Calypso and Lexi that you're supposed to talk before the fair." Likely one of those two would've told the twins. Vivi's the baby, and they've all made it their responsibility to protect her. He holds my gaze, a little less anger in his eyes this time. "This whole thing is really important to her, and *you* helped her create that. It's the perfect opportunity to get your head out of your ass."

"Yes," Knox agrees, nodding to himself. "A grand gesture. I've never met someone who deserves one more than her, honestly." I couldn't agree more with that.

"Not only that, but both of our moms will also murder you if you're the reason they can't spend Christmas together for the first time in, what? Twelve years?" At least twelve years. The further into high school we got, the more awkward it got between Vivi and I. Especially when we started to date other people. I might be disowned just so they could spend the day together.

"I don't plan on doing nothing, but I've been trying to think about it. I just keep coming up short."

Knox nudges my shoulder with his. "It's a good thing you have a lot of people who love her on your side."

As I'm walking out of the cafeteria with Daisy in my arms and Stella talking Hudson's ear off about how excited she is to start ballet, I'm feeling immensely better than when the day started. I know this sinking feeling in my stomach won't be gone until Vivi's back in my arms, though. But after spending the last hour and a half talking to Knox and Hudson—and Asher, who FaceTimed into the conversation—I actually feel like I have some sort of direction for the first time in days.

I went over everything that happened leading up to the day on Vivi's porch, and Asher pointed out something I'd been overlooking. Vivi never said she doesn't want to be with me, just that she's worried I don't want to be with her. Which is insane, but I can understand where I let those insecurities take root in her again.

I can only hope it's as easy as they seem to think it will be. Yeah, it's me and Vivi, I get it. Getting her to forgive me for years of silence was easier than I ever imagined but this is different. I know that this hurt goes so much deeper. She doesn't have to forgive a stupid teenage boy this time... She has to forgive a grown man who promised her the world, and then made her question all of it. Part of me wouldn't be surprised if she didn't forgive me again.

"*Miller*," an angry voice calls from down the hall leading to the gym. I take a deep breath, knowing exactly who it is just from the way it grates my nerves. "I need to fucking talk to you."

"That's a dollar for the swear jar," Stella tells Harper. He stops a few feet from us and doesn't offer my daughter more acknowledgment than a disdainful look in her direction.

His expression causes Stella to cower, but Hudson immediately puts his hand on her shoulder and guides her behind him.

"Don't swear in front of my daughters or my team," I tell Harper.

"I'm a grown fucking man. I'll do whatever I want. And that starts with *not* wanting to be a part of a dunk tank for six hours straight."

I glance over at Hudson, and after a childhood of friendship, he can read my expression. He nods toward me and reaches to grab Daisy from my arms. He quickly kneels in front of Stella and whispers something to her, nodding his head toward the front doors. She gives me a concerned look but agrees to go with him and takes his hand. Handing off my keys to him, I wait until he's further from earshot.

Turning back to Harper, I glower at him. "If you *ever* scare either of my daughters again—hell, any child at this school—we'll have a real problem, Harper."

He takes another step, closing most of the space between us so we're almost chest to chest. It's a lazy power move, and one that doesn't faze me. "The dunk tank is *bullshit*, and you know it. If you don't change our booth, you and I'll have a *real fucking problem*."

With a firm hand, I push him back a few inches. "If you didn't want me to choose for you, then you should've sent in your ideas when Vivi asked for them in *September*. The committee decided that it was a school-wide mandate for the clubs and athletic teams to participate. If you have a problem with that, you're talking to the wrong person."

"*Change. The. Fucking. Booth*," he seethes.

"And what would you like us to change the booth to, in less than a week? The booth you didn't have to do a goddamn thing for, the last time I checked."

"That's your problem," he retorts like a petulant child. "All I'm saying is I won't be doing a fucking dunk tank, and neither will my assistant coaches."

I roll my eyes, ready to push past him. He can take it up with the committee for all I care. But he stops me with a hard grasp to my shoulder and says in a deceptively quiet tone, "You either change the booth for the football team or I'll have no choice but to go to *Genevieve* about my concerns."

Before I can even process what I'm doing, I grip his t-shirt and forcefully push him into the locker. His eyes widen in surprise before he can cover it up.

"No, that's not how this is going to go, Harper. Do you *fucking* hear me? You will not go around any of my girls, and we both know that includes Genevieve. I don't care about *anything* like I care about those three. And over my dead body will you harass her for another second."

He's simmering against the lockers but stays silent. And as much I'd love to take my building frustration out on someone, especially him, I have no interest in getting into a physical altercation. Even if Vivi decided she wanted nothing to do with me for the rest of her life, I wouldn't let this piece of trash anywhere near her ever again.

"You want a different booth?" I snort derisively. "Fine, I'll get you another booth. But beggars can't be picky, *Derek*."

His face reddens in anger at the use of his first name, but he just lifts his hands in a faux-placating manner and sneers, "That's all I wanted. No reason to get so fucking worked up, bro."

My blood is boiling but I remember the two precious souls who are outside—who need their dad to stay employed and out of jail. Gripping his shirt tighter, I push him back into the lockers again. "First of all, I'm not your *bro*," I snarl, giving him one last quick shove. "And secondly," pausing to look him straight in the eyes, I mutter the words I have *never* told anyone, "fuck you." Then I turn and walk out of the school.

When the doors shut behind me, I take a minute to calm my breathing and get a grip on my emotions. Once I'm ready to face my daughters, I round the corner and instantly some of the lingering tension starts to dissipate. Hudson's leaning into the backseat, over a giggling Daisy, while a very exasperated Stella tries to talk him through how to put her sister *properly* and *safely* into her car seat.

I walk to the open door opposite of Hudson and pull Stella out and into my arms, needing the grounding effect only my daughters have been able to bring me in the last week. She squeals in surprise but instantly melts into my hold when she realizes it's me. "Dad," she pretends to whisper but she wants Hudson to hear her, "Daisy's going to fly out of her seat if Hudson doesn't get it together."

Daisy's still laughing, mostly because Hudson's tickling her while wearing the most serious expression she's probably ever seen on a person, but his eyes meet mine in amusement.

"I bet Lypie could do *way* better," she murmurs. The thought of Calypso doing anything child-related the best makes even Hudson break into a deep laugh.

"I'll fix Daisy's buckle, don't worry, sweetheart."

When I set her back into her booster, she looks at me with sincere doe eyes, "I trust you, Daddy."

It sends a much-needed shock to my heart, putting a little more life back into my system. I drop a kiss to her head and round the car so I can put Hudson out of his misery. He leans against the driver door while I talk to Daisy and get her safely situated into her car seat.

When I shut her door and turn toward Hudson, he's looking at me with raised brows. "You're going to figure this out." With a pat on my shoulder, he walks to his G Wagon and I climb into my Jeep.

After a few minutes of driving in silence, Daisy calls from the backseat, "Daddy?"

"Yes, darling?"

"Can we invite Vivi to dinner?" Her hopeful voice only pushes the knife further in my heart.

"Not tonight, Dais."

She looks at me through the rearview mirror. Her expression is a mix of anger and sadness, just adding to the guilt. "Why not?"

"Because, Daisy, she doesn't want to hang out with us. Isn't it obvious?" Stella snaps. Daisy looks between the two of us, her chin quivering.

"That's not true," I add quickly. "It has nothing to do with either of you."

Stella looks back out the window, her lip starting to tremble. "That's what you think."

Thankfully we're pulling into our driveway because I can't handle them crying and not being able to do anything about it. I quickly put the car in park and turn around in my seat. Stella's already unbuckled and going for the door. "Hold up, we need to have a little talk. Vivi's not mad at either of you. She and I... we had a fight. I'm trying to fix it."

"But it's my fault!" Stella cries. I shake my head, trying to tell her that it really isn't her fault, but she steamrolls on. "I was listening to you and Mommy talk one night... I don't wanna move again. I want to stay here, and I told Vivi that. She *promised* she wouldn't be mad, but she hasn't been around since then. She hates me." Tears are flowing down her little pink cheeks, breaking my heart even more. "I told her I like her, and she *hates* me."

Daisy looks at me, despair clear across her face now. "We're moving? I don't wanna move! Mommy left us. So, she should move here. I have a friend! And he has a gecko!" Daisy lets out on a sob.

Goddammit. I get out of the car, unbuckle Daisy, and scoop her into my arms. I half-expect Stella to walk herself inside but she crawls across the seat, clinging to my other side. I carry them both into the house and get settled on the couch before taking a deep breath.

"We're not moving. We're staying here, in Amada Beach. This is our home now. Does that sound good to you two?" They nod against my shoulders. "Good, me too. Your mom does miss you, but she and I still agree that this is the best place for the three of us to be. Sometimes... even grown-ups get confused, and your mom was just feeling confused. But we're staying here, and your mom will visit every chance she gets. And you two will go visit her and your grandparents every change you get. I promise."

Daisy nods against my shoulder again, wiping her tears on my t-shirt. Stella sits up, looking at me with a guilty expression. "But what about Vivi? You said she was going to be a part of our new lives here. Does she not want that anymore? Because of me?"

I gently push her head back to my shoulder. "No, sweetheart. Vivi loves you two so much. She isn't mad at you. I'm the one who messed up."

"Are you going to fix it?" Daisy whines. "Maybe if you say sorry, she'll come over for dinner again."

"Yeah, Daddy. Just say sorry," Stella pleads. "I'll say sorry too."

I look down at my oldest daughter, trying to read her thoughts but it's never as easy with her compared to Daisy. She holds so much in, trying to protect everyone else. "Do you really like having Vivi here?"

Daisy nods again, "Yeah... I know she isn't Mommy but she's funny and nice. And I like when she dances in the kitchen with us."

"Me too," Stella whispers. "It was hard at first but now... it's hard without her. She made me feel happier when she was here. I promise I won't ever be mean to her again if she comes back."

That makes me chuckle. *Oh Stella, we still have your teenage years.* But I appreciate the sentiment all the same.

"She's like the sun, huh? Always making the world brighter when she's around." The girls don't respond, instead just wiping their tears and holding on to me. But it was more of a reminder to me than anything else anyway.

Vivi is my home. I've known that for a while. What I hadn't realized was she's becoming a comfort for my daughters as well. I was so worried that my relationship with her was hurting them, but it isn't. It's helping them.

It only adds to my resolve to fix this with her. To create a future with her. A family, a home, a life. Whatever she'll give me at this point.

Chapter Forty-Eight
Vivi

When I pull up to my driveway, I see the very last person I would've ever expected. Seriously, Arielle would have been more likely at this point.

Not Blake.

But this is just as nerve wracking, in a different way.

I slowly step out of my car and make my way toward the porch steps. She gives me a small smile, the air between us awkward.

I try to smile back at her, but I think it's more of a grimace. "Hey… uh. Did you get lost?" I'm only teasing but the joke falls flat even to my own ears.

I don't know what she wants, but somehow it involves Grady. I'm sure of that much. But I haven't seen anyone in his family, other than Selena. Even then, I'm trying to avoid her for the first time since high school. If he hasn't told her what happened, she knows something's up.

Blake chuckles, but I know she's only being polite. "No. Surprisingly, I meant to wind up here. I had to ask my mom for your address… She said she'll call the cops if one of us doesn't reach out in an hour."

That actually makes me laugh, my shoulders relaxing a bit. Plopping down on the stair next to her, I ask, "So, what was so important you'd risk jail to talk to me?"

Blake stares forward for a few moments. I have to head to the pier soon, but I can grant her a few minutes. She deserves more from me if I'm being honest.

She taps her thumb to each finger over and over, a nervous tick I remember from childhood. "Being at S.P.A. was… hard." I recognize the acronym as Serenity Prep Academy, the private school Blake attended through middle school and most of high school. "It started as cliques that I didn't fit into and then evolved into… worse." My eyes instantly fill with tears, but I hold them at bay. It's my own emotional distress about her brother and the guilt I've been holding onto for over a decade when it comes to my friendship with Blake that causes the reaction. But I need to offer Blake more than my own emotions right now.

I owe Blake apologies and if she's allowing me the knowledge of all the ways I've hurt her, then I need to listen. Then, and only then, will I properly ask for her forgiveness in the way she deserves.

She started at the private school when I was in ninth grade. Even though we grew apart soon after, I remembered it was a hard transition for her. A lot of the girls who go to S.P.A., even now, have attended their entire lives so *cliques* is probably putting it lightly. Blake's an extremely talented swimmer and was offered a scholarship when she was only in seventh grade, and I remember it being important to Selena's mom that she attend since Selena also graduated from a private, all-girls school. But regardless of how well off the Millers are, it's pennies compared to most of the students there.

"That stuff didn't happen right away. It all just got to be too much, so that's why I finished online. But even before that… I just—I was so fucking angry. At everyone. At my grandma for wanting me to go there, at my parents for allowing it. At myself, for being good enough at swimming to get a scholarship so they had no reason to say no." Her voice starts to tremble, so she takes a few deep breaths.

"I was pissed off at Grady for leaving for college... I was mad at you for caring more about your friendship with my brother than you did about mine."

Fuck. That... that breaks my heart into what feels like irreparable pieces.

My initial reaction is to defend myself, to tell her she's wrong. But that's not true. I know it's not.

It isn't that she meant *less* to me than Grady but... it was just hard. Everything that happened with Grady started to pile up and then I started to date Brody. I pulled away from their entire family, even if they were *mine* at that point. Anything relating to Grady just fucking hurt too much.

"You were my only friend that wasn't my brother. Calypso was like an older sister, and your brothers were two more siblings as far as I was concerned. But *you* were my friend. My best and first friend. I always knew that you and Grady were closer. As soon as I was old enough to understand what a crush was, it made sense. And I wasn't jealous of that, necessarily. But I was mad at you. And I was mad at Grady. And you both were gone so I got angrier. And it consumed me."

"Blake..." I start, trying to blink back my tears.

"Hold on. Let me finish, okay?" I nod, crossing my arms on my knees. "But then that anger turned to embarrassment. Because I was bullied and because of the things they'd say about me, sometimes even to me. Because I had such a hard time making friends. Because my only friend moved on without me. And that embarrassment only made me angrier and sadder and more isolated.

"It wasn't until I graduated that I started to go to therapy. But I realized how I felt about our friendship, was probably how you felt about your friendship with Grady. And I blamed you for so many things that weren't your fault when I reacted similarly. Your family was my family, but I stopped talking to all of you. Including your mom, though she is rather persistent." I chuckle, remembering how Grady told me that she continued to reach out to him no matter the distance he tried to create.

I'm not surprised that my mom treated Blake the same. Selena and Tim gave me my space, but they always welcomed me with open arms—whether I was spending time with them due to my own desires or my mother's demands. And they'd do the same for any of my siblings.

Our families took to each other just as quickly as Grady and me. Our moms have been best friends as long as I remember knowing them. Selena and Tim gave us a family when we so desperately needed one after my dad's death.

My problems with Blake and Grady didn't only hurt us. We hurt our entire families.

I turn toward Blake, silently asking if I can speak now. She nods and turns her body to face me.

"Blake..." Immediately my voice cracks. I don't need to know the details about what happened to her to appreciate her openness and empathize to the best of my abilities—but I hope one day she might trust me enough to confide in me. I take a deep breath, not wanting to make this about me in that way. "I am so sorry. I never realized it got that bad... and I am so fucking sorry." She shakes her head, but it's my turn to stop her.

I hold up a hand and carry on. "Your friendship wasn't less important than Grady's, but I understand that my actions spoke otherwise. It hurt to be around you. *All* of you. I don't fault you for questioning if I was to blame for what happened with Grady. Truthfully, I wasn't all that innocent most of the time. I... I don't know what you went through at S.P.A. so I won't pretend. All I can offer you in that regard is a shoulder and ear whenever you need it. But I understand that anger and embarrassment you speak of.

"I was so fucking mad at your brother," I chuckle again, but there's no humor in it. "I was angry, heartbroken, and embarrassed. It's no secret what our parents imagined for Grady and me. And I felt like I let them down somehow. The worse I acted toward Grady or the *more serious* I got with Brody, the less I could look any of you in the eye."

Tentatively, I grab one of Blake's hands—surprised that she allows it. "I don't mean to make excuses for how I hurt you or try to justify it because there is nothing that can. I *hurt* you, Blake, and I am so fucking sorry. And no matter what happens with me and your brother, I hope that we can move forward from this. I was so scared to let people into my life for so long, which is a big reason why I never reached out. Because I should've been the one sitting on your porch steps. But I'm not scared anymore. I know I can be the friend you deserve if you allow me the chance to try."

Blake shakes her head again, confusion and relief mixed in her watery expression. "I actually showed up here hoping that you'd eventually be my sister-in-law... *finally*... so I'm a little confused about what you mean. What's happening between you and Grady?"

"It doesn't matter, Blake. I want to focus on how to move forward with *you.*"

Guilt washes over her—even though she's the last person who should be feeling any semblance of that. "Did something happen with you two because of me?" I shake my head. Before I can respond, realization washes over her. "Did something happen with Arielle? Is that why you weren't at Stella's birthday?"

I take a deep breath and look up. *This isn't my place.* "Grady just needs to figure some things out with her, but you should talk to him about this. I don't want to overstep."

"Okay," she nods slowly but never takes her eyes off of me. "But you should know… all of that's done. Grady never thought twice about that relationship once all was said and done. And he *never* looked at Arielle, or any other person, the way he's always looked at you."

I huff out a laugh but try to hide my puddling tears. "Can I ask you something?" I take her silence as a *yes.* "What did you tell Arielle about me?"

I look back at her, but confusion is written across her face. "She said there was a picture of Grady and I in a photo album together. She saw it with you…"

Blake snorts, catching me off guard. "Oh, God. I'm sorry… I just forgot about that." With a huff, she leans back on her hands. "Arielle was crazy jealous. It was rare she ever showed that side to Grady, I think. But she used to ask about his high school girlfriend and for any information she could think of." With a roguish grin—her signature that I haven't seen in years—she says, "Most of what I told her was wrong anyway."

"Blake," I laugh. "What did you tell her?"

"It was one of the *few* times she came to visit. Stella was only a couple months old. Anyway, my mom thought it would be fun for Arielle and Adrian to see some baby photos." My brain starts to fill in the pieces, but I let Blake finish. "She started to wonder why there was a little redhead girl in *all* of the pictures with Grady. Even to someone who knows you two, it was weird how threatened she felt by a childhood friendship. But I knew Grady was trying to make this work for Stella and I knew he was planning on proposing soon." She gives me an apologetic grimace. "It had been years since you guys had talked…" No one knows about prom, and few know about the vow renewal. She rolls her eyes, at herself, and I can't help but smile. "And I was still mad at you… so I told her that you were just some girl who lived next door and was obsessed with Grady. *Super* annoying and was always buzzing around him like a fly. But that Grady dropped you as soon as he entered high school."

With each word my mouth drops open. After I second, I break out into a laugh. Blake looks confused for a second, but she tentatively laughs along.

Playfully, I shove her shoulder. "I'm so not surprised but you weren't really lying either. You just made it sound way too one-sided."

Still laughing, she nods. "I know. He was obviously the one obsessed with *you.*"

I roll my eyes, looking forward again. I was starting to believe that maybe Grady was just as in love with me as I am with him. But I can't help feeling like his secret, his second choice. Rationally, in my head, I know the truth about his marriage and divorce to Arielle. He's been so open and forthcoming with any and all questions. I've been the one standoffish and untrusting. But in my heart… the hurt is still bleeding out from the inside.

Seeing the tears brimming, she asks, "What happened with Arielle?"

After a moment, I decide to tell her all about our first meeting with each other.

The look of disbelief throws me off after our heart-to-heart, but she finally breaks the tension. "How is he such a fucking idiot?" It takes me a moment to realize that she's talking about Grady but once I do, I can't help the cackle and nod I give her. "Vivi, dude, he's an idiot. But I *promise* it wasn't anything against you. This is the same man who didn't tell us about his divorce until it was finalized. He likes to handle things privately. And his life isn't Arielle's business anymore."

I tilt my head back and forth, contemplating. "His life will always be partially her business. And who he's dating and bringing around their daughters is also her business. I mean I can understand at first… but the cat's been out of the bag for a month now. I don't know what he expected when she got to town."

"I think he was choosing hopeful oblivion. But please… just talk to him. It doesn't have to be tonight. The fundraiser should be your main focus. But soon after." She takes my silence as a yes. Standing up, she goes to leave but adds, "My dad was right about knowing Adrian was the man for me. So, I believe his *feeling* about you being right for Grady. I've always known it would come back to you two." She walks to her Suburban and waves over her shoulder. "I'll see you at the pier later."

Lexi comes twirling into my room, happier than anyone has a right to be in front of me right now.

Okay, that's mean. I know its mean… and I don't actually feel that way. Except maybe I do right now. A little.

"Why are you twirling around? You look like…" I let the sentence die off, not wanting to talk about Stella or Daisy. It hurts too much.

Never letting me take the easy route, she asks, "Who? Daisy?" She stops and looks at me sitting on my bed, in only a bra and underwear. She gives me an exasperated glare. "Because I'm *happy*, you bitch. Hurry up and get dressed. I'm leaving in ten."

Reluctantly, I walk to my closet. "Why're you so happy?"

"You'll see."

I grab my white sweater and booties before meeting Lexi in my room. "What do you mean, *I'll see?*" Nothing good can come from that phrase out of her mouth.

"You need pants." She walks to my dresser, thumbing through the options.

"I'm wearing the red flairs." I point to the other drawer. She opens it and throws the pair to me. Slipping them on, I say, "Please tell me what's going on. You know I hate surprises."

"Velvet is perfect for a Christmas fair. Good choice." Usually, I can play into her deflection for a bit but I'm at my wits end here, on the verge of a panic attack at having to interact with Grady in less than thirty minutes. And I *know* he's going to want to talk about us. I'm honestly surprised he's given me the week and a half I asked for.

But truthfully, the thought of not talking to Grady tonight is worse.

The small possibility that he's changed his mind since then, that I'm too much and I don't giving enough back, is the outcome that hurts the most.

"I can't do this tonight, Alexandra." We *rarely* use each other's full names, so she knows I'm serious right now. "What the fuck is going on?"

She bites the inside of her cheek, considering letting me in on the surprise. When her hands slip into her pockets, I know that I'm getting an answer.

"Your brothers and Knox helped Grady plan something for you. It's not a *small* gesture but I promise it won't feel like a big, public declaration either. But it's sweet." She gives me a small smile and nods. "And he wants to talk to you. I'm in charge of getting you there." She's been Grady's biggest supporter since he moved back, so I'm not surprised by her change of loyalty.

Rolling my eyes, I finish getting ready and let Lexi drive me to my impending anxiety attack.

Chapter Forty-Nine

Grady

I stand at the end of the pier, only slightly worried that Lexi's more likely to pull a Thelma and Louise than she is to bring Vivi here. She's been a huge supporter of our relationship so far but she's always going to be a bigger supporter of Vivi—as it should be.

Knox, Asher, and Hudson helped me get everything ready. The three of them are further down, staying out of sight so I can have this one moment with Vivi before the fundraiser starts.

I know what tonight means for her and the school, so I wanted to show her that what's important to her, means everything to me.

As my nerves start to grow, I see headlights pull into the parking lot a few hundred feet away. The car turns off, but it takes a couple minutes before I see her bright red hair half piled on top of her head in a messy bun, the rest is in loose waves down her back. With her white and red outfit, she looks like an adorable candy cane. I wouldn't be surprised if that was intentional.

It feels like hours before she finally begins her ascent up the stairs. I hold my breath, counting the seconds until I see her beautiful face. A week and a half feels too long now. Vivi isn't just a part of my everyday life, she's ingrained into the very essence of my soul. Even if she decides she doesn't want to be with me anymore, I know that she will always carry part of me with her.

The moment the top of her head crests the staircase, her eyes widen in shock. She stops with only a few steps left, her mouth opening and closing—searching for the right words. The woman who almost always has a retort is speechless.

"Grady... I—what?" She lightly shakes her head. "How did you do this?"

I give her a small shrug. "I had some help."

"But... in a week you turned our fundraiser into..." She trails off. Her eyes are lit up with awe, but I can't help worrying that I overstepped. I promised her that we would follow all of her plans for this.

And I let Asher talk me into going completely rogue.

"Do you hate it?" I ask desperately, glancing over my shoulder.

She shakes her head, tears brimming her eyes. "No," she says through a watery laugh. "I *love* it." She takes a few steps toward me, toward the winter wonderland we somehow pulled off.

She stops a foot away from me and I watch as she takes in all of the details.

The fair she and I planned was a cute—albeit impressive—event. There were string lights and hand painted signs. More booths than we could have imagined at the beginning of this. Games, food, raffles, photobooths, all of it. But Genevieve was imagining the block parties we experienced growing up. And those went all out, every year.

The entrance arch resembles oversized candy canes leading down a gumdrop path—thanks to the talented art department, papier mâché and washable paint. The booths look like they appeared out of thin air, straight from the north pole—no thanks to most of the coaches. The icicle lights mixed with the fake, biodegradable snow gives the desired illusion, regardless of the ocean below us. Straight ahead, at the end of the pier, is Santa's sled full of the raffle items and ready to be used for photos.

What she's looking at now resembles the Christmas events she always made me participate in growing up. She loved dressing up as an elf for photos with Santa and to hand out toys. I hated the outfits that looked like the elves from the clay version of Rudolph, but I went with her every year, starting my seventh-grade year. My sophomore year of high school was the last time I went with her, but I know she continued to help until she left for college, even though the event lost a little bit of the magic each year.

"Grady... this is amazing. How did you pull this off?" She looks at me like I put every star in the sky for her. It's a look I'll never take for granted again.

"People wanted to help, Viv. Especially when I told them I was doing this for you." I cautiously take a step toward her. To my utter delight, she inches closer in response. "So many people care about you, and I'm at the top of that list. Tonight isn't about us though." Her face falls but she recovers quickly, if I didn't know her so well, I wouldn't have caught it.

"Baby, I don't mean it like *that*," I add quickly. One tear slips down her cheek at the same time the relief hits her. "Every moment for the last four months has been about us, and that's the only way I would want it. But tonight is about what *you* continuously do for the school and for the students. I don't want to take away from that. So, all of this," I pause, waving my hand toward the gumdrop lane, "is just to show you how much you deserve and how loved you are."

Her eyes search my face for a few seconds before she drops her face into her hands. Her shoulders start shaking but her tears are silent. Without thinking about it, I reach for her and pull her into my chest. "I thought you were going to change your mind about me."

I can barely understand her muffled words but my heart breaks as I realize how bad I hurt her; how small I made her feel. I never want to be the reason for her sadness again. Keeping one arm around her shoulders, I use the other to grip the nape of her neck. "No, never. The only reason I was able to get through the last week and a half was by putting all of my extra time into this, for you. I was sick thinking about how I messed this up."

Slowly, she slips one of her arms around my waist, continuing to hide her tears from me. "Thank you for doing this. I didn't think something this amazing would be possible."

"I haven't even shown you the best part." She must hear the smugness in my voice because she finally peaks through her fingers, showing me her beautiful hazel eyes. The green is brighter from her tears. "Do you want to take a tour before everyone gets here?"

She nods, and I hold my hand out tentatively. She slips her fingers through mine. I give her a small smile, but she doesn't return it quite yet. With as much confidence as I can muster, I pull her down the pier.

We pass concession stands, the cake walks and a caricature stand. There are skee-ball lanes that are now painted to look like snowballs. The baseball team's booth is darts and balloons filled with red, green, and gold paint. Ring toss, DIY ornaments, robots dressed as snowmen to race. There's face painting and raffles with items from many of the local businesses. We pass more games, prizes, and activities. Her eyes light up with every step we take until we reach the end, near Santa's sleigh.

"Um. What is that?" She asks, both unsure and amused.

"*That* is a very special gift for you."

She gives me a curious side-eye. "And what *is* it?"

"Harper didn't love the idea of being dunked, even if the water was heated." She turns toward me, and there are a lot of questions in her eyes. "I promise to tell you everything about the last few days later. But I changed their booth since he hated the first one so much. Now, Harper and the football coaches are volunteering as the targets for pie throwing. I even got every committee member to sign off on the activities and tables included tonight. So if anyone doesn't want to participate, they'll have to take it up with them." Not letting go of her hand, I turn toward her with an impish smirk. "What do you think?"

She looks at me like I'm crazy for exactly two seconds before her head tips back in laughter, her belly laugh filling the air around us. "All of this is amazing… but this," she points toward the pie booth. "This is fucking incredible."

She wraps her arms around me, burying her face in my chest.

I pull her tight against me and kiss her temple. "I love you so much, Vivi, and I'm so sorry for hurting you. Please forgive me, and I promise I'll spend our entire lives making it up to you."

Tipping her head back and placing her chin on my pec, she tells me, "There's no one else. Never has been and never will be. I'm always going to be yours." She slowly rises to her toes, leaving a couple of inches between our lips. "Kiss me again, Grady."

And without a second of hesitation, I do.

Chapter Fifty
Vivi

After our quick reunion, Grady and I were pulled apart to finish getting everything set up and tend to the few problems that have popped up throughout the evening. Nothing major—it'd be almost impossible with the amount of thought Grady put into the whole event. Just a few little things, like our Santa getting sick but dear Mr. Sparks agreed to finally take on the roll, if only for me. One of the carafes broke but Hudson ran to Brighter Daze to get another one for the hot chocolate booth.

But now, with the event starting to pick up and more guests showing up, it *feels* like a winter wonderland. The soft sounds of Christmas music are the perfect background to the laughs of families and cheers at the games. The only thing that's weighing on my heart is the fact I haven't seen the girls yet, and I don't want to be out of reach from Grady for another second.

I know that there's more to tonight than just he and I though.

"Why do you still look sad, Viv?" Lexi asks, slipping an arm around my waist as I organize the pastries Calypso donated for the cake walk. "Did you two not make up?"

"No, we did," I assure her. "It feels a little up in the air, and we still have things we need to discuss, but I think that's just the timing of everything." I wave a hand in the air, indicating the carnival going on around us. "I just... I wish I had agreed to talk to him sooner."

"I get that." She turns around, setting her hip on the table. "But maybe you won't have to wait much longer." I can hear the smile in her voice, but I still look up to catch the familiar sight before I turn to where she's staring.

As soon as I do, a high-pitched squeal rips through the air at the same moment Daisy runs from her dad's side. Straight to *me*.

I crouch down, catching her in my open arms as she springs into my embrace. "Vivi!"

"Daisy," I murmur into her hair, holding her close. "I missed you, little lady."

"I missed you so much. Are you still fighting with Daddy?"

I pull back to look at her as Stella quietly slips into the spot next to us. I open an arm for her, and warmth fills my chest when she slips an arm around my neck and settles closer to my side. "No, we aren't fighting anymore."

"Oh, *good*." Daisy lets out a big breath, and I can see her shoulders relax.

Stella nods in agreement. "You'll visit again?"

"Whenever you want me there, Stella girl."

"Tonight!" Daisy shouts. I can hear Lexi and Grady's chuckles off to the side. "Come over *tonight*."

I glance up at Grady, looking for confirmation that *he* wants me there tonight. "I don't kno—"

"Christmas Eve is tomorrow. You have to be with us," she whines.

Grady finally moves closer to kneel in our small huddle, joining the reunion. "She's right, love. We're making new traditions, and that includes you."

"Yeah! You're our new tradition!" Daisy nods emphatically. Laughing, I pull Stella a little closer when she rolls her eyes at her sister's misinterpretation.

"You said whenever we want," Stella whispers after a second.

I look her in the eye and can feel more than just a fondness radiating off of her. "There's nowhere else I'd want to be."

"Then you're coming home with us," Grady states.

"But first, *Santa*," Daisy emphasizes.

"We can't miss Santa," I promise. "But I need to go check on the Yearbook's photo booth first," I admit regretfully.

"We'll go with you," Stella instantly says, grabbing my hand tightly. Daisy interlaces her own with my other hand.

I turn to tell Lexi I'll talk to her later, but she cuts me off by leaning over my shoulder to place a quick kiss to my cheek and winks at me.

After a pit stop at the hot chocolate station—even though all three of us girls agree it's *nowhere* near as good as Grady's—I make sure that my assistant supervisor on the Yearbook club has it under control and that one of my editors-in-chief are there too. We've agreed to a staggered schedule, so I have the first half of the evening to wonder the booths with the girls and Grady.

Stella's surprisingly great at darts, winning herself the largest stuffed polar bear among the baseball team's prizes. Daisy, on the other hand, is still learning hand-eye-coordination so she hasn't won anything for herself, but she hasn't given up. While I'm playing a couple rounds of skee-ball with Daisy, Stella and Grady make their way back from the bathroom… but a smile tugs on my lips when I see what Stella's carrying, and that she didn't really need to go to the bathroom.

"Another one?" Daisy asks when she sees the giant penguin that Stella's carrying. Her voice tries to stay excited, but I can hear the undertone of jealousy that her sister won *two* stuffies.

"Do you like it?" Stella asks, softly and tentatively. Daisy nods, trying to hide her disappointment. "I won it for you, Dais."

"Really?" She instantly lights up. Instead of grabbing for the toy, she reaches for her sister's free hand.

Grady's arm snakes around my waist, pulling my back to his chest. "These are my favorite moments to watch," he whispers. "They've always reminded me of you and Lyp." I smile at the scene playing out before us, knowing Calypso would've done the same for me growing up.

"Of course, I did. It's only fun when we can play together," Stella confirms.

"You. Are. The. *Best*. Sister," Daisy swears, emphasizing each other.

My lips pull impossibly wider as I watch the girls share a hug.

After we finish at that activity, we make our way to the cake walk because Daisy's determined to win something for herself tonight and this one looks *easy peasy*.

Knox is already there with his family, along with both of my brothers. The team captain Jeremy and Lexi's brother Johnny were handling the dart booth for the team, allowing the coaches to walk around and check on things throughout the night. So, this is the first time I've seen them since the event started.

I slip between my brothers and wrap an arm around each of their waists. "Thank you," I whisper and lean my head on Asher. "This means everything to me." I make eye contact with Knox, so he knows my appreciation extends to him as well.

"We were happy to help, Viv," Knox amends.

"Still," I breathe, a little watery from my growing emotions.

Hudson places a kiss on my head before both of my brothers disentangle from my clutch, but Grady slips right in to hold me close again.

"I need you to stay right here," he leans down to murmur into my ear.

Turning my head into his chest, I nod and take a big whiff of his musky amber scent I've missed. We stay there with my siblings and friends until Daisy and Matty both won a cake, then we move to Santa as a group—where we find Blake and our moms. And the rest of the evening goes similar to that. We make our way from booth to booth as a group, sometimes breaking a part—but never me from Grady and the girls—and always make our way back to each other.

When it's time for me to take my shift at the photo booth, Grady insists on coming with me after Knox assures us that he'll take over with the baseball team for the remainder of the evening. We offer to let the girls go with Blake, but neither of them seems ready to let me out of their sights just like their father.

And after almost two weeks of the horrible distance between us four, I only want to be here with them.

By the time we got to Grady's house, it was almost midnight. We tried to get the girls to go with Selena while we cleaned up but neither of them was having it. Daisy even started to cry, though I think that had more to do with exhaustion by that point.

We stopped by my house so I could grab their gifts and bring Cinnamon and Vanilla with us. After one *small* piece of the funfetti cake Daisy won, the girls are now in their own beds, each with one of my cats curled up to keep them company. I even went to tuck them in with Grady for the first time. Daisy told me that he doesn't do *snug as a bug in a rug* nearly as well as me. As if that wasn't one of the best compliments I've ever gotten.

Grady's standing next to me in his bathroom as we brush our teeth. Even though his arm is resting along my shoulders, we keep making googly eyes at each other through the mirror like two kids with a schoolyard crush. We've been mostly quiet since getting home, both content to be in each other's presence again. I can't speak for Grady, but I'm feeling more relaxed than I have in weeks.

When we're finished, I let Grady guide me to my side of the bed and he already has it set up with the extra charger, glass of water and a hair tie waiting. Once we're settled next to each other, I turn so he has full access to my long, wavy locks and he instantly starts to work the knots out.

I can feel myself drifting off to sleep when Grady lazily starts to place soft kisses along the exposed skin of my neck and shoulders as he finishes off the braid. I lean back into him, letting his safe arms and warmth wrap around me.

"Grady…"

"Hmm?" He hums in between kisses.

"I don't want you to think I *don't* want this because I do… I just—I'm so tired," I admit, taking a shaky breath.

His hand wraps around my jaw and tilts me to look at him. "Have you been sleeping?"

I shake my head truthfully. "Not very well… and I'm just so tired, Grady."

His eyes redden but he holds me tighter and settles us on the mattress. My legs tangle around his and my hand lazily strokes over every bare inch of him. "All that matters is you being here, in my arms and my bed. Everything else can wait." I nod against his chest and let my eyes close, already feeling sleep wash over me.

"Get some rest, baby. I'll be here when you wake up."

"Mm, I love you," I mumble sleepily.

"I love you so much, Genevieve."

Chapter Fifty-One
Grady

Waking up to Vivi's familiar vanilla berry scent and soft curves wrapped around me, feels like I'm in heaven. Even though I know we aren't there yet—and my daughters definitely aren't either—I know without a doubt that this is what I eventually want every day.

But I know I still owe her a conversation first.

So I lay back and enjoy the feeling of her body tangled with mine while she sleeps a bit longer. I'm careful to not wake her up as I pull her closer, needing the physical contact I always crave from her. Yesterday was a long day for both of us but from what Vivi said last night, I know that anxiety of the last week and half has been weighing heavily on her.

I never want to be the reason she can't sleep again.

I want to be the person who calms her mind and heart, that gives her a space to always feel safe and loved.

Closing my eyes, I listen to the sound of her breathing and the low hum of the neighborhood waking up outside my window. At some point, I must have fallen back asleep because I wake to featherlight touches along my chest. Glancing down, I see Vivi watching her fingers make patterns that feel like words but I can't distinguish what she's trying to write along my heart.

Brushing a lock of hair off her forehead, I murmur, "Good morning, love."

Tilting her head up, she offers me a sweet, sleepy smile. "Good morning, Grady."

"How'd you sleep?"

"Much better. What about you?"

I run my fingers up and down her spine, soaking in the view of her in my bed again. "I always sleep best when you're here."

She rests her chin on my chest so she can look me in the eye. "Really?" There's so much insecurity and vulnerability in that one word.

"Yes, Genevieve. *Really*." She silently nods and bites the inside of her lip. Using my thumb, I gently pull her lip free. "We should talk, though."

Reluctantly, she sits up and crosses her legs but stays close to my hip. "Yeah, we should… I have questions."

I settle my body against the headboard and rest my hand on her thigh. "Whatever you want to know, I'll tell you."

Nodding again, she thinks it over before meeting my eye. "Did you talk to Arielle?"

"Yes," I quickly reassure her. She listens as I tell her every detail about our conversation and the very clear boundaries that have been set between Arielle and me. I tell her about our plans for the girls over the next six months and when she can expect to see Arielle again, no surprises this time. "She wants to talk to you," I decide to tell her.

Her eyes widen in shock. "Me?"

"Yeah, *you*. She wants to get to know the woman who will be in Stella and Daisy's lives. But it's more than that. She wants to apologize to you."

"I mean… that's not necessary," she says slowly but I can see that Arielle's words are still weighing on her.

Shaking my head, I give her thigh a squeeze and tell her, "No, it is. She was out of line and she knows it. I know I'm mostly to blame here, and I don't expect you guys to be friends, but if only for the girls, I hope you two can get along."

Vivi bites her lip and thinks it over. "I wouldn't *mind* being friends with Arielle. I'd do anything for Stella and Daisy, you know?"

"I know," I quickly reassure her.

She offers me a soft smile and visibly relaxes a little. "I just don't want to be an inconvenience to any of you, so I'm willing to let it go with Arielle if that's easier."

"It's not easier for me, and I'm not willing to let it go." She reluctantly nods. "But it doesn't have to be today or even this week. She's going to visit at the end of January to spend her birthday with the girls, so we can cross that bridge then. Right now, I just want to focus on us and making new traditions with the girls."

With more confidence, she nods again. "Me too."

My eyes move over her face, trying to understand where her head is at. "You have another question." It's more of a statement than anything, but I can practically see it forming on her mouth before she voices it.

"Are you sure this—" She waves her hand between us. "—is still what you want? Because if being *friends* is less complicated for you then I think I can do th—"

"I can't do that, Genevieve." I lean forward and lightly clasp my hands around her neck, pulling her close enough to rest my forehead on hers. "I don't want to just be your friend. And whatever you need for me to prove that, I'll do it." If I have to spend every morning and night giving her the reassurance she needs, then I'll do it. As long as she's here with me. "Is that what you want though?"

"No, Grady, I don't. I want a future with you." She runs her fingers along my scruffy jaw and places a soft kiss on my lips that ends too quickly. Pulling back, she looks me in the eye and searches my expression. "But I need you to be completely transparent with me. I don't care so much about other people—we can figure that part out *together*. But you have to let *me* into everything that's going on. I want to be a team, a family. And I can't be blindsided like that again…"

"You're right. That's something I promise to handle better in the future, because being a team is the only option. Which brings me to my last point, therapy." Her eyebrows raise. I know that Vivi went to a therapist for a few years when she moved back to Amada Beach after college. She's always been the more self-aware one between us, even if she might disagree with that. But her need to constantly make herself "better" is proof enough. "I found two child therapists—one for each of the girls—and they're going to start going to bi-weekly sessions in the new year. But I also found a family therapist, and I'm going to go with the girls every other week as well."

Her smile blooms into a full grin, one of pride and happiness. "Grady, I think that's great. It'll only help the girls in the long run. I'm sure of it."

"I know, baby. I should've done it sooner." I trace her full lips with my thumb. "And you've been nothing but the brightest ray of sunshine in our lives these last few months *but* if you wanted to maybe go with us, even once a month, I'd love that. Because I'm trying to build a life with all three of you."

She gives me another sweet kiss, but this one is more alive and passionate than the last. "I'd love to go with you. Anything I can do to support you three is all that matters to me."

"And what matters to me is making sure that *all* my girls are happy."

"I don't doubt that I will be as long as I'm with you, Grady." A breath of relief escapes me, and I didn't know until this moment how much I needed the reassurance. She must see it on my face because she adds, "I couldn't imagine my life without you again. I don't want to even try. Nothing for me has changed—if anything, I'm more sure now than I was before. And you're only confirming the things I was already feeling."

I nod, swallowing down the overwhelming emotions trying to break free. "Good. I never want to be the cause of your pain again, Viv. I'm going to do everything in my power to be the man worthy of your love and the partner you deserve."

Lightly, she pushes me back onto the pillows and crawls into my arms, laying on my chest. It isn't sexual, but intimate and comforting, like she needs the contact our bodies have been missing these last two weeks. "You're already doing the work Grady. I see the effort in your actions, between setting those boundaries with Arielle and everything you organized for the winter wonderland. I appreciate all of it more than I can put into words."

I kiss the top of her head, hoping it conveys enough of the gratitude I'm feeling for the patience and understanding she has given me. Pulling her closer, needing that connection too, I ask, "What do you think about a few more minutes in bed, then we go see what the girls want to do to start our first new tradition today?"

She lets out a little sigh. "Sounds perfect to me."

Me too.

Vivi and I laid in bed for another half hour before I pulled her up and into the shower. We washed each other's bodies and made love under the spray of the water—it was passionate and carnal. Her quiet moans and sweet nothings drove me into an almost frenzy, needing to be as close as possible to her just to remind myself she's really here.

The girls have been slow to make their way out of their rooms. And as much as I'm trying to hold onto hope that it's solely for the fact that each of the cats took up residence in the beds and how late they were up last night, I can't help but feel a little bit of anxiety the longer Vivi and I wait, drinking our coffee at the island.

Around nine o'clock we finally hear the small pitter patter of feet walking down the stairs though. Vivi gives me an encouraging smile, but I can see the apprehension on her face too.

It's been a lot for both of my girls the last few weeks, and we have to take each moment at a time right now. I know they've missed Vivi and invited her to stay with us, but they can also change their minds at any second.

Daisy lets out her trademark squeal when she sees Vivi sitting on a stool and Stella lets out a big sigh at the same sight. Almost as if they were worried, she'd disappear in the dead of night.

I kept her firmly in my grip all night, irrationally afraid of the same thing. And when I first woke up, she was wrapped just as tightly around me.

"You're here," Daisy breathes out, beaming at us.

"We're making traditions, right?"

"Yes," Stella nods resolutely and climbs onto the spot to Vivi's right.

But Daisy rounds the island and pulls on my shirt, glancing up at the cabinet behind my head. On a chuckle, I lift her into my arms so she can present her gift to Vivi. She tries to sneakily grab the item but accidentally slams the door shut. Daisy peaks over her shoulder, and even though I saw Vivi glance this way, Stella's doing her sisterly duty by trying to keep her as distracted as possible.

Setting Daisy on the counter, sitting with her legs crossed in front of Vivi and Stella, she holds her hands behind her and is practically shaking with excitement.

"What you got back there, little lady?" Vivi asks.

Shoving the oversized ceramic mug in Vivi's direction, she says in one breath, "This is for you. I made it a couple days after Stella's birthday when Daddy took me to sign up for classes at the pottery place."

Vivi places her hands over Daisy's, so she can pull the creation closer to her while keeping that contact between them. Both of their eyes fill with happy tears as Vivi takes in the giant pastel green mug. And I mean, it's *huge*. It could probably hold a large, iced coffee, which is coincidentally perfect for Genevieve. Especially because Daisy forgot to add a handle, so you'd need to wrap it in something if you wanted to drink something hot anyway.

"Do you like it?" Daisy tentatively asks.

Moving one of her hands so she can trace over the shaky letters, she nods. "I love it *so* much, Daisy. Thank you for making this for me."

Daisy preens at the praise, gaining most of her confidence back. "It's all of our letters!" She points out, but she means our initials. She asked me to write out *G+V+S+D=a heart* so she could carve in the design. "But I forgot to add a handle," she admits sheepishly, glancing at Stella who had pointed it out to her when we went back to pick it up.

"I drink my coffee cold anyway, so it's perfect." And I take that as my cue to grab the cold brew I picked up at the grocery store a few days ago, with the hope and intention that Vivi would be here soon to receive her gift. Sliding the bottle toward her, she happily swaps me for her mug of brewed coffee and fills her new cup after I drop a few ice cubes in the glass for her. "So, what are we thinking as far as traditions go?"

And that's how we ended up outside of her brother's house with a car packed full of all the winter beach picnic essentials—a picnic blanket, extra blankets and sweaters, hot chocolate in a Yeti tumbler, UNO, a few picture books, and a basket full of sandwiches, fruit, goldfish, and Daisy's cake from last night.

It's probably more than we need, but the girls were so excited at Vivi's suggestion that we wanted to make sure we had enough so we can stay out as long as they want. Or until it gets too cold, and we'll have to bribe them with the promise of a blanket fort and Christmas movies at home.

Either way, it does something to my heart knowing that my daughters are going to experience one of the most special things of mine and Vivi's entire friendship—something we've only ever shared with each other until right now.

Asher's lived in this house since around the time my parents renewed their vows, and while I know he had originally bought it with the intention of moving in with his ex-girlfriend, it *feels* like Asher—small beach bungalow with an attached shed for his surfing gear and a back gate with access to a fairly secluded part of the beach that also happens to have some of the best waves in the area. He always lets his siblings park their cars here to avoid the tourist traffic at the main shores. I understand why he never sold it.

"Ready?" Vivi steps up to my side and looks up with the prettiest smile.

"Ready!" Daisy calls from Vivi's arms as Stella raises her own for me to pick her up. With our lunch in one hand, my daughter in the other arm, and Vivi carrying Daisy only a step ahead of me, we make our way around the house and start our first of what I hope are many traditions to come.

"Ready," Stella and I agree at the same time.

Epilogue
Grady

End of May, last day of the school year...

For the first time in what feels like hours—but has really only been three—I let out a deep breath. Asher and Knox are hanging the last strand of fairy lights, while Hudson helps arrange the multiple bouquets of peonies I bought from Sunday Blooms. It's a little late in the year for them but they're Vivi's favorite flower so I would have spent thousands just to get a few arrangements. But whether it was luck or possibly a little dose of fate, there was a surplus in blooms this year.

That's not everything though. The flowers and string lights accent the large tent, decorated with layers of blankets and pillows. There are two chairs in front of the entrance, giving us a spot to sit and watch the meteor shower tonight. There's an ice chest full of our favorite ciders from Clear Horizons as well as her favorite sushi from a place in Ocean Beach. Calypso made a lime pie with berries–a seasonal favorite of Vivi's.

But the most important piece is sitting in a velvet box in my pocket.

A white gold band decorated with five pear-shaped diamonds

that are slightly different sizes and arranged in a way that makes a dainty flower. As soon as I saw it, I knew it was the right choice for her. It's unique but simple and so perfectly Genevieve.

My small backyard has been transformed into—hopefully—the perfect proposal. Simple, private, and nostalgic.

It was in her backyard, on the last night of school, huddled in sleeping bags and cloaked in darkness, that I realized my feelings for Vivi had grown into more than friends. More than I was able to understand as a kid. So, I've known for months that this was where I wanted to ask her to marry me.

One month ago, I sat down Vivi's family—and Lexi, of course—to ask for their blessings. Sure, Bonnie's is the only one I *needed* but I knew I had it. I could have asked for Vivi's hand in marriage at ten and our parents would have viewed it as a legitimate binding contract. But these are the people who have made up so much of Vivi's time over the last few years. If anyone knew of a reason I shouldn't ask her, it would have been the four of them.

But each one gave me a nod of encouragement, one right after the other.

"That's everything," Knox says, walking up next to me. "When is she getting here?"

Asher and Hudson come to stand with us, giving our effort one final look over. It's perfect.

Taking a deep breath I say, "Lexi and Calypso should be dropping her off in the next twenty minutes. You guys should get out of here before she sees you."

"We'll see you for brunch tomorrow though, right?" Asher asks. He's been the most excited of her siblings, but that fits their dynamic to no one's surprise.

I nod. "Yeah, we'll be there with good news, fingers crossed."

Hudson pats my shoulder. "Don't be nervous. She's wanted to

marry you since she was six years old. You just needed to get your head out of your ass." His comment is teasing but the sincerity in his voice calms my nerves a little.

"We'll see you tomorrow. Good luck, but you don't need it," Knox adds.

Asher shakes my shoulders in excitement before pulling me into a brief hug. "You've always been our brother but it's about to be official."

Their support, and my nerves, have me choked up so all I can do is nod my head. They leave me in the backyard and exit through the side gate. The same one that Vivi will enter through. The path of seashells I saved from many summers spent at the beach will lead her back here. And now we wait.

Fifteen minutes later, I hear a car pull into the driveway and three voices, but I can't make out the words. It doesn't matter though because I would recognize that sweet teasing lilt anywhere. I stand from the chair and wait for the love of my life to come around the corner.

After about ten seconds that feel like a lifetime, she slowly walks to the back. "Grady, are you—" her question dies on her tongue the moment she sees me standing in a familiar setting. "What is this?" She takes another step forward, taking in the scene.

"I wanted to have another backyard sleepover with my best friend." I hold my hand out for her, lightly tugging her toward me once it's in my grasp.

"You did all of this? When?" she asks quietly. Her eyes are flitting around, in disbelief that all of this is for her.

Cupping the back of her head, I murmur against her lips, "This afternoon but I had some help."

"Oh?" Her voice is breathy, almost inaudible. She's confused, I can see it in her furrowed eyebrows. She's wondering if there's more but doesn't want to get her hopes up.

Placing a soft kiss on her lips, I whisper, "I love you, Genevieve."

She fists my button up. "I love you, too, Grady. This is perfect. *You* are perfect."

"Viv, baby. *I love you.* I love you so much that I only have one plan for my life—to spend it with you." Her eyes slightly widen with her sharp inhale. Taking her hands in one of mine, I slowly drop to one knee in front of her. She's holding back a sob before I pull the ring box out of my pocket. "Genevieve," I start.

"Yes," she says immediately.

Laughing, I shake my head lightly. "Let me do this correctly please."

She tries to breathe through her choked sobs, mixing with her impatient laughs. She nods and wipes her cheek with one of her hands.

"Genevieve Briar Davies, I have been infatuated with you since I was five years old. I had no idea that the little redhead girl who saw me playing alone, and brought me a plate of hotdogs, was going to be the most important person in my life. For so many years after that, my days started and ended with you. Those are the memories I hold the closest to my heart.

"Somehow, I was lucky enough to have a second chance with you. Then a third chance. But I've known my entire life you were it for me. Throughout everything we both have been through, my heart has always been yours, Vivi." I take the ring out of the box and hold it at the tip of her finger. "For the rest of our lives, I want you to be mine. I'm ready to start the life we've dreamed about, the one we grew up pretending to have when we were only kids playing house. I want to love you, support you and cherish you every day for as long as you'll have me. Genevieve, love… Will you marry me?"

She drops to her knees in front of me, nodding. "Yes, *yes.* Grady, I love you. I love you so much. I want you. Forever."

Tears fall down my cheek, but I hardly notice them. My focus is on sliding the ring onto her finger and pulling her into the tent. The food and the rest of the world can wait.

Right now, I'm going to show Vivi a glimpse into one of the ways I'll always take care of her. Forever.

Vivi

The next morning, Vivi's birthday…

I don't think I've stopped staring at the gorgeous ring sitting on my finger in the last sixteen hours. The hours I was sleeping or making love to Grady don't count.

Everything about last night was perfect. I couldn't have imagined a proposal that was more intimate, or felt more right, for Grady and me. Then to wake up to him with my coffee order—Lexi dropped it off—and a single cupcake with one candle on top.

He asked the question I hadn't heard in over a decade but imagined every morning on my birthday. "What's your wish for us this year?"

Over the last few months, a lot has changed. In January, I sent in my application for the University of California, Aurora Hills school administration graduate program. I had spent the entire day after Christmas wrapped up on Grady's couch, watching TV with the girls, while I finished my essay. I wrote about Grady and all the ways he's changed my life, but I also wrote about Stella and Daisy. How they're the best parts of both of their parents, while still being uniquely themselves, reminding me to hold onto that unconditional joy and innocence we so often lose into adulthood.

In February, I moved into a one-bedroom apartment ten minutes away from Lexi and sobbed like a baby for weeks before *and* after. I was worried that it'd change things between us, but I still see her almost every single day. Both Grady and I felt it was still too soon to move in together, but I stay with him and the girls most nights. Often enough that Cinnamon and Vanilla live with them full time now. We both knew where this was going with the way Christmas Eve played out.

At the end of March, we took a family camping trip—partly a late birthday celebration for Asher and Hudson, and an early birthday celebration for Blake. We've slowly started to spend more time together, enough that I don't have to question if I want to ask her to be a bridesmaid. I *know* I want her to be a part of mine and Grady's day in one of the most important ways.

In April, I received my acceptance letter for the School Administration graduate program at UCAH. Apparently, the essay was a deciding factor when considering me and how I would fit into their program. It's just another addition to the endlessly growing list of things I'm so thankful to the three of them for.

A few weeks later, the High Tides' baseball team made it to the final round of playoffs.

Two weeks ago, Grady and I held our second school fair. This time the money was allocated between each of the clubs—excluding sports because they receive funding each year. We didn't require any of the teams to participate but to our surprise, almost all of them wanted to help out regardless. With the very obvious exceptions. But Harper hasn't bothered me since his confrontation with Grady in the hallway. Unfortunately, I can't say every other teacher or student has been so lucky.

It hasn't deterred us from continuing to do everything we can for the school, though.

After Grady set the bar high in December, we went all out for the second time. The theme was May Flowers. It was whimsical and magical and as big of a hit as the winter.

The winter fair is what brought Grady and I back together and has allowed us to give back to the school and students in a fun way. We came to a quick agreement that for the foreseeable future, this is something we plan to continue going forward. The fall's theme will be for Halloween instead.

With a watery smile, I leaned forward and blew out the candle, not having to think about it at all.

I wish for the rest of our lives to be this full of love and happiness, for us to overcome the hard times as a team, for decades of memories together.

Just like when we were younger, Grady hasn't stopped bugging me to tell him what I wished for. But I won't budge. Not because I'm embarrassed of his reaction, not anymore. On the off chance that telling your wish will cancel it out, I won't risk it. Plus, I know Grady is hoping for all the same things as me.

Last night Stella, Daisy and their cousins started their own end of the year tradition—a bonfire and movie night at their grandparents' house. Grady told them ahead of time what his plan was, so they wouldn't be surprised. He said that for once they cried *happy* tears during their conversation about him and I. So, they're waiting with everyone else for my birthday brunch. Grady's entire family is there, plus mine, Lexi's, and Knox's.

When we walk to the backyard, we are greeted by cheers, congratulations and so much love. But there's only two reactions I care about right now, even if Grady's been trying to soothe my nerves since last night.

Crouching down in front of Stella and Daisy, I grab each of their hands and give them a long, affectionate look. "How are you feeling today, little ladies?"

"Happy," Stella nods emphatically, not trying to cover the tears that are rolling down her cheeks.

"I'm so happy, too, Stella girl." Turning to the uncharacteristically quiet Daisy, I ask, "What about you? Are you happy?"

"I'm *so* happy, lovey. I don't know what to do with all of it." She shimmies her shoulders for emphasis, like all the emotions are about to burst from her little body.

With new tears cresting my eyes, I ignore the large audience we have and focus on my two favorite girls. "Lovey?"

Daisy nods. "Do you like it?"

Stella's eyes flash behind me to Grady before dropping back to mine. "Dad calls you his love all the time… and we just figured, you'd be *ours* now too, right?"

"I love it, almost as much as I love you two." It's fifty-fifty when they say it back, but Grady told me that each of them has admitted that they both love to hear me say it. They still get nervous or need to go at their own pace sometimes, and we're allowing them the space they need without any pressure. "I'm yours as much as I'm your dad's, okay?"

With big smiles and a lot of tears, we hold each other for a few minutes while everyone else around us disperses to give us some sense of privacy. When we break apart, Grady kneels to lift both of the girls in his arms, whispering *I love yous* and other endearing phrases.

Once we settle in our seats, Grady and I prepare for the tirade of questions we know our moms will have.

"When are you thinking about having the wedding?" Selena asks as she places French toast on plates for each of the kids.

"I already have it in my planner for November eighteenth. Two weeks before Thanksgiving." I talked to Grady about it this morning, not wanting to wait too long. We've waited decades now.

Next, my mom asks, "Where are you going to have it? Who is going to cater? You need to plan this, Vivi."

Grady chuckles, "Bonnie, I know you know your daughter better than that."

She laughs good-naturedly and looks at me for answers. "We actually want to have two of the food trucks cater. Most likely Gringo Tacos and Finger Lickin' BBQ. As far as where we wanted to have it… I had a kind of different idea."

"Okay…?" They both ask slowly.

I look at Grady, confirming one more time he liked my unconventional idea. He smiles and nods, just like he did this morning. "Everything about the last twenty-four hours has been so nostalgic that I can't help but want to continue the theme. Sooo, I was thinking we could have the wedding here. Mom, your backyard is perfect for a group of people to watch the ceremony. We don't want more than fifty people. Plus, with the side gate, we can park both of the food trucks and fit a bar in the backyard afterward. And obviously, we would want to use your porch for dinner and there would be room for a dance floor on the grass." I turn toward Selena and Tim. They look a little shocked but not like they want to say no. "So many of our biggest moments happened here together. It feels right that we get married here next."

There are tears in both of their eyes and a huge smile on Tim's face. When they don't say anything, I ask, "What do you think?"

"It sounds like we're planning a wedding," my mom announces.

Selena holds up her glass to the table, and just like that, everyone chooses their roles for the next few months. Every person wanting to help Grady and I make it the happiest day of our life.

And for the first time in years, I believe that I'm going to have everything I spent years dreaming about.

Acknowledgements

There are so many people who have supported, loved, and encouraged me through this process. And if it weren't for them, I'm not sure you'd be sitting here, with this book in your hands.

Lily, I've told you a million times, but if it weren't for you, I probably would've never written this. My entire life I've said how *"I'm going to write a book one day!"* But you were the first person I ever told about Grady and Vivi and Amada Beach. It was your support and encouragement that filled me with enough courage to start this journey. Thank you.

Christana, you are an amazing editor and an even better friend. Thank you for treating these characters with so much love. You helped to make this book what it is today—something I am *so* proud of—and I'm so grateful that I have you in my corner every step of the way. I wouldn't want to do this with anyone else, and it's only the beginning for both of us!

Hillary, you are the moonlight to my sunshine and one of my greatest friends. You cheer for me, calm me down, and never judge me. Thank you for letting me rant endlessly and loving me unconditionally. You are stuck with me forever.

Lyra, you've been my biggest hype man and one of the best additions to my life. Thank you for answering all of my questions, making me laugh when I need it most and showing me an endless amount of support.

Alaina, you're such a bright light of support, love, and joy in my life. Thank you for yapping your way into my DMs and not stopping since. You constantly show me a new perspective and can build me up when I need it.

Lorah, in so many ways, you know these characters just as well as I do. You treated them as if they were as real as you and me when I asked for help with creating their birth charts. Their readings were full of love, respect, and attention to detail. Grady, Vivi and everyone else are who they are because of you. Thank you for your help and knowledge but also for your friendship.

Kyle, thank you always instilling the belief that I can do anything I set my mind to. You've always made me feel like anything is possible. So much of you is in these pages.

Thank you to Mel, Sav, Bri, Grace, May, and Abby for your friendship, and taking the time to read this early on. So much of writing the book was an extremely personal experience but you've made this feel like *ours* by your endless support. It means more to me than I can articulate.

Thank you to my parents. I believed in myself enough to chase my dreams because you always have. Thank you for everything you've done for me and continue to do for me. I don't have the words to properly articulate how grateful I am to all of you. Both for the safe space to always land when I need it, and for the support to keep trying when I feel like I crash. (But if you're reading this, I wish you weren't lol.)

Thank *you*, lovely reader. This story and these characters now just as much yours as they are mine. I hope you love them fiercely. I hope they bring you some form of peace. But more than anything, I hope you know how thankful I am that you took a chance on my novel out of millions. You have a piece of my heart forever. Thank you.

Dicktionary

Please use the guide below to modify your reading experience at your discretion. Your mental health and comfortability is always the most important thing while reading.

🌶🌶🌶

Chapter Twenty-Five
Chapter Twenty-Nine
Chapter Thirty
Chapter Thirty-One
Chapter Thirty-Three
Chapter Thirty-Eight
Chapter Forty-One

About the Author

Ashtyn Kiana is an indie author whose day job doesn't leave a lot of room for creativity, so she started writing her first novel as a way to express that side of herself. Ashtyn writes loves stories that are heartfelt, emotional, and swoony with a good helping of spice! When she's not writing, she's probably walking her dogs, making macrame, or at a local coffee shop.

Instagram: @ashtynkiana.author
TikTok: @ashtynkiana.author

Made in the USA
Middletown, DE
09 November 2024

64185079R00268